A Legacy of Blood

Salena Lee

Copyright © 2017 Salena Lee

All rights reserved.

ISBN: 9781522017950

Print: Independently published

To mum, forever the light amid my darkness, I love you.

This book is a work of fiction. Names, characters, places, and incidents are either products of the author's imagination or used fictitiously. Any resemblance to actual events, locales, organisations, businesses, or persons living or dead, is entirely coincidental.

Warning: Intended for adult readers only: Contains scenes of death, sex, violence, and occasional bad language.

Front cover designed by Salena Lee, copyright2017

A legacy of blood, written by Salena Lee, copyright2017.

Prologue

What am I? I am many things, a curse, an abomination, a tragedy… you decide. All I know is that my guardian called me half breed… What the hell is that supposed to mean? … Painfully, I learned quickly, never to ask.

I know very little about myself, my heritage, but I do know this: My parents are dead, at least that's what I have been told. Whatever family I have remaining, I've never met. Since they are the ones who arranged my execution, I'm not eager to do so.

For unknown reasons they have forsaken me, decided that I must die. Fortunately for me, their chosen means for my demise refused to carry out the execution order, becoming instead my guardian and only companion. Unfortunately, his refusal to kill me has meant that my entire life has been spent running, fighting, and hiding, until finally my guardian vanished, and my worst fears have come to life… I am alone.

Who am I? I am Mara, and for as long as I can remember I have been hunted. There hasn't been a day that has gone by in which I haven't felt their breath upon my neck. The breath, although often imagined, promises a violent death. It's safe to say I am paranoid, but then experience tells me I should be. As I look upon the world I have never truly belonged to, I crave normality. I want to be the girl next door, student, friend, or at least what I understand those things to be.

Whatever ungrateful individual claimed that normal is boring, has no idea what it's like to look upon the sun's light, to see its warmth just within your reach, and yet, when you try to move towards it, you cannot. Trapped, you are a shadow, so close to the light, to warmth, and yet so far away. The shadow is coldness, another world completely.

With my guardian gone I should run like I always have, there is safety in what has already been tried and tested. I don't know anything else, I should, but I won't. Not this time. For the first time in my life loneliness can mean something, something I have never had, and never believed I could have. Freedom, and a chance to leave the shadow behind me.

New Beginnings

So here I am. Somewhere in Scotland, not far from Loch Katrine. This is where I learned to train and fight as a child. Ti, my guardian, would make me spend days out amongst the dense woodland and fog covered hills. Conditioning he called it.

"Warmth will only make you weak, better to grow accustomed to the cold little one. Shadow and ice Mara, it is the nature of what you are, embrace it, and you will never need fear." he would say.

The longest he ever left me was over six months. I was about eight at the time. I could have gone to a local village; modern day Scotland isn't as remote as it once was. It wouldn't have taken me long to find someone who could help me, but I was afraid. Even as a child I understood that both Ti and I were different. Ti was stronger than the mortals who surrounded us, they couldn't protect me like he could, nor could they keep me safe from the hunters who plagued my nightmares and haunted my every waking hour. If that wasn't enough of a reason, I knew that Ti was watching me, he was always watching, waiting for me to grow complacent, expecting it. I knew this, and yet still, somehow… it found me.

I was skinning a rabbit, preparing it for dinner, when the energy that surrounded me changed. The crisp winter air had become charged with static. It was unusual, dark, and made me pause. Before I had the opportunity to study the changes, the presence of another entity pressed against my life force. The sensation, sinister, made my small heart race. Whatever it was, it wasn't friendly, and it was close, too close. I remember a faint impression of something familiar, almost as though we had met before, and yet my young mind couldn't place it. It felt wrong, unnatural, and I was deeply afraid.

A flash of adrenaline warned me that whatever the unnamed threat was, it was here for me, that I was prey. I didn't know what to do, panic flooding my mind. Instead of hiding, I remained still, my eyes nervously scanning the surrounding area.

I didn't hear it approach, I didn't hear anything. I should have known then that something was wrong… nature is never silent. Drawing in a deep breath, my eyes were instinctively drawn to the edge of the woods… it was there, watching me.

Staring, for what at the time seemed like an eternity, I noticed a cloud of mist forming. It was small at first, not unlike a warm breath that had been forcefully expelled against the winter air. Growing rapidly, the cloud rolled in, signalling its hushed approach. The mysterious dense hue clung to the grass, the branches, and even the midges, as one by one, I watched them stop mid-air, freeze, and fall to the ground. The sight reminded me of snowflakes dancing chaotically as though caught in a breeze, and yet there was no breeze, no wind, just an eerie silence.

Nothing moved as nature decreed it should, everything seeming to slow down in a jumpy and hectic manner. Petrified and unsure, I watched in horrific detail as small tendrils of fog took form and reached out towards me. Like fingers of smoke they unravelled, stretching, searching. Frozen with fear I didn't move, but waited. What I waited for, I couldn't say. Stupid girl! I should have run.

The fingers of fog found me easily, wrapping themselves around my limbs like ivy would a branch. A terrifying coldness, like a whisper of death, raced along my skin, seeping into my blood. It felt as though the tendrils had somehow injected themselves into my veins, the chills the jabs generated, like shards of jagged edged glass, swimming through my blood stream. The force of the flow ripped at my insides, causing my immature body to convulse painfully.

Bit by bit, my body locked into place, held by the mysterious force. It was how I imagined turning to ice would feel, I could almost envision tiny particles of ice clinging to my skin like frost along a window pane. It was torturous, brutal.

Air I had unconsciously been holding was ripped from my throat, creating a cloud of steam that sizzled against the arctic air. Now completely immersed in a frozen vice, a new and creative attempt on my life, I discovered I was paralyzed, unable to move. Suffocating, I tried to gasp, scream, anything, but nothing happened. I had only my sight, for once I longed for the darkness to sweep in and obscure my view, wanted to close my eyes. No matter how hard I tried I couldn't.

Desperate for rescue I called repeatedly for Ti, my guardian, but like my attempts to move, the call remained idle, trapped within the confines of my mind. After trying for what I thought was the hundredth time, the fog and ice started changing, becoming something else.

I will never forget those eyes, like the ice that imprisoned me they promised death. Greys and silvers swirled within their hideous depths. They were mocking me, laughing at my fear. I felt warmth then, the only time I have ever felt it. I could not move to look but I could smell the ammonia as I lost control of my bladder. Its evil eyes followed the scent, quickly returning to meet my gaze. Disgust marred its muzzled face, quickly turning into anger, contempt, both equally terrifying.

A snarl escaped the beast, the disturbing sound corrupting the air about me. It carried on the air as though it was an extension of its body, slowly creeping along my skin, invading my thoughts, and claiming my life as its own.

The darkness when its mind melded with mine was beyond my comprehension, it took control of my every thought, whispering repeatedly of the pain yet to come. It was a declaration, a promise… My fate was sealed. There would be no escape, no rescue. Despair flooded my entire being, the unknown threat lingering within my mind. The twisted voice the beast emitted, repeated the words, 'you have lost' the impact of the statement, horrifying.

Images flashed before my eyes, his images, that was the moment I knew it was a 'he'. Many of the things I saw I could not understand, what I did begged for me to flee, to be stronger, but still, I couldn't move, so weak, what chance did I have? Ti had often mentioned such things, knives, hooks, devices of torture he called them, used to inflict horrific pain. A moment of clarity set in, tears fell from my eyes, freezing, and remaining glued to my cheeks. I knew what awaited me, and there was nothing I could do to stop it. With that revelation, I found my breath again, and screamed.

I remained the beast's prisoner for over two years, constantly kept in the dark and always in pain. When I eventually woke from what can only be described as a nightmare, the light, like the hot pokers he used to mar my flesh, burnt my eyes. As the pain eventually passed, Ti was there waiting.

"You have learned from this I hope, never to grow complacent again?" He said coldly, his expression as always, unreadable.

It is safe to say, I did.

Looking across the peaceful stillness of the Loch, it seemed like so long ago. A memory of a life I fully intend to leave behind. Now is the chance for new beginnings. The girl next door I mused. Time then I suppose to find a neighbour.

Brig 'O Turk isn't the biggest village and the population is definitely minimal, but it's a start. One step at a time. My house or rather cottage is… perfect. Just like the ones I had seen on biscuit tins at Christmas, white rendering, thatch roof, secluded. Quiet. Mine. All I need now is to make it habitable. Furniture, CCTV, weapons, and possibly a few ingredients for some homemade explosives. Preparation is the key to everyone's survival, and I intend to survive.

Unable to find the supplies I needed locally I set out for Glasgow. As I often do when driving I lost myself in thought, internally mapping every inch of my cottage for the correct placing of key security features. Completely engrossed in my plans and with the music playing on the radio, I didn't initially recognise the presence of another's thoughts. Normally such a presence would cause alarm. However, instead of fear or aggression, an unfamiliar feeling passed over me, like a jolt of electricity, a flutter. Excitement perhaps? It couldn't be, I rarely get excited.

"You're here, finally! I've been waiting forever. Seriously, like I dinnae have better things to do!" a female voice squealed.

Alarmed, I slammed on the brakes.

"What the ff...!"

The car screeched nosily to a halt, the sudden loss of momentum propelling me forward, straight into the steering wheel. The pain from the impact was excruciating, it laced its way through my body, instantly making me feel nauseated. Blood filled my mouth, the metallic taste only adding to my discomfort. Raising my hand shakily, I knew that blood covered my quickly swelling face. A broken nose, Great!

Dazed, I couldn't make out much of the sounds swimming around me, but I thought I could hear the complaints of the other driver I had unintentionally sideswiped. Doing my best to focus, my head ringing, I sluggishly recalled the cause of my crash. That overly excited squeal. Scanning the car, I found no one, but then I would have known the minute I got in if there had been someone else in the car. Annoyingly, the radio continued to play the same song unaware of the accident that had just taken place. The bass thumping in perfect synchronisation to my now accelerated heartbeat. I don't make mistakes. I know what I heard. Unless….

"You're nae mad. Seriously! Why does everyone always jump to that conclusion? Never heard of a psychic. You know it amuses me, it's easier to believe you're mad, or that I'm a ghost, which by the way I'm nae. And aye I..."

That voice again, loud, too loud. Wincing, I didn't appreciate the assault on my ears, another wave of pain racing along my face, neck, and head. Mentally cursing, my grip tightened on the steering wheel.

"Do you always talk so much"? I asked, my jaw clenching.

"What? Oh, no, nae really no, I mean, you just would nae believe how many times…"

"You could have killed me" I snapped.

"Hardly, nae like your human, and besides, it's nae your time to die. Also, were like BFF's as the Americans would say, you know, birds of a feather stick together and all that. I would nae harm you! So, what you doing bestie?"

"Crashing! And no, I don't know what you're saying. Who are you?" I asked dangerously.

Head still pounding, I noticed the approach of blue flashing lights in the distance, police, fantastic! I placed my cross bow that was currently lying fallen on the passenger side floor, under my seat. The last thing I needed right now is to draw attention to myself. The police I could deal with if I had to, the witnesses too, but those sirens! Damn it! They were not helping with my headache. Grunting as irritation swamped me, I attempted to calm myself… it was difficult. I clenched my jaw tightly and tried to focus on the police's approach, I couldn't. There were too many noises, and with my mind half-heartedly attempting to piece together the information I needed to process my current predicament, I nearly lost the invaders name.

"Did you say Donna?"

My voice was not as threatening as before, good! I'm getting back my calm.

"Aye, I said Donna. Are you ok?" she asked, her voice lowering to a more tolerable level.

"Not surprisingly I have a bit of a headache." I responded, my eyes taking in the scene around me.

My car was crumpled up like some discarded crisp wrapper, the steering column trapping my legs, which surprisingly hadn't been broken. Had I have been human, I would be dead, or at least critically injured. I sighed, my mood growing foul again. Perhaps finding and killing the women who caused my crash would abate it somewhat? Something to consider, as any kind of emotion should be avoided, it gets you killed.

"It's one thing to speak to someone telepathically, it's another to squeal suddenly whilst that said person is driving." I said flatly.

I didn't like having someone in my head. It didn't feel right, and it was making me more volatile than usual. What is this? I don't do emotions of any type, and yet my emotions seem… chaotic. Probably the crash I told myself, looking out the window to gauge how far the police were.

"I was nae squealing, I was joyous, and I dinnae know you were driving." Donna defended, her voice still merry held mild notes of concern.

Joyous? The word sounded foreign. I tried to recall if I had ever used it. Donna continued talking, her words lost on me.

"Joyous." I whispered the word aloud, like its meaning might suddenly make sense.

"What? Aye! Joyous. You know, happy. Anyway, as I was saying…"

"Happy." Another unused word, but at least I knew what this one meant. Happiness is something I have never had, something I craved, or think I crave at least.

"Aye. Happy. I knew you're were different, nae human that is. You're minds map is completely foreign, but I dinnae think you would be... I mean honestly hen, you would think

you had never heard of the word... You have heard of it right? I cannae tell, your thoughts seem confused. Are you injured?"

Ignoring her question, I snapped my nose back into place. Pain shot across my bruised face, traveling across my brow and head. A low menacing growl followed, goose bumps erupting all over my body. Did I just growl?

"Did you just growl!? I'll take that as aye your injured then, shall I?" Donna asked with a faint giggle.

I just growled. Since when do I growl? Confused, I breathed in a deep breath and massaged the back of my neck. The pain was lessening, which was good, it meant I was healing.

"I will be fine in a minute" I replied finally, still shocked at my response to the pain.

I've never growled before. Ever.

"Are you sure! Normally people dinnae growl. Just saying. Do nae take offense or anything. What are you anyway? I mean, I know you're nae human, but growling. Now I'm super curious!"

"I'm Mara" I answered simply, trying to make sense of whatever the hell just happened.

"Mara! What's a Mara?" she verbally pouted, disappointment marring her strong Scottish accent, I could almost visualise a frown.

"Not a what. Who. My name is Mara." I sighed, my attention distracted by the policeman who had just knocked on the window.

Guess they have arrived.

"So, you're a mystery. How exciting! I'll meet you at Maccy Dee's, just off great western road." Donna ordered, certain of my acquiescence.

Irritated, I nearly snarled, who did she think she was telling me what to do? But the policeman, who was desperately trying to get my attention, made me think it was probably not the best idea. A woman snarling and shouting at herself after a high-speed crash, doesn't look good... crazy much. I don't want to be forced to kill him. If I'm going to give normal a shot, I need to stop killing… death diet.

"You ok lass? Bring the paramedic! What's your name?" The officer called, trying to open the jammed door.

Great! Now there's two voices bouncing around my head. Why was everyone so bloody loud?

"The police are here. I can't speak to you and him, I'll …"

"You ok lass? Can you hear me?"

"Ok, no bother, see you there at 8.00pm. Oh, I'm so excited. Finally, all the fun stuff I saw us doing is actually going to happen!" Donna squealed.

I winced again, my head can't take this. Rubbing my temples, I tried to ease the pain.

"Miss! Paramedic now!" shouted the officer.

Damn it! I didn't want to have to kill him but if he didn't shut up... deep breath. At least Donna was no longer in my head, just breathe Mara.

"Miss! Can you hear me?" the police officer continued, his faced etched with worry.

Sighing, I nodded, my head protesting the action. At least the bruising and swelling were now completely gone.

"I'm ok, just a little shaken." I lied.

It took over two hours to deal with the police and paramedics. Finally, after giving my statement and fake details, I was allowed to leave. Other than my blood soaked top, you would never have suspected that I had just been in a crash that totally destroyed my car. One of the few perks of being me, I'm an exceptionally fast healer.

Curiosity getting the better off me, and knowing that the shops were all now closed, I decided to go and meet this Donna. She had gotten into my head literally, and no one has ever done that before. Also, she claimed to know things about my future. She did say she was psychic, and if I didn't like her, I could always kill her. The thought made my mouth twitch, which is as close to a smile as I could get.

The Taxi pulled up just before eight. As always, the fast food restaurant was busy, those famous golden arches lighting up the darkened sky. I have seen those arches all over the world and have always wondered why the humans love it so. Only ever an outside observer, I felt liberated, I'm finally doing normal stuff. Amused with myself, I entered the fast food restaurant. It didn't take long to locate Donna, she was the only person sitting on her own. I walked over to her conscious of the gazes that followed me. I hate being watched, I knew the humans were assessing me, what they saw I couldn't say, some dark part of me wanted to kill them… huh… the pull was stronger than normal. With exceptional difficultly, I resisted, and instead of killing everyone, I focused on the low rumbling sound that had started building low in my throat. I'm going to growl again. What the hell! It was some kind of warning to everyone around me, I was sure of it. Not sure what to do about it, I quickly covered my mouth with the back of my hand, with the hope I could contain it, and cautiously made my way towards Donna.

Reaching Donna's table didn't take long and was uneventful, despite my initial reaction to kill everyone, nobody died. Standing Before her I studied the women who had ruined my day. She, Donna, wasn't what I expected. Her voice had hinted at someone who was overly colourful and eccentric. Instead, she was dressed as though she was about to hit the town, high fashion. She looked like one of those women who grace the front of a magazine. Her long brunette hair was pinned up in a style favoured by women in the 1920s. She looked out of place sitting in the middle of a fast food restaurant.

"Donna?" I asked, my voice deadly, was devoid of emotion, and overly calm.

I raised my eyebrows slightly surprised, it wasn't a voice I could ever remember using before.

Snapped out of a daydream Donna looked up. Her eyes met mine, the action instantly followed by a warm smile that lit up her whole face, and enhanced her rather envious cheek bones.

"Mara?" Her eyes scanned my body, her smile quickly turning into a scowl.

"That's nae what your wearing is it?" she asked.

Her jade green eyes seemed to plead, I hope not.

"I wasn't aware a change off wardrobe was required." I said dryly.

And I thought I was strange.

"Never mind, we're nae meeting them until ten thirty we can quickly run back to mine, I'll do some magic, you'll look amazing. Not that you are nae pretty or anything, because you really are. But looking like you've just committed murder will nae help me land the guy, if you know what I mean." She winked. "Are you aware you're covered in blood? Never mind."

Blood? My nose. No wonder I was getting odd looks, silently glad I didn't kill anyone I returned my attention to Donna, as she continued to speak with little to no pauses.

"I will only meet him if you're there, so let's get a move on, shall we?" she said, standing up from the small table.

Before I could form a response, Donna grabbed my hand and was pulling me swiftly out of the restaurant. Normally such an action would guarantee her a smack in the face, but today had been a day of firsts, and instead, without any idea why, I decided to follow. I trust instinct, it's the only thing I do trust, and instinct was screaming follow.

Exiting the restaurant, we stopped at a white pristine Audi R8 that was parked just outside of the entrance. After pulling out her keys from what I assumed was a designer bag, big and gaudy, she opened the car and signalled for me to get in. Somewhat confused by my desire to do so, I got in without any thought for my safety or the ones who hunt me. It should have bothered me, it was reckless, for all I knew she was one of them, and yet I wasn't bothered, not even a little. Odd.

 "So where are we going, and why will that man you intend to meet only be present if I'm there?" I asked, my voice surprisingly no longer containing any semblance of menace.

I was my normal calm self. About bloody time. A big grin lit Donna's face.

"Well. I've gone over the different scenarios again and again, and no matter what I do, he only appears if you're with me. I have no idea why, but I fully intend on meeting him. Tall, Short auburn hair, body chiselled and firm like some Greek statue. Dreamy… And if that is nae enough, he has all the look and aura of a very naughty but deliciously good boy! If you know what I mean. I plan on making him all mine." She winked. "I have definitely waited long enough".

"I see. That would explain why you're all dressed up." I said with just a hint of sarcasm.

She caused my crash because she wants to meet a guy! I should slit her throat my inner beast coaxed. Sighing in disappointment, I dismissed the idea almost as quick as it had surfaced, she does have information after all. All I need to do is stick around long enough to get some answers. Then I can do what I want. Patience is a virtue I thought, another twitch of a smile flashing against the corners of my mouth.

"Aye, one look at me and he will be smitten. Well, he will fight it, men are notoriously stubborn thinking they know best. But eventually he will admit that he cannae live without me. He will come around to my way of thinking, my terms." She explained happily, whilst utilising the Audi's engine capabilities to its best advantage.

Donna's driving reminded me of the time Ti decided we would play cat and mouse on super bikes, a thousand cc's, and eight daggers each, of course I was the mouse, I always was, but still, her driving was reckless, she wasn't being hunted, and she was mortal.

"I see. So, your psychic and saw him coming, and me apparently. What are you exactly? I wasn't aware humans had such psychic ability. I've heard of a few mediums, especially amongst the gypsies, but I've never encountered anyone strong enough to enter my mind. Especially over a distance." I said, holding on to the door handle for dear life.

"I'm a witch. A very good, very talented, and exceptionally gorgeous witch. Although I look like a human, and my body is as fragile as a human, and I'm mortal like a human. I'm still…"

"A witch." I cut in.

She really does like to talk.

"A very beautiful witch". She added laughing.

I'd never heard laughter up close before, it felt good, like a wave of darkness was being pushed back, just a little. Interesting that such a simple act would have an effect on me at all. A day of firsts. What next? Wondering at the possibilities, I looked out of the window and took in the sights.

Glasgow at night was magnificent. The lights and music escaping the clubs and bars brought the streets to life. My senses were wonderfully overwhelmed. Drawing in a deep breath, the smells off Indian cuisine, alcohol and various perfumes clung to the night air and filtered through my senses. Even from within the car I could detect the individual spices of cumin and coriander. The exotic fragrances appealed to me and reminded me that I hadn't eaten yet today. I would need to eat soon, lack of food always made me aggressive, more so than normal anyway.

Passing pedestrians and store fronts at alarming speed, Donna didn't seem to care the streets were narrow. Speeding around corners, she barely avoided cars and railings by mere inches. Scotland's city roads are not designed for speeding.

"I know what you're thinking. I'll have you know I'm an excellent driver. Never hurt a fly." She grinned.

Wait did she… "You can read my thoughts?" I asked, menace creeping back into my voice.

Telepathy is one thing, invading my thoughts another!

"No, unfortunately mind reading is beyond my capabilities, but I'm working on it. I can only read a surface thought, I cannae invade your mind. Another hundred years or so though, and I reckon ill have it in the bag." She claimed confidently.

"Ok so…" Wait, a hundred years? "I thought you said you were mortal." I accused, my eye brows pulled taunt as I suspected a lie, I hate lying.

"I am. But as I said before, I'm a witch. Witches in general are mortal. But if like me you're exceptionally talented, and beautiful, it's possible you can become powerful enough to live as an immortal. I'm working on it." She said, taking another corner at break neck speed.

"I see, and you just happened to know I was thinking about your driving how?" I asked, holding on to the door as if my life depended on it, which it might.

Had she forgotten I had already been in a car crash today or was she purposely trying to make me relive it?

"I could tell by the glare you were giving me. Are you always so serious? You look like a maniac might jump out at you any minute. Relax! I might not be able to see every minute of every day concerning the future, but I've relived tonight so many times, I practically know it off by heart. I assure you, no one is going to attack you, nae today anyway! We're here." She announced happily, pulling sharply into an underground car park.

The bright lights which hung on the huge concrete celling, stung my eyes, the blinding glare making me frown. Blinking in an attempt to adjust my vision she parked in bay forty-three and got out. There must have been a dead rodent nearby because the smell of decay was strong. Sniffing for other threats and happy to discover there were none, I followed. Donna's high heels echoed nosily as she crossed the vast car park to reach the lift. My footsteps, as always, were silent.

"This is where you live?" I asked as the lift doors opened.

"Aye, home sweet home. Your room is ready, you really like the décor, I did an excellent job." She claimed, the lift doors closing.

"What?" I asked, unsure if I had heard her right. "My room? I already have a house."

Is she insane? I hardly know her.

"Exactly, a house. This is your home, he will nae find you here, my home is warded" she replied happily.

"Who won't find me here?"

"The one that hunts you. He cannae see me or my kin. We are hidden from him, so too are our dwellings and our familiars. As long as you stay close to me you are as good as invisible to him." She announced, her voice adopting a more serious tone.

Staring at me thoughtfully, her eyes pinned mine. She looked as though she was falling into a trance. The rich green of her eyes glazing over. A film of white coated the iris, like green glass that had suddenly became frosted, except they held no coldness. Wave after wave of warmth, each wave warmer than the last, peeled from her body. Like a sauna, the lift filled with heat. I could see it in the same way a snake can see its prey, I should have felt it too, I wanted to, but I couldn't. Always it pushed against me, trying to find a way in, but nothing. Like the sun, it was a reminder that I belonged to the shadow. Even hot drinks felt like ice pouring down my throat. I can only recall one time I had ever felt warmth, once a long time ago. Ti made sure I would never feel it again.

Donna's urgent voice pulled me out of my daze. She looked worried.

"Hello! You ok?" she said slowly.

"Yes. What did you do?" I asked, unable to keep the suspicion from my voice.

"What? Nothing I've called you three times, you just kept staring at me. You sure you're ok?" she asked, really observing me this time, I didn't like her inspection.

"You did something. Your eyes glazed over and you started releasing this heat…"

"Oh that. I was just making sure your aura was hidden, so he cannae see you. Be careful though, the cloaking spell is tethered to me, if you move more than two hundred feet from me, it will snap and unravel. Thus, you will nae be hidden from him anymore. Quickly now, we are running out of time."

Pulling me yet again, we made our way quickly down the corridor until we reached the door at the far end, number forty-three.

The sight upon entering Donna's home was how I first imagined her to be, when she hijacked my mind and caused me to crash, homely and colourful. Large sofas which looked like they could swallow you whole, dominated the room. Like her car, it was tidy, and smelled of freshly baked cherry and vanilla pretzels. I liked it, everything about her apartment, from the colour of the walls, to the plush furnishings, was inviting and warm. My body might be unable to enjoy warmth's touch, but I could see it and appreciate its beauty. Soaking in the room's atmosphere, the red and beige tartans caught my eyes, I've always liked the pattern. A small tingling sensation started to build from somewhere within my chest, it was a new feeling, although good, it was making me weirdly uncomfortable. Doing my best to ignore it, I continued the flats appraisal. Stag embossed cushions and faux fox throws reminded me of the country I love, and am accustomed too. A sense of longing filled me, there was nothing as beautiful as Scotland's wild and diverse landscapes and everything about this flat reminded me of that beauty, and of what has been my only real home. A gentle tug pulled at my mouths edge, dragging its corners upwards. My muscles were unused to the new demand placed upon them, and as such the action was slightly rigid. I raised my hand cautiously to feel what was happening. Am I smiling?

A Squeal of excitement.

"See, told you, you would love it!" Donna said happily. I'm smiling, awkwardly, but still!

"Wait till you see your room!" she squealed again.

Donna practically skipped to the room. With a huge grin, she opened the door. I peered inside, that same unfamiliar feeling rising again, this time causing the hairs on my flesh to stand to attention. It was as though they were alive with electricity. Logically, I knew it was just a room, but what a room. It was designed in the same style as the living room, one whole wall had a photographic mural of a forest which opened up to reveal a loch, still and calm, the moon and stars reflecting upon its surface. It was beautiful, and there was a bed!

"There's a bed." I said.

"Aye. It's a bedroom." Donna replied sarcastically.

"I've never had a bed." I whispered.

I reminded myself that this wasn't mine, I had a house, Donna was a stranger, Psychic or not, I don't trust people, ever. I would never just move in.

"Never! Where did you live? A stable?" she said.

"Sometimes." I said matter of fact.

Donna burst out laughing.

"And there I was believing you lacked humour. A stable, funny! Next you'll say your bed was a manger!"

Giggling noisily, she left the room. Confused at her outburst I followed her out. Hovering unsure in the hallway, I was amused when a song about how tight a girl's pair of jeans were, started to blare from what I assumed was Donna's room. Unsure if I was meant to follow her in, I started memorising her apartment for threats and defence possibilities. Within a matter of seconds, I knew every place suitable for both protection and attack. I had also seen at least sixteen items that would be suitable for use as a weapon and were easily accessible.

"Mara! What are you doing? Would you come and get dressed, were running out of time" Donna called impatiently.

Was she always so bossy or just eager to meet this man of hers? I didn't reply as I walked into her room.

"Your dress is on the bed." She shouted from within her walk-in wardrobe.

When she said dress, I was expecting something slightly more substantial. I picked it up from the bed like you would pick up a dead mouse.

"Are you sure that's a dress?" I asked, biting my lower lip.

It looked like one of those underwear dresses I had seen hanging in, 'adult only' shop windows. A tiny White baby doll dress I think they are called, the fabric was so thin it was nearly see through.

"Aye it's a dress, I got it just for you. You will feel incredibly uncomfortable in it. But he, not my he, your he, will love it. You will thank me later." She claimed on a gentle laugh.

What? I was trying to work out what she had just said, when she came bowling out of her wardrobe, her eye brows drawn together tightly.

"Quickly, get dressed and let me doll you up, we have to go." She ordered, grabbing various grooming items from her white high glossed dresser.

"But my bra is black, you will see it, even I know that's tacky." I added quickly.

I should probably leave, this is getting weird. I didn't really care about the bra, I'm not shy when it comes to my body, flesh is flesh, but where will I keep my knife? I don't like being unarmed, I've already had to hide my crossbow.

"You do nae need one, the material there is thicker. No one will know." She smiled, turning on some sort of heating instrument.

Questionably resigned, and extremely confused as to why I wasn't objecting like I should be, I put on the dress, minus my bra and knife. If the need arises I will have to improvise. Sighing. I wondered again why I was agreeing to this? I was beginning to miss the feeling of mistrust, where the hell had it gone?

With the dress on, the material revealing more than I would normally reveal, I sat down on the bed feeling somewhat defeated. Donna immediately pounced, applying makeup and various perfumes and stuff I didn't recognise. I felt like I was trapped in an outlandish dream, why is no one dying?

After half an hour of Donna pulling my hair and curling it in that heated instrument, she was finished. My face coated, felt similar to the effect mud had when it dried on your skin. Uncomfortable and hungry, I couldn't stop the low rumble that surfaced. Fortunately, Donna had left to get my shoes, so she didn't hear it. Placing my hand on my stomach, I gently rubbed it, an unconscious effort to appease my hunger. I muttered when I realised what I was doing, it was pointless. Since when did rubbing your stomach appease hunger? Irritated with myself, I waited for Donna to return.

Less than a minute later Donna entered the room, she was carrying a pair of high heels that were easily five inches high. They looked really good, those heels could defiantly cause a lot of damage. Maybe that why she wasn't concerned regarding the likelihood of trouble, she thought ahead, weapons that are easily concealed, clever witch. Silently impressed, I strapped the heels on. When I looked up, a look of self-satisfaction covered Donna's face. She was obviously pleased with her work. I on the other hand was completely out of my comfort Zone. I'm not the sort that needs a pretty little dress to kill. Although the prospect of using those heels was exhilarating. Secretly, I was now hoping for a little trouble. Hungry, sceptical, but slightly excited, I followed her as we left to find this man of hers.

After spending what felt like an age parking, we headed up a street called Renfield. The night was busy, every club, bar, and restaurant, like earlier, was full and humming with life.

"We're here". She grinned, her eyes scanning the surrounding streets looking for something.

Probably this man she keeps going on about. We stopped just outside of a nightclub called Revolution. The queue was long, and I didn't like the attention I was getting. A lifetime of hiding meant not standing out in a crowd. An unwanted rumble low in my stomach reminded me that I needed to eat and pulled me from my thoughts.

"Do they serve food here?" I asked, that same gnawing growl growing stronger.

"Aye, bar food. You hungry?" she asked, her eyes quickly glancing at my stomach as if she could somehow see its complaints.

"I need to eat soon." I explained, just as the growl I had been desperately holding in, escaped. Thankfully no one but Donna seemed to hear it. What is happening to me?

After staring at me with a puzzled expression, Donna moved from the back of the queue to the front. Ignoring the protests from the women, and the wolf whistles from the men, she attempted to walk straight past the door men with all the familiarity of someone who owned the place. The door men clearly shocked by her boldness tried to prevent her entrance. Without looking at the men, Donna raised her hand and flicked her wrist like a dancer. A slow pivot that pulsed with electric blue energy, flickered across her palm, the mini forks of lightening she created, jumping from finger to finger. Captured in time, the door men, every person, and every song along the entire street just stopped. It was like someone had hit pause. For the first time tonight, I really wondered about Donna. Just how powerful was she? And why wasn't I concerned? Turning briefly at the club's entrance, she smiled.

"Come on then. Let's eat." She winked mischievously.

My questions and doubts forgotten instantly, I followed her lead and entered the club.

The smell of alcohol and sweat invaded my nose instantly, the foul stench making it twitch indelicately. Coughing gently, I tried to rid my nose of the putrid invasion, it didn't work. When we reached the bar, Donna flicked her wrist once again, the pause button lifted, the world springing to life. A loud rhythmic beat reverberated through the room, like a low purr of bass rubbing along your skin. It felt good, even though hundreds of bodies danced, seemingly locked together, and consuming every inch of space. It was making me feel anxious, far too many people, anyone of them could potentially be an assassin. Sneezing loudly, I shook my head gently. How anyone could stand the smell was incredible, I silently prayed my sense of smell would adjust, whilst rubbing my nose to prevent another sneeze from escaping.

Ignoring the annoying itch, I watched Donna speak with the bar man. Bodies of strangers kept bumping into me, invading my much-needed space. Every wink, every comment, was playing havoc on my temper. It was not like me to lose my calm like this, I was always in control. Something is wrong… very wrong. Looking at Donna talking with the bar man, I meditated with the idea that somehow, she had done this to me. A spell maybe, or the tether she spoke of. The thought of ill play caused a low threatening snarl to erupt from somewhere deep inside me. The crowd of people that stood closest to me quickly retreated, a semi-circle of floor forming, separating me from the rest of the room.

"If someone tries to caress me again, I will break something." I warned, dark thoughts suddenly swirling around my head and contaminating my thinking.

It was like a sleeping beast was waking, and despite my best efforts, I was powerless to prevent it. A small sliver of fear burst forth as the idea presented itself as a truth. Shit! What did that mean?

"Here."

Donna slid a plate containing a large burger and chips over to me. How did she get that so quickly? Staring at her in wonderment and then staring at the plate in the same manner, I noticed that her studying gaze never left me, nor did her hand leave the plate. Aggravated by this, my already volatile mood rose a notch higher, forcing a primitive and foreign part of me to challenge her. It's mine the inner beast threatened, followed by another vicious growl that had even my heart racing. Donna quickly let go of the plate.

"It's all yours." She grinned.

Suddenly she burst out laughing.

"You really are hungry, aren't you? I think for the sake of the general population you should keep a snack bag or something." She giggled.

Tucking into the food I ignored her comment.

"I honestly thought you might kill me for a burger." She glared, a huge smile dominating her face, vivid green eyes cheerfully relaying her amusement.

I wanted to reply that it wasn't the case, but the way I was gulfing down my burger suggested otherwise. What the hell is wrong with me? Donna was still laughing to herself when she placed a tray of several small glasses in front of me, each containing a rich amber liquid. There was also a small plate of sliced lemon and a small pot of what smelt like salt. Licking the last remnants of my meal from my fingers, I took note of my surroundings once more.

"What's this?" I asked.

"It will help you relax." She smiled.

Licking the top of her hand she picked up the salt pot and shook it over the wet area of skin she had just created. The small grains of salt clung to her hand. Is she seasoning her hand? What does she think I am? I was just about to tell her I wouldn't bite, when she picked up one of the small glasses of amber. After wedging a slice of lemon between her fingers, she grinned even wider.

"Here's to a friendship that will last forever, slainte." She said genuinely.

Lifting her hand, she licked the salt from her skin and then immediately drank from the small glass, emptying it in one swig. After pulling an unrecognisable face she placed the lemon in her mouth and sucked on it. Another funny face. Not sure what to make of her strange ritual, I continued to stare at her quizzically.

"Well, what you are waiting for?" She asked amused.

She picked up the salt pot and pointed to my hand.

"Lick your hand then. The salt will nae stick otherwise." She explained.

"I see, I'm supposed to repeat your ritual? That makes more sense." I answered dryly.

I wondered if this was a normal thing people did. A quick scan of the bar suggested it was a witch thing.

"Is it some kind of spell?" I asked warily.

"Spell?" she smiled.

"No. It's nae a spell. It's a toast between friends."

"Toast?"

"Oh hen. What kind of life have you had? A toast, in the words of the great and all-knowing dictionary, is when a person or persons propose a toast/drink to someone's health or in someone's honour. In this case, I propose a toast in honour of the friendship we will share." She explained with a knowing smile.

Lifting another glass from the tray she said.

"To us… Slainte."

Sceptical, I licked the back of my hand and mirrored the ritual. The amber liquid was rich and welcoming. A combination of the salt and lemon creating an exciting explosion of flavour. Each taste was new and fascinating. Refreshed, I finished the rest of the tray.

"This is good, what's it called?" I asked, licking my lips.

"Tequila gold. Nice, isn't it?"

Before I had a chance to answer she pulled me into the middle of the dance area. Once again people started pressing up against me, their bodies moving in the same groping manner they did on that dance TV channel I often watched when I was lucky enough to be staying in a hotel, of course Ti got the bed, but still, it was a luxury.

Rigidly, and suspicious of everyone around me, I observed the room, allowing the foreign atmosphere to sink in. Different coloured lights were flashing in beat to the music, capturing my attention. The room felt alive…I felt alive. Despite my hesitation and with the burger appeasing my temper somewhat, my body couldn't help but join in with their dance. For the first time in my life I was dancing, and it wasn't a dance of death. Donna laughed as she danced with me, her body swaying and dipping in perfect sync to the music.

"You're a natural" Donna claimed.

"Natural what?" I frowned, not understanding her statement.

"Dancer."

Oh…I wasn't surprised, dancing wasn't all that different to sparring, and in that I excelled.

The longer I danced the more I relaxed. I could hear my pulse racing with every new move I made. A flutter that started low in my stomach spread its way up to my chest and then across my collarbone. It was the same sensation I got when I first felt Donna's presence in the car. Excitement. But this time it was definitely mine. I smiled. I could get used to normality, like it even.

"They're here." Donna squealed, her excitement contagious.

Still dancing she leaned in and whispered.

"Their hearing is as good as yours, watch what you say. And remember, although they appear to be like you, they're nae. Say nothing." She warned, her green eyes twinkling with delight.

"Who are they?" I whispered.

Like Donna I didn't stop dancing. Dancing I decided made me feel free, and since Ti wasn't around to punish me, I would make the most of it.

"The Keltoi. Hunters. They do nae play well with strangers, especially strangers they cannae account for." She explained.

At that exact moment, she decided to dip low, rising slowly, her stomach curving seductively. A growl of appreciation sounded behind me. Donna bit her lip before drawing me closer to her.

"Told you he would love me. In a moment, he will nae be able to resist coming to me. Remember what I said, say nothing about what you are or what you can do. Just keep close and keep dancing. Oh, and turn around, your, 'he' is dying for a better look." She added whilst wearing a mischievous grin.

My what? Swaying slowly, she moved back from me. Pulling my hand forward she spun me around, my body mimicking hers. The music hummed through my body, I didn't miss a beat. It should have bothered me that we had an audience, but it didn't, I was dancing for me. I would sooner stab a guy than dance for him, men in my opinion are over rated.

"You should see the way he's looking at you. It reminds me of the look you gave me when you thought I might nae give you your burger." She whispered, barely containing a laugh.

"Unlike you witch. I have no desire for, or need of a man. But I wish you all the luck in acquiring yours." I replied, uncaring.

I have never understood a woman's need to be with a man. I honestly can't see what they have to offer. But then I have never been near a male other than Ti, and the beast, perhaps there is some secret to them that women crave. None the less, one cannot miss what one has not had.

A tingling feeling at the back of my neck pulled me from my thoughts. Danger! A Low threating growl undetectable to humans reached my ears, and like the predator that I am, I ached to call him out. He growled a second time, a warning to everyone nearby to get out of the way. Slowly a circle of sticky black floor formed around me and Donna. I doubt the patrons even knew what they had just done, still unaware of the threat they danced unfazed. The killer that I am has never responded well to threats, neither have I ever ignored them. So much for Donna's theory of no trouble. Maybe I will get to use my heels after all. Anticipation coursed through me, putting every sense on high alert. He was getting closer, like a vulture circling its prey. Focused, I readied myself to attack.

"Mara! I give you my word he seeks me, nae you. Please do nae give yourself away. He does nae see you, but if you attack he will! Along with his companions. Please

Mara, his interest in me is nae violent. He will nae harm us." Donna pleaded, an unspoken request that filled my mind, her face full of reassurance.

It is not in my nature to back down, and yet for whatever reason I believed her. Unsure why I was trusting Donna, I allowed his approach. Every muscle in my body wanted to betray the illusion of calm I held. With all the demure of someone unaware of his presence I danced slowly away from him, exchanging places with Donna.

As I ignored the hunters approach the innate need to hurt someone was making me restless, I was going against every principle and lesson I have ever been taught, and I couldn't explain why. Because a witch told me so… A witch I've known for less than a few hours!

"Thank you." Donna said silently, her smile one of gratitude.

Hesitant, I watched the stranger like a hawk, if he did just one thing wrong he was fair game. Disappointingly, and on a long sigh, it didn't take long to see that Donna was right. The man that stood in front of me saw only her, the hunter's eyes followed every dip and sway of her hips with such intense focus he seemed lost to everything around him. I wasn't fooled.

Towering above her he was easily seven foot tall. His body was broad and powerful, every muscle tirelessly honed for fighting. He was a warrior. I had no delusions that should this man decide to fight he would prove deadly. Placing his over-sized hand on her waist he brought himself closer to her, his touch surprisingly gently. Licking her lips, Donna turned into him, her hand resting on his chest. Layering her body against his, she continued to dance with him as though she had known him her entire life. But then she did say she saw him coming. Thirsty and still hungry I made my way to the bar, leaving Donna and her newly discovered boy toy dancing. Once at the bar I signalled to the bartender.

"What can I get you sweetheart?" The bartender asked.

"A tray of Tequila please. What food do you have?"

"Here. I'll get your drinks while you decide what you would like." He said, handing me a menu.

"What do you recommend?"

I stared at the menu indecisive, my brow raised.

"Personally, I'm a dessert man. Ice cream sundae all day long." He winked.

Dessert man? Grinning, he went to get my drinks. Did I just miss something? Frowning, I focused instead on my next meal. Scanning the menu, I realised I didn't know what most of the food listed on it was. What's bangers and mash? Surf and Turf? None of it made any sense. When the bartender returned with my Tequila I asked for the ice cream sundae. At least I know what ice cream is, even if I haven't tried it. Thirsty, I finished all the tequila, several empty glasses littering the bar.

"Thirsty!" The bar tender chuckled.

"Very."

Why he thought this funny was beyond me.

"Would you like some more?

"Yes, another tray please." I answered dryly.

It goes without saying, if I'm thirsty, then of course I want a drink, idiot.

Following the bartender's movements as he readied my drinks, I couldn't help but feel like I was being watched. It was a fleeting feeling that went nearly as soon as it came. Looking around the room and seeing nothing obvious, I pushed the thought aside and waited patiently for my ice cream.

After finishing my third tray of tequila, my ice cream still nowhere to be seen, I thought about my night so far. It had been… weird, confusing, surreal. I had so many questions, but as I attempted to answer them, I found myself failing terribly. Deciding that no information was worth the headache, I stood to leave.

"You're not leaving, are you?" The bartender asked, placing a large bowl of ice cream in front of me.

Staring at the ice cream and finding its scent irresistible, I knew I had to sample it. Sitting back down on the stool with a, 'flash of a smile', I decided I could always leave after…I will leave after.

"Not a chance." I hummed.

I eyed the ice cream as though it was the only source of water in a baking hot desert. Biting my lip, I twitched another, 'not quite' smile. If it tasted as good as it looked, then I was going to enjoy this. The bartender smiled and was about to reply when he was called off. I didn't care, Mara had a date with ice cream.

The dessert, invitingly sat before me, was huge. Several scoops of strawberry and vanilla ice cream sat on top of each other, forming a creamy pyramid of lushness. Spirals of sticky red sauce laced its way across the ice cream, creating intricate patterns that looked delicious, mouth-watering. Thoroughly enticed I placed a spoonful into my mouth…it was amazing! The flavours were sweet and delectable. Thick creamy coolness coated my tongue, it was heaven in a bowl. Coolness wasn't a new thing, everything I ate was cold, but this was different, sublime even. Who knew that such a creation could invoke so much pleasure? Slowly, I devoured my ice cream, making sure to savour every mouthful. When I reached the bottom of the bowl I couldn't help but feel disappointed. Using the tips of my fingers, I carefully scrapped together the last remaining drops.

"Did you enjoy that?" A stranger asked me, his voice, rich and deep, contained Irish notes that vibrated teasingly along my flesh.

A burst of desire exploded from within my chest, shivers of anticipation swimming up my spine. Surprised, the nearly invisible hairs that coated my body to stood to attention, the whole bombardment of sensation, new to me, exciting. Intrigued by my reaction, I turned to face my questioner. Instantly my eyes found his, and wow… they were mesmerising. They were green, but not just any green, they were like the rich greens of the forest, vibrant and magical. This pleased me…a lot, apparently, I'm partial to green eyes and an Irish accent, I could practically hear the internal purring when his gaze captured mine.

Watching the stranger intently, I unconsciously licked the remaining ice cream from my fingers and lips. A low hiss sounded from the dark-haired stranger, his captivating eyes following my every move. With the stranger occupied, I thought it the ideal time to assess him further.

I immediately recognised him as a fighter, there was a lethality about him that made you pay attention, the man was dangerous. I should probably make my excuses and get the hell away from him, but I found myself overly curious, and surprisingly, not that fearful. Odd when I knew with absolute certainty I was gazing into the eyes of a killer. As for his looks, his face was…what's the word? Beautiful? No, handsome. Whatever, I liked looking at him.

He wore a low dark stubble that clung to his jaw, highlighting stark but beautiful contours to an otherwise masculine face. An angry red scar ran from the top of his right brow down to his temple, the angry wound standing out against smooth skin. It was a knife cut, recent, and not yet healed. I have one of similar design on the inside of my thigh that for some reason never completely vanished. Finally, a man that warranted a minute of my time. I wasn't the only one who thought so either. Some of the women surrounding the bar were desperately trying to get his attention. One of them even went as far as to boldly place her hand over his shoulder before running it slowly down his chest. In a low sultry voice, she whispered in his ear.

"Why do nae you come and play with someone your own age. The young ones are always a disappointment, they lack the knowhow. I give you my word, I will nae be a tease." She promised, her tongue flicking out to gently caress his ear.

Play what? Uninterested in her display and remembering Donna's warning, I moved to leave…again. What's my issue? Since when has leaving a place become such a damn challenge?

"I'm not interested." The stranger responded flatly, his words and hypnotic tone instantly making me halt my retreat.

Tipping his head slightly to the side, the woman's mouth no longer at his ear, he proceeded to move or rather shove her hand away. Not once did his gaze leave mine. Affronted, the women cursed and moved off, mumbling something about men and their obsession with younger women. Staring at her questionably I remembered he had asked me a question. Curiosity getting the better off me I decided to reply, the notion to leave, forgotten.

"Yes, very much." I said simply, and a little late.

The intensity of his gaze should have made me uneasy. Instead a new awareness coursed through me. It wasn't fear or danger, but something else.

"I can tell. What's your name darling?" He asked, a small smile fixed to one corner of his mouth.

"Mara." I replied cautiously.

I quickly looked for Donna. I'm certain this is one of the companions she spoke about. A hunter, he's defiantly not human. I should have had a look when they came in.

"That's a beautiful name, it is old Norse." He said, wearing that same, 'almost' smile.

"Ok" I answered uncertain.

What are you supposed to say to that? I wondered again about leaving. I'm really not the conversation type, regardless of how intriguing I found him.

"Are you not curious as to mine?" he asked, his eyes taunting me, trapping me.

A sudden need to please him surfaced, it was as though his opinion of me mattered more than anything in the world. It annoyed me, and yet still I remained fixed in place, compelled even.

"Am I meant to be?" I asked seriously, and slightly confused.

Current emotions aside, social behaviour was never high on Ti's training list.

"Normally when somebody asks you your name, one would inquire as to the others name also." He claimed, his eyes seeing more then I liked.

A hunter? A sudden memory sprung to mind, Ti had spoken about them before. A race of immortal warriors, enforcers meant to keep order and maintain the balance. Extremely dangerous. *"If you ever encounter a hunter Mara. Run!"* Ti warned.

"It is only polite." He continued.

I couldn't detect a lie. Scanning the floor quickly for Donna and finding her still safe and sound, I decided it was probably ok to continue with his line of questioning. I couldn't help but wonder about this man, despite Ti's warning. Also, if I ran now he would only grow suspicious. Again, another warning from Ti resurfaced,

"Never give yourself away. Never reveal your true thought. Think. Think ten moves ahead." He would say.

Good excuse to stay, wouldn't want him getting suspicious now, would I?

"I see. What is your name?"

Was my voice lower than usual?

"Conlaóch, but my friends call me Col." He replied eloquently.

His Irish lilt felt good, like a soft breeze that wraps itself around you. It reminded me of a feathers caress, barely there, and yet your whole body reacts to the slightest touch. Trying my hardest not to shiver I asked him my own question.

"Your friend over there, whose hands are all over my friend. What's his name?"

Did I just say friend? And yet… the word felt right, like somehow It just was. Instinct. What's going on? It's as though my subconscious has already decided, but had failed to tell my conscious mind. This is messed up.

"His name is Aengus, and you're friend's name?"

His eyes still firmly locked onto mine I couldn't help but suspect he was searching for something? That his gaze saw more than just the physical.

"Her name is Donna. Why are you looking at me like that?" I asked wearily.

Why do I care?

"Like what darling? You need to be a little bit more specific." He said gently, his grin widening ever so slightly.

"Like I'm some kind of puzzle you fully intend on solving." I answered, inadvertently edging closer to him.

"Do I make you nervous Mara?" he asked, whilst moving, or maybe stalking towards me.

It was subtle, but I could detect the slow advance. It reminded me of a fox that patiently creeps up, so it didn't startle the hen it was about to steal. A low hum of danger whispered in my mind, yet it was a danger I didn't recognise, a danger I found thrilling. Col's eyes shone with an intelligence beyond the years he appeared, they seemed to whisper, 'you should be', and yet I remained unconcerned, calm even. Instinctively I knew he wasn't going to hurt me, not yet anyway. Why then should he think I'm nervous? Confused by his question, Donna, and my entire day, I tried to think of a way I could leave but still get information. Maybe kidnapping? It had worked for me in the past. As quick as that idea surfaced, it fled. I doubt I could get him out of here without injury to myself or without his friend's knowledge, and as for Donna, I don't know enough about her, especially after her display earlier, for all I know she could zap me into oblivion. She's already convinced me, a career killer, that we're friends.

"Are you not going to answer me darling?" Col asked softly.

He looked in that moment as perplexed and intrigued by me as I was about him.

"I was thinking. No, you do not make me nervous. You have no intention of harming me, that much I can tell. Should I be?" I asked him frustrated, the conversation was beginning to give me a headache.

"Harm you? Why would you assume that was my intention?" He frowned.

"You're a warrior, don't you live to fight? What else would you want from me?"

Obviously, he thinks I would be a worthy opponent. Which I would be.

"Even if I am a warrior." he said, a flicker of a smile flashing against the edges of his mouth.

He really wasn't doing a good job at hiding his amusement.

"I am also a man. Men have many needs." He finished, his eyes following the length of my legs leisurely, hungrily.

"And what need is it you hope to have me fulfil? You have one I assume, or you wouldn't be talking to me?"

What aren't I getting? Maybe I should go ask Donna.

"Darling, I can think of many things I would love for you to do for me, with me. However, it's becoming increasingly evident that you're an innocent. Perhaps on this occasion we can dance instead?" He said, offering me his hand.

Innocent. Why on earth would he come to that conclusion?

"Innocent? Hardly. I've killed hundreds of men." I explained frustrated, and ignoring his hand.

I'm missing something, damn Ti. I speak, read, and write, in over twenty languages, several of which are no longer used, I can solve equations at university level without even thinking about it, and yet I can't piece together his cryptic speech.

"Yes. But how many have you kissed?" He asked, his heated gaze focusing on my mouth.

Kissed! What's that got to do with anything? I have seen people kiss. Joining their mouths together, sometimes placing their tongue inside. From what I gathered it was one of many forms of affection, an outward display of love or regard. I always thought it was similar to a hand shake or hug, just a wetter version with a higher degree of affection attached. Why would you want someone's saliva in your mouth? If you cared about someone that much you should give them something useful, like throwing daggers, or a blow torch. The perfect gift.

"I don't understand. If my intention was to kill them, why would I kiss them?" I asked bewildered.

I really do like his eyes. Those damn eyes! Maybe it's part of a hunter's allure. I have the same abilities although I rarely use them. Lure them in to make the kill easier. I always thought it made it too easy, where's the fun in that?

"I don't mean the men you've killed darling. Have you ever been kissed by a man, ever?" He asked patiently.

That same secret smile was beginning to bother me. I had a sudden urge to flee which only annoyed me further. People fled from me, not the other way around. Except the one who hunts me, but that's a different matter.

"No. never." I said bluntly.

Why would I?

"Not that it would have made any difference, I am glad. To be the only one means more to me then even I imagined." He replied, his Irish lilt adopting a more thoughtful tone.

"What? Did we change topic?" I asked bemused.

Again, I marvelled at women's need for men. I can't for the life of me understand them.

"No anam cara." He grinned, his hypnotic gaze sweeping the length of my body. A low growl of appreciation followed. "We did not, but I am happy to discuss any topic you choose." He added temptingly.

"Mara, time to go!" Donna shouted from a few feet away, interrupting whatever this was.

She looked red faced and flustered. Standing with her hands on her hips she ignored the giant behind her. She's upset with him, angry with him. Cross with myself for not noticing something had obviously taken place, I stood and growled. Like before its effect reached everyone in the room, anger flared.

"What did you do to her Giant?" I snapped, my voice, low and menacing, sent chills coursing along my spine.

A red haze began filling my vision, the temperature around me plummeting. I remember this happening before, the last time I inadvertently lost my temper. It was the day before Ti disappeared and left me alone. It felt like a blanket of ice was forming, wrapping itself around me, protecting me like frost protecting a flower from the freeze. Quicker than the eye could see, Col stepped forward, grabbing my arm, my eyes meeting his. I didn't know what he saw but it was enough to pull a dagger from his back and silently place it against my throat. The metal like the air around me was cold and all too familiar.

"Remove your blade Conlaóch before I remove your heart." I hissed quietly, my eyes holding his.

"Mara! Please. I was nae harmed. Let's just leave. Crap! Why dinnae I see this happening?" Donna said, mumbling the latter.

"What are you anam cara?" Col asked me, his voice no longer containing any traces of humour, instead they held deep concern, his eyes desperately searching mine for the answer.

"Pissed off." I growled dangerously, my eyes flickering between him and Donna, ice forming on the floor beneath me.

"Mara let's just go. I do nae know what's happening, I'm completely blind here, but I swear idiot that he is, he dinnae hurt me. Aengus! Like his name sake, is a bull… He might taste good, but ultimately, he's thick headed and stupid. But he would nae harm me." She announced angrily, her tongue hitting the inside of her mouth.

"I'm nae a bull lassie, and I'm certainly nae stupid" Aengus rumbled.

His Scottish accent was heavy and thick. He was staring at Donna with a look of absolute astonishment. Obviously, he has never been called stupid before. My guess, nobody dared.

"On the contrary Aengus! You're exactly that." Donna huffed.

The sight was confusing, I didn't know what to make of their spat. I was angry because she was hurt and, yet I was convinced Donna wasn't in any immediate danger. Quickly assessing the situation, I focused instead on the man in front of me, who at present still held a wickedly sharp knife against my throat.

Everything about the hunter's stance suggested a swift and violent death should I provoke him. Eyes so vividly green before had taken on a shadowed hue, like a cloud of smoke swam within the iris. You could believe that such a cloud would obscure his view, but I knew better.

I struggled to let go of the anger I knew was unwarranted, but whatever the darkness was, lurking beneath the surface, it wanted control, was fighting for it. My confusion level suddenly grew as an unexplainable need to taste blood left a metallic taste in my mouth, the surprisingly alluring sensation almost overwhelming my ability to think cohesively. For a brief moment, I thought I felt my body ripple, the sensation followed with a nauseated feeling of teeth gnawing away at my stomach. It was as though some unknown terror was desperately trying to get out. What's the hell was happening to me? I had to get out of here!

With a speed undetectable to the human eye, I grabbed the blade pressed against my throat and reversed its trajectory. Dipping low, I spun, catching Col's legs, and propelling him backwards towards the floor. Straddling him, I leaned in close, pressing the knife against his jugular. Surprise flashed in his eyes. Abruptly the concern he had been wearing vanished, replaced instead with amusement. He grinned!

"What about this do you find amusing" I asked in a voice I didn't recognise, half human, half something else.

Inching the blade closer, I drew blood. The scent, all male, was intoxicating. Slowly I licked my lips, my eyes drawn to the tiny beads of claret that rested upon the knife edge. Col hissed, his eyes following the small gesture before answering.

"No one has ever done that before. What an intriguing woman you are. I shall greatly enjoy unravelling your secrets. However, consider this a warning anam cara, I learn quickly. You will only ever catch me off guard the once." He promised, his half smile tugging at something deep within.

Confused, and before I could attempt to decipher his words, one of his hands found my waist, the other regaining ownership of the knife. Flipping me over, I found myself neatly tucked between him and the floor. The pressure from his body felt… good. But then I have always loved a fight, born for it.

My hands free and aware of the knife he now possessed, I prepared my escape. Using everything I had I elbowed him hard in the face. I felt the snap as bone gave way, the barely audible crunch making me grin. A broken nose will be the least of his worries. Grunting, he released the knife and attempted to pin my arms. With the knife no longer visible, now was the time to leave.

"Enough. I have no intentions of hurting you darling."

"I've heard that before." I confessed, slamming my knee between his legs.

"Damn it Woman!" Col growled loudly, attracting the attention of the humans.

"You need a hand their boss?" Laughed one of the hunters.

"Not if you know what's good for you Finian" Col grunted, successfully pinning my hands above my head.

He was strong, much stronger than me, but I was fast. Wrapping my legs tightly around his waist I utilised every muscle to its best advantage, and swung suddenly to the left, managing to throw him off to the side. Releasing his hold on me to regain his balance, I swept down both my hands, hitting him in the side of his head.

"Feisty one, isn't she?" Mumbled Aengus, who had also begun laughing.

"Oh, shut up, meat head." Donna snapped.

She was now stood behind me, her voice hitched as though at any minute she might start cheering me on. I grinned at the prospect and then grinned even wider when I remembered I wore high heels. With a second blow to Col's head, followed by my heels being repeatedly stabbed into his legs, I managed to wriggle free and regain my footing. Had he actually attempted to hurt me I would have been in serious trouble. My initial assessment was correct, he lives to fight, he's stronger than me, and more experienced than me, and he's not alone. With a final stamp to the back of Col's head, I grabbed Donna, and delivered a hard kick to Aengus's crotch, successfully paving a way for us to pass. When in trouble use every advantage. A loud growl followed, then a curse, then another round of laughter. Without looking back, I ran for the fire exit, dragging Donna behind me.

"Are they following witch?" I asked.

A hundred different escape scenarios racing through my mind.

"Urm aye. The scary looking one with the knife is up and now in pursuit, followed closely by two others. Aengus is still moaning on the floor with the remaining one laughing at him. You know I want children right, you should nae have hit him that hard, poor baby." She exclaimed mournfully.

Really! I thought she was angry with him. Clear of the club and with the fire exit now blocked, thanks mostly to Donna's casting, we ran up the street back to the car. Out of breath Donna got in the driver's seat and started the engine. Col and two of his companions raced after us. So much for the block.

"Wow they're fast." Donna announced.

Yes, they are, faster even than me. I needed to ask Donna just what the Keltoi are capable of. Slamming her foot on the accelerator she flung the car into reverse and started up the road. Col was practically on us, the look in his eyes a warning, a silent declaration, 'You dare run from me'. I felt like a sparrow who was trying to avoid the talons of a hawk, I should have been afraid but instead I was excited, the thought of Col capturing me was worryingly appealing.

Reaching the end of the street, Donna pulled up the hand brake, spinning the car a hundred and eighty degrees to face the other way. Her foot never leaving the accelerator, the car spun forward with a screech. Col and his companions hit the back of the car, smashing the back window. Fortunately for us not even a hunter could out run an Audi

R8. Before we knew it their hold on the car was lost and we quickly gained ground, their silhouettes the only proof they were in pursuit. That and the smashed window.

"We need to dump the car." I said, ignoring the urge to return to him.

"What? Why? I'm not dumping Percy" she squealed outraged.

"Percy? You named your car Percy?" I asked stunned.

Must be a witch thing.

"I name all my cars. I happen to love Percy. Why do I have to dump him anyway? Which I will nae by the way." she exclaimed, her faced scrunched up in disgust.

"They wouldn't have pursued us out of the club if they didn't intend to catch us." I explained, the thrill of getting caught returning. "It wouldn't require much effort to trace your number plates."

"Oh." She smiled.

"Well in that case nae need to worry I put a glamour on the plates. The numbers and letters change periodically, none of which are actually genuine. Basically, they cannae trace it."

"And you just happened to have that in place?" I asked surprised.

It was definitely a skill that might come in useful.

"Well you might have noticed I like to speed. I do nae like receiving speeding tickets." She laughed wickedly.

"I see." I smiled, trice in one day. The witch is growing on me.

Hunters

"So, where are they?" Mumbled Aengus, one hand supporting his crotch the other resting lazily against the wall.

Watching the red-haired hunter, I was struggling to form a response. The stench that permeated the air was foul, stale ale and refuge had my nose revolting in protest, it was so potent you could almost taste it. Of all the places to park the car, Eoghuan had to choose an alley crammed with restaurant bins.

"We lost them." Eoghuan said.

"How the hell did you manage that? They are a pair of wee lassies." Aengus grunted annoyed, his bearded face full of disbelief.

"A pair of wee lassies with a car." Ansgar answered, leaning against our black 4x4, scanning the police radio for reports of a white Audi R8 speeding.

The witch was reckless, she was mortal, a kick in the head could end her life, let alone speeding in a high-performance car. It's probably best I hadn't mentioned it to Aengus, her driving habits will only anger him.

"A nice car at that." Eoghuan added.

"That just makes it easier to trace. Have you run the plates?" I asked Finian, my mind still replaying tonight's events.

Mara… my anam cara. Finally, after nearly two millennia I found the one that is to be mine, the one every hunter waits for... and she ran from me. Not exactly how I envisioned meeting my soul mate.

"Yeah. Whatever plates were on that car were duds." He replied dryly.

The raven-haired warrior looked surprised, but then in our experience civilians didn't think about such things. Just who are these women?

"And cars matching the description?" I asked, unable to keep the frustration from my voice.

"One hundred and four. Within a forty-mile radius." Finian announced, flicking through pages on his tablet.

"They could be from anywhere." Ansgar yawned.

"No, the witch said she was local. Judging by blondies temper when she thought I'd hurt her, she keeps close to hand, maybe even living together. A bodyguard maybe, she has definitely had training." Aengus grimaced, his hand no longer nursing his crotch.

"What did you do to piss off the witch anyway?" Finian grinned, his navy-blue eyes mocking Aengus as he often did.

"I know where this be going Finian, do nae be blaming me now. None of this was my fault. Well… maybe concerning Donna, but that blond psycho is nae on me." He hissed.

Slowly lifting his hands above his head, he stretched backwards, cracking his back. Tilting his head to the side the hunter grinned widely.

"The witch is a stunner, isn't she nae? Those never-ending legs and pert wee mouth!" He boasted loudly.

"She is that Aengus. I'll shall greatly enjoy bedding that one." Finian taunted.

"I swear pretty boy, if you touch her, I'll kill you!"

Now stood to his full height, my giant of a friend, glared at Finian murderously. Laughing un-perplexed Finian walked to the back of the 4x4 and climbed into the back seat.

"I was just jesting you idiot. Like I would touch your anam cara. Unless of course she was begging for it, like your last girlfriend, then I can't be deemed liable. Gentlemen that

I am, I can't leave a lady wanting now, can I?" He smiled, his laughter deep and throaty could be heard from inside the car.

This is all I need, last time Finian pissed off Aengus he ended up completely naked, hung up by his ankles, in full frontal view of several hundred humans who were visiting the Eiffel tower. The amount of mind control needed to fix that problem left us near dead from exhaustion for nearly three days. Aengus grunted dangerously, we needed to go.

"Enough Finian. We need to find the women. They are anam cara, I have never heard of two being found within two hundred years of each other, let alone on the same night, it's unheard of. For their own protection, they must be found and returned to the estate."

Sounds simple, and yet I couldn't shake the feeling that this might be harder than expected. For one I'm not finding them to kill them, and protecting people who don't want your protection never ends well. Witches are notoriously stubborn and like to stay close to their coven, and as for Mara, I don't know where to begin. I know every species upon the face of the earth, their strengths, weaknesses. I have studied them, hunted them, some to destroy, others to protect. When you have lived as long I have you recognise them for what they are, know their breed, anticipate their movements. Until Mara that is, what is she?

Normally I could read her mind, ferret out the truth, but as my anam cara I can't read her thoughts, her secretes hidden from me. I could ask one of the others to read her but to read the thoughts of an anam cara, yours or another's, is a crime. Without such an advantage, I know only that she is neither one species nor another, but a combination of two. I can detect a darkness residing within her, it is silent, and yet I can sense it is powerful, and more alarmingly, eager to be free. It worries me, it's not a quality one would expect to find in the anam cara of a hunter. Especially mine. As Lord of the Keltoi it is my duty to seek the destruction of any who dwell in the dark and hide amongst its shadows. How then can she, tainted as she is, belong to me? Mara is shadow born, of that I have no doubt. I should destroy her, and yet I knew the moment I saw her she was my anam cara, my Soul mate.

Like the males of all of the immortal races, the Keltoi are born with the knowledge that enables us to recognise instantly the keeper of their soul. Just one look at her is all it took for my soul to hunger for her, ache for her. But she was supposed to submit to me, recognise me as I did her. A woman of my kind would know this instinctively, they would not run. In less than a second Mara has captured my full and undivided attention, and I don't have a clue what she is or where she is.

"What of Sköll? he is close, I feel him." Ansgar frowned, his voice, quiet, cutting through my thoughts.

Another issue I'd have to deal with. We have been hunting Sköll for years. It is the reason why we're here in the first place.

"You are all aware that like us he is hunting, he has done little to hide his presence from us, either he wants us to find him which is highly unlikely, or he has found his prey and with his prize in sight, no longer cares if we discover him."

One hundred and nineteen years we have been tracking him, always we've remained one step behind. Prior to that time, he was but a legend that had for whatever reason disappeared from the sight of man, only to suddenly reappeared like a virus hell bent on destroying life in any of its forms. After ninety-eight years of perusal his travel patterns suddenly changed. It became evident that he himself had started his own hunt. During this time not once had the ancient ever been complacent, and then, two weeks ago, he became easily traceable. He could have left a trail of breadcrumbs that would have been less noticeable.

"Maybe after living since the dawn of time he's feeling suicidal." Finian mused from the back of the car.

"I doubt it. The trail of mutilated bodies he's leaving all over the place would suggest he's still rather fond of living, or rather, the living." Eoghuan added grimly.

"Aye, all the more reason to locate the lassies and bring them in. Should he discover their anam cara he will certainly take them. Especially blondie." Aengus warned, worry creasing his forehead.

No doubt he was worrying about the witch as I was Mara.

"Aengus is right Conlaóch. No one hates you as much as Sköll, should his spy's have seen you with the girl… For years now, you have lived only for the hunt. Any report that you were interested in a woman would warrant his attention." Finian said, his voice adopting a more serious note. "Found them."

"Who? my witch?" Aengus asked, his huge body coming to life, deep blue eyes, focusing on Finian.

"Answer me you cocky Irish bastard." Aengus called impatiently.

"Give me a chance!" Finian grunted. "I want to make sure. You know me, nothing but thorough." He added smugly.

"Aye, I know you. Young, arrogant, impulsive." Aengus accused, moving at speed towards the car.

His body, tense and coiled, was ready to beat the information from him should the need arise.

"Don't forget intelligent, handsome, and God's gift to women." He winked, the gesture clearly visible in the rear-view mirror.

"God's gift? Please!" Mocked Eoghuan.

"It's true, when I leave, women across the world mourn the loss of me." Finian continued.

"Keep telling yourself that Finian, but let's face it brother, when it actually comes down to it, a woman will always choose a man to a boy, experience rather than flattery."

"On the contrary brother. With a face like yours, no woman alive would care for your experience." Finian chuckled.

Aengus reached the car and slammed his over-sized hand against the roof. The noise echoed loudly through the alley, causing a cat to screech loudly before running off.

"Your identical twins you pair of idiots. You're both inexperienced and equally as ugly, and if that's nae bad enough, you're Irish. Now you going to tell me where you found my wee witch, or do I have to teach you another lesson on respecting your elders" Aengus grinned wickedly.

"The women Finian?" I asked impatiently.

We can't afford delays. No one is safe with Sköll around.

"Of the hundred and four cars matching the description only two were registered under a Donna. One of whom is thirty-two and married, the other is twenty-four and single." He said, pleased with his discovery.

"She wore no wedding band." Aengus added possessively, his face barely concealing his anxiety.

His concern mirrored my own. They may not know it yet, but they belong to us, ours, and ours alone. I remembered being sceptical as a youth when we were taught about ones anam cara, they claimed it was life altering. Just one look they said, and you will be theirs forever. I always thought it an exaggeration, meant to discourage promiscuity. After all, it was only recently that freedom to choose lovers was accepted by society. Guess I've been proven wrong, I don't mind, it rarely happens, but this sudden need to possess her alarmed even me. The desire is so potent, it's as though poison has been injected into your body, its presence sent to oversee your destruction, your only hope is to possess the cure, to possess her.

"What's the address of the younger one?" I asked.

With any luck, they would believe themselves free and clear. They won't be expecting us.

"She lives in Merchant city, less than a mile from Argyle station." Finian answered

"The time?" I asked.

"11.24pm." Eoghuan added, climbing into the car to join his brother.

"We will wait until 04:30 hours, they should be asleep by then. Eoghuan, Finian, go scout the building, I want every exit covered. They have already run once so you can be certain they will attempt to run again. Stay on your guard, the witch will undoubtedly have the house warded. She might have other traps in place also. Make sure the CCTV is out of operation. Aengus, you secure Donna, I'll get Mara. Ansgar cover our backs. Do we still have the warded cuffs for the witch?" I asked Eoghuan.

The last thing we needed was the witch casting.

"I'll have them ready boss. Just out of curiosity where are we going to keep them? I can't imagine them being model prisoners. A witch and a, 'whatever' the blond one is, are not going to go quietly or remain quiet." Eoghuan added from within the car.

Good point.

"Ansgar you still own that land up at the Cairngorms?" I asked.

"Aye, boss." Ansgar responded happily. "Be glad to visit the place. It's been a long while."

"Electricity?"

"Aye. I have made sure everything is up to date. Satellite, supplies. It's all there."

"Good. You all know what you have to do?" I asked.

"Aye"

"Yeah, we got it."

"Then let's move out".

The Chase

After returning to Donna's apartment it wasn't long before the witch fell asleep. She wasn't kidding when she said her body was like a mortal's. I had originally planned to get information from her, about my future, about the Keltoi, but instead I watched the witch clearly upset with the red headed brute, fall swiftly asleep.

With Donna sleeping, the events of the night kept replaying through my mind. Something was happening to me, something that I didn't understand. A darkness, foreboding and evil was stirring. I should have been afraid, instead I was intrigued. Just what was I becoming, and what would it mean? Pain was obviously a precursor for my change, not long after my vision was brought back under control, the red haze abated, pain started lashing at my insides, the sickening sensation like acid burning me from the inside out.

By the time we had reached the flat, several of my bones had broken, only to reset and break again, and I had no idea why. I wanted to tell Donna, but exposing a weakness is stupid, especially when Donna was still a question. I wanted her to be all that she claimed to be, but I was still unsure. Unable to do anything about the pain, I focused on Donna asleep on the sofa. Her long chocolate brown hair was a mess, tendrils of feather soft hair, clinging to her porcelain skin in soft curls. I never knew normal people could be so restless when sleeping. I thought it was only me, the damaged one.

I wanted to wake her, to rescue her from a nightmare, but I didn't even know if she was having one, she didn't look afraid, so I left her. Constantly moving she was making me feel tetchy, her erratic and sudden jerks reminding me too much of the sleep that had plagued me and the reasons I fought it.

Frustrated, I wondered for the hundredth time today why I was still here. Unable to placate myself, or answer my own questions…again. I went to the room Donna had designated for me and ignored the pain that was relentlessly coursing through my body.

Moving around languidly, I looked for hidden traps, cameras, anything that could pose a threat and prove that Donna wasn't what she claimed to be. A potential friend, my first friend, possibly even my only friend. After twenty minutes of coming up empty, I finally resigned myself to the fact that maybe she is what she proposes to be, and gave into the temptation of trying out the bed. My bed.

Laying down slowly, I allowed the luxurious fabrics to mould against my body, gently cocooning myself within the lush silks and expensive cottons that had my senses purring in gratitude. I was so comfortable, so at ease, I couldn't help but run the folds of rich delicate fabrics against my exposed skin. It felt good, and as hard as I tried to ignore the urge, I couldn't stop myself from stretching out like a cat across the bed. Unconsciously, my body began to relax and uncoil, my tension easing. I wished the pain would too. Pulling the duvet up over my legs and arms, I revelled in the feeling of safety, genuine or imagined, and thought that for the first-time sleep might actually come easily. Perhaps this time when I closed my eyes the nightmares will remain absent, a first I would gladly embrace. Allowing my eyes to fall shut, I let sleep prevail. My last thought before the darkness took over, Col, and those damn green eyes.

An explosion that shook the apartment, and by the sound of it, the entire building, dragged me from my sleep. Donna screamed! I jumped out of bed and ran out of the room to find her. Just as I exited the bedroom, fire alarms began ringing, bursting my ear drums, and leaving me temporarily deaf. The unexpected condition forced me to halt. Quickly healed, and adjusting to the pitch, I cautiously continued into the front room.

I saw Donna on the floor besides the sofa she had been asleep on earlier. After checking the room for an intruder and finding the apartment empty, I moved to help her get up from the floor. Out of nowhere water began to pour from the ceiling, in what could only be described as mini torrents. What the hell! It looked like a storm had broken loose within the confines of her apartment. Soaked through, my head ringing, and my body still in agony, I helped Donna to her feet. She was confused and still half asleep. She must have fallen from the couch and was only just realising water was ruining her dress and all her furnishings. The look on her face was priceless.

"I'm going to kill that bull-headed brute of a man!" Donna screamed.

Now fully awake, she took in the sight of her apartment, her face marred in annoyance. Ignoring my discomfort, I ran to the kitchen and armed myself with some knives, this time I will cut first and ask later.

"What's happening?" I asked Donna.

"They have come for us! They have chosen to follow the path in which they have deemed us fragile little flowers who need to be shipped off for our own protection." Donna huffed loudly.

"Fragile?"

Hardly!

"Aye! Of all the possibilities, they have gone and chosen the one I dislike the most. Now they're going to discover why it's nae wise to piss off a witch!" Donna screeched. "Look at my house!" She added despairingly.

"So, you're saying they plan on kidnapping us?"

Idiot men!

"Aye! That's exactly what they intend. But nae worry, I planned for this even though I hoped it would nae come to pass." Donna declared wickedly. "The explosion was a warning." She continued "Right now they will be breaking through a door they wrongly believe is mine, they're going to be disappointed. I did nae just set wards, I created a whole new floor above my own." She said, whilst moving frantically around the flat looking for something

"You created an illusion? Clever!" I grinned, impressed with the witch's cunning.

"Aye, however they're hunters, it will nae take them long to figure out the type of spell I used. We need to get to Gilbert quickly." Donna explained, whilst hurriedly throwing clean laundry, make-up, her phone, and iPad into the bag she had now found.

"Who's Gilbert?" I asked curiously.

"My other car." Donna smiled.

Oh, why did I ask? Amused, I smiled back.

"Ok, so, down the stairs to the garage, get into Gilbert and drive like the wind?" I asked with one brow raised.

"Aye, that's the plan, oh and I intend to leave them a little welcoming, or rather, leaving present! Now they will know what it feels like to see red!" She grinned, her eyes gleaming menacingly.

What does that mean?

"They will have the garage watched. You should go out first, make it seem as though you're on your own. When I see the lookout following you, I will come up behind him and take him out."

"Got it! Do nae kill him though, he is nae out to kill you." Donna said, standing ready at the door.

"Fine, do you have any rope, chains?" I asked disappointed.

Although she is probably right, killing would be unnecessary on this occasion.

"I have magic. You detain him, and I will conjure you up some chains that nae even a hunter can get out off." She claimed, her eyes mournfully appraising her beloved home.

"Ready when you are."

Determined she left her apartment, me in tow.

Wet through and eager to teach the hunters a lesson we made our way down to the low-level garage. A knife in both hands, I moved silently. Half way down the stairs my vision started to flicker, blues, greens, yellows, and reds were the only colours I could see, each of them forming the structures around me. A flash of bright red caught my attention. My head instinctively swung following the vivid blur. I quickly identified it as a rat. It ran past the door at the bottom of the stairwell leaving a bright trail of oranges and yellows in its wake. Panic flared, what the hell, I could see heat normally, but this was a whole different level. Blinking my eyes rapidly I tried to switch my vision back to what I knew, what I understood, nothing happened.

Quickly but carefully we rounded the corner exiting the stairwell, my fears momentarily pushed aside, my face revealing nothing. Grabbing Donna, I pulled her to the floor. Using my head, I pointed to the left indicating that the lookout was there. His positioning was downhill to avoid me scenting him, but I could see the same red and orange glare the rat had, only on a much larger scale. Nodding, she stood and boldly made her way over to Gilbert, while I remained crouched waiting for the hunter to approach her. It took only moments before the hunter spotted Donna and began to follow. His hesitant movement suggested he suspected foul play. Scanning the area where I was hidden he searched for the threat. I thought our plan had failed, that somehow, he knew I laid in wait, but thankfully he didn't. Passing me without so much as a second glance, the hunter followed Donna. Perfect.

Pausing at the car, Donna pretended to fumble with her keys, allowing the hunter to approach. Following him silently, I waited for him to make his move. Donna yelped surprised when the Hunter grabbed her right arm, placing it in a metallic band. Desperately, but without fear, he tried to fasten it onto her left arm, in an attempt to bind the two together. Struggling when Donna kicked him hard in the shin, the hunter shoved her against the car, the action making her grunt.

Silently, and pissed he had just hurt her, I moved in behind him. With one knife pressed dangerously into his kidney, I placed the other tightly against his throat. A hiss of annoyance was his only response to my presence.

"Release her hunter and I will let you live." I breathed against his ear.

"There be nae need for this now lassie. I nae intend you any harm." He answered calmly

"Says the man who was in the process of abducting my friend."

"It be for your own protection."

"We do nae need protecting, nor do we want it." Donna glared angrily

"May haps nae, but you are in danger. An ancient one named Sköll will undoubtedly be coming for you." He warned.

"And why would he be interested in us?" Donna asked, when he released his hold on her.

"Because you are Aengus's anam cara. If you die, he dies. Witch or no, you're the easier target."

Spinning around to face the hunter, Donna was surprised, her body shimmering with power.

"You dare lie to me of such." she accused outraged.

"I speak truth little one." He said patiently, lifting his hand protectively in front of him.

Staring at him for what seemed like minutes, Donna finally calmed down and let out a slow steady breath.

"Aye… As much as it pains me I can see you speak truth, I dinnae know the bond was that strong." She said quietly, thoughtfully, her mouth gently pursed.

"This Sköll, he has seen us?" I asked, fear fluttering down my back, the sensation far from pleasant.

I cannot afford another creature hunting me. Sighing inwardly, I constantly scanned the car park for the others. It was only a matter of time before they appeared.

"I have nae reason to doubt. He has his creatures spying everywhere." The hunter added disgusted.

Great, that's bloody brilliant.

"You are hunting him?" I asked the hunter.

"Aye, it's the reason we're here."

"Aengus dinnae come for me?" Donna asked disappointed.

"No. We had nae intentions of entering the club, but Col detected a presence, something cloaked in shadow. He thought Sköll was attempting to mask his presence, disguise himself as another like he has done in the past. Instead he found you." The hunter said, the latter directed at me.

That would explain why the witch only met him if I was there I thought silently.

"She nae be evil! At least nae wholly. Now that she has me I can help her control it, let her other side surface." Donna said proudly, defensively.

Other side? I have a good side?

"She is Col's and as such she is his to be dealt with." The hunter announced arrogantly, like it was fact, a truth I had no choice in.

It pissed me off, a sudden need to punch him dominating my thinking.

"I belong to no one hunter" I said icily, the knife I held against his kidney drawing blood, the allure like before, so very tempting.

"Your fate is the same as hers. You cannae escape it."

"I'll have the rope now if you please" I said to Donna in a low growl of annoyance.

"Aye, I'm with you." She grinned mischievously. "You can release him now, I have immobilised him." She added, her gaze thoughtful, studied the hunter.

Relinquishing my hold on him, I took the rope that had appeared out of thin air and fasten it around his wrists. Satisfied my knots would support his weight, I threw the other end of the rope over a steel support beam, lifting the hunter to rest a foot above the ground.

"This is pointless you will nae get far." The hunter threatened, as he calmly hung mid-air, like it was a normal everyday occurrence.

Ignoring him I tied the other end of the rope onto a neighbouring cars tow bar. Conscious of the time spent detaining him and sure he was stalling for time I decided it was probably best to go.

"You ready?" I asked Donna, who was staring sweetly at the hunter.

It was obvious she found his predicament amusing.

"Aye, but first I want to leave a message for Aengus. Will you give it to him Hunter?" She asked.

"Aye, but it will make no difference."

Donna tapped her fingers on her lips gently.

"Tell him… I am willing to forgive him for the damage to my flat and the insult to both mine and Mara's intelligence in believing we are helpless fawning women, who need a man in order to survive. If...! Aengus and the rest of you sexist medieval brutes are willing to treat us as equals and allow us to accompany you as such, if you give us your word that we will remain free and under no circumstances will you detain us, we will come with you, without a fight." She said confidently.

"We will?" I asked, my tone full of disbelief.

Ti's warnings rang loud.

"Aye, but you must also promise that despite what you may or may nae learn about Mara, she will nae be hurt in anyway, that by your own laws, both Mara and I will be protected. I want Conlaóch's word as lord and overseer of your people, nothing less will be acceptable." She quickly added, sensing my uncertainty.

"Anything else witch, Scotland perhaps!" The hunter mocked, a small smile trying to break free from the otherwise stoic form of his mouth.

"Now that you mention it, aye, there is. You tell Aengus I am rather fond of diamonds, white gold, or platinum mounts, nae yellow gold. I look forward to receiving my gift of apology so much so, that I give him my word… The bigger the diamond, the bigger the kiss. And if he should include an emerald I might just let him choose where." She smiled sweetly, her eyes twinkling brightly with mischief.

Kissing! I didn't understand the relevance? Aengus must be fond of it, that or she knows they won't take her up on the offer.

"Anything else?" The hunter asked, clearly amused with Donna's demands.

"Nae, we're good, if they accept my terms they need only agree. I will know, and we will come to you!" She replied.

"And what about you lassie, what do you want?"

Impressed with Donna's boldness I answered.

"A blow torch would be useful."

Opening the passenger side door to Donna's Land Rover, I got in.

The hunter burst out laughing, deep and raucous it echoed around the cavernous garage. I almost wanted to laugh with him, this whole idea of me agreeing to travel with five hunters was hysterical, but I didn't. Sliding into a plush leather seat, my dress damp and uncomfortably clingy, the hunter called out

"And what will you give in return"

"I have already given a gift. I spared your life." I said smugly, before closing the door.

Driving out of the garage, Donna sped up the street, my vision finally returning too normal.

"So where are we going now?" I asked.

"Somewhere that even they would nae dare to follow." She replied on a giggle.

"And that is?"

"My coven." She grinned.

Illusions

The blast was unexpected, but not as much as running into a room that was actually nothing but wide-open sky. Aengus was the one who entered the false room first, which is why it was now me who was desperately trying to maintain my hold on the roof, as well as trying to hull Aengus's large arse, up, and over the edge. Clever witch! She had created a whole bloody floor on the roof as a decoy. I should have been pissed, but when you have lived as long as I have, it's not often you're surprised, I couldn't help but be a little impressed.

"Damn it! Bloody witch near on killed me!" Aengus mumbled.

I pulled him up onto the safety of the roof. Standing to his full height of seven foot four, he was a foot taller than me. The giant of a man, my friend and fellow hunter, looked torn between being appalled and being proud.

"I wouldn't take in personally, all lovers quarrel at some point." I grinned.

"Aye, but she is nae yet my lover. I cannae help but feel a bit cheated." He grumbled. "A dive off a roof and I've nae even had a kiss." he added, feeling sorry for himself.

Amused at his sorry face, we raced back towards the stairwell. With an explosion of that magnitude the element of surprise was lost. We needed to act fast, before they decided to flee. Reaching the correct floor, the illusion no longer in effect, we moved swiftly and quietly along the flooded corridors, until we arrived at Donna's apartment door, a mirror image of the false one above. This time Aengus paused before opening.

"I'll let you take this one old friend." He smiled.

"Too kind" I grinned, the faint gesture laced in sarcasm.

Mentally counting down to three I kicked open the door. It came flying off its hinges, traveling at speed and landing on a glass coffee table. Shards of glass erupted everywhere, scattering, and then sinking beneath the pool of water that covered the floor.

"I hope she nae like that table" Aengus said quietly, entering the apartment.

"I wouldn't hold your breath."

A low growl was his reply.

"Col!" Finian called.

Why the hell was he here? Turning to face the entrance way and consequently Finian I knew something had gone wrong.

"What is it!" I asked coldly.

"They're nae here!" Aengus roared frustrated, returning from what I assumed was the bedroom.

"There is no good way to say this, so I'll just get on with it. The Witch! She has to be psychic, the security room was warded too." He said surprised.

"We went and took out the CCTV like you said. Just as we were leaving this blue vapour started rising from the floor attaching itself to our legs. One minute we're trying to free ourselves from the fog the next we're waking up only to find five minutes had past. I sent Eoghuan to help Ansgar and I came to warn you. They're not here, and if they were, they're gone."

"We've under estimated them" Aengus said flatly, smoke curling in his eyes.

"They are our anam cara, we should have known they would be exceptional" I sighed, scanning the apartment needlessly.

"Exceptional is one word for it!" Finian complained.

"We regroup." I said.

Annoyed we made our way back down the corridor. Where would they go?

Click, click, click, click….

"What's that?" Finian asked

"GET DOWN!" I snapped.

I flung myself down into the water, just in time. Small sporadic explosions erupted the length of the hallway, one after another they ejected puffs of claret red powder that filled the hall.

"What the bloody hell is it?" Aengus asked, rising from the water warily, his brow creased in annoyance.

Studying the powder, I lifted it to my nose, inhaling its scent, it wasn't hard to identify.

"It's dye" I answered dryly.

"Why dye?" Finian asked standing.

His clothes were ruined, no doubt that was the point, we ruined her things, she ruins ours.

"They're women! Nothing they do makes sense" Aengus said, wiping water from his face.

His face, like Finian's, was coloured a vivid blood red. The water and dye combination creating a stain that coated our skin. I held no hope that I had escaped it, we can only pray it's not permanent. Thoroughly pissed and no longer impressed with the witch, we headed to the garage.

"And I thought I had it bad" Ansgar said, attempting to contain a smile.

Given the mood I'm in, he would be wise to do so. I can't remember the last time I felt this angry. The woman was mine! And I wanted her back.

"Yeah you should have seen him. Mara hung him up like a prized turkey! While the witch made ridiculous demands" Eoghuan said astounded.

"Demands?" I asked in a low growl.

Does she not realise she's fated to me? There is no negotiation.

"What kind of demands?" Aengus asked, clearly stunned.

"I'm nae sure you're going to like them boss. But I have to say the lassies have brass." Ansgar grinned.

Brass? I used to think that was good quality.

"There's nothing like bad news when you're having a bad day, out with it." I snarled.

Wiping what dye I could from my weapons, I listened to the demands.

"Are they mad? They want us to let them accompany us while we hunt Sköll in return for their compliance." Finian hissed.

"Don't' forget the part where we're supposed to allow them to do whatever they want!" Eoghuan added.

"I'm more interested in the part about the kiss, diamonds aye? And I can choose where?" Aengus hummed thoughtfully, a huge grin dominating his face.

"Damn it Aengus, focus!" Ansgar scowled.

Ignoring the conversation, I thought about the demands. The witch had me backed into a corner and I hated it. Hated the idea that Mara would be exposed to Sköll, should I agree. Hated that she wanted my word not as Col, but as lord of the Keltoi, securing their freedom should they chose to run. Hated that Mara had already run… twice! But most of all I hated that agreeing was my only real option.

When a witch is in trouble there's only one place she would go, her coven. If I don't accept her terms I will never get Mara out, not unless they committed a crime, and last I checked, running from one's soul mate doesn't constitute as a crime. Angry and frustrated, I walked back across the garage to the car. I needed a fight, needed to vent.

"Boss, you ok?" Eoghuan called out.

I wanted to shout, 'No. I'm fucking not!' Instead I growled, the lethal sound, filling the underground garage.

Pulling my broad sword from my back, I swung it with all the strength and speed I possessed, straight into the roof of a gaudy pink mini. The sound when the blade hit was nearly as deafening as the roar I expelled. The ancient broad sword cut through the mini's roof like it was made of butter. Unsatisfied with the damage one hit did, I continued to stab and cut at it like its death was the solution to my problem.

Magic

The Coven wasn't what I expected. After a sixty-minute drive out of Glasgow we arrived at a castle neatly tucked away behind a group of enormous evergreens. The highlands in all their splendour, created a back drop that was nothing short of breath taking. As for the castle itself, it was striking, huge grey bricks forming the castles façade, nature complimenting the stone. It was Beautiful! The sound of birds singing their morning tune only added to its appeal. At first glance, there didn't appear to be any cameras or security, but I knew better. I could feel the hum of magic surrounding the large estate, the castle was heavily warded. There would be traps everywhere, the trick is deducing where.

Getting out of the car cautiously, I followed Donna as she made her way up to the huge grand doors. They stood at least twelve feet from the ground. Arched at the top they were medieval and appeared to be carved from oak. Before Donna had the chance to knock, the doors swung in-wards. On the other side stood a man who looked like he was in his earlier thirties. White blond hair and ice blue eyes glared at me with contempt and undisguised disgust.

"You brought her here?" He asked.

"Aye, I said it was a possibility." Donna answered, walking past him without so much as a hello, how are you.

She obviously didn't like the man, which for unknown reasons meant I didn't either. Staring at him with murder in my eyes, I joined Donna in the foyer.

"Is he a witch?" I asked Donna.

"Warlock!" The man hissed, his manner aggressive.

His cold eyes raked my body, the small gleam contained within them, relaying the fact he enjoyed the view. My dress, still slightly damp, clung to my skin, making me feel exposed. I growled low, not liking his attention. The need to hurt the stupid man was growing fast.

"He is nae important, call him arsehole! Fits him well." Donna replied coldly.

"Nice to see you're still a bitch!" He replied tartly.

"Watch your mouth" I hissed "and look elsewhere!" I warned, the beast stirring dangerously, a fresh wave of pain twisting my insides.

I clenched my fists tightly, my finger nails embedding themselves into my palms. It stung, but the pain was making it easier to maintain control. I really wanted to hurt him, watch as his life faded from his eyes. I'll make it slow, draw it out…

"I'm not afraid of you half breed, I'll look at you whenever and wherever I please." He smirked.

"Ignore him Mara, most do." Donna added, pulling me hastily from the foyer.

My control slipped a bit further, my desire to kill the warlock fierce, like a compulsion I couldn't break, didn't want to break. Ideas, dark ideas on how best to kill him swam through my mind. Should I torture him first, or be merciful and offer him a quick death? Torture… Mercy, torture, mercy.

Donna must have noticed my internal battle as she deliberately bypassed other people who called out to her, dragging me quickly behind.

"Let's get you something to eat, shall we." She said, entering a large, richly furnished kitchen.

Good idea. Sitting down at what I recognised as a breakfast bar, I watched Donna search the cupboards for something to eat. Being away from the warlock was calming, my control instantly returning. Good. Studying Donna, I got the impression that she knew something, or at least suspected something about what was happening to me. The witch was incredibly in tune to my needs.

"What am I?" I asked her, afraid to leave the question any longer.

Returning to place a bowl and spoon in front of me, Donna looked hesitant.

"Truthfully, I do nae know." She pouted regretfully. "I know you want answers Mara, but I am as blind as you are."

She seemed to be searching my eyes for a reaction.

"You said you have seen my future, surely then you would know what I was?"

Donna sighed sadly.

"My visions do nae work like that. I see different possibilities, depending on people's choices. They appear as images, usually in dreams. I can see people speak, but their words are silent and often an image can mean something other than what it appears. It's all very confusing and I'm still only learning to decipher them." She explained, whilst pouring cereal into my bowl.

Disappointed I picked up the spoon. At least my anger was subsiding.

"That's why there was trouble when you thought there wouldn't be?" I asked.

Pouring milk over my cereal Donna grinned shyly.

"Aye, that's my fault. I can see the consequences of other's choices, but not of my own. In none of my visions did I ever see myself angry. When Aengus told me I belonged to him, like a piece of lost baggage, I chose to let it anger me, and as such I altered the path we were on. One I have nae seen before. I'll be the first to admit, I do nae always get it right. I was so focused on how much I wanted to meet Aengus that I dinnae pay attention to the other details. Like the fact they were all armed! I'm sorry for putting you in danger." She said quietly.

"I know nothing else" I answered, tucking in to my cereal.

"As I am beginning to realise" Donna added grimly.

"Tell me about the Keltoi?"

If I can't get answers about my future, then I can at least prepare for the hunters.

"Now that I can help with". She smiled.

The Keltoi, as Donna explained were once neighbours to the Greeks. A hidden secretive people they lived a nomadic life, traveling at will. They were known for their skills as warriors and were widely left alone. At some point in their history they gave up their nomadic life and sought a place to call home, eventually settling in Alba and Eire also known as Scotland and Ireland. Today their ancestors are referred to as Celts and were responsible for the Celtic traditions and values that are still revered and loved. Donna further explained that they are guardians and keepers of balance, balance pertaining to good and evil. It is there duty to protect the world from the ever-increasing evil that seeks to destroy life. Wholly good they live only on what they need and live by old traditions and beliefs. Which would explain why they wanted to protect us and not seek our thoughts on the matter. From what I understood from earth's history, women had it bad. Rarely were they ever consulted. They were told what to do and they were not to question it. Intrigued, I motioned for Donna to continue.

"They are exceptionally strong, more so when they have fully matured. As you may remember they are also very fast. They were created by Gaia, mother earth, to protect life. They eat as we do, and they also need sleep as we do, but they can easily go days, even weeks without it." She said, now eating her own bowl of cereal.

I was on my third.

"And their weapons?"

"They prefer the weapons of old, something to do with the way they were made. Some sort of magical protection I guess." She said, intrigued herself.

"What else can they do? Magic?" I asked curiously.

"Nae, I do nae believe so. But they have all sorts of magical items they have gathered over the years. They are immortal, so they pick up things."

I have seen various magical devices myself, have had them used against me, I wasn't overly impressed.

"Anything else I should know about?"

"They can read minds." She said unconcerned.

Read minds! I spat my cereal back into the bowl. No wonder Col was staring at me, he was reading my mind.

"What! Why would you leave that bit of information as an afterthought?" I asked appalled.

Donna giggled.

"Because they cannae read the minds of an anam cara." She said mischievously.

"Anam Cara?"

I remembered Col calling me such.

"Aye, it's Irish Gaelic for soul mate." She smiled happily.

"Soul mate?" I frowned.

What the hell is that?

"You do nae know what a soul mate is?" She asked shocked.

Shaking my head in response, Donna looked at me with concern.

"But you know what a soul is?" She prodded.

"If it didn't involve fighting or surviving, and it wasn't on T.V the few occasions I actually got to see it, then no! Just assume I don't know anything." I admitted uncertainly.

"Will do."

I could see questions forming in her mind, shaking herself she focused on my question.

"So" She continued "Where to start… A soul is your life force, or is also known as your conscience. Your mind, your knowledge, your personality, the part of you that is nae physical. Here is an analogy for you. I'm nae very good at them but I will try my best." She said, sitting up straight in her chair.

"Ok" I said, my food forgotten.

"Gaia or Jörg depending on where you're from, Mother Earth, created an apple tree. That tree grew big and strong, but it was alone. In order to survive and thrive the tree had to produce seed, to create others. You with me?" She asked unsure.

"Yes, so far."

"Ok. So, the tree produced fruit. Of the hundreds of apples that grew, each one of them was different, nae two alike. For every one that existed only one would grow to become what the tree needed. Without the apple, the tree would stand alone and without the tree the apple wouldn't exist.

Now picture Aergus as the tree since he undoubtedly came before me, and picture me as an apple. Of the hundreds and thousands of women, 'apples', who have been born since Aengus the tree has stood. I am the apple, 'woman' who has been selected by fate to survive and grow. The only one that can be what he needs. Aengus will nae longer be alone, I exist in this world for him and 'he' for I. We are two halves that have come together to be a whole, perfectly selected by nature.

It is a rare few who ever find their soul mate Mara. Most live their lives feeling incomplete, unhappy, and unsatisfied. Nae get me wrong, they have moments of happiness, but they come and go like seasons. Many ease the loneliness by having weans but weans grow and people drift apart. You will never drift apart from your soul mate." Donna said, her face a mask of seriousness.

It sounded Claustrophobic. To need someone that much was a weakness and a guaranteed way of getting hurt, or worse, killed. I'm being hunted, if being close to Col was going to make me vulnerable and weak then I needed to keep my distance, I'm not ready to die.

The issue was, I wanted to stay with Donna, she has for reasons unknown become a friend, one of whom I have barely gotten to know. I don't understand the bond or need to protect her, but I cannot deny that the need to do so is there. In fact, the need to protect her was beyond my understanding, logically it didn't make any sense. Why would she matter when no one else ever has? I didn't even know her. It was an issue, Donna wanted to be with Aengus, wanted the bond that would ultimately tie them together. Having Aengus around means having Col around. As much as I wished I could keep Donna, I can't be with Col, nor would I deny her the happiness she seeks. No one deserves to know loneliness like that, it would ruin her. Aengus can protect her. The best thing I can do is move on, my time with her a memory to look back on when the darkness creeps in, tonight I would leave, I must, before those who hunt me begin to hunt her.

The Deal

It was close to midnight and despite my best efforts I was still reeling. No matter how many times I tried to make the Mara meeting Sköll thing play out as a positive, I couldn't. She is my anam cara! How could I possibly hunt him, defeat him, knowing that one wrong move will kill her because she's standing right beside me. She would be safe with the other women; the clan is protected. Nothing or no one could get in there, not even Sköll, not even his father Fenrir, monster of the river ván, the most feared immortal to ever grace the earth. Not without an army at least.

"Boss?" Ansgar called.

"What" I growled.

"Still in a bad mood I see."

"What do you want Ansgar?"

"We just heard from the clan, they have given us the location of four covens. Murdock coven and McCaffrey coven are the only two to return our calls, both claim the women are nae there."

"The names of the other two?" I asked non-committal.

Just because they say they're not there doesn't mean they aren't.

"McMurtrie and Stewart."

All this information and none of it useful. We were lucky with the apartment, but the surname Donna had registered it under was not her actual family name, and as such finding her coven was proving difficult.

Witches are untouchable in their covens and don't trust anyone. The minute they hear hunters are sniffing around, they will close up ranks and send us on a merry dance. Frustrated, I punched the leather-bound punch bag that hung in our temporary accommodation. The force of the punch caused chunks of plaster to fall from the ceiling, covering the concrete floor and spraying me in a fine powder.

The sound of velcro fastening caused me to turn around. Ansgar was in the process of putting on sparring gloves, his shirt removed.

"What are you doing?" I asked, already knowing the answer.

"It's been a couple of days since I've had a fight, I need to let off a bit of steam. Fancy helping me out?" He grinned.

He stepped into a make shift ring we had built for practice. Ansgar was the embodiment of calm, always in control. He did this for me, not him, and I appreciated it. The raven-haired warrior was the same height as me, his frame too resembled mine, broad at the shoulder and powerfully built. We didn't share the bulk that Aengus possessed but we were in no way disadvantaged. Thousands of years of fighting had honed our bodies fit for purpose. We were designed for war, built for it. Golden eyes searched mine as he waited for my response.

"I would be honoured old friend."

I stepped into the ring to join him. Circling slowly, we studied each other, each trying to predict the others intention. Ansgar was deadly and didn't hold back, for me to do the same would be stupid. Friend or not we would fight as though our lives depended on it. I made the first move. Moving suddenly to the left I faked a hook and instead attempted to take out Ansgar's legs. He didn't fall for it, but then I didn't expect him too.

Dodging a hard blow to the gut, I pivoted backwards a hundred and eighty degrees, leaving me standing at Ansgar's back. A quick elbow to his kidney got his attention, a grunt, the only indication I had hit him at all.

First contact made the fight spark to life. Jab after jab was passed between us as we each gave all we got. Ansgar was good, he had to be to be on my team. We were the elite, the ones that the other male hunters aspired to be. Normally we travelled in teams of four but when Finian and Eoghuan made it through to final selection to replace Kyle, a hunter and friend who now stands on the high council, the two warriors were found to be exceptional. Years of fighting together meant they knew each other's faults and weaknesses, subsequently no one warrior was better than the other. I decided that the brothers would be an exception to the rule, the youngest of the group, they have yet to let me down. To make it on to an elite squad at barely two hundred years was unheard of, I had high hopes for them. A hard crack to the mouth pulled me from my thoughts. Damn that hurt!

A quick inspection of my mouth confirmed I'd lost a tooth. That's what happens when you get distracted.

Using my one thousand five hundred and thirty-year advantage, I brought the fight to an end with an upper cut that connected squarely on Ansgar's jaw. With a thud, Ansgar fell to the ground chuckling.

"Feel better?" Ansgar asked, nursing his now swollen jaw.

"Yes, thank you."

Offering my hand, I helped Ansgar to his feet.

"Come old friend, we have a witch to placate."

I didn't like it, but what choice did I have?

Entering what we have dubbed the lounge, Eoghuan and Finian were busy cleaning weapons. Aengus was nowhere to be seen.

"Where's Aengus?" I asked no one in particular.

"He went out, said he wouldn't be long" Eoghuan answered.

"What could he possibly need at this time of night?"

He should know better than to travel alone with Sköll close by.

"He was mumbling something about diamonds." Finian snorted. "If you ask me I don't think it's wise to panda to women like that. Once you give in, that's it, they start expecting more. He will be broke by the end of the year!"

"Aye, but a happy anam cara is a happy hunter." Angsar added with a wink.

"What about you boss, you going to get Mara a blow torch?" Eoghuan chuckled.

"She'll be lucky if I don't tie her up for running out on me" I answered dryly.

I'm not sure I wanted to know what she needed a blow torch for. As long as it didn't involve kissing, I didn't care. Eoghuan and Finian's laughter filled the small room. The blow torch was an unusual request.

"From the little we've seen of Mara she would probably enjoy that." Finian interceded.

"Aye, as would Col" Aengus roared, storming into the room in a fluster.

That man didn't know how to be quiet. Everyone in the room stopped what they were doing and stared at him. Noticing that the room had just fallen silent, Aengus turned to face us.

"What?" He scowled.

"Where have you been?" I asked.

"Looking for a damn shop that sold diamonds. You would think that living in a day of twenty-four-hour shopping there would be more to choose from. It took a time before I eventually found a pawn shop that was open. None of their diamonds were particularly big. Do you think quantity will make up for size? I got everything they had." Aengus explained, his eyes serious.

"Just how many are we talking about?" Finian asked disapprovingly.

"I cannae be sure, thirty plus." Aengus guessed.

"Bloody hell Aengus! That's excessive. It never ends well spoiling women, I'm telling you." Finian moaned horrified.

"Huh, you wait until you find your anam cara. You will be bending over backwards to accommodate her every whim." Aengus grunted defensively.

"I can assure you, I will not! My woman will desire only my touch and will have no need for such things as diamonds. Also, she will listen to her hunter and stay where she will be safe." Finian added.

Eoghuan was the first to burst out laughing, quickly followed by the rest, Finian was deluded.

"Enough" I said, before Finian could add anything else.

"Donna has placed us in a precarious position. There is little we can do to take them from their coven unwilling. With this in mind I have no real choice but to except her conditions, are we all in agreement?"

"I do nae like it, but aye. I agree." Said Ansgar

"As do I" added Aengus.

"I agree" Eoghuan frowned.

"I guess there's little choice, I agree." Finian muttered with a scornful arc of his brow.

"I agree little witch" I said to the room.

Almost instantly Eoghuan's phone began to ring. We all stared at it.

"Eoghuan?" I called.

Looking at me, Eoghuan nodded. Retrieving his phone, he answered.

"Hello? I understand… Yes. An hour? Ok. What?... Yes ok, I will."

Hanging up he grinned.

"Well" I asked impatiently.

"It was the witch." Eoghuan said.

Of course, it was the bloody witch.

"And what did she say?" I hissed, not stating the obvious.

Normally my hearing would have permitted me the ability to hear, but the witch had obviously placed some sort of privacy spell on her phone. Annoyed, I stared at Eoghuan. If he didn't tell me everything soon it was going to get ugly.

"She said she's pleased we came to our senses and she looks forward to retrieving her gift. She accepts quantity over size and fully intends to keep her promise."

Aengus growled happily.

"She also said we can be there within the hour and that we shouldn't delay. She has text me the address of her coven. Oh, and she said to bring our manacles." Eoghuan finished.

"Manacles?" Aengus asked, his brow creased.

"That's what she said. She sounded a little concerned."

The witch knew something, and I couldn't help but think it had something to do with Mara. Loading the gear into our car, we left leaving nothing behind. The agreement with the witch only stipulated that they could travel with us freely, and that they wouldn't be harmed. It said nothing about leaving Glasgow. Turning off all the electrics we left for the McMurtrie Coven.

The Awakening

After eating what equated to seven bowls of cereal and four pieces of toast Donna spent the rest of the day introducing me to the members of her coven. With the exception of Ewan, the first warlock I met, everyone else seemed just as friendly and welcoming as Donna. Showered and dressed in clothes more like my own, I felt calm, like my normal self. With the castle now silent, all the adults and children having gone to bed, I sat in the huge library absorbing the peace and relishing in the rich woody scent of the books. Books are one of the only positives I could recall from my childhood. Ti was an avid reader, always he would return with a new book, and when he had finished would insist I read it too. Books of history, war, and philosophy, filled my mind from a young age. I love learning. On the rare occasions Ti brought home a book about nature, trees, plants, and animals, was the only time I could ever say I felt content. Of course, it was imperative I hid it from him, should he have known I have no doubt he would have thrown them into the fire. Just as he did Angelica.

We had been returning from Moscow and were in a small village about forty miles out, called Abramtsevo. Ti had travelled here in search of a knife. He never revealed why the knife was so important. Talking was only ever done when necessary, which was not often. Conversation was a definite no.

He left me to wait in the snow under a large spruce of evergreens. Sat on a rotten log, I waited for Ti. After two hours, my body shook uncontrollably, my fingers and toes frozen. Deciding that although I was told to stay here that didn't mean I had to remain seated, I stood.

Circling the small patch of trees, I attempted to warm up. As feeling slowly returned to my fingers I noticed a small piece of red cloth poking up from beneath the snow. Curiosity getting the better of me, I picked the item up, and brushed off the snow, from what I could now identify as a small wooden doll. I had seen other children with such, seen them smile as they ran with them and held them. I had always looked on with envy. Checking that Ti wasn't watching I placed the small Doll inside my pocket, hidden within my jacket. I knew I shouldn't have taken it, that Ti would disapprove, but I was a child and desperately wanted what other children had. Returning to the log, the doll temporarily forgotten, I sat and waited for Ti to return.

I had the doll secreted away within the folds of my coat for over a week. Every morning when Ti would leave to do his errands, I would carefully take the doll out, brushing what was left of her thinning hair with my fingers.

"I thought of your name last night." I said to the doll quietly.

"I'm going to call you Angelica. It is a good name for an angel."

I kissed the top of Angelica's brow. I knew logically she was an inanimate object, she held no life and could not possibly save me, but by some act of magic, I hoped more than anything that she would.

"You found me little angel" I whispered, straightening out her worn clothes.

"Now I am not alone. Like the angels in the big book, can you fly me away? To heaven?" I asked the tiny doll despairingly.

"So, you wish to go to heaven Mara" Ti snarled behind me.

Fear slammed into me, my breathing hitched. Ti's voice, furious, caused me to stumble forward. I dropped the doll, the sound as Angelica hit the ground made my eyes water, my body quiver.

"Well!" Ti spat

"I... I..."

Stuttering, I failed to form my words. My breathing laboured, I started to hyperventilate.

"Look at me girl" Ti demanded.

Turning slowly to face him, I struggled to find the courage to meet his gaze. Shaking, I knew I was only making the situation worse, Ti despised weakness. Gathering myself together as best I could, I lifted my eyes to meet his. Like mine, his eyes were an eerie ice blue, but where mine were filled with fear, his seethed with anger. Lifting me from the ground he threw me against the fire's grill. Hot metal burnt my flesh. The heat was lost on me, but the pain as my skin melted was agonising. Moving quickly away, I tried to curl myself into a ball, tears shamefully falling from my eyes. Ti wouldn't allow such a cowardly retreat. Lifting me roughly by my hair, he forced my head toward the flames. Lashes of fire singed my delicate flesh, omitting a foul odour, that to this day, I would never forget. My terrified screams filled the small cabin, the sound, like the smell, forever corrupting my memories.

"There are no such things as angels Mara. If heaven did exist there would be no place in it for one such as you." He hissed.

Picking up Angelica he threw her into the fire. Forcing me to watch my only friend burn, I silently cried. When the last of Angelica had become nothing but ash, I felt empty. The hope I had foolishly held of a better life, vanishing in a blur of icy resignation. Ti dragged me to my feet, my footing unsteady.

"How long Mara? How long have you hidden this from me?" He asked, his voice carrying a warning.

It said, 'do not dare lie'.

"Nine days, since the stop at Abramtsevo" I replied quietly, my focus steady.

I never wavered as my eyes bore coldly into his. My mind was closed, my heart more so.

"Get my knives." Ti instructed, his eyes every bit as cold as mine.

No longer afraid, I did what he asked. Presenting Ti with the box that contained his knives, I waited.

"Place your hands on the table, fingers spread." He ordered, opening the box.

Knives of all different sizes and designed gleamed menacingly in the low light of the fire. I had an idea of what was to come, but my mind was numb. Doing what he asked, I sat expectantly.

"You took something that you shouldn't." He said to the air, selecting a long-serrated knife from his box. "For every day you disobeyed me, you will lose a finger, perhaps then when you look upon an object you desire, you will remember the cost of such insolence." He snarled.

Unmoved, I said nothing, revealed nothing. My mind blank, I did nothing to stop him.

I have often thought since then that my time with the beast was further punishment for what I had done, but I guess I will never know. Physically, you would never know of the injuries I endured as a child, the scars I wear kept tightly sealed within the confines of my mind.

"What are you doing in here half breed" Ewan, the warlock from earlier asked, his voice laced with disgust, his face more so.

His interruption of childhood memories was welcomed, even if rude. Getting up from the comfort of the chair, I stood before the warlock, my thoughts devoid of emotion.

"I'm waiting for Donna."

She mentioned something about making a phone call and packing some stuff. She seemed really pleased. Not wanting to get in her way, I asked to wait in the library.

"And she just left you to roam? Like some wild savage wolf in a house full of sleeping lambs." He asked contemptuously.

"As you see." I answered.

Bored with his distaste, I proceeded to walk past him and find Donna.

Not wanting me to pass, the warlock placed his hand out to the side, preventing me from leaving. He then aggressively positioned his body to block my exit. Annoyed, a lash of anger spread its way through me, a snarl hovering in my throat.

"Now hold on. You have come in here, unstable, and undomesticated, contaminating our home with what can only be considered filth. You have used our facilities, eaten out food, borrowed our clothing, and yet you have provided nothing in return." He said, gliding his hand over my stomach, his touch callous, causing me to shiver, and not in a good way. "I think payment is due." He smirked.

He edged his hand further up, stopping just below my breast.

"Take your hands off me" I warned, the snarl escaping.

Sparks of sensation burst forth in my mind, the dark and violent spurs embedding themselves in my thoughts and demanding his blood. I imagined him begging for his life, begging for my mercy. I wanted my imagination to bare truth, to be almost prophetic, a glimpse of what will be, what is inevitable. No!

Donna trusted me with her family, the last thing I wanted to do was lose control.

"Normally I wouldn't degrade myself to a woman such as you, but I doubt you have much more to offer than your body and your beauty." He reasoned, his hold on me tightening.

The way the warlock glared at me made me feel uncomfortable, like I was prey, like I was weak. The arrogant assumption pissed me off! I'm going to hurt him, and I'm going to enjoy it. I felt it, felt the rightness of my train of thought, No I can't! I can't do that to Donna!

Ewan's cold eyes remained on my neck and chest as he closed the gap between us. I didn't understand his demand for payment, what he expected me to give him. But the beast within was furious, and I didn't like him touching me. Nobody touches me! Shivering with disgust, I tried to move away from him, but he wouldn't let go. The pain that I had been ignoring for hours grew and spread throughout my body. I panicked, mentally battling to find a solution for this predicament that wouldn't offend Donna or her people, and more importantly, wouldn't result in his immediate and agonising death.

Again, I attempted to move, this time using more force. He followed and positioned himself in front of me, pinning me against one of the large oak bookcases. Trapped, my body rippled sickeningly.

"I will not ask you again, get away from me" I hissed, my voice barely human, dripped with menace.

"Not until you give me my due" he hissed back.

Grabbing my hair, he pulled me harshly towards his mouth. The action making me more furious. Whipping my head angrily to the side, I ignored the pain when my hair was pulled taunt, my scalp stinging. Rage beyond my ability to control sprang forth, the force of its arrival making me feel nauseated and yet somehow elated. Slowly and patiently maturing inside me, the beast finally woke, taking command of my body. It was like I was looking through another person's eyes, my field of vision flickering through various lenses, heat, prism, and red. My senses were in overdrive, sounds and scents all more potent than I could ever remember them being. I could hear a spider spinning its web in the other room, could detect the small beads of sweat that formed on the warlock's head, and smell the threads of fear contained within them. He must have noticed the change, as he tried to back away. He was afraid. He should be. I had never felt so alive, so powerful. It was both terrifying and exhilarating. What am I?

With murderous intent, I stared at the warlock, the temperature in the air plummeting. Like a vacuum, the heat was being drawn from the room, even the glass on the windows began to freeze over. Within my peripheral vision I could see that the books beside me were beginning to form an icy layer, in the same lacy pattern that coated the windows. Like a ripple in the water, it spread, covering the book case, the walls, the floors, the frozen representation of my intent, spreading fast and claiming the room.

"I'm sorry, I didn't mean to offend you." Ewan pleaded.

I dismissed his words, enjoying his fear, delighting in in. I wanted to hurt him, needed to.

"This is bad! This is really bad!" I heard Donna saying from the door way.

"What did you do Ewan?"

Too afraid to speak the warlock said nothing. I shivered pleasurably, my mouth twitching, trying to smile.

"Whatever you do Ewan, do nae run!" Donna warned.

I do not know if the warlock heard her, but he looked petrified. Visibly shaking, tears fell from his eyes, the sight heightening my euphoria. He was weak, pathetic.

"Mara!" Donna called.

I didn't listen, couldn't. Focused completely on the man in front of me, I tilted my head to the side and studied the warlock. The sudden desire to taste his blood was intoxicating, promising me pleasures untold. Dark and forbidden images were forming in my mind once again, they tempted me to do harm, whispered of the hidden treasures waiting to be discovered. In response, razor sharp teeth exploded from my gum, just above my canines. I deliberately and slowly, ran my tongue over them, growling low. They felt good, like a trophy I had dully earned. Purposely stalking towards the warlock, I smiled sadistically, his life was mine!

"Mara Please do nae hurt him… Mara!" Donna called, her tone one of desperation.

I ignored her, Donna's opinion was mute. What she wanted and what I desired did not in any way compare, his suffering was the only possible outcome.

"Run." I snarled at the warlock.

A horrified expression cloaked his face as he attempted to back away from me, his useless gesture amusing me greatly. Trapped between me and the wall, his efforts were futile.

"Nae Ewan, you run, and she will kill you. Mara please do nae do this. Do nae give them a reason to hurt you. Mara, stop!" she screamed, placing herself directly in front of the warlock, just as I was about to launch at him.

"You really think that standing in front of him will save him?" I asked her contemptuously, my eyes never leaving the pathetic man who cowardly hid behind her.

"No. But if you do nae stop it will put us on a path I wanted to avoid. A path that will hurt you. Mara please, you are my friend, I do nae want that for you." She said with genuine concern.

Her pain at the prospect clearly hurt her. A part of me wanted to stand down, I didn't want to hurt her. But the desire to kill the man who provoked me was stronger. He threatened me, and there is only one recourse for that, death.

Ignoring Donna's pleas, I listened instead to the blood traveling around the warlock's body, his heart was beating rapidly, the sound enticing. The fear he was radiating was like a drug, and I desperately wanted to sample it. The beast's needs won out, the minute I let it arise was the minute I lost this fight. At a speed that defied convention, I bypassed Donna and grabbed the warlock by his neck. Pushed up against the wood panelled wall, the warlock attempted to breathe though a crushed windpipe. I discovered that his chest rising and falling, painfully searching for air, was thrilling, rewarding even. The anticipation was too much, teeth now fully extended, ached to penetrate his flesh. Wanting to savour the feeling, I used my now sharpened nail to nick his throat, allowing a small trail of blood to trickle teasingly down.

"I'm sorry Mara." Donna whispered from somewhere behind me.

I didn't respond. I was certain I could hear Donna chanting an ancient language, one that I should have known. But I couldn't make myself care. Hearing briefly the approach of other voices I returned my attentions to the warlock, his rich blood begging to be sampled. Enthralled, I slowly licked my first taste of blood from the dying warlock's flesh. Lavish forbidden flavours greeted my mouth, just as my mind promised it would. Bliss raced along my nervous system, heightening my pleasure, and making me purr. So potent and seductive in nature, I already craved my next hit, craved it all.

Irritatingly, and before I could feast on the retched beings blood, the pain that had been plaguing me since the club began to intensify, my body shifting and rippling uncontrollably. Apparently, my transformation wasn't complete. Instead of small breaks, my bones snapped with a force that ripped a scream painfully from my throat. I hadn't thought it possible to experience a pain more destructive than the pain I had already endured with the beast. I was wrong. Dropping the warlock, I fell back towards the frozen floor, my body contorting as my back snapped loudly. Stomach facing the ceiling, my head rolled back with a loud bang that cracked sickly against the ice. Dazed, bone after bone gave way, the beast attempting to break free. Screaming in agony, I could do nothing. All I could see was blood, and all I could think about was death.

"Mara?"

Was that Cols voice? Green eyes momentarily swam before me only to be forgotten as the darkness swept in.

Lost to the darkness, I floated in nothingness. I kept trying to move but it was as though I had no body, no form. A familiar male voice permeated the darkness, like a small insubstantial light that commanded my attention.

"Col?" I whispered, my voice barely audible.

"Mara?"

It was Col, his soothing Irish accent called to me, reassured me.

"Col?" I called his name again, my voice not working.

"Can you hear me Mara? Open your eyes darling, look at me." Col pleaded gently.

My eyes? A tingling awareness pulled me from what was a dream like state. Every nerve in my body rebooted and sparked to life. My eyes? I could feel them, they were heavy and bruised. My entire body was bruised, pain rolling over me in waves. Memories, hazy, came flooding back to life. The warlock, his blood, Donna! I had hurt her. Not physically, but I remember the look on her face. I wanted to take it back, but I knew it was too late. There is a word for such a feeling, guilt. I have never felt it before, it left a sour feeling in my gut, an ache in my heart. What will she think of me? What the hell am I? My only real friend and I couldn't even keep her a day.

"Wake up Mara."

I didn't want to. A tug on my arm sent a jolt of pain shooting all the way up it, I cursed silently.

"Mara, I know you can hear me, I saw your face when I pulled your arm. Now open your eyes darling or you will leave me no choice but to take drastic measures."

Measures? Funny, like there is anything he could do that would be worse than that which I had just endured.

"Very well, don't say I didn't warn you." He added slyly.

What will it be, water? pokers? My guess, water. Readying for the cold, I was shocked when instead I felt…. Warmth. Just how I remembered it, only in a much better context. Something warm and soft was pressed against my mouth and I could feel it, feel the warmth. It wasn't painful either, it was… I can't describe it, I have never experienced a sensation even remotely close to it. My mind was literally floating on a cloud of unimaginable bliss. How is it possible? What is it? Unable to resist, and desperate to know what could possible provoke such a delectable heat that had my stomach all in a flutter, I opened my eyes.

Col, it was Col. How was it Col? Confused, I saw his mouth was on mine, his tongue pressing lightly against it, seeking entry. Curious, I let it in, the warmth flooding in with it. I gasped breathless, his tongue guiding mine into a slow sensual dance that literally set my body alight, my senses greedy, and thirsty for more. Heat exploded, coursing its way chaotically throughout my body, winding around my limbs, and penetrating my heart. It was like the lights had suddenly come on, and I was only now able to see. I thought the craving I felt for the warlock's blood would haunt me forever, but this was far more addictive. I wanted to pull him in deeper, but my arms wouldn't move, something was preventing them. My mind lost to the sensation of the kiss couldn't recall why this should have been a problem. Wait. kiss! He was kissing me. Pulling away abruptly, I ended it. How dare he! Anger flared, followed swiftly by confusion, realising that I genuinely missed the warmth he had just shared with me, the taste of him in my mouth.

"You kissed me." I accused angrily.

"You kissed me back." He replied, that same half smile he wore at the bar making my stomach do a strange somersault.

"I didn't know I was kissing you, I mean that you were kissing me." I answered confused.

"But you enjoyed it, or you wouldn't have kissed me back."

"I wouldn't have kissed you back if I knew it was kissing" I claimed, unsure if it was the truth.

"Known or unknown, you enjoyed it" He said matter of fact.

"I never said that."

Like I'm going to admit to liking being kissed. I don't kiss, period.

"You didn't deny it either darling." He added cockily.

"Believe what you wish hunter, but let's be clear, do not ever attempt it again!" I warned, with absolute conviction.

I need to get out of here. Trying to move I realised I couldn't. Not my arms or my legs, looking up I discovered why. My arms had been shackled, a quick glance to the floor told me that my legs were also chained. Furious, I pinned Col with a look of complete disdain.

"You chained me up, so I couldn't move and then kissed me without my permission! There is a name for men like you." I growled.

At least I think there is, I'm sure I've read something about it.

"Now hold on darling, when you put it like that it does look bad. Perhaps it wasn't the best time to kiss you, but let's think for a minute. You wouldn't be in chains had you not run from me in the first place." He said, leaning casually against the far wall. "Also" he added before I could argue. "You then ran from me… again, straight into a witch's coven where you shifted in to a blood crazed killer, impervious to magic, forcing the little witch to ask for my assistance. Powerless to do so herself, it was I that had to retrieve you and prevent you from killing the warlock. Who was her brother by the way?" He finished.

"Brother?" I whispered.

Allowing everything to sink in Col said nothing further. The silence should have been uncomfortable, instead it was strangely reassuring, familiar, like the chains holding me.

"Did I kill him?" I finally asked.

Donna must hate me.

"He will survive."

Piercing green eyes, like before, were seeing more than just the physical. Pacing, he came to stand before me, his closeness inadvertently reminding me of the kiss we had shared. I couldn't stop myself from looking at his mouth, it was so soft, welcoming. I bit my lower lip as the memory of it resurfaced. He growled.

"Careful now darling, continue that train of thought and you might just convince me you need another kiss." He said seriously, whilst gently running his thumb over my bottom lip.

The flutter in my stomach returned instantly, so did the warmth, I purred. Purred!

"Don't touch me!" I warned, pulling back as far as I could, which wasn't far thanks to the bloody wall.

The concrete was cold, I welcomed it, the heat Col was generating was making me nervous. What did it mean? As much as I desired the warmth he offered, I was suspicious of the implications that arose with it. Cold I knew, cold I could handle. Raising his hands above his head in surrender, he stepped back.

"As you wish!" He said simply, his eyes watching me closely.

A knock on the door interrupted whatever this was, and I was grateful.

"The door is unlocked" Col said, his eyes refusing to leave mine.

Donna walked in. She smiled shyly and looked worried.

"Donna?" I asked, the question unknown.

A single tear fell down her cheek, the sight opening a small part of me that I thought was forever closed. Why when I don't care about anything? Running to me she flung her arms around my waist. The pain was incredible but surprisingly I welcomed her embrace.

"I'm so sorry Mara. I tried to stop you. I dinnae want this to happen." She sobbed.

"Sorry? For what? It is I who was in the wrong." I grimaced.

A weird feeling hovered in my throat, like a hiccup that wouldn't come. The sight of Donna crying made me think of all the ways I could stop it, remove her pain. I had ideas, but I doubt they would actually offer any kind of comfort, I seriously doubt a blow torch would mean to her what it would to me.

"No, I knew the risk. I saw what might happen, it was one of the possibilities. My brothers a dick." She said bitterly. "He could have walked away. I thought that he would. He's my brother, I never thought he was capable of that."

"Capable of what!?" Col growled darkly.

Letting go abruptly, Donna turned to look at Col, who was clearly agitated.

"I'm sorry Col, I dinnae know he was capable of that. I honestly thought it was a mistake, that I dinnae see it correctly. It was only one possibility, and I dinnae think it would happen." Donna said regretfully, her manner remorseful.

"What did he do?" Col hissed, his gaze calculating, was piecing together the small bits of information Donna had supplied and was making his own assumptions.

He was furious with his discovery, Col angry, was fearsome to behold. His eyes, like before, had taken on a shadowed hue that demanded Donna's collaboration. She must have been terrified, I needed to distract him, to protect her.

"Nothing." I interjected, fearing where this may lead.

His eyes quickly flashed to mine only to return to Donna's just as fast.

"Donna." He said smoothly, and ignoring my comment.

Damn it! Donna's arms clutched on to me, she was afraid, her fear invading my senses, her heart racing.

"He tried too…" She stumbled, struggling to find her words.

"Tried too?" Col prodded as he took another step towards her, his manner lethal.

"He wanted her, and he dinnae care that she dinnae want him." She said finally, her hold on me never wavering.

A growl, so low, so deadly, was Cols initial response. Clenching his jaw, he placed his hands in tight fists, struggling to maintain his control. His body was coiled with tension, the sight of which excited me. He was so strong, so predatory, I liked it. Angry because someone dared touch me, I wanted to reward him for his vigilance.

"Col" I called, requesting his attention.

Obliging smoke-filled eyes fell on mine, their depths compelling. I wanted him to see me, see how his protectiveness pleased me. I can't explain why; the reasons were foreign. With Col momentarily distracted, Donna ran from the room, not bothering to look back. The barrier between us gone, I watched Col thoughtfully. His gaze unnerved me, but in a way, that intrigued me, drew me in. Not understanding this sudden need that gnawed inside, I bit my lower lip hard, a small layer of blood coating my tongue. His eyes caught the gesture, he growled again, my heart racing. I knew how I would reward him.

"Kiss me."

Kiss Me

Enraged that someone would dare lay hands on my anam cara, I struggled to comprehend Mara's request. 'Kiss me.' The words filtered through my anger, appeasing the hunter within. Instead of anger, a different emotion surfaced. Unmoving, captured in thought, Mara gazed at me, her expression filled with longing. She bit her lip again. I hissed, appreciating the implication of what to her was such an innocent act, but to me, so very carnal. Moving slowly, so as not to startle her, I studied the perfect form that was Mara. Long golden hair framed a face that was stunningly beautiful. Her eyes, the colour of glaciers, were captivating, ethereal, adding to the magical allure she naturally imbued. Edging closer, I allowed myself the pleasure of admiring a body that although toned still held the desirable curves indigenous to women. With restraint, I positioned my hands to rest on the wall behind her, encasing her within my arms. Fearful of her innocence, I dared not touch her.

As much as I wanted to pull her against me, I knew she had never been touched, doubted she knew what was happening, or what it meant. To take from her that which she didn't know she was giving was criminal, and yet my mind hummed with all the possibilities. Eager to sample her taste once more, I slowly brought my mouth to rest on hers. Warm velvet lips brushed against mine, the contact sending waves of heat that pulsated about me. Trembling with need,

I battled the urge to pull her possessively against me, it was too much, too soon.

Debating whether this was the right time to attempt such, I tried to move away from her. Still recovering from my anger, my ability to be gentle, to be patient, had been dangerously compromised. Mara wouldn't allow my retreat. Sucking my lip hungrily, she coaxed my mouth back to hers. Unpractised, and yet irresistible, her tongue claimed mine, slowly and firmly, sucking its tip. Shit! I was a prisoner to her touch, the thought to preserve her close to being forgotten. Stroke after stroke she moulded me to her whim, delectable I craved more, wanted more.

"Boss, a word?" Ansgar asked, his interruption, like icy water being poured all over me.

Obviously, it had the same effect on Mara, as she pulled back, the look on her face one of bewilderment. No doubt she just realised that we had been kissing, again. Stepping away, I couldn't help but grin. I should have been annoyed at the interruption, instead I was grateful. She was chained up and untouched, what was I thinking?

"You did it again" She accused angrily, her face one of surprise.

"I only did what you asked darling." I said, backing towards the door where Ansgar waited for me.

I needed to get away from her, the hunters desire to claim her was to strong, to tempting. This was something I needed to build up too, and prepare her for.

"I… I'm not myself." Mara explained disorientated.

"I'll have someone come and bring you a drink" I said lamely, walking out of the room.

"Thank you." I said to Ansgar.

Shutting the door behind me, we made to leave the basement.

"Nae worry about it. Figured you needed a distraction." He replied, his expression unreadable.

"You could say that."

I hated the idea of leaving Mara in there, chained and confused, but I wasn't sure how I could explain what was happening without confusing her further, or worse, having her run out on me again.

"You gave the witch a fright." Ansgar smiled.

"The reason that Mara lost control at the coven was because Ewan tried to rape her." I hissed, the anger I held earlier, returning tenfold.

"Bloody hell!" Ansgar cursed.

"I was not my intention to frighten Donna, my anger was directed at her brother."

If we hadn't just journeyed so far north, I would go there now and kill him… it will not go unpunished.

"You may need to speak with Aengus, explain. He's nae very happy that she came running upstairs crying. She will nae let him in her room."

"Crying?" Just what I want "I'll go see him. Can you do me a favour?"

"Aye always, what do you need?"

"Can you release Mara? I was going to ask Donna to come and see her, but given her state it might be wise to release Mara instead. They are friends, Donna will let her in."

I hoped. I've never been good with tears, no matter the cause of their appearance. We entered the kitchen to the sound of Irish folk music, the soothing music helping me focus.

"Aye, you may be right. I'll go get her." Angsar agreed, before headed back the way we came.

"Ansgar."

"Aye?" He answered, stopping mid step.

"I recommend telling her about Donna before you release her, and watch yourself, she may attempt to run." I warned.

"I hear you." He smiled unconcerned.

The music that drifted through the cabin was calming and uplifting. Soft melodic tunes native to Ireland played, reminding me of the home I love and missed. It had been too long since I had visited my homeland. Eoghuan sat playing the guitar while Finian sang the intricate Gaelic lyrics that have stood the test of time. Retrieving my fiddle, I joined in, and wondered what our next move was going to be. Sköll was a problem, and a danger to us all, and Mara as much as I wanted her, only added to that danger. She was unpredictable, and had obviously been shoved into a world she didn't know anything about. Whatever lessons in life she had received, they didn't include relationships of any description. I would need to think long and hard on how I was going to breech the fact that she belonged to me. Allowing the music to carry me away, I pondered on our future and begun to make my plans.

The Birds and the Bees

"Damn it woman!"

Ansgar cursed loudly as I ran from the room they were holding me in. Donna was upset and needed me. At least I think people cry because they need someone. I would rather be hurting someone, but I wasn't going to let her down. Still annoyed that Col had left me in there chained up, even after he had kissed me… twice, I flew upstairs, leaving the hunter who had been left with the unfortunate task of releasing me, on his knees, nursing his crotch. How odd that men who are supposed to be the warrior race would be created with such a weak spot, I mused. Nature's way of maintaining balance perhaps?

As I reached the top of the stairs, I was greeted with the sound of music, it was mystical in nature and made me pause momentarily, curiosity once again getting the better of me. Moving stealthily, I crept along the kitchen counters, and towards the music. Ingrained habits had me scouting for threats, even though I knew I wasn't in any danger. I wasn't a prisoner, and the only reason I was detained in the first place was because I lost control and had placed Donna and her family in danger.

Standing at the doorway to what I assumed was the living room, I watched enthralled as Col and two other hunters played and sang music that was truly captivating. It was so sad in its melody, and yet it made me think of all the beautiful things I had seen, it was distracting me, 'Donna'. As much as I wanted to watch the spectacle, I left to find her.

With the cabins layout unfamiliar to me, I had to rely on my senses to locate her. The smell of cherries and vanilla clung to her clothes, betraying her whereabouts, and reminding me of her apartment. Standing behind the closed door, I heard Aengus trying to placate her. Soft muffled cries made my heart skip a beat, as I tried to determine how best I could help her. How does one stop crying? Tapping lightly on the door I waited for her answer. It didn't come.

"Donna, its Mara, can I come in?" I asked her quietly.

"Mara?" She asked, the bed creaked, hurried foots steps following.

The door suddenly sprung opened, Donna peering at me uncertainly. I smiled at her reassuringly, at least I hoped it was reassuring.

"Can I come in?"

"Of course." She smiled.

Walking into the room, I followed. Standing just within the doorway Aengus stood uncomfortably, he seemed happy that I had arrived.

"Aye, well I'll leave you two lassies to have a wee blether then, shall I?" Aengus mumbled, before quickly leaving the room, his face etched with relief.

"They let you go? I was worried they would nae keep their word." Donna said, sitting back down on the bed.

"What's a blether?" I asked, the word throwing me.

"What, oh, it means chat." She smiled.

Oh.

"Do you want me to hurt him?" I asked her seriously.

"What? Hurt who?"

"Col."

"What, no. Why would I want to do that?" she asked, her brow arched quizzically.

"Because he upset you. Isn't that why you're crying?" Smiling widely, she replied.

"Oh no. Men do nae like crying generally, so I figured if I did enough of it they would release you sooner. Col was going to wait until he knew how to educate you, which would have been a disaster." She said, whilst resting casually on the bed, all pretence of sadness gone from her face.

"I see. It worked." I smiled surprised.

Donna was a marvel.

"Aye, I had no doubt." She giggled.

"What do you mean Col intends to educate me?" I asked, sitting down on the bed beside her.

"Oh well, urmm… Let's go and get a wee drink first, then I will tell all."

Walking to her suit case I watched her silently take out various grooming tools and articles of clothing. Oh no!

"Please tell me they aren't for me." I complained rigidly.

Humming happily, she looked at me excitedly.

"We cannae attend a party without getting all dressed up." She answered mischievously.

"Party?" I sighed.

"Aye, there's a wee party at a nice local bar, twenty miles from here. I thought we could go have a wee drink, then I'll tell you everything you want to know." She said, pulling off her original clothes.

"And besides, for a reason I still cannae figure, we're supposed to go there." Donna added.

"And what about them? It doesn't take a genius to know they have no intentions of letting us out of their sight." I reminded her.

Donna threw me a gold backless dress that I caught with ease.

"Aye, that's true, but they have taken an oath that we were to remain free to do as we wish and that they cannae punish us. So, the way I see it, we just go and do as we like, and they have no recall to do or say anything" She said, wriggling in to a black tube dress.

"They will only stand behinds us all intimidating until we get annoyed and leave." I clucked, reluctantly undressing.

"Aye, that's why we're nae telling them. By the time they realise we're nae here and activate the car's transmitter, we will already be there having a drink. It will take them just under an hour to get to us if they run fast, and do nae stop, that's plenty of time for a wee chat and a few drinks." She added.

"Twenty miles? More like ten minutes, if that." I said unconvinced.

I put on the dress, like before it was too tight and uncomfortably clingy, what the hell are women thinking wearing such unpractical and revealing garb?

"Twenty miles if they cut through the mountain range, not including mountains they will have to go over, or around. You could add a couple of minutes for every one they have to climb, another couple for every one they have to go around." Donna smiled, shrugging as though it was of no bother.

"I take it then there is no road through, we're driving around?" I grinned.

I was beginning to feel a bit bad for Aengus, she obviously does what she wants and damns the recourse. We were more alike than I thought. Despite my initial thinking, I wasn't truly alone in the world. She was in many ways just like me, but good, like the version of me I could be, if I wasn't a habitual killer.

I didn't care that that hunters would have to run miles over mountain ranges. It's their own fault for deciding we were delicate. After all, if they viewed us as they did each other, they would just wait for us to return.

"It's a good plan, but how are you going to fool them into thinking we're still here long enough for us to reach our destination? And how are you going to stop them hearing the engine start?" I asked, my brow raised.

I sat on the bed and fastened on another pair of ridiculously high heels. How did she know my size?

"Look this way and I will reveal all my precious." Donna said, her voice animated to sound like an old woman.

Hunching her back, she shakily pointed to the bed. The duvet begun to rise like a balloon. Two shapes that resembled bodies, rose on either side of the mattress. Once they had reached the appropriate height, the formed shapes begun to rise and fall, gently mimicking breathing. I couldn't help but smile. The action felt good, I hoped that unlike my small wooden doll, it would last. Standing up, all animation from her voice gone, she gave me a wink.

"Do nae underestimate my mad skills. With the lights off, it will be enough to pass a quick inspection. The only reason they will discover us gone before midnight is when they do their rounds and find the car gone."

Donna giggled at the thought, no doubt she was picturing it all in her mind, or actually watching it happen.

"Are you not worried about me losing my temper, I didn't fair to well last time we were out." I said, sitting back down on to the bed, so Donna could start fiddling with my hair.

"No. Even when you were lost and no longer visible in your eyes you dinnae hurt me. You are stronger then you could ever believe Mara. The times you did lose control was because you were threatened, not because you wanted to kill everyone in sight. You were protecting yourself, from those who intended you harm." She finished, spraying sticky stuff on my head.

A knock at the door caught our attention.

"Aye?" Donna called, her gaze watching the door cautiously.

"I was checking in to see if you were ok." Aengus answered from behind the door.

"Aye, thank you Aengus, we're just undressing for bed. I would invite you in for a good night kiss, but Mara is naked and I'm already in bed. Perhaps I could wake you with one instead." Donna said suggestively, winking at me, and grinning wickedly.

A low growl was his only response. Aengus rustled outside, probably wondering how he could tempt Donna to go to him now.

"You nae hungry?" He finally said, his voice low.

"No. I ate just before Mara woke, and Mara's fine as well. We're just tired, but thank you my love." Donna said sweetly.

She really was good at manipulation. I should ask her to teach me.

"If you need me I will be in the other room. Sleep well anam cara." Aengus said softly.

"And you my love."

Satisfied that we were where we were meant to be, Aengus moved off in the direction of the lounge.

"You think he suspects?" I asked Donna, who had returned to doing my hair.

"Not a clue." She giggled again.

Twenty minutes later, Donna deemed us ready.

"Hold on a minute. It was close to midnight when Ewan walked in on me. Surely nowhere will be open." I said, wondering why I didn't ask her earlier, before she painted my face.

"Oh, I probably should have told you, but that was yesterday. It's around nine pm the following day." She said guiltily, her mouth pursing.

"I was asleep for that long?" I asked surprised, I don't normally sleep for that long.

Gauging my shock, another wave of guilt swept across her face.

"Urmm, Col used a sleeping dart on you, several in fact. I do nae think he was coping to well with the amount of pain you were in." Donna added, flicking her wrist, the action causing the bed to come alive in the same fashion as earlier.

He didn't?

"Come on then, and be quiet." Donna instructed, as she gently pried open the window.

Quiet, was she kidding! Of course, I wasn't going to make a sound, she should be worrying about herself. Not saying anything I followed her out.

Now stood outside, Donna pulled the window back down and turned off the lights, using nothing but her thoughts. At least that's what I assumed, as I failed to see any gesture to indicate otherwise. Silently, she signalled for me to follow her. I did. Twice before reaching the car Donna tripped. If it wasn't for the music the hunters were playing, I'm certain they would have heard us. Next time Donna decides to go sneaking about I might have to carry her, Donna does not do stealth.

Reaching the Land Rover safely, Donna retrieved her keys from her bag. Before she attempted to unlock the car, she closed her eyes and uttered a word that was again familiar, and yet I didn't recognise it, like a language I know, but couldn't hear. Placing her hand on the headlights, she continued to speak in the unknown language. What she did to the car I couldn't say, outwardly it appeared the same. Happy with her efforts Donna stood back from the car and unlocked it. Normally the car would beep and the lights flash, indicating that the car had been opened, but instead, nothing happened. Whatever she had done to the car had been successful. Getting in, I thought no more about it, Donna was a wonder, and I was beginning to expect she could do just about anything. The thought triggered a memory.

I remembered something Col said earlier about how Donna couldn't stop me. That she had to ask him to retrieve me.

"Why didn't you use your magic to stop me earlier?" I asked as she started the now silent engine.

"I tried, but nothing I did worked. I can use magic to aid you, like cloaking you, but for whatever reason, I cannae use magic against you." She frowned, backing the car slowly up the drive.

"What do you mean?"

Glancing at me briefly, she pursed her lips in thought.

"For example, I could nae bind you with magic and I could nae immobilise you with it, and Ewan sure as hell tried to hurt you with it, but nothing that was directed at you worked. However, when I placed a spell on the room to prevent you from leaving, or a cloak on your body to stop you being seen, it worked. So, basically, I can use my magic to help you, and I can use it to throw things at you, but I cannae use it to hurt you. At least not directly. Your aura just soaks it up, as if you're the very source it originated from in the first place."

Donna steered the car onto a proper road, tarmac, not mud, and turned on the cars head lights.

"To be honest, it freaked me out a bit, never seen it happen before." She continued, speeding and taking corners as though she was in a rally tournament.

"So, magic can work for me, but not against me?" I asked, as I tried to sum it up.

"Aye, basically."

No wonder those magical trinkets that were used against me were useless, they have zero effect on me.

It took us just over an hour at break neck speed to reach the little village that Donna intended us to drink in. It was called Aviemore, and the pub which was in full party mode was named the Winking owl. I was going to speak more with Donna in the car, but before I got the chance she turned on the radio and had tunes blasting out of the speakers the minute she deemed us far enough away from the hunters so as not to be heard. Singing loudly to the music, she started dancing in her seat. Amused with her antics I couldn't help but enjoy the journey. It must be nice to be so carefree, so happy. The more time I spent with Donna the more I believed I could have it too.

"Quickly, they're about to cut the cake." She said, jumping out of the car.

I followed, cake. Walking with all the poise of a runway model, Donna bowled up to the pubs entrance, me in tow. The pub was warm and welcoming, music that was in a similar style, but a lot more upbeat to the music the hunters were playing earlier, filled the small space. A live band played on a small stage towards the back of the room, sounds of laughter and conversation filling the air with warmth. Everyone was happy, their merriment, infusing the room, was contagious.

"I love weddings." Donna smiled.

Grabbing my hand, she walked purposely towards a woman in a white gown and a man in a Green tartan kilt. Standing before them, she took an object from her purse, a silver clip with Celtic drawings carved into it. It was beautifully designed and undoubtedly expensive. If not before, it was now anyway, as it contains a wad of fifty-pound notes.

"It's such a delight to see you both again. Thank you so much for inviting me to share in your special day." Donna said, handing over the clip to the confused women.

As soon as the women saw the gift she no longer looked confused, with a quick look at the man besides her, she smiled brightly, accepting the money offered.

"Thank you so much, it's a pleasure to see you too, I hope you enjoy the night." The woman smiled.

"I will, I wish you both a long and advantageous marriage."

Donna turned and winked, grabbing my hand.

"You know her?" I asked, making our way towards the bar.

"No, never met them before in my life." She grinned.

"Then why?" I tried to ask.

"Because I love weddings, and it's traditional to present a gift, especially if you do nae want to get kicked out for gate-crashing." She said, finding a small gap at the bar.

Leaning over, she put up her hand seeking service.

"Gate-crashing?"

"Aye, when you attend a party or celebration you have nae been invited too."

Ah that makes sense. A bribe.

It didn't take long for Donna to get noticed, apparently when you're beautiful that means you get priority. Doesn't seem fair, but then no one seemed to be complaining. Maybe she has cast another spell. Personally, I wouldn't allow such a slight, when the bartender arrived, a stupid grin on his face, I sniffed distastefully.

"What can I get you?" The young bar tender asked Donna, his eyes blatantly enjoying the view she presented him.

"I would like a white Russian. Mara?"

White Russian, that's a beverage?

"Tequila gold, a tray, and one of your white Russians." I told the bar tender, my tone letting him know I wasn't overly fond of him.

"Why do nae you go grab some food from the buffet table while I get our drinks. It's been awhile since you last ate and it's best not to tempt fate." Donna said on the verge of laughing, probably reliving the first time we went out.

"You going to manage all those drinks?" I asked her, curious as to how she would carry that many glasses, and the salt, and the lemon.

"Huh, Like I will be carrying them. There is plenty of strapping young lads in here who would love to help me." She smiled sweetly.

"Ok then, I'll be sat over there."

I grinned as I eagerly made my way over to the buffet table, I'm starving.

Moving to sit at the little table at the back of the room I discovered Donna already there waiting. Drinking through a straw, she looked up at me and grinned, her eyes sparkling with glee.

"What?" I asked, pulling out the seat opposite her.

"That's a serving platter, nae a plate." She laughed loudly.

I quickly glanced at my plate, it was piled high with various foods, some of which I had never tried before, I frowned back at her, confusion no doubt marring my face. Serving platter?

"It's an over-sized plate you can place lots of food on in order to share with many people. By the size of that one, I would say it was designed to feed six." She explained, still laughing.

Oh, I see, that would explain the heated glare I was getting from the old couple sat near the buffet table.

"I won't waste any."

"I know" She giggled "that's what makes it's so funny."

Not sure what to say further I started eating instead, I'm hungry, hardly my fault. So many new things to be explored, I couldn't help but relish in the diversity the buffet offered. All of it, so far, was delicious. I wondered briefly just what was happening to me, I've always had a healthy appetite, but I've never eaten this much, it was though my stomach had become a bottomless pit. Glancing at my stomach quickly, I considered where it was all going. Outwardly my stomach still appears its normal flat self, my legs maybe…no, they looked fine too.

"They have realised we're gone." Donna said unexpectedly.

"You had better ask your questions Mara, they have located the car and are preparing to cross the range as we speak." She finished, stealing a strawberry from my platter.

I growled possessively when I realised what she had just done, which only made her start laughing again. Ignoring the fact, she just stole my food, and the urge I had to fight her for it, I thought about the things I wanted to ask.

"I don't know where to begin, I have many and I doubt thirty minutes will cover it."

"Well, start with the one that has been bothering you the most and we will forgo this lovely party and take our drinks on a wee country stroll. After arriving here to find the car, it should take them another thirty minutes or so to find us if we go off grid." She grinned.

"We could get far in an hour and the fresh air might be the last we see for a while." She finished on a long sigh.

"They're angry?" I asked, already knowing the answer.

"Aye, more than a wee bit. But a kiss can placate at least two of them." Donna winked, before finishing the last of her drink.

The mention of a kiss brought all the memories of Col's kiss back to life. Without realising what I was doing I ran the tip of my finger over my lip. Despite the anger and the confusion, I wanted to feel the warmth again. Col? I knew what my first question would be.

"You said earlier that Col wasn't going to release me until he found a way to educate me, what did you mean?" I asked, standing to leave, my platter empty.

"Well… What do you know about the birds and the bees?"

Putting her arm through mine she led me back out towards the pubs entrance. Birds and the bees? This is what Col wanted me to teach me?

"They both fly?" I guessed, wondering if that was the answer she was searching for.

Sighing, she pulled me in close for a half hug.

"I can see why he was concerned. Let's see… Do you know how babies are made? How we have children?" Donna asked, watching me closely.

"Yes, I have read about it, reproduction. Every living species does it, otherwise all life would die off." I answered, pleased I had read a book on life cycles.

"Aye! Well that's positive, at least I don't have to tell you about the consequences." She hummed happily.

Consequences? I have a feeling I won't ever look at a bee the same way again.

We exited the pub, her arm still linked with mine, passed the land rover, and entered a field through a gap in the barb wire fence before she spoke again.

"Do you know how we reproduce? As in the physical act of reproduction." She finally asked.

I tried to recall what the act was called in the book and weather it had directions as to how the act was accomplished. Just as I was about to answer Donna stopped to remove her shoes, the smallest amount of mud coating her heel. Her shoes in her hand, and satisfied I had her complete attention, I answered.

"We mate."

Donna smiled.

"Aye, that's one word for it. Do you know how we…mate?" She winked, walking up a small hill towards the woods.

"No." I answered quietly.

I guess I'm about to find out.

"Well!" Donna grinned. "A man and a woman decide they like the look of each other. Then nine times out of ten they kiss. It always starts with a kiss!" She winked.

Col kissed me! Does he want me to have a baby? I am not having a baby.

"Then hands start to roam and the next thing you know your both naked."

Naked? Col naked...

"And then they kiss you in places other than the mouth…"

Really, you can be kissed anywhere?

"Then there's the stroking and the rubbing. A good lover will pay attention to the whole of your body Mara. Do nae let them cheat you." Donna said seriously, like it was a huge offense should they do so.

"Don't let them cheat." I muttered to myself, not wanting to forget.

"Aye, and then when you cannae stand the foreplay any longer, and if you're into it, you let him have sex with you." She said matter of fact.

Foreplay?

"What's foreplay?" I asked.

"Oh, the stroking, rubbing, and kissing on the body part. The bit that leads up to sex." She grinned.

"Ok, and what does the sex part entail?" I asked, my mind swimming with all the images she had just placed into my head.

"well…" She smiled.

The Winking Owl

After checking in with the clan and receiving intel on Sköll's movements we settled down to eat. Eoghuan had made dinner with rabbits he had caught earlier.

"You sure the women don't want anything to eat." I asked Aengus

"Aye, I asked before Eoghuan started cooking. They said they were tired and were going to sleep."

"Together?" Finian grinned.

"Whatever images you have just concocted, I strongly suggest you get rid of them." Aengus growled warningly, a deep crease lining his brow.

"Donna's car is gone." Eoghuan said, racing into the room.

"What"

Gone? Standing up, my food forgotten, I raced towards the witch's room, Aengus on my heels. Opening the door without knocking, I walked in and switched on the lights. Two shapes that looked like bodies were rising and falling lightly as though in sleep.

"There still here." Aengus said relieved, behind me.

I doubt it, I'm going to murder that damn witch. Staring at the bed I focused not on my sight but on my hearing. Something was missing, no heart beats. Walking angrily towards the bed, I pulled the duvet off, leaving it heaped on the floor. Nothing! The bed was empty. The roar that followed the discovery was deafening. I was furious. What the hell are they thinking?

"Damn bloody witch!" Aengus roared loudly, storming out of the room.

He looked as livid as I felt, jaw clenched tightly he begun muttering in Gaelic, the string of curses, far to kind. When I get my hands on them…

"Ansgar!" I roared.

Grabbing my gear, I readied myself to hunt for Mara, again! It was getting old. If it wasn't for that damn oath I would be permanently restraining her upon returning.

"I hear you boss! Trackers got them at Aviemore, in a pub called the Winking owl." He said, strapping on the last of his daggers.

"Of course, they would be in a pub." Finian added sarcastically.

I growled warningly, now wasn't the time to be a smart arse.

"It will take too long to drive around, we will have to cross the mountains." Aengus rumbled unhappily.

"If memory serves. there is a pack up by Aviemore." Ansgar said to the room, his brow creased with worry.

"Varúlfur?" I asked dangerously.

Fucking brilliant!

"Aye, about five miles to the west of Aviemore, Caggan. Its highlands territory."

"And you dinnae think to mention this when we got here?" Aengus scowled, his voice laced with venom.

"Why would I, we're miles away on the other side of a mountain range, and they do nae cross the river that lays to the east of Aviemore. We're completely separated from them." Ansgar stated factually.

Aengus grumbled in-cohesively.

"Do you think the witch knows about the wolves, or is it merely coincidental?" Aengus asked, his grumbling ceased.

His eyes, like the rest of ours, had taken on the smoky hue prevalent to our kind. He was pissed, as we all were. But more than being angry, I was afraid for Mara. The Varúlfur were not a tolerant species. Created by Fenrir, they were born to serve him, and were bred for their savage tendencies. Many of the wolf packs later betrayed their master, helping to imprison him, rejecting the darkness they were born too. However, there are still those who remain loyal to the dark one, those who have fully embraced the dark.

"Do we know their loyalties?" I asked Ansgar.

"No. They are secretive and keep to themselves."

"Then I hope for their own sake they do nae leave the pub." Aengus hissed.

It took us just under forty minutes to reach the river separating the mountains from Aviemore. Racing across the wild landscapes of Scotland we were all grateful that it was not yet winter. Even in autumn the terrain was demanding, by the time we reached the river bordering Aviemore our muscles ached, and our lungs burned. We would recover within minutes if we paused to stop, but with a pack so close to our women, neither Aengus or I were prepared to take the risk.

"What is it with your women and water? Or perhaps I should be asking what is it with your women and running off." Finian muttered.

Unamused, he waded into the river that separated us from them, his expression marred in annoyance. Ignoring his questions, and his sarcastic tone, I followed his lead and stepped into the river. Fuck! It was freezing. It might not be winter yet, but the river is fed from the mountain, and up there it's snow and ice. Sucking in a deep breath, we made our way across the icy waters. Soaking wet we emerged from the other side, not one of us remotely impressed. They will pay for this, I'll make sure of it.

Although it was late, the small town was still busy. With pubs and newsagents still open, there was still a small trickle of people walking along the brightly lit streets. Soaking and fully armed, we were bound to get noticed. It is exactly for reasons like this we were given the ability to influence another's mind. Moving quickly through the streets to reach the car, and ultimately Mara and Donna, who was quickly becoming a pain in my arse, we silently sent commands to nearby pedestrians to look the other way and remember nothing about us.

From the river to the car park, where Donna's car sat, it took less than three minutes. Leaving Eoghuan and Finian by the car in case they decide to piss me off further and run again, myself, Aengus and Ansgar entered the pub. The atmosphere that greeted us was vibrant. Music in the style I love was playing loudly, wedding guests dancing to a traditional Gaelic song. Laughter filled the full room, the air muggy with heat. With their whereabouts not obvious, we each took a different direction and went in search of them independently.

After spending the next couple of minutes with no luck, I tried to identify Mara's unique scent from the bombardment of others. Assuming if they had been here they would have at least used the bar once, I started there. Moving slowly along the bar I tried to detect her aroma through the prevalent smells of alcohol and sweat. In full hunter mode, my senses were working overtime. Each spirit, each beer, had its own smell unique to its brand. It was nearly impossible to search for her this way, especially in a bar that was full to the brim. There! Just at the far end of the bar. Ignoring the speculative looks I was receiving from the patrons, I commanded them to forget me, and lowered my nose to rest above the bar, drawing in the scent that had caught my attention. The smell of woodland and rain travelled along my senses, carrying an image of Mara to my mind. The trail was small, virtually invisible, but It was enough for me to follow. Moving purposely from the bar I moved through the crowd to stand in front of a buffet table. The small particles that contained her scent rested upon various plates, each containing a different food. So much for not being hungry, bloody woman!

"You found her?" Ansgar asked, coming up behind me.
"Yes, but the trail is thin."

Not speaking further, I continued to follow her path. The trail led me to a small wooden table towards the back of the room. Her scent was stronger here. She had obviously sat for a while. Donna's scent was strong too.

Aengus moved in, standing on the other side.

"Good to know they are still together." He grumbled, his blue eyes scanning the room.

"Yes."

But where? Turning to face the entrance, I followed her scent back out of the door. I should have tried to locate her scent upon entering, I could have saved us time. Growling low, we left the way we came, empty handed. Sighing, I cursed the fresh mountain breeze, her small thread of scent, lost on the wind.

"Looks like we will be hunting old school." Finian smiled.

"Aye, it would appear so." Aengus added, pleased with the prospect.

There is no greater feeling then that of a true hunt, as you slowly but surely close in on your prey. With modern day cities and towns covered in concrete and man-made stimulants that confuse your senses, it's not often we get to hunt in the old style. Using every gift a hunter possessed, we will track their movements the way we were designed to. A broken twig on the ground, a strand of hair snagged on a tree branch as they passed under it, a minuet bead of sweat that had fallen only to cling to a blade of grass, a foot print amongst the dirt. Nothing will escape our notice. We may control it well, hide it well, but at our core we are predators, and like all predators, we live for the hunt... and for our prey to be our anam cara, delicious. Both Aengus and I growled low with anticipation. By the time we reach them the hunter will be fully dominant, our behaviour more animalistic than usual. Five hunters who have lost themselves to the hunt, bearing down on an innocent should have made me cautious. But after the way Mara responded to the deadly hunter earlier, I'm convinced her response will be favourable. Grinning at the notion, my anger fading, the calm and deadly hunter sprung to life. Time to hunt.

The Alpha

"Are you sure you're checking Mara." Donna asked, just as she tripped over an exposed root.

"Yes, I give you my word, I will not allow you to step in crap." I grinned.

Donna was struggling to see, the tall dense woodland obscuring the moon's soft glow and plunging the woodlands into an impenetrable darkness. I on the other hand could see just as clearly as if it was the middle of the day. I was in my element being back in the wilds of Scotland, of all the places I have visited over the years, here is the place I felt like I belonged, here was home. Scotland was magical, the air humming with power and mystical allure, the rugged and dramatic landscape only adding to its appeal. When the Scottish mist formed, slowly rolling in on the glens and lochs you could practically see its ancient history coming to life, visualise battles that had taken place, and hear the calls of men passed, their souls restless, searching for peace. Some might find it eerie, but I find it mesmerising. Scotland is steeped in legend, the power embedded permanently in the land. I have learned some of its history but always there is more to discover, a never-ending story that captures your heart and imagination.

"Damn it, they have already realised we have taken a wee country stroll."

Donna scowled as she continued to walk laboriously up the hill.

We must have walked at least four miles out whilst Donna explained the so-called birds and the bees to me in vivid detail. Some of the things she described I had difficulty picturing. She assured me that although my first time may seem uneventful it gets increasingly better, and that I should insist he use his tongue thoroughly before allowing him to enter me. Sceptical, I reserved judgment. The whole thing seemed invasive and messy. Furthermore, spreading my legs wide open whilst completely naked just for him to pin me down and invade my space, and body, seemed like a really submissive thing to do, and I do not do submissive! Ever. Nor do I want Col.

"I need to sit; my poor wee feet are hurting." Donna said, her curt statement disrupting my thoughts.

"There's a log over there." I said, ducking under a low hanging branch.

"Ah good." She sighed happily.

Sat for only a few minutes, the night air refreshing, a tingling sensation buzzed at the base of my neck, the prickly uneasiness spreading along the length of my spine. I recognised the signal, Danger!

"We are not alone Donna." I said quietly, my beast stirring.

Donna didn't say anything but remained quiet, listening as I did. A twig snapping to my left caused me to swing around, my eyes finding the direction of the disturbance easily. Crouching low, ready to attack, I let out a warning, a low terrifying growl that made Donna's heart race, cutting through the night.

"I know you are there. I hear your heart beat as I hear the heart of your companion beat behind me." I announced menacingly, my new-found canines erupting once again.

Opening my snarling mouth, I allowed the scents of the woods to swim along my sense receptors. Like a neon light they flickered to life with all the information I was receiving. A rabbit hid frightened behind the log Donna sat on, ten feet away an owl was perched watching us intently, its large eyes seeing everything, and a wolf stood several feet away, its coat matted with blood. Another wolf laid threateningly behind, hidden amongst the undergrowth, ready to attack. With a yelp of pain, the wolf that was covered in blood shifted, taking the form of a man, his eyes remaining those of a wolf.

"You are trespassing girlie" The wolf man said, his fangs bared warningly.

The blood that matted his coat clung to his skin, it was sticky and fresh. I licked my lips as memories of the warlock's blood came rushing to mind. Shivers of excitement exploded as I savoured the memory.

"You own the highlands?" Donna asked sarcastically.

Bravely and without fear she remained on the log unperplexed. The wolf didn't respond but instead, slowly moved towards us. His eyes were golden and wild, and were unmistakably alpha.

"We dinnae know werewolves occupied the area." Donna added, standing up from the log.

Wiping imagined debris from her dress she folded her arms across her chest defensively. She looked bored.

"Now you do, and as such you will have to come with us, so we can determine whether you are a threat to the pack." The wolf said calmly, his eyes wary, were watching me closely.

"Unfortunately wolf we are being pursued by five hunters, so it probably would nae be such a good idea, I imagine they will be here soon, correct me if I'm wrong, but they are nae so keen on the Varúlfur." Donna smiled wickedly.

"Hunters aye? Hunting you?" The wolf grinned, several more wolves slowly emerging from the trees surrounding us, their warm breath creating clouds of mist that hissed against the cold autumn air.

"It is the truth, but if you want us to lead them back to your village, then by all means, be a good doggie and lead the way." Donna huffed.

The wolf snarled, he probably didn't like being referred to as a doggie. I don't blame him, comparing a dog with a wolf is a sure way of getting killed…was that the point? Ah I get it, an insult.

"I can kill them." I said to Donna, a hint of a smile edging my mouth.

"No Mara, you will run the risk of losing control."

She placed her arm on my shoulder, the action making me pause.

"Just follow them, it's nae like they will have us for long." She added.

"You want us to follow a pack of wolves to a village where many more wolves reside?" I asked her surprised.

Has she got a death wish?

"I do nae think you're understanding me, you're coming back to the village is nae a request. You will follow us." He said flatly, the rest of his pack closing in on a tight circle, Donna and I standing in its centre.

The beast trapped within my flesh roared defiantly, its demand for release sending waves of pain coursing through me. It wasn't keen on being told what to do, neither was I. Fluidly, I positioned myself to be closer to Donna, my neck weaving side to side, slowly studying the packs movements. They were communicating with each other, I could sense it even though I couldn't hear it. The killer in me recognised the man wolf standing in front of us as the one in charge. He would be the one to kill first.

"Damn it! Mara!" Donna said alarmed, her face full of scorn.

"Behave yourself. They would nae hurt us, we're women. No doubt there hoping to persuade us to bare a litter or something, everyone knows they're short on women." She scowled.

"Do nae flatter yourself girlie. We would nae contaminate our blood lines with witch." He said disgusted. "Now move that way." He added sharply, pointing in the direction he wanted us to go in.

"Witch!" Donna hissed outraged. "And what's wrong with witches?" She said, finally jogging in the direction she was instructed.

Apparently, I was meant to follow. For someone who didn't like being submissive, I was appalled and somewhat amused that yet again Donna had me following her lead. What was it about the witch that had me trusting her so completely? Because she's protecting you from yourself I whispered, and because she cares about you I added. With that thought I forced the growing need to rip the wolves throats out, at bay.

"Bossy, loud, troublesome things, who are useless at hunting. But she? Now there's a woman we could use. A predator to the core." The wolf man claimed, a suggestive wink in my direction.

Donna started to giggle out of breath.

"Aye she is that, but I'll wager you a million pounds that you will be submitting to her before she will ever submit to you."

"I do nae doubt your right witch. Whatever she is, it's beyond me. But then I'm only a scout and the men with me only a hunting party. The pack leader, and our generals however, are a different matter. Compared to them, I'm just a pup." He smirked.

Donna stopped mid step, her smile fading.

"You're nae the alpha?" She asked quietly.

"No. I will one day become such, but I am only a youngling" He answered arrogantly.

"Nae bother, the hunters are close, and she is Conlaóch's anam cara. You have heard of Conlaóch? You know, the leader of the Keltoi, most feared hunter alive…" Donna said, stumbling down the trail.

"Again, with the hunter's." The wolf hissed unbelieving. "If she was his anam cara she would be claimed, and yet I can sense her innocence."

Moving towards me he grabbed my hair and pulled it out of the way, my neck exposed. Holding my breath, it took every ounce of restraint not to attack the stupid man.

"Nor does she bare a hunter's mark." He added.

Turning, he continued towards his village.

"Why do you think they are hunting us? He has every intention of claiming her." Donna said exhausted.

The pace the wolf set must be too fast for her. The blood covered wolf didn't answer. Instead he sent a silent command to half of the pack, at least that's what I suspected, as there were now only eight wolves surrounding us, the other six speeding off in the direction we came from.

"We shall see if there is truth to this claim soon enough." He said calmly.

When Donna tripped yet again the werewolf growled frustrated.

"Sit down witch and wait for your so-called hunters to come for you. You are too slow, and I care only for her. She will be greatly received."

"I will not leave her." I snarled, a wave of anger weaving across my chest.

"My pack hates witches, it is better for your friend to remain here for her rescuers, than stand before my leaders." He said, reaching for me.

I growled warningly. Pulling his arm back quickly, he looked impressed.

"Oh, they will defiantly like you. I may even get a promotion for this." He smirked.

Donna fell to the ground, the look on her face that of someone defeated.

"Mara, I'm nae as physically adept as you. I cannae go any further… Aengus is near. If you refuse to go they will only get violent, and then you will lose control… And the beast will hurt you, maybe even try and prevent your return. It's nae worth the risk, just go. I will be fine… Col will come for you." She claimed matter of fact, her eyes closing and opening slowly.

"I've ruined my dress! I love this dress…" She added sadly.

"I will not leave you." I stated plainly, my anger, the pressure that was building, insisting that I pay attention. I pulled in a deep breath, my jaw, every muscle in my body, clenching tightly. I was close to bursting, close to murder, an unrealised growl, vibrating in my throat.

"If you stay I will get seriously hurt in the crossfire, going is the better option... I will be out of the way when all hell breaks loose." She said, a small smile lighting up her face, her head falling gently to the side.

Hurt?

"Give me your word that none of your kin will hurt her in anyway, or by any means, and I will follow you without incident."

"You have my word woman." He grinned happily.

I hated that he thought he had won, I wanted to carve a permanent smile into his face. But the thought of Donna so fragile getting hurt, bothered me. If I lost control… I let the thought dissolve as an ache began to form in my chest. I had no doubt she could use her magic, but she didn't because she wanted to protect me. Any kind of fight would awaken the beast, and she wasn't prepared to aggravate it, even at her own discomfort. She was being a friend, a good one. Smiling back at her, my body slowly relaxing, I motioned for the wolf man to proceed.

"I will see you soon bestie." I promised, reusing the term she had used for me when we had first met.

"Aye you will Mara."

Her eyes were now fully closed, her soft voice barely audible. I increased my pace to a run, matching the pack. Silently we ran through the trees, my thoughts with Donna. I was certain that she had fallen into a deep sleep, I prayed the hunters would find her soon

The village was hidden in a valley, the unspoilt, and rugged landscape, obscuring its existence from unwanted eyes. Until you come directly upon it, you would never know it was there. There was no road in that I could see. Slowing down to a walk, we stepped onto a loose cobbled path, it's dated rural appearance reminding me of the small villages I had visited as a child in Bulgaria and Romania.

There didn't appear to be electricity of any description, the lanterns lighting the narrow streets and paths were made with fire, just like the small bonfires adorning the narrow walk ways, pots of food cooking above them. Their homes seemed to have been built into the valley's face, with large wooden doors standing in periodic intervals, reminding me of church doors. Instinct told me it wasn't actually that archaic, but they wanted whoever came across it to believe that it was. The six wolves who had been following me suddenly shifted to become men, they did it with such ease, low grunts and sighs were the only indication it caused them any discomfort.

"Where is everyone?" I asked.

The village appeared empty, which was odd since there was an abundance of food cooking.

"Waiting for you in the great hall."

Waiting for me? How would they know I was coming? Oh, pack mentality, they can communicate with each other telepathically. It wouldn't surprise me if they saw everything that had occurred in the woods. Donna, they hate witches.

"To be sure, the witch will not be touched!" I growled.

"Aye, the pack has given their word." He said as we approached a large wooden building.

It was easily the size of five double storied houses and was sat in the middle of what looked like a large communal garden. The grand entrance reminded me of Donna's coven, it was in the same style, medieval.

Sounds of hushed talking escaped the building, I wasn't sure what to expect but the beast hovered ready to escape should it be given the opportunity. Wearing the gold backless dress, and uncomfortable heels, I felt uneasy and overdressed, what I wouldn't give for my weapons and leathers.

Breathing in a calming breath, the night air refreshing, I entered the hall, the wolves falling back to stand behind me, and blocking any retreat. Hundreds of golden eyes fell upon me, some belonging to women, but most to men, all of them overly curious. Low growls, grins, and frowns, swept the length of the room, as they ushered me up the aisle to stand before a panel, of who I assumed was their leader and generals. Their gazes were heated and somewhat primal, I wasn't quite sure how to react. My beast however approved and responded in kind, a low growl bursting free, the sensation pleasing. My body trembled with pleasure, I didn't have a clue why I was so pleased, only that I was.

"I am Hamish, laird of Caggan. Welcome Mara." The man who sat central said, with a commanding Scottish accent.

A smile on one half of his mouth reminded me of Col, the laird was looking at me like Col did too, seeing beyond my skin, and into the very depth of my soul… if I have a soul. He was studying me, so I studied him back. He was a hundred times more powerful than the alpha who brought me here, his power seemed to radiate in waves that I could somehow detect. It reminded me of a road on a hot day, when the air seemed to bend and shimmer above it. I found myself looking at it like a cat would catnip, it was almost hypnotic. Dragging my eyes reluctantly away, I looked at the man instead. Like most immortals I have yet to encountered, he was tall and powerfully built. His chestnut coloured hair was long and was partially tied up with a leather band. He wore a short tidy beard that clung to his square jawline, enhancing his untamed look. Golden eyes, the same eyes shared by all the wolves, beamed with intelligence. Hamish hissed as he appreciated my assets un-restrained. Raising my eye brow speculatively, I realised Donna was right, men do have a weakness for a woman's body. I could use that.

"What can I do for you my lord" I smiled sweetly, mimicking as best I could, Donna's smile, when she succeeded in appeasing Aengus. Hamish grinned, pleased with my response. It worked! Huh, this is easier than I thought.

"I'm in need of a mate, one worthy to bare my sons." He announced loudly, standing to join me.

Mate! Babies, sex. Do all men think alike?

"Apparently I belong to another." I replied, thinking of Col.

A flash of annoyance raced its way along my body. Ppfft, I don't belong to anyone, damn men!

"He too implies such." I hissed.

"Aye, the hunter. My hunters have seen them. The witch dinnae lie." He said in a bored tone, indicating he didn't seem remotely bothered by the fact.

"Conlaóch could be a problem, but he has nae marked you, as such you do nae yet belong to him. I could impregnate you now while you are yet unclaimed. You are a powerful women Mara, a litter born to you would be a great blessing to our pack. We will raise them if you prefer not to."

He now stood directly in front of me, his tall frame forcing me to look up at him. Using his hand, he moved the hair that covered my neck. Not feeling threatened, I allowed him. Lowering his mouth to my neck, he breathed in deeply, absorbing my scent.

"Aye, so very powerful, an alpha, a queen." He announced, surprise flickering briefly in his eyes at the latter.

The hall instantly erupted in whispers. The wolves muttered amongst themselves, many lowering their eyes to the floor to avoid my gaze. Those who would look at me, did so in a, 'what are you' manner, that irritated me.

"Quiet!" Hamish roared.

The room instantly fell silent. Hamish looked uncomfortable, and a little confused, as though he suddenly realised he shouldn't be propositioning me at all. What had changed?

"The hunters are here?" I asked him, my heart skipping a beat at the thought of seeing Col all worked up and overly protective.

No Mara, you don't want to see Col, remember!

"No, the pack took Donna to the south, leading them away from you." He stated, his generals coming down to meet him.

One of them was on a phone, speaking urgently into the receiver in Old Norse.

"You said you wouldn't hurt her." I spat angrily, my body reacting oddly to all the attention.

I had the sudden urge to flip my hair back like those T.V women selling shampoo. I didn't, but I really wanted too.

"We have nae hurt her. We merely put her to sleep and had one of my hunters carry her to the south, we left a trail for the hunters to follow, one they should find easily. They will realise soon enough, but we hoped it would give us enough time to persuade you." He said, looking guilty and a little ashamed.

A minute ago, he couldn't care less, again I wondered what I have missed. Hamish's brows were drawn together tightly, concern swimming in his eyes. One of his generals came and handed him the phone he had just been speaking on. I should have paid more attention to the call, but my mind was distracted with the news they had just surrendered. Sleeping, they put her to sleep, how? Magic, drugs? No wonder her eyes were closed! I thought she was just tired. Angry at myself for not noticing, my fangs erupted, the small pang of pain a welcomed perk. Teeth bared, I snarled dangerously. Hamish and his generals turned to face me, their shimmering eyes instantly filling with heat. They raked my body hungrily, their golden eyes overly pleased with what they were seeing. Apparently, they liked aggressive women. Confused by their reaction, I crouched low, ready to attack. I thought I heard Col roar from outside, but to many thoughts invaded my mind, as I tried to do what Donna had asked and maintain control.

"Was that her?" An unfamiliar voiced growled, his tone sinister and thoughtful, sounded from the other end of the phone.

Again, he spoke in Old Norse, one thing I could thank Ti for I guess, it was one of the first languages I was taught, English was the fourth.

"Aye" Hamish said through gritted teeth, purposely moving away from me.

"She is strong, bring her to me, she is close. I can hear the urgency in her voice." The stranger demanded.

"And Conlaóch?" Hamish asked, his muscle straining as he stared at me regretfully, a look of longing and shame shaping his expression.

"Bring her to me Hamish, do what you must… Do not disappoint me." The unknown man ordered, the lethal edge to is voice promised death should Hamish fail.

Passing the phone back to one of his generals, Hamish spoke silently with them. I wanted to know what they said, what they were planning. Donna said Col would come for me, she said I would see her again, I believed her. Struggling to maintain my hold on the beast, I roared my frustrations. Despair and desperation echoed around the vast room, the residue of which sent waves of goose bumps racing across my body. Many of the women and some of the men got up and left abruptly, I don't know why. Those who remained looked at Hamish for instruction, their eyes if possible holding even more desire for me than before. Forty plus Lycans began moving in to surround me. Feeling trapped, my claws ripped into the floor, leaving deep gouges upon its surface. I should have felt threatened, but instead anticipation and excitement coursed through me. It made me think of Col, for some reason I knew he would know what to do, knew what I needed. The smell of blood reached my nose, my beast reeling with an urgent need, the need, whatever it was, lost on me.

"She's bleeding" One of the generals called, his voice low, contained notes of excitement.

The blood is mine? Searching my body, I found the source. A small, 'barely there', trickle of blood, ran down the inside of my thigh. I don't remember injuring myself. This must be yet another change, again I wondered what was happening to me. Another low growl flew past my lips, this time it was a plea… for Col. The werewolves growled in response, some of them taking the shape of a wolf. Teeth snarling, both mine and theirs, I didn't expect the sharp stab of pain that originated at my neck. Moving my hand to inspect, I pulled a small feather dart from my flesh.

"What…?" I growled viciously, two more darts flying through the air, one hitting me on the top of the arm, the other one in my thigh.

Enraged, I flung myself forward, eager to engage my attacker. Before I could reach him another two-darts embedded themselves into my flesh, flecks of darkness filling my vision. I fell to the ground hard, for fuck sake…

The Hunt

Silently we crossed the forest floors, following the small trail that was Mara. Crouching low, I breathed in the faint scent that clung to a bramble, it was fresh, we were getting close. Running at speed, we passed a herd of highland cattle, startling them into a run, their complaints echoing loudly between the trees. Breeching a small incline, we halted, crouching low, danger! Scenting the air, we listened for the threat we knew lurked below. Varúlfur! They have gone and walked right into wolf territory.

Silent, so as not to give our position away, we signalled to each other our intention, and within seconds had formulated a plan. Eoghuan and Finian separated, one going to the left, the other to right, so they could scout ahead and flank the wolves. Slowly we made our way down the hill. The wolves knew we were in the woods, their sense of hearing and smell was as acute as ours, but so far, we have managed to remain hidden from them. Unlike our eyes which absorb the light, a Lycans eyes reflect it. Like stars in the night sky they gave themselves away, flashes of gold illuminating the dark under growth.

I counted six. Drawing in another intake of air, I searched for Mara. A fallen trunk that sat atop a small hill caught my attention, they had spent some time there. Her scent lingered on the ground, forming small circular patterns usually associated with the movements of someone who was defending themselves. I growled low, if anything has happened to her... Three of the six wolves began whimpering in response to my displeasure. Only lesser wolves would react in such away. A hunting party. They must have come across the women whilst gathering meat for the village. Aengus stood beside me, giving away our position.

"What are you doing?" I asked, standing up with him, crouching would have been pointless now, they would have spotted us immediately.

"If the Varúlfur had let the women go, they would have come back the way they came, and straight towards us." Aengus snarled angrily. "They have taken them."

Furious, Aengus flung himself down the hill. Roaring in outrage, he went straight for the closest wolf, a grey mottled one that was hiding behind a small dip in the ground. When the wolf spotted Aengus, it turned and fled. It was a useless move, hunters were faster, and Aengus was fuelled with rage. While Aengus went to retrieve the wolf, Ansgar and I went to the log that Donna and Mara had occupied. Studying the ground, the disturbed soil and leaves revealed the story of all that had taken place. Donna had been sitting on the log while Mara stood in front of her. The witch was bare footed and had at some point developed a small limp. Probably got a splinter or cut. Since I couldn't detect blood I guessed splinter. Fourteen wolves had surrounded them. I grunted, unamused with the revelation, why do women always manage to get themselves into trouble? It almost makes me believe they enjoy it.

"They went in that direction at a run, the women surrounded. It does nae look like there was a struggle." Angsar said surprised.

"They followed freely, Donna would have persuaded Mara not to fight." I said to Ansgar, as we continued to follow their trail.

Aengus strode up besides us, dragging what was now a man behind him. The Lycan was unconscious.

"Because Donna would have gotten hurt?" Ansgar figured.

"Donna's hurt?" Aengus sniffed the air for proof.

"No, they followed freely without a fight. I was just saying, Donna would have persuaded Mara not to fight, to prevent herself from getting hurt in the exchange." I explained.

The wolf Aengus held, began to regain consciousness. Fully coherent, the wolf struggled against Aengus's hold, desperately trying to wriggle free. Lifting him up as though he weighed less than a feather, Aengus forced the wolf to meet his gaze

"Look at me boy, I know your leaders can see me. Listen well, the women you have taken are anam cara, they belong to us, and you will return them immediately. Should you refuse, we will take them by force, killing whoever dares stand in our way." Aengus promised, his normally concealed power sparking furiously about him.

The wolf, a witness to his fury, was shaking in fear, stuttering, he struggled to find his voice.

"They… The."

"Speak before I snap your neck." Aengus roared, frightening the wolf further.

"To the south… The… The witch is… South. One mile. She is… There."

Relinquishing his hold on the wolf, the Varúlfur landed with a thud, shifting back into its wolf form, it scampered away, the smell of his fear invading my nose. Immediately Aengus left to retrieve Donna, Eoghuan and Finian emerging from the trees and filing in behind him.

Less than twenty feet in to our journey, I stopped, the others stopping slightly ahead.

"What is it?" Finian asked, crouching low and sniffing the air for threats.

"I can scent Donna, but not Mara, she didn't pass this way."

Back tracking, I attempted to pick up her scent again.

"She would nae leave Donna." Aengus said, eager to continue.

"She would if Donna insisted." I bit back annoyed.

Donna may be his, but Mara was mine. Where she goes, I follow.

"I cannot detect her either." Finian sniffed, moving to join me.

"Finian, Eoghuan, with me. I'm going to the village. Angsar stay with Aengus."

Not waiting for them to follow, I set off to find Mara.

"It could be a trap" Angsar warned.

I didn't think it was, they wouldn't be that stupid. I should have marked her when I had the chance, to touch ones anam cara once they have been marked carries a death penalty, in which execution is delivered swiftly. There are few laws that include all the immortal species, most having their own, governing themselves. But along with exposing yourself to the mortals, touching another's anam cara or their variant of it, means death. Not even your own can protect you from it. The Vanir will issue the execution order, if the perpetrators own people don't deal with it, we will.

Stopping, I breathed in the aroma of the surrounding woodland, Mara scent so familiar to our surroundings made it difficult to distinguish, but I was certain it was her. She had passed through here not that long ago, eight wolves in tow. Each of us grunted with satisfaction, we had located her, and she was close. Running at full speed, we passed trees and shrubs so fast their form was lost to us. Creatures of all kinds scurried for the safety of their dens, the woods instinctively responding to the threat we carried. They were fools to take Mara, they will pay heavily, and with their lives if she has been harmed.

We knew we were close the minute wolves started throwing themselves in front of us, an idiotic attempt to prevent us reaching her. Flinging a charcoal coloured wolf against the trunk of a tree, its back snapping loudly, we reached the edge of their village. It was quiet, the small walkways empty, which meant they were waiting for us. Slowing down cautiously, we paused momentarily, assessing the situation. Every door and window along their dated cobbled road could potentially hide a wolf. I roared a challenge that said, 'this is your last chance', no reply was given. Cracking my neck, I watched for movement.

"You ready?" I asked the brothers.

Their low growls and languid movements told me they were. Ready, we began our assault. Running at full speed, we pulled our favoured weapons from our backs. A broad sword in hand, I made my way up the street towards the large hall, where Mara's scent was the strongest. She was in there, I knew it.

After passing the third bonfire, the wolves descended. There must have been at least fifty of them racing up the street to engage us. The fact that they were doing so proved they had no intention of giving her back. Pissed, and desperate to reach her, I slashed and diced at any wolf who dared try and stop me. Just as I predicted they would, wolf after wolf came pouring out of the houses, closing us in. It was chaos, the whole street a funnel of snarling teeth and razor-sharp claws, that tore into my flesh. Fangs that are rarely ever used sprang forth, the animal in me enraged. A growl, so low, so deadly, erupted from Finian, garnering my attention. Someone had stabbed him through the shoulder. Seeing his brother in trouble Eoghuan ran to his aid, a bloody mess following his advance. Chopping of the leg of a new attacker, I heard Mara's anguished roar. My heart stopped as her consciousness called to mine, she needed me, and she was mine to protect. Fury welled as I tried to cut a path through to her, the smoke in my eyes curling, and flickering with flame.

Frustrated at my slow progress, I was glad when Ansgar came flying above the fray, reaching my side. How he got to me I wasn't sure, but his presence was welcomed. With a sword in both hands he helped me carve a path to the hall's entrance. Covered in blood, most of which was wolf, we reached the doors just as they were trying to close them. Pushing through, we entered the hall and searched for Mara. She was unconscious and was being ushered out of a door manacled. Thoroughly pissed with what I was witnessing, I roared, my heart pounding.

"Do nae breathe in Conlaóch." Ansgar warned, as he assessed the situation.

These wolves were not foot soldiers, they were elite.

Ignoring Ansgar warning, I drew in a sharp intake of air, Mara's blood dominating my senses. Lust hit me hard as I realised the source, she was in heat, and my body, like the Varúlfur, responded to her in kind.

"Focus! Look into their minds, they want her Conlaóch, desire her, they steal her away from you, so another can claim her."

His words, curt, cut through the lust, my anger reaching new heights. Disbelieving that one would dare steal her from me I searched their minds, the result of my probing an explosion of clarity that had me running for her regardless of the risk. I heard Ansgar roar behind me, felt him at my back. Dodging and throwing my assailants away I entered the same door Mara had only moments ago. Her blood was a temptation I could have gone without, shaking my head I battled to keep my lust at bay, it wouldn't help her, wouldn't help me get her back.

A Varúlfur that had been lying in wait came bursting through the wall, a sword in hand, he tried to push the blade through my stomach. Furious, I threw him away from me, the wolf crashing hard against the floor and taking me with him. Getting up almost instantly, I swung my sword around, the tip of it connecting with his jaw. With a sickening thud, the lower half of his face dropped to the ground. Screaming in agony, I left him behind and exited the hall, not caring for his condition.

Stood outside, the cool air pushed the last of my lust aside. Seven new Varúlfur waited for me, another two placing Mara into the back of a helicopter, a bearded man holding her against him. The look he gave me was one of regret, he didn't want this, wanted or not he would pay dearly. My eyes meet his, every ounce of my intent carried in my glare. He closed the helicopter's doors, his face unreadable. Hoping my strength and speed would be enough, I threw myself at the seven wolves that stood between me and Mara. Instead of breaking through, the wall of Lycans had me spiralling backwards, my shoulder dislocating as I hit the ground. Ignoring the injury and with my desperation reaching new heights, I threw myself against the wall again. Knives and claws stabbed and ripped at my flesh, the wall refusing to fall. In time, I knew I could get through, but time was a luxury I didn't currently have. When the helicopter started up, I went wild, despair, grief, and fear, gnawing at me, the thought of her being taken, gripping at my heart.

"Mara!" I called, hoping she would hear me, that she would know I came for her.

"Boss, go get her!" Angsar shouted, before he too, threw himself at the wall, his eyes murderous, wild.

One by one the wolves began to fall, the barrier weakening. As hope began to flare the helicopter lifted from the ground, the sound of its departure deafening. I hissed frustrated as one more wolf blocked my way. Grabbing his arm, I attempted to side step him, bending his arm back in the process. I felt his arm give way, heard the bone snap. Expecting him to let go I was surprised when I found I couldn't move. The wolf had grabbed me with his other arm, and was pulling me to the ground. Arming myself with a dagger, I stabbed the wolf in the chest, his warm blood bubbling over the hilt and coating my hand. Coldly shoving the wolf aside, I leapt for the helicopter.

The helicopter's lights flashed mockingly, my blood coated hands struggling to maintain their hold on the undercarriage. Wiping what blood I could from them, I pulled myself up and reached for the door. Smashing it with my fist, the glass gave way easily, shards of it piercing my flesh. Before I could gain entry, what was left of the door slid open, the movement un-expected. Mara lay asleep in the bearded man's lap, his mind impenetrable. Before I knew what was happening, he pointed a barrel of a gun to my head.

"This is beyond me hunter. I cannae disobey him." He said, pulling the trigger.

I felt the burn of the bullet entering me, before I heard the shot. Roaring in agony, one of my hands lost its grip on the rail, my body hanging dangerously. Three more bullets were fired, my body inflamed. My remaining hand gave way, blood running freely from my wounds. With nothing to hold onto, I fell to the ground. I watched powerlessly as Mara moved further and further away. The pain from my wounds was insubstantial, the pain of losing Mara, soul destroying. Watching her fade into the distance, the flashing lights paving her departure, I felt nothing but loss… I'd failed her.

Captive

Disorientated, I woke, my head pounding. Lifting my hands to massage my scalp, I attempted to stand. Dizziness swept over me, nausea followed, the sensation overwhelming.

"You really shouldn't be standing." A small female voice offered from beside me.

Trying to locate the source, I searched the area around me. Several times I tried to focus only to be greeted with a mirage of colours that blurred together un-recognisably. Defeated and about to throw up, I sat down.

"You were drugged, you had at least eight darts in you when they threw you in here. If you ask me it's a bit excessive, I mean, what do they think you are, a T rex?" Another voice added dryly, in a broad American accent.

"Where am I?" I asked, my head held tightly in my hands.

I tried to recollect my thoughts, but every time I thought I was beginning to remember something, it slipped from my mind. Frustrated, I glared at the blurred shapes.

"We don't know where we are. Like you we haven't been here that long." That same small voice said.

"I think I've been here for a day, but I can't be sure." The American added grimly.

"You were already here when they threw me in, a couple of hour's maybe." The women with the quiet voice said.

"You know nothing about how you got here?" I asked them, my sight was beginning to return to normal, my headache lessening.

I could now faintly distinguish the outline of the two women.

"No, like you, we too were drugged. One minute I was shopping, buying these killer heels, the next I was pulling a small feather dart from my backside. Then nothing! I woke up here with a headache, all on my lonesome." The American women explained, her tone one of indignation.

"Similar to myself. I was on my way to meet a friend for a coffee, next thing I know I was stung on the arm, and then again on my neck. I didn't even have a chance to react before I felt myself give way." The other woman said disbelievingly, as though she thought this was a dream and couldn't possibly be happening.

"What about you?" The American asked.

I tried to recall the events that had led up to this point. The Varúlfur! Hamish. I growled.

"Werewolves are what happened to me!"

"Lycans?" The American snarled angrily. "I hate the dogs" She continued.

"Why would they want us? I have never even met one." The other woman asked thoughtfully.

"They asked me to have a litter for them." I explained, disgusted with the fact.

Bloody wolves, I'll kill them all!

"A litter... as in babies!" The American squealed outraged.

"We're here to be brood mares?" The quiet one squeaked at the same time.

"I cannot be certain as to why you're here, but I have no other reason to offer. They asked me if they could impregnate me. When my anam cara came for me, they darted me, and now I'm here."

The women gasped simultaneously, my vision greatly improved.

"They stole you from your soul mate?" The quiet one asked appalled.

The American's eyes were wide in shock, her mouth slightly open.

"Yes, apparently." I answered flatly.

At least I thought I heard Col. No, I know he was there, I felt his presence. He came for me. The thought made my stomach flutter, my heart race… Odd, why would that excite me? Somewhat irritable, I realised that for every hour passed since meeting him, I have thought about him increasingly. I tried to decipher why that was, especially when I had already decided I didn't need him. Lost in thought, the American came and sat beside me, she then proceeded to pat me gently on the back. I wasn't sure what to make of the gesture, so I just sat there, my body stiff.

"I'm so sorry! You must be so worried." She said sorrowfully, her teary eyes filled with concern.

"Col will come for me." I said confidently, surprising myself.

How could I be so certain?

"Yes! They say your soul mate can find you anywhere, and they will never give up looking for you." The quiet one smiled excitedly.

"When he comes for you, will you take us with you?" She asked hopeful.

I couldn't see before, but the quiet one was a red head, not auburn like Aengus, but a vibrant red. The vivid colour reminded me of cherries. Peering at me with rich amber eyes, she watched me expectantly. Oh, she's waiting for an answer.

"I will take all that wish to go." I promised.

I meant it, and I will kill every damn Varúlfur too. The women smiled, their eyes full of hope.

"Since we're stuck in here together, we should probably learn each other's names." The America decided, a small smile on her face.

"My name is Gabriella, Gabriella Tepes."

Years of distrust suddenly reappeared since leaving Donna. For all I know these women could have been placed here to learn more about me, to gain my trust. I contemplated not revealing my name, but then I remembered Hamish already knew it. There was no point in not revealing it, but I would say nothing more, at least not until I was sure they could be trusted.

"Mara." I said, trying to stand.

This time I was steady, the effects of the drugs no longer having any bearing on me at all. Perfect.

"Just Mara?" Gabriella asked me, her eye brows raised in suspicion.

"If I have a last name, I don't know it." I said truthfully.

She didn't look convinced, but she said no more about it. Looking at the quiet women we waited for her to reveal her name. She, like me, looked unsure. She doesn't trust us either, which in my book meant she was in the same situation.

"Asta, of the house of Thura." She said eloquently, her voice small had an accent I wasn't familiar with. Which is unusual as there aren't many places I haven't been.

"Thura! You are Vanir, fey!" The American said excitedly.

The fey, I knew them as elves. Ti had spent just one-day teaching me about them.

'They are a private secretive people Mara, who would attack one such as you on sight. They are creatures of the light and cannot abide those who live in the shadow'.

He went on to speak about their home and their ability to manipulate the elements, and that was it. He said they would offer no aid and as such it was pointless ever engaging with one.

"My parents were adamant the fey existed, but I never believed them. You're powerful, you can control the elements, you could get us out of here!" Gabriella added hopefully.

"I'm sorry, I am only seventeen, we do not have access to our power until we have grown into our immortality." She said regretfully, her eyes lowering.

"Oh" Gabriella said deflated. "At what age is that?"

"Usually between twenty-one and twenty-five, later for males. When we have reached our peak physically we will remain forever unchanged. It is at that point our ability to channel manifests." Asta answered nervously, as though she was revealing more than she intended.

The small sliver of hope which had been present in Gabriella's eyes, died, her shoulders slumping. The hope was genuine. Which means they are both like me, a prisoner. At least I could be sure they were in the same situation as me, even if I was still unsure as to whether I could trust them or not.

"I will get you both out of here, I swear it." I heard myself-saying.

Why are you being an idiot Mara? You don't care about them, you don't care about anyone! Save yourself, my mind complained. Hope flashed in their eyes. Damn it!

"First I must gather information." I sighed, somewhat resigned.

Searching the room, my vision restored, I noticed it was carved out of ice, and yet neither Gabriella or Asta appeared to be cold. Ice cave. Mountain. My mind began puzzling together information in the same methodical way I had been taught to. There were many places on earth that had ice caves. But the general at the village was speaking in old Norse. If only I could be sure that he remained in the area indigenous to the language. If so that would place us in Norway, which is full of bloody ice caves. Wait. Hamish. The look in his eyes when he was told to bring me. Regret. He did not want to, and yet he did it anyway. There was something Ti had taught me about the Varúlfur, something I needed to remember. Hamish was a leader, an Alpha. All wolves defer to the alpha, they must, why…?

"We will help you. Tell us what kind of things are important to remember." Asta said, interrupting my thoughts.

"If you are ever taken from the room remember room locations. If they blind fold you, remember to count your steps and remember what direction you were taken. Listen for noises, for example an area where there are loads of voices or machinery. Are there coded locks on the doors? Look to see the code or listen to the tune as they dial it in. Windows, names, everything is important, everything can give us a clue as to where we are." I said, studying the room further.

It was simply furnished. Four single beds lined the walls, each with a small bed stand. A huge bear skin rug lay beneath me in the centre of the room along with smaller wolf pelts near the beds. Probably so you didn't get out of bed just to stand directly onto ice and burn your feet I deduced. As far as prisons went, this was better than most of the places I have lived. So, our captor wanted us to be comfortable? Or maybe he just liked playing games and this was just a taste of what we could have if we co-operated.

"I can do that, I have excellent hearing." Gabriella said confidently, brushing her, bobbed, honey coloured hair with her fingers.

I smiled at her statement. She was a vampire, of course she had excellent hearing. As well as other talents I could use, I thought to myself, and inspecting the door for weaknesses. Nothing, it was magically warded. Frustrated, I began searching the draws for tools or weapons. Coming up empty, I snarled wickedly, the sound made Asta jump.

"Are you ok?" She asked bravely.

Trying to calm myself, I drew in a long deep breath.

"It has been a while since I ate. I have been increasingly angry and short tempered; my body has been changing in ways I don't understand. Furthermore, things are happening to me that have never happened before, feelings of attachment, regard, regret, none of which I knew until… four days ago. I now find myself here, a prisoner, trapped. I should be tearing the wall down and killing everyone that would hinder me, it is what I would normally do, it is my nature. Instead, I am making promises to help two strangers, who I may, or may not be able to trust. And Col's eyes, his damn green eyes, are haunting me. I think of him constantly. A man I have already decided I do not want." I burst out.

Frustrated and surprised by my own admission, I sat down on the closest bed and breathed in another long breath. What the hell is happening to me? And since when did I become chatty?

"If I'm not mistaken, you are in heat. As I remember it, irrational behaviour is to be expected." Gabriella grinned.

Heat?

"You have obviously never been in heat before or you would know what is happening to you. Which means you have reached your immortality! Your true self will manifest, your strengths and weakness revealed. All of your abilities surfacing, basically, you will be bad ass! And very fertile."

It would explain much but it still didn't answer the question as to what I am, or what I'm capable off.

I snarled, angry with my current situation, my nose twitching.

"But I don't know what I am." I confessed.

Restless, I stood up, I needed to be doing something, hurt something.

"Oh, well, between the three of us, I'm sure we can figure it out, at least enough to put you at ease." Asta said confidently, a small smile of reassurance enhancing her delicate features.

"What could you do before you started changing?" Gabriella asked.

I couldn't help but glare at them both. They hardly knew me, and yet despites Ti's claims A Vanir and a vampire wanted to help me. For the first time, I began to wonder just how much of what Ti had taught me had been truth. Having looked into the eyes of men who want only for their own gain, their aid fuelled only by their own desires, I knew the women in front of me held no such emotion, their declaration to help was genuine and selfless. They reminded me of Donna, I couldn't help but hope Aengus had found her, and that she was safe. Against my earlier warning of revealing too much, I began telling them everything. Starting with my childhood and Ti. We were prisoners, if I was ever going to escape and take them with me, I needed to know what I was capable of, and I needed to know now.

The Alliance

I grunted loudly as the last bullet fell from my body, the crumpled-up shell casing ringing on the floor like an unwanted penny. Unlike its entry, the exit was agonisingly slow, the muscle and sinew knitted together, pushing the foreign object back out the way it came. Thirty-six hours! That's how long it has been since Mara was abducted, and I was still no closer to knowing where she is. My mind was chaotic with images of her being beaten, tortured, or worse, raped. Best case scenario she was in a cell, but I was afraid for her. They wanted her, I saw the lust in their eyes, saw the things they wanted to do to her in their mind, and I was here, useless to help her, powerless to stop them.

"You really think Mara would allow someone to touch her. You're her anam cara, and she didn't exactly roll out the mat and welcome you." Donna said loudly from across the room, her brows drawn together in a scowl.

Ever since the witch awoke to find Mara missing she has fluttered between angry and woeful, blaming herself for her inability to fully understand her gift of foresight as the reason for Mara's abduction

She was young, just shy of a quarter century. I have seen Vanir thousands of years old still learning to decipher their dreams. She was too hard on herself, it was my fault, I should have marked her.

"Damn it, do nae look at me like that Conlaóch. Hypocrite! Like your thoughts are any different." She shouted.

Standing, she started pacing around the room, her energy fiery and toxic. Wait! Did she just read my mind?

"Calm yourself anam cara." Aengus said.

Standing, he folded her into his arms. Reluctantly, and with a sigh, she relaxed against him. Weeping quietly, Aengus rested his head on hers, pressing a gentle kiss on the top of her head.

"We shall nae stop looking for her my love. You friend and Conlaóch's anam cara will be found." He said to her soothingly, and with conviction.

She wrapped her arms around him, comforted by his declaration. I couldn't look, Mara should be within my arms, she should be safe. With a heavy heart, I turned and walked out the room, a trail of dripping blood following me. Standing out in the fresh air, I searched the trees for calm. Focusing on the gentle sway of the tree tops, I watched as the wind carried them back and forth in a hypnotic manner, my temper slowly defusing.

Rubbing a hand across my forehead to clear the anger which had firmly taken hold. I started to analyse the events that led up to Mara's abduction. I had searched the minds of the Varúlfur to determine whether or not Ansgar's claims had held merit. I saw then their lust for her, it was strong, her menstrual blood an aphrodisiac to them. But at least one of them had to be following some kind of order, or they wouldn't have been able to organise her kidnapping.

Sitting amongst the tall trees that surrounded our cabin, I started to peel back every thought I had seen within their minds. Images flashed quickly, as I flipped from wolf to wolf in an attempt to discover something useful. Shame. One of them was ashamed by his involvement in taking her. No, several of them were ashamed, those who knew what would happen to her. They were ordered by one who was more superior then they were, an order they were physically unable to ignore. Pack hierarchy… Alpha's have a hold on those below him, a compulsion that they must obey. They cannot stop themselves from obeying, bar from killing themselves they will carry out the order even if they did not want to. It is the reason that so many of them have set up their own communities, separate from the royal household. The royal household… The bearded man's words echoed in my mind 'I cannot disobey him, even if I wanted to'. Yes, he was definitely under compulsion. From his king? Or someone else?

The village did not appear to be loyalists, I would have recognised the stench of evil upon entering. The absent of such darkness would indicate that they, like many of their kin, have forsaken their master Fenrir. This would also explain the shame of taking ones anam cara, at least I hope it would. Taking ones anam cara was widely considered the same as murder, the minute you look upon them and recognised them as yours is the moment you will never recover from the loss of losing them. If it didn't kill you straight away, then it was only a matter of time. Determined to find her, I searched my memories to discover who of the Varúlfur was more powerful than the bearded man? If I could discover his name, I could find out who his superior was. Nothing! No one was thinking of his name, I have learned nothing.

Growling, I stood and punched the nearest tree. The bones in my hand broke, but I didn't care. Frustrated, I sat back down and drew in a long breath. I had to find her, had to find something that would lead me to her. I started searching again.

After two hours of methodically searching every useless thought, I went back inside to contact the Keltoi and see if the Vanir had discovered anything.

"Finian?" I snapped, my temper short as I envisioned Mara being tortured.

Livid with the thought I struggled not to lash out.

"Nothing." He answered apologetic.

"I may be able to locate her." Donna said, her eyes full of hope, her demeanour calmer than before.

"How?"

"I have just spoken with my coven, they said if I can find something that belongs to her I could attempt a location spell. I dinnae have anything that belonged to her. A few clothes at my house but nothing that was important enough to establish a link. But then my mum just pointed out that I have the most important thing to her, and I dinnae know it. I've wasted so much time, I'm so sorry!"

Her eyes began to water.

"Donna?" I asked impatiently.

Aengus glared at me unhappily, flames dancing in his eyes.

"Oh, you! You are the other part to her soul." She said, looking up at Aengus, her emerald eyes full of wonder.

"Do it." I said desperately.

I had to find her.

"Aye, I need your blood, fresh." She said, studying the dried blood on my clothing.

"Done."

After retrieving a knife and bowl from the kitchen, I placed the bowl on the table and ran the blade across my palm. Blood poured from my hand into the bowl, the pain nothing more than a necessary nuisance. I would endure much worse if it meant getting Mara back. When I was finished, the bowl practically full, I passed it to Donna.

Using her fingers, Donna made a large circle on the floor, using the blood. After marking the inner circle with ancient symbols, she stood and assessed her work.

"It is ready. Sit within its centre." She instructed.

Doing what she asked, Donna left the room, returning moments later with an iPad.

"Why do you need an iPad?" Finian asked.

"I need the world map, unless you have an atlas on you." She said without looking at the warrior.

Finian didn't answer but watched closely.

"No one say anything, I need to focus." Donna warned, her mouth pursed in concentration.

Sitting in front of me, but outside the circle, she closed her eyes and began speaking in the language known only to those with the ability to channel magic. Almost immediately the windows in the cabin flung open with a crash, wind that wasn't present moments ago, flooding the room. Un-moved by the display I watched the witch intently. Her eyes open, I noticed that her irises were coated in a thin film of white, it reminded me of frost, and was transparent enough to show that her eyes beneath were a vivid green. Chanting softly, the words Donna uttered started to resemble a song. The blood that surrounded me slowly came to life, moving in a circular motion around my body. Picking up speed, the blood started to rise from the floor, one drop at a time, like rain that had reversed its trajectory and sort the sky instead of the earth. Unsure if I should touch it, I remained still. When the blood had risen above the height of my head, it stopped mid-air and began to gather into one large pool that hovered directly over me. With a speed that not even my eye could follow, it flew into the iPad, my blood trapped beneath the glass. Flicking through images of the world, the blood travelled the length of it, Iceland, Canada, America… Page by page it flicked through earths nations until finally my blood rested on Norway. Creating a circle like the one I had been enclosed in, I watched as the area within the circle zoomed in, showing first cities, then towns, and then smaller still, the villages, until finally it revealed Mara's exact location, and I knew exactly where she was! A deafening roar filled the room, my roar, Donna lost the connection. My blood poured from the iPad, as though it had been cut and was bleeding heavily.

"That was fantastically creepy." Finian said, staring at Donna in wonderment, and ignoring my outburst.

"Varúlfur's!" Angsar spat angrily, capturing my attention.

Moving quickly to retrieve his swords, he headed to the front door. Pulling in a deep breath, the room filled with the forest air, I searched for the wolves' location. Two miles out, coming in from the west. At least twenty elite and forty plus foot soldiers, and they were moving fast.

"How long?" Eoghuan asked, both he and his brother arming themselves.

"Two minutes." I said angrily.

"Ward this room Donna, now. I must fight with my kin, but I will not have them take you. Nothing gets in!" He ordered, moving to cover the back door.

"Like you have to ask. I'll burn every last one of them!" She said furiously.

Waves of electric blue energy pulsated dangerously across her body, the minute she began to chant, the magic that danced along her skin, skimmed across the walls, floor, and ceiling, boxing her in, and keeping the wolves out.

"We're counting on it little witch."

I wanted all the Varúlfur dead for what they have done. Leaving the house through the front door I waited eagerly for their arrival.

One by one the wolves emerged from the shelter of the trees, their pelts varying shades of blacks, greys, whites, browns, with the occasional red drawing the eye. When the lesser wolves had surrounded our cabin the elite came forward, their power rolling off them in waves that manipulated the air around them. Growling low, I recognised them all as the men who took Mara, but in better health than when I had left them. Surrounded, my eyes found and remained solely on the bearded wolf who stood in the centre, his face like before was unreadable. Fury rose. Staring murderously into the eyes of the man responsible for Mara's captivity, I moved to attack.

"We have nae come here to fight with you hunter." The bearded man said grimly.

He stood before us unimpressed, he didn't even bother to arm himself. It was a rare thing for one to stand before us and not be afraid. I grudgingly respected his level of fearlessness, if I wasn't going to kill him, I could have found a use for him.

"The penalty for taking ones anam cara is death" I said, my voice calmly hiding my anger.

The Varúlfur's leader sighed regretfully.

"I could nae do anything about taking her, my orders were clear. But he said nothing about helping you get her back." The wolf answered defiantly.

"Who?"

Who would dare take her from me?

"I cannae speak his name. None of us can." He said angry with the fact.

I growled frustrated.

"Then what use can you possibly be, I already know where she is."

I had already tried to read his mind, but he must have been expecting it, his thoughts guarded. What information I could gather without physical contact was limited. Looks like attacking is the only way I'm going to get answers. Lifting my sword, I jumped from the porch, and towards him.

"Wait!" The werewolf growled, his golden eyes betraying his frustration.

"I said I could nae speak his name, I dinnae say I could nae mention he is my brother. I have been building my strength for years now in the hope to challenge him and put an end to his reign. It is the only way we can be truly free of his rule. When Mara came, I thought only of her bearing a litter, I had fully intended to give her back." He said factually, like impregnating ones anam cara was nothing important.

Angry, I took another step towards him.

"Damn it hunter. It was cocky aye, but I was nae going to harm the girl, and if she had said no, I would have released her instantly." He claimed defensively, as though he didn't understand my reaction.

"Then what went wrong?"

I could sense he spoke the truth, but he was still the one who took her. I wanted to make him feel the loss I felt, the pain I felt.

"It was her scent." He sighed.

"Explain"

"My brother has been collecting women. He searches for one's powerful enough to produce an heir worthy of his master's approval. A queen, or if not a queen, a woman he can place in his harem for breeding. He has taken women from across the species. Varúlfur, Valkyrie, Nosferatu, maybe even Keltoi... He sent his soldiers to every wolf pack and ordered us to take any female who contains a unique power, and to contact him directly should we find one with the makings of a queen." He finished.

He wasn't telling me everything.

"Out with it wolf."

"I do nae know how to tell you this hunter." The Lycan confessed, anxious to speak further.

"Just say it."

The wolf dropped the guards to his mind, allowing me to see the reason why she was taken. No! He is mistaken.

"Fenrir's blood runs in her veins." He said, his thoughts closing off again.

Pity swam in his eyes.

"She is a direct blood descendant. However, she is too young to be Fenrir's daughter therefore she must be the daughter of one of his sons Sköll or Hati."

No, I refuse to believe it, and yet I felt it in my heart, felt the truth of his claim. It was the very reason I entered the club in first place. I detected a darkness that reminded me of Sköll. Why? Why would fate give me the daughter of my enemy, whose blood is tainted by a darkness so thick, it cannot comprehend the light. No wonder she ran from me when another anam cara would have given herself freely. She was born to a monster.

"Idiot! You should be ashamed Conlaóch!" Donna shouted, bursting out of the cabin, her glossy hair catching in the wind.

Aengus growled with disbelief.

"Get back inside woman!" He hissed warningly.

Staring at Aengus with daggers in her eyes, she ignored him, her attention returning to me.

"We will talk about your use of the word, 'woman' later, but right now, Conlaóch!" She spoke, staring at me with the same amount of scorn she had just directed at Aengus.

Mentally sighing I knew I was about to be lectured.

"Her father is but one half of her parentage! If his pervert brother can steal women for his breeding purposes than why cannae her father have done the same?" She added, rolling her eyes dramatically to land on the wolf leader.

"Bloody witches!" One of the Varúlfur spat.

"I do nae claim she has nae got bad in her. Aye, she has a darker than normal dark side, but she also has a good side. It just nae been nurtured. If she was like her father, whichever brother it is, she would nae have been able to be a friend, to care." She continued, her voice gradually quietening.

Her eyes gleamed proudly as she no doubt pictured Mara in her mind.

"Have you nae thought that she was given to you because you can help her nurture it. I mean, a hunter, a guardian of the light, to protect the one woman whose ability to see the light is a daily battle. You are her anchor Conlaóch, a constant source of light that will prevent her from ever getting lost in the dark."

"Aye it makes sense friend. I know no other man who could be what she needed. For thousands of years the mother Jörg has been preparing you for her… Think about it, we belong to the light and yet we hunt the creatures of the dark. We understand them, their needs, how they think, you are perfect for her." Angsar said, his golden eyes daring me to contradict him.

Sighing, I realised there was truth to their words. The darkness was within her of that there was no doubt, but I had witnessed her regard for the witch. Sköll has no regard for anything, and as far as he who hates, Hati. He is every bit as malevolent as his brother.

"I know." I said unperturbed.

"Could have fooled me." Donna muttered sarcastically, a small smile lighting up her face.

"I was merely processing little witch."

I returned my attention to the Varúlfur, Donna huffing indignantly behind me. Ignoring her, my face revealed nothing.

"So what kind of begrudging alliance did you have in mind?" I asked.

Rex

We must have spent hours discussing all the known species, their strengths, and their weaknesses. Asta was certain I was half dark entity and half-light, which is why she thought I was so volatile and quick to anger. She had also concluded that my light side was like her Vanir. Apparently, if you looked deep enough I contained an inner light that all Vanir can recognise within their own race. As to the dark part of me, they were both at a loss.

The realisation that I was half fey caused a lot of excitement. Apparently Asta could teach me to tap into the part of my nature that had so far remained un-used. She also believed that all my new feelings were a result of my immortality, the fey don't get access to the inner light they carry until they have fully grown, and now that I have, it is likely the reason I have started to feel things… emotions. It would make sense, I guess… feeling stuff only started happening when I started changing, so it's a possibility. Looking at the delicate elf I had difficulty picturing myself as such. She was so gentle and timid, and I was confident and lethal.

"Honestly Mara, you can do it. Your guardian Ti only taught you those things which pertained to the dark. You can learn to understand the light, you just never had the opportunity." Asta said, her face full of reassurance.

"I agree with her. In fact, I half suspect he didn't want you to. It's probably the reason why he kept you always in the cold and why you can't feel warmth." Gabriella added, fetching the jug of water, that had at some point before our arrival been placed in the room for us to drink.

"Have you not ever wondered why you wanted a normal life? I mean if you were purely bad then surely you wouldn't care at all." Asta frowned, taking the full jug of water from Gabriella, and placing it gently on the floor in front of me.

"Fine, what have I got to lose?"

Uncertain, I stared at the water.

"Excellent, lesson one. Basic levitation. Focus on the water, see it, every particle of it, and imagine what it feels like to touch. Focus on its texture and the way it would move within your hands. When you are sure you have remembered every detail, envision it rising from the jug. Will it to move, order it to, in the same way you would command a warrior in to battle." Asta instructed, her eyes brimming with excitement.

Command it? Sighing loudly, and biting my lip, I focused on the water in the jug. Doing what Asta said, I started breaking the water down into separate stimulants. Utilising my highly-evolved senses, I committed the scent of the water to mind. I could detect the earthy notes within it as it travelled along the bedrock before reaching the lake. Tiny threads of varying minerals had attaching themselves to the minute particles that formed the greater volume, the variety teasing my scent receptors and defining the waters true essence. Satisfied I knew the waters fragrance I opened my eyes to study its structure. I imagined it within my palm, as Asta had instructed. The sudden feeling of water running through my fingers soothed and calmed my breathing, and more surprisingly, lessened my pain. The more I concentrated on the feeling of running water the more the sensation spread. No longer restricted to my hands, I felt the water caress my body in the same way it would, had I'd been standing beneath a slow pouring waterfall. Immersed, the water found its way into the smallest of spaces, filling the gaps, and forcing the trapped pockets of air to be expelled back into the atmosphere. Completely enveloped in the feeling of immersion, I saw for the first time a pulsing energy that swam within the waters depths. I could hear it as though it spoke to me, it's language familiar. Awareness hummed as I saw the same energy within the ice walls that surrounded me. Returning my gaze to the jug and the water contained inside, I started to picture it rising. Using the same language, the water had just taught me, I commanded it to rise from the jug.

The water lifted from the jug with ease, the action making me feel elated. I am part Vanir! Watching so intently, afraid of losing the connection, I didn't respond to Asta and Gabriella's gasps of shock, my eyes remaining fixed on the water that floated in front of me.

"Mara?" Asta whispered, her voice full of wonderment.

"What?" I asked just as quietly.

"Look at the walls!" Gabriella breathed, her soft tone laced with excitement.

Reluctantly I tore my gaze away from the blob of water suspended mid-air. The walls! Thousands, no millions of drops of water floated a foot from the entire area of wall. Like small crystals they shimmered, the lanterns light reflecting from surface to surface in a captivating dance of light. The low illumination bounced between each drop, in the same way the sun's summer rays shone through a heavy down pour of rain. It was beautiful. I was doing this! Focusing on the ice wall, I wanted to see just how much I could do. Commanding it to dissolve and melt, I was silently surprised when water began falling freely from the walls. The whole room filled with droplets of water, that grew increasingly bigger. With nowhere to go the water pooled at our feet, and was rising rapidly.

"Urm Mara!" Gabriella squealed.

"What?" I asked, too enthralled to be aware of the danger.

"As pleased as I am to discover you have talent for water manipulation, I do not fancy drowning only to regenerate and drown again, forever!"

Ah… I winced. Unsure how I could create a place for the water to run without alerting our captors, I did the only thing that came to mind and commanded the water to return to its previous form and location. It worked! Staring at each other quietly, all of us struggling to find something to say, I noticed later than usual the approach of footsteps. My eyes whipped around to land on the door.

"I hear them too!" Gabriella hissed, her fangs bared. "Four of them." She added without needing to.

I had already deduced as much.

"Stay behind us Asta." I instructed.

I suddenly understood what it must feel like for Col when I placed myself in dangerous situations. Compared to his big frame, I would have appeared to him just as Asta did to me, dainty and small.

"What's that other noise?" Gabriella asked, her head tilting slightly to the side as she strained to decipher the peculiar noise.

I recognised it, memories of my captivity with the beast surfaced un-welcome, my fangs making an appearance in response to the negative memory.

"They are dragging someone."

No doubt another woman for the last bed. Standing back from the warded door we waited for them to enter.

When the door flung open, the doors opening outward, I wasn't prepared for the sight that greeted me. Expecting another drugged woman, as we had been when we arrived, I was appalled to see that they were dragging a young, badly beaten girl. She was unconscious and in poor condition.

"What did you do to her?!" Asta shouted, her voice filled with grief.

Running forward, against my warning to stay back, she pulled the young girl into her arms and carried her to the bed, ignoring the danger to herself. With the girl out of the way, I grabbed the nearest wolf by his neck, lifting him easily off the ground. I growled, the whole situation, emotionally provoking. The flare of aggression inadvertently stirred the beast, rage welling like a tsunami, one-minute calm, the next complete desolation. Consequently, I broke the wolf's neck with a sickening crack, damn it.

Dropping the wolf with a thud, I sped lightning fast and grabbed the next one in line. Gabriella snarled beside me, a wolf held firmly in her grasp, her hand deeply embedded in its chest. Ripping his heart out with an eerie sucking noise, she dodged a hook from the remaining Lycan, blood covering her now dried clothes. My only thought was that the water really did return to its original location.

Placing the thought aside, and not pondering on the weird directions of my thinking, I returned my attentions to the wolf I had pinned to the ground. He looked confused and shocked by the turn of events, he was supposed to. He was at least three foot taller than me and powerfully built, but he was a foot solider, so subsequently, no match for me. Copying Gabriella's approach, I punctured the wolf's chest and placed my hand over his beating heart. The smell of his blood delighted me, so did the growl of pain he omitted the moment I pushed through his ribcage, capturing his heart. Held in an iron clad grip, each retched beat angered me further.

"Tell me Lycan, does your master see me?"

I knew that if his master chose to he could view me through his soldier's eyes. I hoped that he would.

"He sees you." The wolf snarled, his golden eyes now containing the presence of another.

"I will not be kept. I will walk out of here with the others and you will be wise not to prevent me." I demanded, my captivity giving my beast more power, more sway.

I felt her rising, felt her need to kill whispering throughout me. A malevolent, twisted laughter sounded from the wolf, the action causing his heart to jolt within my palm. My beast purred, the sensation pleasing. It was like a tease, like someone ran the tip of a knife along the sensitive inner of my thigh. I wanted to crush it, to feel it give way within my hand, the warm blood and sinew pumping through my fingers. But then the pleasure it would bring me would end to soon, so I held back… reluctantly.

"Tell me wolf, what amuses you?" I snarled, my grip tightening on the wolf's heart.

"Mara… So strong… so ripe for the taking. My loins ache with the promise of you." The wolf smirked, his master's words making me cringe, I didn't understand all of it, but I got the general gist.

"You will never possess me!" I replied, my voice hedged with venom.

"Ah… But I already do Mara. The room is warded, you cannot pass without an escort of those who are loyal to me. Since the vampire has killed two, there are only two left." He laughed mockingly.

"If there are two left, we can leave." I smirked.

Lifting the werewolf that I currently had pinned to ground, and with his heart still held firmly within my grasp, I moved to walk out of the door. Laughing loudly the wolf within my palm wrenched himself free, the force of his departure placing him outside of the room, his heart still pumping furiously in my hand. Disgusted more than shocked, I dropped the heart and turned to face the remaining wolf, our last means of escape. He was now stood, his neck healed, Gabriella holding him. Staring at me with an empty smile he continued the laughter that was only moments ago coming from the dead wolf.

"Apologies, one wolf left." The wolf smirked arrogantly.

As annoyed and angry as I was with his game, the beast in me enjoyed the spectacle. I almost wanted to join in and laugh with him. Shaking my head at the thought, I suddenly recalled what Ti had said about the Varúlfur.

'A wolf has no choice but to follow his master Mara, it is ingrained in their blood. They are creatures of hierarchy. The only way to be free of an alpha is to challenge him and win. Then you can take their place. Lose and they will kill, and make an example of you.'

No wonder the wolf committed suicide, he was ordered too, I almost felt pity…almost. Grinning, I now understood why he was laughing, he was going to kill the remaining wolf too, this is fun! Gabriella must have realised already, because she was holding on to the remaining Lycan for dear life.

"What's a matter? You are so afraid of me you would cower behind your lesser wolves? You are pathetic. So weak you can prey only on defenceless children." I hissed, the tone indignant.

I was deliberately provoking him, I wanted him to send for me, that way I could kill him. The idea pulled out my best smile, which probably didn't look as good as I envisioned. He growled, the sound terrifying to the others made me hum pleasurably. How long would he play this game? Excited, I skilfully hid the shiver of anticipation that swept through me.

"Raping the girl was merely a distraction, something to bide the time until you woke. It was hardly worth my time. Although her desperate attempts of escape did bring me a moments worth of enjoyment. But only a moment. Soon enough I will come for you Mara, I can hardly wait. Perhaps I shall come for your friend's first, warm up so to speak." He said, his voice bored, lacked emotion.

It must have upset Gabriella as she screamed with rage before ripping the head from the werewolf's shoulders, instantly severing the link to the alpha. Growling angrily, I kicked the Varúlfur's head out of the room, she ruined the game!

"You do realise he was provoking us, so we would kill our only means of escape."

"Shit, sorry! He raped the girl! And then threatened to rape me, us." She added, throwing the remaining wolf's body from the room.

"I heard him." Was all I said.

Irritated, I went and sat by Asta, Gabriella sighed heavily behind me.

"I really am sorry, I've always had a problem with my temper."

"You are a vampire, it is in your nature to be so." Asta offered sympathetically.

Standing, she went and fetched the jug of water from earlier, she didn't seem upset.

"Don't worry about it. All it means is that we have to wait a bit longer." I sighed, feeling a little guilty.

Guilty about my words or about how fun I found the whole situation? I sighed again, like I didn't have a temper problem of my own. With nothing left to say I pondered on what to do next.

I watched Asta as she ripped off a section of her t-shirt and placed it in the jug to absorb the water. Rinsing out the excess, she started to clean the blood from the young girl's body. As she wiped the blood away she sang a soothing song, it was the kind of song a mother would sing to a baby in an attempt to calm them. The girl wept softly. Had she been awake the whole time? Studying her swollen face, I noticed her eyes were still closed. The swelling was bad, maybe she had been awake, but just unable to open them.

"My name is Asta, the vampire is Gabriella, and this woman who sits beside me is Mara. The monster who hurt you, can't hurt you any longer. We will not allow it." She promised, her voice sure and confident, seemed to appease the girl.

Her crying turning instead to soft sobs.

"You are one of us now and we protect each other." Asta continued.

Her voice was filled with such warmth and kindness, I wondered whether I was capable of such. I quickly decided that I could never be that way, it was a weakness that would get me and the people I have come to care about dead.

I stood restless, and placed my hands on the frozen wall. Listening to the water within. Just as I had before, I allowed its voice to calm me. If I was going to get us out of here, I needed information. We were in ice caves, everywhere was formed from water.

Closing my eyes to concentrate, I asked the walls to reveal their secrets, asked them to show me a way out.

To my astonishment my demand was met. Images started flashing through my mind, the water filtering through my consciousness as though we were one and the same. The location of every room, every tunnel, and every exit within the mountain was clearly formed within my consciousness. It was like I had walked the very mountain myself and had been in each of the rooms. I saw the Lycans travel from room to room, could see what they wore, hear what they were saying. The knowledge filtered through to my brain and permanently infused itself within. It was exactly what I needed to know to get out of here, I couldn't stop the smile that formed on my lips. As the images flicked through like photos on a camera roll, I noticed there were other rooms like ours, they too held women captive, some screamed with rage, others wept begging for help, and many more lay broken, their eyes vacant. The sight angered me, I had no idea how long they had been subjected to the alpha's perverse games, but I made an oath, I would not leave here without them all.

"Show me the alpha." I asked the ice politely, my heart full of conviction.

Like someone had just turned on the T.V, the water revealed the alpha. He had started raping another woman, her clothes torn, her body bloodied. The sight made me growl, the sound somehow echoing within the alpha's room, his attention briefly interrupted.

The distraction allowed the victim to distance herself from him. She was a Valkyrie like the young girl they had just brought in, but she was grown and as such she had her wings. With her large feathered wings extended, she desperately tried to avoid his reach. Her soft ivory feathers brushed against the ceiling, the ice relaying the small caress, I shivered, her frozen cage preventing any retreat. The alpha laughed at her while he removed the remainder of his clothing. He was toying with her, but this time, I wasn't fond of the game. Staring at the alpha, I couldn't help but be reminded of Hamish, the only difference was the colour of his eyes and the shape of his nose. A relative perhaps?

Instead of the golden eyes I associated with the Varúlfur, his eyes were completely black. Opaque, they held and reflected no light. They reminded me of obsidian, the iris barely noticeable, was devoid of emotion. Completely naked, he stood fully erect beneath the angry women. His long chestnut hair was tied up in a ponytail whilst the lower half of his hair was shaved short, revealing his scalp. Offering his hand to the woman like a gentleman would a lady, he smirked at her, a flicker of amusement crossing his face.

"Come now, you're only making it harder on yourself. Fighting me will only prolong your suffering. I enjoy spirited women."

"I will never willingly give myself to you." The Valkyrie screamed.

"Yes, as others have claimed before you. A week, a month, a year, they all break eventually. It is of little importance, there are always more to be had." He smiled darkly.

"You're sick!"

"Yes… And you're about to discover just how much."

Contorting his face into a half man, half wolf configuration, the alpha coiled and leapt for the woman. With nowhere to go the Valkyrie didn't stand a chance. He yanked her out of the air, the force and speed of his movements whipping her into a spin, her head smashing against the ice. The impact was so hard, the floor cracked nosily, the ice like before carrying the sound to me. Unconscious, the woman lay still. Lifting her up effortlessly, he flipped her over, her stomach facing the ground. Blood covered the back of her head, and coated her thick hair. Snatching a handful of it, he ran the length of it beneath his nose, breathing in deeply. Prostrating with pleasure he waited patiently for the woman to wake, he didn't wait long. Regaining consciousness she started to move beneath him, the alpha snarled, his saliva drenched muzzle dripping onto her back. With what sounded like a contented yip, he ripped her wings from her back. The woman screamed, her pain and agony somehow infusing itself into the room, the air surrounding the alpha blackening. The grey, black, mass, he emitted, absorbed all the light from within the chamber… and from within the woman. How? Not sure what I was witnessing I couldn't tear my eyes away. Inhaling deeply, the alpha drew the dark vapour into his lungs, power radiating about him. The woman's screams slowly died, just as the last of the vapour vanished, her eyes fell vacant. Uncaring, the alpha continued his assault. Unable to watch anymore, I severed the connection. Dizzy, I fell back into the room. What did he just do? … What did he take?

"Mara!" Gabriella called out frantically.

Growing Doubt

Hamish spent over two hours explaining his plan for infiltrating the Varúlfur's royal stronghold. He explained the layout, the security precautions, and the patrols. It wasn't necessary, after spending so long in our company they were no longer able to hide their thoughts.

"I don't understand how the Vanir didn't know what Leif was doing?" Finian said displeased.

"He has yet to steal one of their own." Hamish muttered.

"You suggest then that they knew but did nothing?" Finian asked, while he relaxed on the couch.

"Aye, that's exactly what I'm saying."

Hamish's eyes were filled with anger, disgust shaping his mouth.

"It is their job to care about all the races." Aengus claimed, Donna sitting on his lap.

She smiled up at him, love in her eyes. I couldn't stop myself from feeling envious, on the few occasions I caught Mara looking at me, her face contained a mixture of confusion and annoyance. Except for the one occasion when she looked at me with desire. Allowing the memory to surface, I sat with my eyes closed and relished in the memory of our first kiss. Heat greeted me harshly as I recalled it all too well. With a room full of people, I quickly let the memory drop. Placing my head in my hands, I cursed. Looking up, I caught Finian grinning at me.

"A cold shower and a firm hand might be just what you need boss." Finian added, amusing everyone but me.

With a low growl, I stood and moved to look out of the window.

"If I wanted your advice, I would ask for it." I said coldly, my back to him.

"Just a friendly suggestion, after all, you're releasing so much sexual tension even I'm beginning to look at you in a new light." He joked, whilst trying to contain a laugh.

Eoghuan didn't succeed in containing his. Hissing with annoyance, I turned to face Finian. I knew he was just attempting humour, but the fact was the need to claim Mara was slowly eroding away at every thought, bar the ones that contained her naked and beneath me. I could understand a man in his youth being so lustful and impatient, but I had lived for millennia.

"You should have said that you wanted something large shoved up your arse Finian, as it happens, I need a new scabbard for my sword." I responded callously.

Picking up my broadsword, I slowly ran my finger over its tip.

Eyes wide, Finian tensed. Eoghuan and the room burst out laughing.

"When are you going to learn boy, do nae piss off your elders." Aengus chuckled.

"How old are you anyway?" Donna asked Aengus, taking the attention from me.

I was grateful.

"I was born in the year 1014AD, during the winter solstice."

Aengus grinned when her face dropped in surprise.

"You're ancient…" Donna added quietly, her mind racing with questions.

"Conlaóch and Angsar are older." Aengus claimed defensively.

Donna's mouth was pursed, her brows drawn tight, she was obviously trying to work out just how old that made him.

"Were you celibate all that time?" She asked him, a small measure of hope tinging her voice.

Aengus coughed loudly in response, his face flushing.

"I'll take that as a no then." Donna said, suddenly anxious.

Standing before him she placed her hands on her hips.

"You do realise." She said, counting on her fingers.

"That based on one women a month for every year you have been alive, that's at 12,012 women you have slept with!" She breathed, her face scrunched up with disgust.

"I dinnae have a woman until I was fourteen." Aengus said stupidly.

Standing up he tried to bring her back to him.

"Aye, but I'm guessing you had more than one women a month in your youth." She scowled, annoyed with his confession.

Aengus coughed and mumbled. Donna huffed angrily, her eyes brows raised in a vexed arc.

"More than one a week?" She asked, eyes wide.

"I… This is nae relevant, you were nae even born." He added, not refuting Donna's question.

"You did, you had more than one a week. One a day?" She continued.

"I will nae answer." Aengus grumbled.

"Aye you will Aengus McCormac, I insist upon it!" She said angrily.

"I have nae wish to hurt you." He pleaded with her.

"I want to know."

Aengus grunted, his face etched in annoyance.

"Very well."

I winced along with half the room, idiot! He was falling into a trap, he should say nothing and leave it at that.

"Aye, sometimes more than one a day, sometimes two, sometimes two at a time. And sometimes, I went days, weeks, months, years, without one. Again, you were nae born, you dinnae even exist." He said, as though that would put an end to it.

"You must have known that one day you would meet your anam cara." She said sadly, her cheeks reddening.

"Aye, but I was a boy, it's hard to ignore those kinds of urges." He explained uncomfortably.

Watching your anam cara on the verge of tears because of something you did must have been painful. I pitied him. I doubted Mara was the weeping type, thankfully.

"But you dinnae even try to avoid women. You just said you were fourteen!"

"Your twenty-four and you dinnae wait." He said agitated.

Idiot! I winced again, a low hiss escaping. Hamish and his men chuckled amongst themselves. Donna slapped him hard across the face.

"What the…" Aengus started.

He grabbed Donna's other hand before she could slap him again.

"I was nine when I dreamed of you. I knew then what you would be. My soul mate… Despite what men think, women have needs too… Do you know how many men I have turned down? Hundreds Aengus! And why did I deny myself when I really dinnae want to? Because I was your anam cara and that meant I was to be yours and yours alone." She sighed, her initial anger turning instead to disappointment.

"You're a virgin?" He said surprised, followed quickly by shame. "But you know so much about it, I just assumed…" He continued awkwardly.

"Arsehole, you thought I slept around." She accused.

"I… Damn it Donna, I will nae continue with this line of questioning." He answered, not denying her accusation.

"I know about it because I live in the twenty first century, Sex is everywhere. T.V, magazines, conversation. I cannae believe you thought I slept around! Take your bloody hands off me."

Donna stormed out of the room furiously.

"Blasted women!" Aengus roared before leaving in the opposite direction.

Stunned, the room sat quiet.

"Shit, I hope my anam cara isn't a virgin." Finian said, clearly shocked by the argument.

For once his interruption was welcome as it broke the awkward silence.

"Really! You would rather have a woman who had been touched and tasted by another?" Eoghuan asked dubiously.

"I've already had women who have been touched and tasted by another." Finian winked.

"You know what I mean." Eoghuan grinned.

"Honestly little brother I would just be pleased I found her." Finian said, all humour gone from his face.

"Me too." Eoghuan added thoughtfully.

"And there I was convinced you would never grow up." Ansgar smiled at the brothers.

"Now be good lads and go jump in the car." He ordered, in the same manner a parent would a child.

Watching the brothers leave, my thoughts once again returned to Mara. Would Mara care that I, like Aengus, had a history with women? Probably not, she didn't seem to care much about anything.

"Now that you have finished demonstrating how bad the Keltoi are at handling their women, can we get back to the matter in hand?" Hamish scowled.

"We already know the plan." I said, strapping on the last of my weapons.

"Aye, but are you or aren't you going to inform the Vanir?" Hamish asked.

He was referring to an earlier conversation about family coming forward to claim the women in captivity.

"The Vanir are concerned that if women are retrieved by family before we reach them, a war will break out, and the women will get hurt in the crossfire." I explained.

I agreed with them. If everyone turned up at the Varúlfur's front door with the intent to kill, it would be the innocent victims that got hurt. Stealth in this case was definitely better than strength. Hamish obviously didn't agree, leaving with a grunt to make a phone call.

"Can we trust him and his agenda?" Ansgar asked, his gaze following the Lycan leader as he left the cabin with his men.

"His hatred for his brother is genuine. But keep an eye on him just in case." I cautioned.

I didn't really think he would be a threat, but the lust he felt for Mara was nearly as strong as my lust for her, and it bothered me. He may not have an agenda concerning his brother, but I was certain he hadn't given up on Mara. I tried to read his mind again, but like me he was an ancient and as such he had developed tactics to keep us only in the parts of his mind he allowed. I was hoping that like the rest he too would reveal all.

"Ansgar." I called to the hunter, just as he left to catch up with the others.

"Aye." He turned to face me.

"You once said I could count on you for anything." I said, my statement leading.

"Aye I did, and I meant it. What do you need me to do?" He asked, his intellect ripping apart my sentences, his golden eyes missing nothing.

"I want you to read Mara."

I gave him a minute to digest my request. Watching the hunter, it was clear my request was unexpected and un-welcomed. His tongue hit the inside of his cheek in an attempted to quell his anger, his left eye slightly twitching.

"You have always spoken truth old friend, do not stop now."

"You are asking me too break our own laws." Ansgar answered, his jaw clenched tightly.

"Yes."

"Why?"

"I need to know why she runs from me."

"Have you tried asking her?" Ansgar snapped, surprising me.

He had never done so before.

"I have deduced enough to know that she will never share her past. That and she doesn't seem to hang around long enough to actually hold a conversation." I said frustrated.

My anam cara should be able to share everything with me.

"Nae now, but give her time and she will." He grimaced, noticing my frustration.

"Time is something we don't have old friend. If I am to claim her freely and without force I need to know why she runs from the bond. I need to know why she fears the connection."

Irritated, I started to pace the length of the room.

"It is an invasion of privacy! There are reasons that we created the laws forbidding us to read the minds of our own and of their anam cara. You should respect her choice nae to share, no matter the cost to you. Her past is hers to divulge, when and if she pleases." Ansgar hissed, his anger returning.

"And if she was a woman of the Keltoi I would agree! But she is the daughter of our enemy. She could be fighting it out of fear of discovery, she may be protecting her father, may be helping her father." I accused coldly.

The words left a bitter taste in my mouth. She was my anam cara and I had just accused her of being as twisted as Sköll.

"You would use your anam cara to hunt our enemies? Use her as bait? Without her knowledge?" Ansgar fumed.

"It is my job to do whatever I must to rid the world of his vileness. His and his brother. You have heard of the prophecy, Sköll and Hati are destined to free Fenrir. You would unleash him on the world?"

I knew what I asked was wrong, but Fenrir was the most feared creature to ever grace the earth. It is foretold that should he ever escape his prison, all of earths occupants will be enslaved, the earth cast into an eternal darkness, where no light will ever again exist. I hated myself, but if Mara hid from me because she remained loyal to her grandfather then I had a duty to know, the lives of everyone depended upon it.

"She is your anam cara Conlaóch, how could you believe such of her?"

"She knows nothing about the world Ansgar, nothing about goodness or laughter. What else am I to think other than she has been kept in the dark purposely, slowly nurtured and manipulated to become what they want her to be. Can we say with absolute certainty that her being in Glasgow with Sköll was merely a coincidence? For all we know her being my anam cara was unforeseen and as such disrupted their plans."

"Where is this coming from Conlaóch? Even if there is truth to it, which I do nae believe there is, she is yours. Fight for her, win her, love her, and her heart will belong to you forever, she will be beyond their reach or their influence." Ansgar implored, his right hand rubbing the back of his neck in frustration.

His advice as always was honest. But if there was a chance, even small that Mara was under her father's rule, then I had to know. I am the leader of the Keltoi, I have a duty not only to my people but to all of earths inhabitants. I must be certain, if that means betraying her privacy and stealing her secrets, then so be it, it must be done.

"Will you do it or not?" I asked him, a hollow feeling forming in my chest.

"Aye, because you asked it of me, but I warn you no good will come of this. The whole thing leaves a nasty taste in my mouth. Damn it Conlaóch, you're the last person in the world, who I thought, or could ever, steep this low. She is your anam cara!" He spat scornfully, and walking out of the room, his whole-body, rigid, and tense.

Sighing heavily, I left to follow him.

"Forgive me Mara."

The Call of Darkness

"Mara?" Asta called softly.

Opening my eyes, Asta's face hovered above mine, her pixie like features etched in worry.

"Good, you're awake." She smiled relieved.

"I've been sleeping?" I asked, sitting up on the bed.

"You fainted!" She reproached.

I scowled doubtful.

"I don't faint."

"Well you do now, you definitely fainted. I don't know what you were doing holding on to the wall like that, but whatever it was, it over taxed you."

She frowned at me in what I assumed was a reprimand.

"I was studying the layout of the tunnels, so we could escape." I explained.

Yawning, I stood, stretching my back, it cracked pleasantly, the sensation pulling a smile from my lips.

"The water showed you?" She asked stunned.

"Yes."

"But I've never met anyone who could do that? You didn't even know you were part Vanir!"

Her eyes were wide, a weird 'what the hell is going on' look about her, it was almost comical, I grinned.

"When I placed my hand on the ice I heard the waters voice, so I asked, and it answered." I offered in explanation.

"It takes hundreds of years to learn how to do that." She claimed, her fingers tapping furiously on the mattress of the bed she had just occupied.

"Maybe the other half of me allows for the Vanir part to be stronger?" I frowned, unsure why she found being strong a bad thing. Especially given our current situation.

"Maybe? But Mara you should not channel anymore, not until someone can teach you to use it properly. You fainted! If you draw too much power in, you can burn out." She warned.

Gabriella looked confused… and hungry. How long can a vampire go without blood?

"Burn out?" I asked aloud.

Should I offer her some blood, or would she be insulted? Would I taint her?

"Burn out, combust!" Asta warned.

"You mean she could blow up." Gabriella squeaked.

"Yes, and us with her." Asta cautioned.

"I don't want to die." A softly spoken voice added.

Who? oh. The girl was awake, she was sitting on the bed, her arms wrapped around her legs.

Her hair was the same colour as Gabriella's, but unlike Gabriella's short bob, her hair fell in long waves that rested on the mattress. Her wounds were healing physically, but the real pain was evident in her eyes. They were hazel and were coated in a constant wet sheen, as though she could cry at any moment. I remembered what the alpha had done to the other Valkyrie. To think that he would have done the same to this girl made me livid. I clenched my jaw in an attempt to defuse my anger, I couldn't wait to get my hands on him.

"What's your name?" I asked her, doing my best to keep the anger I felt from my voice.

Instead, like lava in a volcano, it seethed furiously below.

"Siri." She said quietly, her eyes not meeting mine.

"I am Mara, how old are you?"

"Thirteen." She whispered.

She pulled her legs in tighter, her fingers locked together so tightly, her knuckles had turned white. Rage boiled, I'm going to enjoy killing the alpha, I'll do it slowly, deliberately prolong his suffering. Moving cautiously towards the girl, I sat on the bed beside to her.

"I will not harm you. Look at me." I asked, with all pretence of calm.

Slowly she raised her eyes, her gaze darting around the room nervously. She doesn't trust us, or me at least. I don't blame her, I wouldn't trust me either, I'm…inherently bad, maybe with small moments of good?

"You don't need to be afraid of Mara, she is going to get us all home." Asta said confidently.

Her warm smile must have reassured the girl, as her eyes finally met mine. Yeah, she definitely doesn't trust me. Looking in to Siri's eyes, I tried to relay with emotion the promise I was about to make. Since emotion is a new concept, I hoped I succeeded.

"The man that hurt you… I have seen him. I give you my word he will never hurt you again. I know this because I am going to kill him. Killing is what I am good at, do not doubt that I will succeed, because I will. When he is dead, his life mine, I will take you home. Do you understand?"

She looked unsure, a small tear clinging to her ivory cheek.

"I understand." She choked on a small sob.

"I will have to leave this room to do this, but Gabriella and Asta shall remain to watch over you. There is a chance that the Lycans will come into the room. You must not be afraid, you must stand and face them, without fear."

I can't leave them here unarmed, thinking quickly, an idea formed. Hoping it would work I instructed the ice to form three identical daggers… Perfect, it worked. Grinning, I studied the small weapons, the blades on each of them were heinously sharp. Pulling one free from the wall, I tore the hem of my dress and used it to wrap the hilt.

"The ice will not melt, nor will it break." I said to the girl, who shakily took the knife.

"You are Valkyrie, you are strong and like me born to fight" I reminded her.

She clutched the blade to her chest protectively.

"I could not stop him." She admitted ashamed.

My stomach squirmed uneasy, a strange feeling in my heart.

"He is an ancient who has lived for thousands of years, and you a child. You were not meant to win. But you must remember, just because one fight was lost, it does not mean that all fights will be. One thousand and three times is the amount of fights I have lost as I grew and learned to fight. Do you know how many I have won because I refused to give up?"

"How many?"

"Three thousand two hundred and eighteen." I stated with a small smile.

"Really?"

A spark of life returned to her eyes. In answer to her question, I nodded.

"You can only lose if you give up." I added.

I threw the remaining two blades across the room, one embedding itself into the wall near Asta's head, the other Gabriella caught with ease, and was now flipping skilfully through her hands.

"Now, do not pretend you don't know how to use that." I grinned.

Walking to the door I wrapped one of the wolf pelts around my shoulders the wolf's head resting upon mine.

"Show me how we kill a werewolf."

Siri stared at the wolfs head and then at me. After a few seconds of uncertainty, she stood from the bed bravely, her stance steady. Taking aim, she threw the dagger with pin point accuracy, striking the wolf square in the mouth, the wolf pelt lodged to the door. Moving away, I inspected her handy work.

"And that is why the Valkyrie are to be feared." I smiled.

"You will protect Asta, while Gabriella protects you." I instructed.

Siri's eyes quickly darted to Asta's.

"But she is older than I?" she announced as a question.

"Yes, but she is not a fighter, and love and kindness won't kill our enemies."

Asta smiled, her eye brows raised in gentle reproach.

"Mara is right. I can use a bow and arrow, but that's as much I have bothered to care about combat.

"I will protect you." Siri said with a slight nod, her shoulders held high.

"Good. Now it's time for me to go kill a wolf." I hummed.

"How do you plan on getting out of here? Even if you parted the ice, the room is warded to prevent us leaving without an escort." Gabriella frowned, the others looking at me with a puzzled expression that said they were wondering the same.

"I plan on getting angry."

Prepping myself for the beast and the pain, I began rolling my neck side to side, allowing my pent-up anger to surface.

"Angry? Somehow I don't think they will care." Gabriella snorted sceptically.

"The wolves that took me were rather fond of me angry, the worst I got the more they couldn't seem to resist me."

I bit my lip, confused as to why that was the case.

"Oh of course, you're in heat! You've been so calm since the water thing I completely forgot." She smiled, her face brimming with excitement.

"You're forgetting something." Asta said gently.

"What?" I asked impatiently.

I wanted to be gone already, I can't stand being caged, not after the beast. Granted, it was so far, 'less painful' than before, but still it was mentally grinding.

"You're right, being in heat will attract his attention, but just as you release pheromones that will attract him, he will release them to win you." She scowled.

"What do you mean, win me?"

She can't honestly think I would consider such a vile creature, if Col isn't getting anything then he's definitely not.

"I mean, of all the Varúlfur here, he will release pheromones that will appeal to your base needs. Your inner animal won't care who he is, only that he is the strongest and therefore the better choice. The angrier you get to attract him the more self-control you will lose." She warned, her lips pursed, the gesture reminding me of Donna.

"Are you saying that she will be attracted to him and jump into his bed willingly?"

Gabriella's eyes went wide, her face turned up in disgust.

"She may, yes. Unless by some miracle you turn out to be stronger than he is. If not, you will submit to him."

Asta shivered.

"I cannot wait around doing nothing while he continues to rape other women. I will take the risk."

Should I? I was suddenly unsure. My thoughts sprang to Col and those 'bloody' green eyes. What would he do? He was a hunter, he would do what was necessary to protect those who needed him. Running my finger along my bottom lip, I remembered our kiss, would he forgive me should I fail in resisting the Alpha? My gaze returned to Siri, I had promised to take her home. I had to try. I knew Col would come, but how long would it take for him to find me?

"There is no other way. Stay towards the back wall and do not approach me. Say nothing and draw no attention to yourselves." I warned.

I wasn't sure what would happen when I finally let my beast free, I hoped to all the gods I didn't harm any of them.

"Come back to us Mara." Gabriella said, a nervous half smile edging one corner of her mouth, her eyes encouraging.

I didn't answer. Turning to face the door way, I let the beast rise.

Pulling in a sharp intake of breath, I readied myself for the pain I knew was coming. Since connecting with the water, the discomfort I had been carrying around for days had lapsed somewhat, almost as if the water had pulled me from that dark part of me and bathed me temporarily in the light, but I knew it would return the minute I called it forth, it would always be there waiting.

I growled low as the first wave of pain hit like a hammer to the head. Agony coursed through my body, my bones like before, breaking with an impact you would expect from a high-speed crash. Screaming in response, I fell to the ground, my back bending unnaturally and then snapping completely. Distantly, I could hear Asta as she fought the urge to come to my aid.

"Do not." I growled, the sound truly terrifying.

Writhing in untold torment, my teeth exploded, my vision turning red. I snarled as pleasure replaced the pain, the darkness pushing me out, corrupting my thoughts. Looking through eyes that no longer contained the version of myself I knew, I roared, a defiant edge to the sound. My arms snapped, my body hunched. It felt as though someone was ripping the flesh from my body, revealing instead, a brilliant white coat of fur that covered me from head to toe. Following the sight with my increased vision I noticed that my arms were no longer arms but were paws. Black razor-sharp claws protruded the pads of my feet, of which I now had four.

I thought briefly that I was a wolf, only to be distracted by the scent of blood. My blood. I was bleeding again. The scent pleased me, I thought of feasting on the blood of another, pictured it flowing smoothly down my throat, quenching the unbelievable thirst that had suddenly prevailed upon me. Blood! My hearing told me that it pumped behind me. Turning my head, I faced three deliciously tempting meals. My vision switched, the different lens an automatic response to my desire to seek and consume. I now viewed them in the same manner a reptile would its prey. Reds and oranges revealed the pathways of their blood as it travelled throughout their bodies. Their bright red hearts pumped furiously, they were afraid. I could taste their fear, and it tasted good.

Saliva filled my mouth, my teeth bared. Snarling, their fear fuelled my rage, my desire to commit harm, my need to make them suffer. Stalking silently towards them, I knew exactly how best to enjoy them. Sat on my heels I readied to pounce. Frustrated, the door opened behind me, the movement distracting me from my meal. Growling sinisterly, I turned to face the intruders. My anger, loosely held, was ready to exact revenge for their un-welcomed interruption. Four golden eyed men stood before me, their eyes burning wickedly. Instead of killing them, I purred approvingly.

Snapping at them playfully, and forgetting my prey, I moved to join them. I could detect another within them, a master, and they the puppets. His dark seduction called to me, demanded I follow, curious, I did.

I ran the length of the tunnels, my wolf form returning to that of a human, I briefly wondered why, but was again distracted by the strong scent of power and masculine allure that radiated from the room I now stood before. Entering, I had a brief feeling of contempt, the thought quickly altered to one of desire. Green eyes flashed within my mind, only to be lost when my eyes landed on the man who stood naked at the base of a large wooden bed.

His dark empty eyes raked my body arrogantly, before stopping at the level of my thigh, and the trickle of blood that ran down it. He smirked, before slowly moving towards me. I hissed, a warning that disputed his closeness. He did not like this, his displeasure infusing the room and thickening the air. He looked at me, really looked at me, his savage eyes burning into mine, a challenge...so be it.

He grabbed me unexpectedly, the speed of his advance, a blur that had me spinning. Pain laced it way across my body, my back locked against his stomach. He yanked my head to the side, a vicious hiss scraping against my ear. Cold breath ferreted across my neck, shivers of excitement, of trepidation, swimming side by side, immersing, and coating my flesh. I rubbed myself against him, prolonging the sensation, before running my claws sharply up his sides. Blood coated my fingers, the scent ensnaring. Lifting them to my mouth, I slowly licked the blood from them, the rich flavour… compelling. Moaning with pleasure, the alpha placed his fangs upon my neck. No, my mind screamed, he cannot!

Confused, I pushed him away, crouching low, ready to attack, defend myself. The threat was unknown, but instinct insisted the threat was real.

"Give yourself to me, allow me to sate your need." The Alpha commanded, his low tone reverberating through my mind, a compulsion that demanded I obey. I shook my head, anger replacing my desire, I didn't appreciate his presumptuous tactics, the compulsion he attempted to use upon me.

"No"

"Very well, I will make you submit." He smirked coldly.

"You can try." I baited.

Laughter, my laughter, dark and foreign, echoed through my consciousness, his arrogance and self-importance, truly amusing. He is nothing compared to me, a sardine, and I, the shark. He didn't know it yet, but he was about to die. Leaping for me as I anticipated, he threw me onto the large bed that stood in the middle of the room. Before I could turn he was on me, his teeth sinking into the lower of my back. Pain greeted me, along with pleasure that had me stalling his death. Arching into him seductively, I allowed him to move my leg to the side, my emotions and wants, shifting full circle.

His claws sank into my flesh, pinning me in place. Prostrating teasingly, I spun and threw him off me. I smiled, this had the makings of a great game, and I wanted to play. Frustrated the alpha released a musk into the room, it's scent and power beguiling me to move towards him. It wasn't working, but I would go along, a sadistic glee running through my blood.

Slowly running my hands, up, and across my hips, I proffered him my leg, opening it slightly to the side. Approving, he growled pleased with my sudden cooperation, and knelt before me. He placed his head between my legs, his mouth resting on the soft inner of my thigh. Taking his time, he licked the evidence of my heat from my leg. When he was finished, he stood, forcing me back, and onto the bed, his action aggressive, deliberate. I found myself liking his cruel administration, so decided, I would allow this…for now, play the game.

When my back hit the furs that lined the bed, green eyes flashed within my mind, the image, confusing, familiar, making me cover myself with my arms. Panic welled, but I didn't know why. Irritation rode alongside my panic, I growled angrily. The Alpha noticing the change, placed a strong arm across my waist, preventing my retreat, his other arm prying my arms away from my body. I didn't move as confusion took hold, an agonising light infiltrating my mind, those green eyes scorching holes through my games, my plans, the alpha's death… the darkness. Nothing was making sense, everything becoming unclear, incomprehensible.

I felt the alpha's tongue on my flesh, the delightful sensation bringing a moment of clarity, pushing the light aside, vanquishing it, banishing it. I arched my back, pulling his head closer, the mysterious green eyes forgotten, my focus was returning, my goals, once again, clearly defined.

Sharp fangs punctured my flesh, the pain welcomed. It laced its way across my back, chest, stomach, and made me ache for something more, something I was failing to grasp but wanted badly. Frustrated, I sunk my claws into the alpha's shoulders, ripping at his flesh. he hissed delighted, blood streaming from his back. No longer satisfied with my thighs, the alpha moved, his lean body resting between my legs, his powerful hands pinning mine to the bed.

Eyes as black as night bore into mine and challenged me to move… He would dare! The arrogant display of dominance, of superiority, made me furious. He honestly thought I was the one who was going to submit, that I would defer to him? Foolish man, it is he who will do as I wish. Snarling angrily and no longer interested in playing his game, I attacked him, throwing him from the bed. The impact of his body as he hit the wall, shattered the ice. I smiled, now this is something that pleases me.

"You dare challenge me!" He spat furiously, his expression announcing the fact he was un-affected by my display.

"I am a Queen, you will serve me."

The idea of having the alpha and other lesser Varúlfur worshiping me, worshiping my body, caused me to hum excitedly. Shivers of anticipation coursed temptingly as I wondered if they would fight me, or whether they would obey blindly.

"Stupid woman. I would have let you be my queen, but now that you have challenged me, I have no choice but to kill you." He explained, a glimmer of annoyance reflecting in the black pits of his eyes.

Yes, I had felt the presence of the others, but they like him, will serve.

"You are mistaken pet, you will submit, and I will rule you." I stated calmly, rising from the bed with all the grace and demure of a dancer, my thoughts, dark and vile.

"Unless of course, you wish to die, your heart's blood, pouring down my parched throat." I teased.

He roared angrily, the tantalising sound echoing loudly across the walls, it made me wince, my eardrums complaining painfully, my wolf smiling

"The only thing going down anyone's throat, is my cock down yours."

Enraged, he took the form of a large wolf, his coat like his eyes was completely black, small transparent discs only minutely illuminated, were the only indication he had eyes at all. His large snarling mouth dripped with saliva, the sight horrifying, was exhilarating. I purred with want, pity I was going to have to kill him I thought sadistically. Pouting in displeasure I let my power and malice permeate the room. Like a mirage the air bent and flexed around me. I growled my superiority. Responding to my claim, the black wolf attacked, his aura one of pure hatred. Engaging the alpha with equal vigour, we battled for dominance. Images and thoughts of the other Varúlfur swam through my mind, as they watched to discover who would reign. Missing a decapitating blow from the Alpha, I swung low opening up his stomach. The alpha un-perplexed as his entrails spilled from his gut, did not let up his attack.

A flash thought from the mind of a sentry caused fury to lash at my insides. Familiar faces were entering the mountain and attacking the Varúlfur. They had come for me. Picking up on a brief moment of fear for the newcomers, the alpha commanded the wolves to engage, with the order to kill everyone. Roaring rebelliously, I increased my attack and shifted painfully back into the form of a white wolf. The increased speed and strength was a welcomed advantage, my body begging to tire. My senses were alive, the air around me seemingly static, alive with magic, with a dark seduction that called for me to give no mercy, to destroy, claim his throne as mine. Heeding to the call, I savagely tore into the alpha's body, blood filled my mouth, it's rich taste cleansing my palate and heightening my desire for more. Covered in blood, my body sore, the black wolf began to ebb. Noticing instantly the weakness I pressed forward, eager for the kill.

The triumph when the alpha fell was demonic, violent, his blackened aura contaminated the air around us. The black mist seeped into my body and blended with mine, his power, so potent, now belonging to me. Already fallen, already lost, I could have stopped, some other part of me screamed to do so. But I didn't listen. With the wolf below me keening in pain, defeated and pathetic, I ripped brutally into his neck. Blood, once powerful, poured helplessly down my throat, just as I predicted it would. Relishing in my victory, I allowed my human form to reappear. Bathed in my enemy's blood, an unholy balm of darkness, clouded the room, congratulating me, worshipping me. Euphoric, I devoured what was left of his blood, every mouthful of the rich liquid, increasing my thirst for more.

The Light that Binds

It took us less the three hours to get to Norway from Scotland, another two hours to travel to the Ice caves at Jostedalsbreen, the Varúlfur's ancestral home. They called it Fritjof, the meaning 'those who steal peace'. Ironic I thought, since peace is what they were now fighting for. When the word of Leif's practices reached the ears of those who have had loved ones taken, they would come for the them. Unless they put an end to Leif's rule, every wolf would become a target.

One by one the sentries guarding the mountain fell, the powerful effects of the sleeping drug putting them to sleep. With the entrance dealt with, we moved in, Hamish and I at their head. Entering the vast mountain, the ice walls gleamed and reflected the shapes of Lycans lying in wait.

Hamish raised his hand, halting our advance.

"Something is wrong." He frowned, his gaze finding mine.

Searching his mind, he showed me all that he was witnessing through the pack link. Mara was naked, standing before the alpha, blood clinging to her thighs. Lust hit hard at the sight of her naked followed quickly by fear as I questioned why she was naked and bleeding.

"Did he?" My heart stuttered.

My mind refused to believe what the image was suggesting.

"No, but he is trying too." He answered truthfully, guiltily.

I need to find her. Placing my fears aside, since they would only hinder me, I readied to move again.

Hamish prevented me, his arm pressing against my chest, forcing me to stop. Turning to face me, he looked alarmed. Frustrated, and before I could curse and shove him aside, he spoke.

"She has challenged him to the right to rule, with all of us as witness." He claimed astonished, and deeply concerned.

"She did what!"

What has she done?! If she lost, he will kill her. I have to reach her.

"You cannae interfere with the challenge." Hamish warned.

"Watch me." I snarled.

I might question her loyalties, but she was still mine to protect. Before he had a chance to stop me I ran in the direction that would lead me to her.

"Conlaóch!" Hamish shouted after me.

I didn't listen, nothing would stop me reaching her. Just as I was about to turn a corner, werewolves came pouring out of all the side rooms, all of them in their wolf form, attacking, teeth bared.

I didn't doubt that Leif was trying to prevent me from reaching her, he knew she was mine, knew I would come for her. As the wolves attacked un-wavering, I could see in their eyes that they did so reluctantly, they were being controlled. It was Leif's ability to control the wolves that had us all detouring back to Donna's coven, wasting even more time. Every Lycan received a charm that would prevent Leif from manipulating their minds. Unfortunately, it didn't prevent them from having their minds read. As such, the minute we entered, Leif knew about it.

Putting the thought aside, I dispatched the Varúlfur efficiently, trying my best not to inflict permanent harm, and instinctively clearing a path to Mara. Racing through the frozen tunnels I knew I was close when the smell of a woodlands under the cover of rain filled my mind with images of Mara. Those images quickly became sinister as the smell of blood, Mara's, and another's, drifted into my conscience.

Trepidation greeted me, what would I find? I knew she wasn't dead, if she was, I would have felt it, but allowing her darkness to come forth didn't bode well. Drawing in a hesitant breath, I walked in to Leif's chamber. Like most of the rooms within the mountain, it was carved from ice. A large bed dominated its centre. I was glad to discover Mara wasn't on it. Walking around the large bed, I searched for the source of the blood. Leif lay upon the floor, his body shredded, deep gore's that made it impossible to define any features. Staring at the Lycan who attempted to rape Mara and had succeeded in raping others, I couldn't make myself pity him, regardless of his current state. His retched heart was still weakly beating, which irritated me, she should have finished it and ended his life. Instead she left him to endure a merciless and torturous end, forcing me to finish what she didn't. Driving my sword through his heart, I felt nothing. It was justice, his fate inevitable, with a small grunt Leif's rule had ended and I doubt anyone cared.

Relieved to find Mara had come away the victor, but ignoring her questionable methods of doing so, I studied the floor and followed the small footprints of blood that led off to a small tunnel, neatly tucked away in the far end of the room. Mara's scent was strong, but unlike the scent I remembered, it carried a hint of something else, something all too familiar and something I immediately associated with Sköll. Darkness in its most putrid form, like burnt sulphur it burnt my nose with its foulness. Grief hit me, fearing what I would find. If Mara has lost herself to the darkness, if I couldn't retrieve her… I would have no choice but to kill her, and subsequently, myself. I did not fear for my own life, I had lived for longer than I wished to, but Mara was so young, there was still so much she had never seen, never known. I wanted to show her the wonders that life could bring, wanted to show her earth's beauty and her place amongst it. She cannot be lost…not now, not before I'd had a chance to love her, to give her all the things she never had, a safe haven, a home, happiness. Saying a silent pray to the mother Jörg I took the last few steps towards her.

The small tunnel opened up into a room that was equally as big as the chamber I had come from. Its walls shimmered magically, the large pool of heated water reflecting upon its surface. At first, I thought I had lost Mara, as she didn't appear to be in the room, however, as I walked towards the pools edge she rose from the water, her body bare, glistened sinfully.

Desire burned wildly, unable to stop myself I watched the water roll easily over her smooth skin before falling back into the depth of the pool. Envious of the water I couldn't pull my gaze from her.

"Hunter." Mara called, her voice barely recognisable.

Hunter? She cannot recall my name.

"Mara." I replied, unable to quell the lust in my voice.

"You are so strong hunter… so desirable."

She grinned, a seductive edge to her mouth. Exiting the water, she came and stood before me, her hand gently resting on my chest. Reluctantly tearing my eyes away from her body, my gaze found hers, my heart stuttered, uneasiness prickling against my skin, fear coating my heart. The eyes that looked at me were not Mara's. Instead of the cool blue that I had come to think of daily, grey eyes, like the greys you would find in the depths of a storm swam coldly within. Stepping away from her was the hardest thing I had ever done, the hunter who recognised her need for me was furious. She was my anam cara, the hunter did not distinguish between Mara and the Warg that resides within.

"You do not want me hunter?" She asked.

She followed my departure, her hand deliberately falling down my chest, pausing, and remaining temptingly on my groin. My teeth locked, a hiss escaping. I tried to disguise the pleasure she ignited…I failed, my body responding involuntarily to her touch.

"Not like this." I managed to say.

My mind was chaotic, I needed to remain in control, penetrate the darkness that had taken hold of her. I needed to save her, but I also needed to claim her. A battle waged within, did I give in to the carnal urge to claim what was rightly mine? Or did I ignore that urge and banish the darkness?

"Come now hunter, I will allow you to have me any way you choose." She said, like it was a great honour, which to me it was.

"Any?" I asked, an idea to ferret Mara out, coming quickly to mind.

"Any." She answered pleased, a vindictive smile claiming one side of her mouth.

Placing one hand on her hip, the other at the nape of her neck, I pulled her against me gently. I dared a glance into the swirling grey depths of her eyes before pulling her mouth to mine. I played a dangerous game as my lips brushed lightly against hers but did not fully connect. Irritated with my, 'almost' kiss, Mara pulled me towards her, growling when I refused once again to commit to the kiss both she and I desperately wanted.

"What game do you play hunter?" She hissed, her body curving against mine.

"I will give you what you want when you agree to my terms." I said heatedly.

"No… I agree to no one's terms. You want me, I can feel it, sense it." She purred.

"I do not deny that I want you, only that I want you to agree first."

My jaw tensed, my body betraying my words. I want her now and she knew it. Damn it.

"You want this." She grinned, her chest resting against mine, her hands burning trails along my back.

It was torture, I could not allow her to touch me. Lifting her up, I wrapped her legs around me and walked her back into the pool. Warm water cloaked my body, causing the clothing I had failed to remove, cling uncomfortably against my skin. Groaning in frustration, I wished the clothing gone. With a low snarl, I placed Mara on the inside edge of the pool, her waist at the same height as my chest, and ran my hands along her thighs.

"Yes hunter." Mara hummed, before leaning back and opening her legs for me.

I hissed, the sight of her so vulnerably exposed belittling every fantasy I have ever had. Fangs exploded within my mouth, heedfully seeking entry to her flesh. I needed to taste her, to own her, brand her mine. If anything could quell the darkness it would be my claim, but to claim her she must first give her permission. Lowering myself to rest upon the water's surface, my head now in line with her parted legs, I hungrily moved in to study the yet to be explored inner of her thighs.

A scar marred otherwise perfect flesh. Deciding it was the perfect place to start I ran my tongue along its length, my teeth grazing enticingly. Mara moaned, the sensational sound fuelling my pleasure. Her innocence will be mine to corrupt, mine to own. Cursing inwardly, I mentally reminded myself that I couldn't. I had to remain in control, it was the only way I would get Mara back, the only way to save her. Using every ounce of discipline, formulated over the years, and picturing the faces of every hideous creature I could fathom, I fought for the resolve to do what needed to be done. Moving up her thighs, her scent addictive, I lowered my mouth onto the soft folds of her core. The reaction, instant, had Mara coiling with pleasure. She pulled my head closer, her finger digging into my scalp. Savouring her taste, I increased my attention, sucking leisurely, and relishing at the sound of Mara's breathless gasps.

"Enough hunter, bring me release." She ordered.

"Agree, say yes Conlaóch when I ask it of you."

"No."

"No? You wish me to stop?" I asked, placing a finger inside her.

"Yes." She pleaded, pushing down on me.

"Yes? You want me to stop?" I asked again, placing another finger inside.

"No, no, do not."

"Say yes when I ask it." I insisted, slowly moving my fingers in and out, my tongue caressing.

"No." she growled wildly.

"No? Stop?" I grinned, withdrawing my fingers.

"Do not!" She snarled tortured, her body coiled tight. She was close.

"You will say yes, when I ask it?" I hissed breathless.

My control was slipping. Mara growled in frustration, her anger, and annoyance, shimmering in her dark eyes.

"Your word hunter that you will bring me release." She hissed, sliding her own fingers within herself, her head rolling back invitingly, neck bared.

The sight was perfection, I growled low, my body hard, eager.

"You have my word." I murmured against her flesh.

Gazing at me, her eyes needy, she licked her lips. With a sensual moan, her eyes a chaotic grey, she reluctantly succumbed. Relief coursed through me, the sensation only heightening my desire.

"Say when hunter" she moaned, the breathless gasp laced with vexation.

Knowing that it didn't matter where I marked her, and not wanting to cause suspicion, I returned my attention to the inside of her thigh, more precisely, the silver scar that marked her flesh. Hoping she did not understand modern day Irish Gaelic, as I suspected she may be familiar with the ancient dialect, I uttered the oath that would tie her to me and bind her to the light.

"Before Jörg, I claim you Mara as mine. I will love you without restraint, will protect you from all who would do you harm, your enemies are now my enemies, your allies, my allies. This I swear before all the gods, good and bad, before you, before the light and the dark. Anam cara, will you be for me what I swear to be for you? Will you accept me as yours and yours alone, and will you be only mine forever?"

"Do you agree Mara?" I asked in English, my mouth hovering above her flesh, my fangs ready to brand her mine.

"Yes hunter" She moaned impatiently.

Her interest, only for her release, was unaware of the oath I placed upon her. It's was all I needed, her permission given. Mara is mine. Without pause I pierced her thigh, my fangs sinking in deeply. Euphoria in its purest form exploded from within, the light I carried seeping into her body, binding with her soul and abating the darkness that had taken hold. It was merely a temporary solution, like human marriage consummation was required to make it permanent. It would have to do, I would not take more until I was certain she knew what she was giving. Pulling away, I waited for her to return to me. It was the hardest thing I had ever done, my body rejecting the notion.

"Mara?"

Her body was shivering when she finally looked at me. Her eyes once again the captivating ice blue I had come to love, but within their depths a desperate plea for help lingered.

"Col?" She pleaded.

My body, if possible, grew harder. I understood her plea, knew exactly what she needed. Growling low and unable to resist, I pulled her into the water and kissed her.

Anam Cara

From a dark twisted existence, I woke to a dream. I wasn't alone either. Col was with me, his green eyes, warm, and filled with desire, were fixed to mine.

"Mara?" He called to me, his voice like velvet wrapping itself around me, instantly making me feel safe.

I hummed with longing, my body pulled taunt, I needed something my mind was struggling to decipher.

"Col?" I whispered, my thinking vague, dream like.

My body was on fire, my lip locked firmly between my teeth, the pain it caused, telling me that this was real, that this was actually happening. What is this? I felt lost, without direction.

With a growl that set my heart racing, Col pulled me into the water, the heat of his touch blanketing my frozen body. It felt good, the warmth, him. Pulling me closer, he placed his mouth firmly on mine, the kiss pushing the last remnants of cold from my body. I gasped, the sensation staggering, insurmountable. Why then would he try to move away? He can't…no! I needed this, needed to forget the coldness the alpha had subjected me to. I felt empty, my skin crawling with a thousand insects whenever I remembered the alpha's vile touch. Col's touch was nothing likes his, it was inviting, addictive, but more than that, it made me feel clean. It was as though the fire his touch ignited consumed the alpha's dark taint, rescuing me from the hell I knew awaited. Pulling him closer, afraid of losing him, I placed my mouth almost aggressively against his. The fiery kiss left me breathless, my mind whispering of the inevitability of our union, it said, 'nothing I could do could prevent it', nor did I want it too. Without my permission, my body melted against his, my mind memorising his taste and basking in his touch. There wasn't anything I could compare it to, it was breath taking, and I wanted it to never end.

Removing one of his hands, that was only seconds ago cupping my face, he ran it slowly down my back before resting it firmly on my hip, his fingers digging in deep, holding me to him. I nipped his lip teasingly, he hissed, his other hand finding and griping my other hip. Lifting me easily, my body glided against his, the friction sublime. Instinctively I wrapped my legs around his waist, moulding myself further to him. Unable to resist the urge and not really wanting to, I arched my body against his, my hands heedfully exploring his lush, firm muscles.

I allowed my head to fall back, the tips of my hair tickling the lower curve of my back, increasing my sensitivity. So when his hot mouth landed on my neck, I was powerless to stop the cry of ecstasy that followed. Interpreting my cry as a signal to increase his attentions, I lost myself to his expertise, it was all too much.

"Please… Col?" I pleaded, my body trembling.

"Do you trust me Mara?" he asked, his Irish lilt, teasing, seemed to caress me in the most intimate of places.

Annoyingly he left my neck to hover above my mouth, my hunger unsated, driving me insane.

"I trust you." I answered almost instantly, my words, breathless, were confident of my claim, skilfully masking the desperation tore through my thoughts.

He was not the Alpha, he would never hurt me. Searching my eyes to determine the truth for himself, he smiled when he discovered my statement true. His smile had my stomach doing somersaults, my heart missed a beat, I couldn't help but smile back.

Lifting his hand, he reverently ran his thumb across my lips, as though he wanted to ingrain my smile permanently into his mind, the gesture was, I don't know what it was, but I liked it.

Claiming my mouth again, he gently moved my chin to the side, exposing my neck once more. With my neck bared, he lowered his mouth to rest above my pulse. I could feel my increased heart beat pulsating against his lips, I shivered. Sharp fangs pierced my flesh, the deeper they travelled, the greater the flame that grew. My wolf approving, I clenched him tightly with my thighs, drawing him ever closer. It wasn't close enough. I wanted him, needed all of him.

"Please." I practically begged, my body demanding.

Growling deeply, Col removed his mouth from my neck, a brand that burnt pleasantly even after his withdrawal. A small trail of cold blood trickled soothingly down, offsetting the heat that Col had stoked. It was refreshing, the cold, it reminded me of all the years I had missed out on, never again. By partaking in Col's warmth, I could leave the darkness behind me. Hope flared, my eyes stung as I remembered Angelica. Col was my angel, he could save me, could free me from the shadows hold.

Held tightly against him, he carried me out of the water, his sculpted body visible through his clothing. Biting my lip hard I pulled the hem of his shirt up, eager to remove it. In silent celebration, his shirt removed, I admired his form. He was perfect, powerful, his muscles firm and tempting, I couldn't help but wonder what the rest of him looked like.

Lowering me gently onto a pile of fur rugs that laid heaped on the floor, he placed his body tenderly over mine. Leaning back to gain a better look, his eyes raked my body, before slowly, teasingly, removing the rest of his clothing, my eyes missing nothing. To say I enjoyed the spectacle was an understatement, he was a predator, my predator, and nothing would have prompted me to divert my gaze. When all his clothing was removed, I was unable to keep the surprise from my eyes. He grinned his teasing half smile, the gesture only adding to my pleasure. He was fully erect, his body firm. I wondered about the possibilities, my mind working overtime. Suddenly the things Donna described suddenly made sense.

Licking my lips slowly, I wondered what he would taste like. His eyes watched me greedily, his body jerking irresistibly. Leaning down, his body covered mine, his powerful arms resting one hand on either side of my head, gradually lowering until he rested on his forearms. A brief moment of panic flared as I felt trapped beneath, I thought that the wolf would stir, but instead it purred encouragement.

"Look at me Mara." Col commanded, his Irish lilt reassuring.

Compelling greens eyes held mine, his body pressed against me. Using one hand he spread my legs further apart, his entire body resting upon mine. Nervously I bit my lip again, a habit I had formed whenever I was unsure. It was not like me to be nervous, I felt like a coward. Glad that he couldn't read my thoughts, Col growled, the low sound making me feel feverish, fresh chills racing along my skin. Pushing forward tentatively Col readied to claim what was his, I couldn't move, my mind absorbing everything incredulously.

My gaze remained solely on his, his knowing eyes holding me to him and making everything else seem somehow insignificant. Lost in the moment, I felt cheated when Col halted his advance. His eyes painfully relayed the difficulty of what he had just done, his anguish evident on his face. So strong, and yet he fought to be tender, fought to take his time. I was about to tell him that is wasn't necessary, but before I could utter the words he spoke.

"Mara, you know what this will mean?" He asked through a strained voice.

"Yes." I answered, it meant I was his anam cara, that it would no longer be, 'just Mara', but instead, it would be Mara and Conlaóch. I would never be alone again, it meant that for the first time in my life, I would be safe, wanted.

Pleased with my answer and without hesitation Col claimed what was only ever meant to be his, a sharp stab of pain followed, my body involuntary tensing. It was barely noticeable compared to the pain I normally endure, and yet still I winced.

The discomfort was lost instantly, replaced instead with unimaginable pleasure. Slowly he moved back and forth, the sensation truly stunning. Gasping breathlessly, my body was inflamed, new levels of heat sending my mind into a near melt down. Intertwining my legs through his I pulled him deeper inside, the length of him filling me completely. Col growled, the low vibrations sliding over my skin, a dominate insistence that said, 'I belonged to him'. Shivers erupted as I heeded to his claim, the beast purring happily. I had no concept of time, my mind captured in a euphoric state, but at some point, the need we shared had become alarmingly urgent. Increasing his movements, each thrust seemingly deeper than the one before, I felt as though I was burning up, as though the sun had finally acknowledged me, reached me, sheltering me from the darkness, enlightening me with its rays. It was too much, my mind unable to comprehend the measure of my pleasure. Desperate, my body coiled tightly, this new, yet to be discovered need, finally reaching its climax, bringing with it, my release, and my wonderment.

I tried to conjure up a thought to describe, to process, but I was a prisoner to my body's wiles. Col's continued movements, still as urgent as before, were torture. Waves of pleasure continuing their assault relentlessly, my body shaking uncontrollably. With one last agonising thrust Col found his release.

His passionate roar filled the chamber, the sound thrilling, sent waves of heat that offset the sudden chills that fluttered through my chest. Trembling in what I thought was admiration, Col remained within me, his hands holding me to him, his eyes never leaving mine.

"What has been done cannot be undone." He said breathlessly, his eyes searching mine.

Did he think I regretted it?

"I know" I replied with a small smile, I wanted to do it again.

"Good, then you will not run from me?" He asked with all seriousness.

"It is an ingrained habit, but I shall endeavour to do my best."

"Endeavour? I would rather a promise." He said, his fingers running sensually down my sides.

I shivered again, another wave of heat prompting me to kiss him. Promise… promise! Siri, Gabriella, Asta. Guilt struck me hard as I realised they were still locked up. I promised I would release them and here I was bathing in Col.

"I have to go." I said, wriggling free from underneath him, the need to kiss him forgotten.

"Not even a minute and you are running again." Col said with disbelief, standing to follow.

"I'm not running. well I am running, but I'm not running from you." I called, starting down the small tunnel.

"You're naked Mara!"

Stopping abruptly, I looked down. I was naked, I was also bleeding slightly from my neck. Probably not the best way to show up. Turning around the way I came, and bypassing Col, who was in the process of putting on his trousers, I walked back into the pool. Quickly rinsing myself off, I walked back out, the water without Col's presence having become cold. I picked up his t-shirt. Putting it on, it fell to rest just below my bum, just.

"You look good in my clothes." Col growled possessively, his ripped body glistening invitingly.

Unsure what to make of his comment, I walked up to him, my fingers hooking the top of his trousers. Pulling him against me, I kissed him deeply. It was a mistake, as the heat he afforded me returned tenfold. Burning, my body eager, I pulled away.

"You are a distraction, I need to be somewhere." I said reluctantly.

As tempting as it was to leave them locked up, just so I could partake of Col, I couldn't, I had made a promise.

"You need to be with me." He said with a half-smile, reaching for me.

"I need to free my friends."

"I will come with you, just to be sure."

To be sure? He thinks I won't come back. I couldn't stop the small grin that surfaced, I left the shadow only to be followed by a new one.

"I will return to you anam cara." I promised, nearing the tunnels exit.

"Say it again." Col pleaded.

The tone of his voice made me turn around, it was that damn emotion, the one I couldn't figure but was overly curious about.

"I will return."

"No, what did you call me?"

What did I call him?

"I will return to you anam cara." I said with a small smile, my acknowledgment of being his anam cara pleasing him.

He smiled, my heart flickered. I would have to remember his reaction, remember how much this pleased him for the next time I inadvertently annoyed him.

"I will always find you. Be warned Mara, I will never let you go." He said as a promise.

I believed him.

To Love

As I watched Mara move steadily through Leif's chambers, I was concerned when she didn't even glance at the broken and discarded king. It unnerved me, the bond was no longer a temporary solution, it was a permanent one, and yet she failed to react to the king, her walk almost callous. Ignoring for the moment her lack of emotion towards Leif and her less than dressed body, I couldn't stop the bombardment of thoughts that were overwhelming me. She was now mine, as elated as I was with the fact, my worry for her remained vividly acute. I felt the bond form, felt ownership of my heart become hers. The love was unfathomable, pure, and instantaneous. It should have been the same for her, but the only emotion I saw in her eyes was desire, trust, and hope. Frustrated, I sighed, I may have won her body, my mark forever upon her, but I did not possess her heart. The knowledge made me think of Fenrir, so dark he could not comprehend the light, is it possible her blood tainted with his prevented her from giving me her heart. Can she love?

"Col?" Mara called, pulling me guiltily from my thoughts.

"Yes."

"You look worried, what is it?" She asked innocently, her eyes searching mine.

Could it be she just hasn't loved before? That she doesn't know what it is, I mused hopeful.

"Have you ever been in love Mara?" I asked, her eyes instantly filling with confusion.

"Love."

She used the word like it was foreign. That would be a no then.

"It is to care for someone?" She surmised, relief flooding her face.

"It is more than caring for someone."

"How so?" She asked anxiously, her ice blue eyes fixed to mine.

"To love someone is to give them your heart, to want them, need them more than anyone or anything else in the world. They become your life, your reason for living. You would do anything for them. Have you ever felt such for another person, do you feel it for me?" I asked optimistically.

Like earlier I wanted her to say yes, more than anything I wished to hear the words spoken. Instead she looked at me unsure, her mind racing to find something to say. Disappointment grieved me, my heart felt heavy.

"Mara! I thought I could hear you, are you alright?" An American vampire asked, flying around the corner at exceptional speed.

"Gabriella." Mara replied happily, her face betraying just how glad she was for the interruption.

Annoyed with Mara's reaction, I looked for the mark hidden on the inner of her thigh. It was just about visible, and it was my mark, a black intricate Celtic knot encased within my family signal, three interlocking hounds. Seeing it on her flesh filled me with pride, determination. Mara was mine, I won her body, I will win her heart.

"Who's the hottie?" Gabriella asked Mara, the vampires eyes heatedly glaring at my topless body.

"Conlaóch, my anam cara." Mara answered, a small grin forming when she used the term, 'anam cara'.

Damn women had already learned that using such a title would lighten my mood and distract my thoughts. I wanted to remain stoic, to diminish her ploy and prove to her that I could not so easily be won over, but I couldn't. Hearing her call me that, hearing her acknowledge it, made my heart swell, along with other areas of my body. Growling, lust making me forget why I was annoyed, I couldn't keep my eyes from her bared legs. She wore nothing underneath, the knowledge had successfully altered my thoughts, annoyance swiftly replaced with desire.

"Conlaóch, as in the Conlaóch, the lord of the Keltoi Conlaóch?" Gabriella asked, her eyes studying.

She made me feel like an artefact on display in a museum.

"Yes, what coven do you hail from vampire?" I asked coldly, wishing her gone.

"Gabriella." Mara rebuked, her eye brows raised in a manner that said, 'don't be so rude'.

"Apologises, Gabriella." I corrected, my tone appeasing Mara and warranting a smile from Gabriella.

"Tepes, I'm impressed Mara, Lord of the Keltoi and you have him whipped." She winked at me and patted Mara on the back. Whipped?

"Whipped?" Mara asked.

"You know, when you can make someone do whatever you want. He would do anything for you. Even apologise for being snarky to a vampire."

"You will do whatever I asked you too?" Mara asked me, her eyes twinkling in mischief.

I grinned as I tried to determine her train of thought, with any luck it matched mine.

"What do you have in mind?" I asked, my mind swimming with enticing possibilities.

"Oh, my goodness, you're blatantly thinking about sex. Typical man!" Gabriella added aghast, her face scrunched up in fake disgust.

"Mara?" I asked, ignoring the American, who's positioning was annoyingly disrupting my view of Mara.

"Later." Mara answered, chewing her bottom lip, the action having the same affect it always did. Uncomfortably hard, I moaned when I registered her use of the word, 'later'.

"Really! I'm standing right here." Gabriella interjected, her hazel eyes, amused, flickered between myself and Mara, her brow falsely disapproving.

The gesture reminding me of Finian. Who the hell was this vampire anyway? With a mournful sigh, Mara walked down the hall in the direction the vampire had come from, the vampire linking her arm through Mara's.

"So, this red headed hunter, he didn't give his name, was shouting down the corridors that the Rex Leif was dead, and as such the wards that hold us will no longer do so, and that we are free to leave. At first we thought it was a trick, you know, because the alpha is twisted like that, but then I heard all these women leaving the rooms, whispering amongst themselves, and no one was dying. So, we followed suit. We figured you must have succeeded, but we were worried about your condition. Anyway, long story short, Asta and Siri went in one direction, and me in another. I'm so happy to find you in one piece. I owe you my life Mara." Gabriella said, her eyes filling with tears.

"You owe me nothing Gabriella. I was only able to succeed because of you and Asta."

"No, we just made it quicker. Eventually you would have met him and killed him never needing our aid."

"Maybe, but maybe not. Are Asta and Siri unharmed?" Mara asked her friend, a small crease in her brow relaying her worry for the named women.

"They are fine. Admittedly you scared the shit out of us when you changed, I honestly thought you were going to kill us. But we're ok, no harm done." Gabriella added, her voice carrying the truth of her claim and of her fear.

I carried the same fear for Mara.

"You took a different form, fully?" I interceded, drawing their attention.

Turning her head to face me, a look of confusion covered Mara's face.

"Yes. A white wolf. At first, I thought I was part Varúlfur, but somehow I know that I am not." Mara added, her face regaining control, closed off any traces of emotion, and yet the bond we shared told me she was fearful of the knowledge.

"You are not part Varúlfur." I said, confirming what she already suspected.

How could I tell her what she really was?

"You know what I am?" She asked, no doubt the bond betraying me as it did her.

"Yes." Was all I could bring myself to reveal.

"It disgusts you!" She accused.

"Now is not the time to speak of such things."

"You did not deny it." Mara said, a brief flash of pain shooting across my mind, her pain.

I had hurt her. Hissing on a silent curse, I turned to face her.

"Mara." I began to say.

"Now you pity me!" She growled, suddenly angry.

Fantastic, now she's pissed.

"Ok well, I should probably go and find Siri and Asta, let them know you're ok." Gabriella cut in.

Mara's eyes blazing, didn't leave mine but waited.

"I will come with you." Mara snarled, before turning to leave with Gabriella, her eyes rolling in the process.

"Mara, we should speak of this."

She refused to look at me, instead she proceeded to lead Gabriella past me, the vampire's body acting as a barricade that blocked me from getting to her. Ignoring my request to talk, Mara said nothing and continued on her path with the vampire. Frustrated with how things had suddenly gone from blissfully good to bad, anger got the better of me. Why couldn't the blasted woman do what I've asked for once?

"You said you would not run from me. You so easily break your word?" I hissed, my voice, too cold, was contemptuous.

I sneered at my own stupidity, I had undoubtedly made the situation worse. Too late to take it back, both Gabriella and Mara stopped. Proof that my statement and tone of voice wasn't the wisest course of action, was clearly visible in the manner their shoulders rose, their chests pulling in a sharp intake of breath. Shit! How do I fix this? Gabriella un-linked her arm and moved to the side, her face full of reproach. Wisely she said nothing, if only I had done the same. Mara's eyes blazed dangerously. She was pissed, really fucking pissed.

"Let me make clear your meaning Conlaóch. First you deny me, your anam cara, a truth you know I earnestly seek, then you show me that such a truth disgusts you, but still you do not share it. Then you pity and disrespect me, after which you immediately follow with an accusation that I am being deceitful and not honouring a promise..."

"You put a negative spin on things." I interrupted, garnering another abrupt intake of breath, her eyes seething, burned wickedly.

"And you interrupt me… I have things to do, you would be wise to stay clear of me, least you discover my fist in your face." She snarled furiously.

The statement stung as I knew she meant every word. I should have said nothing further and allowed her time to calm, and myself time to think about how best I could repair the damage, instead, I permitted anger first say.

"You may leave when I have finished talking to you."

I regretted my choice of words instantly. The Bond informing me of Mara's displeasure and of her unrestrained anger. You would not know that below the surface such fury seethed, her face remaining skilfully serene, but I could feel it. With a look of pure defiance, Mara threw a punch that landed heavily on my jaw. The impact was sickening, my lower jaw separating from the upper jaw. Grunting with pain, I fell to my knees, my hand unconsciously moving to support my dislocated mouth.

"I'd say you were done talking, wouldn't you?" Mara said calmly, the undertone deadly.

The vampire coughed ineloquently into her hand, an attempt to disguise her laughter. I couldn't believe she had just hit me. Saying nothing further, Mara turned, pulling the vampire with her.

"You deserved that hunter." Gabriella smirked, before disappearing around the corner.

Standing up, I growled angrily, the sound reverberating through the tunnel. Drawing in a breath, I readied to pop my jaw back into place. With a steady hand, I manipulated the lower jaw back into the joint, and using force, pushed it back in with a nauseating crunch. Testing my mouth was once again realigned, I rolled my jaw in a circular motion. Happy it was in the correct position, my mood positively foul, I left to find the others. Mara, I would deal with later, preferably when she wasn't in heat.

Betrayal

Still reeling in anger at Col's lack of words, and misuse of the ones he did use, I entered what could only be described as a vast frozen cavern. It was easily big enough to fit an entire football pitch and was packed full of werewolves and women of every species. Hundreds of golden eyes instantly fell on mine, sensing my presence through the alpha's bond. I stopped and stood still, wondering what to do with my newly acquired pack. I didn't give much thought as to what I would do once I killed the alpha and took his place. Sighing, I searched the crowd, my eyes falling on a familiar face. I snarled loudly, Hamish! This was all his doing. Noticing my glare, he moved forward, separating himself from the others, his face betraying nothing. Standing only a few feet in front of me he moved to rest on one knee, his head bowing before me.

"Long live queen Mara!" He shouted in old Norse, his voice echoing loudly, skimmed across the ice.

It wasn't what I was expecting, and I didn't know how to react. I didn't want to be a bloody queen. I was about to tell him as much, when every Varúlfur in the room adopted Hamish's position, falling to their knees, their heads bowed.

"Long live queen Mara!" The wolves shouted in unison.

What the hell was happening? Expecting them to stand after their unwanted proclamation, I was unsure what to do when a minute had passed and the Varúlfur remained on their knees, their heads bowed. What do queens do? Rule.

"Arise." I projected loudly, my voice surprisingly calm, reached every inch of the cavern.

The wolves heeding my command stood. I looked over the Varúlfur, their golden eyes seemingly waiting for me to speak further. There had to be at least seven hundred wolves present, not to mention thousands within the world and they now looked to me for leadership. What had I done? What I needed to, the beast whispered mockingly.

"What would you have us do your majesty?" Hamish asked, startling me from a daze, the whole situation left a lot to be processed, where do I begin?

"Where are the children?" I asked Hamish, my gaze lingering on Col as he entered the room with the other hunters.

"Children?" Hamish asked confused.

"These women were part of a harem? What did he do with the children he produced?" I asked him impatiently, I hated being the centre of attention.

"I have nae been here in over one hundred years, I do nae know." He said plainly, his eyes filling with pity.

Pity for the children no doubt, I could just imagine what kind of father the alpha would have been.

"If I may speak your majesty, I know where they are." A female wolf claimed, stepping forward from the crowd.

"Your name?" I ordered coldly.

I knew the children weren't kept in the mountain, the ice would have shown me earlier.

"Ylva." She said confidently.

"And how is it that you were not part of his harem?" I asked, watching the power she wore like a cloak spark wickedly around her. She was strong, the kind of woman Leif would have taken.

"I have found my one, I can bare only his." She said, her eyes filling with sorrow.

Why would such sadden her?

"Your anam cara?" I asked, whilst looking up at Col, despite my best efforts not to do so.

Damn bond, I loathed it already, especially when he grinned at me as though he had just won some kind of fight. Annoyed, I grunted, my emotionless gaze returning to Ylva.

"Yes, although we refer to them as our elska. Leif imprisoned him to secure my compliance. I attended to the young."

"Secure your compliance? I thought you had no choice but to follow the alpha?" I asked thoughtfully.

"There is always a margin for interpretation." Ylva grinned slyly.

"For example?"

"We were ordered never to speak his name. But he said speak, which allowed us to write his name. He ordered us to report anything of importance. What does he deem important? Most of us attempted to defy him when we could. He wanted my complete cooperation, so he took what meant the most to me to secure it."

"I see. I can expect the same then?" I asked speculatively.

"I could not determine other's intentions my queen." Ylva answered cleverly, something to ponder later.

"But you know where he kept the children?"

"Yes, my queen."

"Those children belong to Fenrir bitch! Betray them to her and he will kill you and all yours." A wolf spat furiously from within the crowd, several other wolves growling and hissing in agreement.

Fenrir. Why does that name sound so familiar? And why was Col suddenly staring at me accusingly.

"I am your queen. You will swear fealty to me and me alone, any who would betray me can rip out their own hearts." I shouted angrily, scanning the crowd for the wolf that dared speak out, my temper once again getting the better of me.

The phrase be careful what you say, came dizzily to mind, before I could do anything to stop it, wolf after wolf started tearing their hearts out, some remaining silent, while others screamed in agony as they attempted to fight the unintentional command I had just placed upon them. Frustrated and appalled with my careless words I looked on emotionless, my default setting when everything was going to hell. It was stupid to reveal themselves as they did, like any of them had a choice. If I wanted to, I could have forced them to tell me all them secrets, it's what Leif would have done. Fortunately for them, I abhorred such practices.

Col's unrelenting gaze captured my attention, his expression filled with concern, his mouth stern, as though he wanted to intervene, tell me off. It was clear he didn't like what I had just done. I didn't intend for it to transpire as it did, I had in my anger forgotten the link to the pack. Unsure if should tell him such, I ignored him instead.

"Where are they?" I asked Ylva, my eyes leaving Col's eyes and returning to the avid determination held amid hers.

"Those he deemed worthy to live are kept in the neighbouring mountain. It is warded, only those privy to its nature can gain entry. The children that disappointed him were destroyed." Ylva shared mournfully.

As queen, I could see her thoughts even before she spoke them. She wanted no part in it, nor did Hamish want any part in my abduction, which was the only reason he was still alive.

"Do you have records of what child was born to what mother?" I asked hopeful.

"Yes. The mothers who pleased him with strong offspring where visited regularly."

"Should the mothers want their children returned to them, then do so. Those who are not wanted will remain under the care of the Varúlfur, free and innocent of their father's crimes."

"As you say my queen, and my husband?" Ylva asked, hope flaring in her otherwise guarded eyes.

"The alpha. Leif as you called him, was evil, I can only then assume that his prisoners are not. You will release everyone."

A sudden gust of blood filled air, infiltrated my nose, the scent from the dead wolves appealing. It made my stomach grumble, my wolf practically salivating. Bloody stupid wolves, the scent was making me hungry.

"Thank you, my queen, I swear for this kindness you will always have my loyalty. Ask anything of me and it will be done."

I didn't know what to make of her declaration. Why would she declare such when she would have to do it anyway? I was her queen, none of the wolves had a choice. Perhaps she meant she would not fight me?

"Take who you need to get the job done, I leave you in charge of this endeavour."

"It will be done." She said, a small smile forming on the edge of her mouth.

Turning to face the crowd, she motioned for several of the Varúlfur to follow. She wasted no time as she left to free her husband and carry out her duty. It felt liberating to know I had done something good, my wolf on the other hand wasn't overly impressed. In a brief flash of menace, I nearly called her back to deny her the happiness I had just ensured, but then I saw Donna waltzing into the room in an indignant frenzy, her ere, aimed entirely at Aengus.

"If you ever do that again, you big baboon, I swear I will hex you!" She shouted, me and the rest of the room wincing.

I didn't notice initially, but her arms were bound in the same metallic band the hunter had tried to place on her back in Scotland.

"Release me now!" She screamed.

"Donna" I called, torn between being amused and being angry for her.

Fool of a man had probably locked her in the car and cuffed her, so she couldn't use her magic to get out.

"What… Mara!" Donna squealed delighted, her face suddenly full of joy.

Forgetting her predicament, she ran towards me, slipping on the icy floor. Just as she was about to hit the ice Aengus had her cradled in his arms.

"Damn bloody woman, are you trying to get yourself killed? Can you nae just do what I bloody say?" Aengus mumbled.

Donna blushed, finally realising that she was stood in front of hundreds of onlookers.

"Oh… Urm… Damn it Aengus, put me down and release me." She whispered frantically.

I smiled genuinely pleased to see her. Shocked, I realised I had missed her. Other than a favourite knife I lost a few years back I couldn't remember ever missing anything. Walking over to greet her, my heart felt different, erratic, and fuzzy, I almost mistook it for static shock, but it was more pleasing, and not uncomfortable.

"Release her hunter, before I feed you to the wolves." I said, secretly amused by my choice of words.

My statement had no effect on Aengus, stubbornly he refused to un-cuff her, or put her down, regardless of her protests. Could he not see he was embarrassing her, I was growing annoyed for her.

"I will no. This is nae place for a woman of her beauty, everyone knows the Varúlfur are lustful uncontrollable beasts. And since she is forever getting herself into trouble when using magic, I forbid it." Aengus declared, his powerful body daring me to refute his words.

No longer struggling for release, Donna stilled in his arms, her eyes rapidly changing from annoyed, to a livid fury that reminded me of a hurricane.

"Forbid it?" She asked, her voice the calm before the storm.

Aengus must have seen what I saw, as he placed her feet gently on the floor, as though any sudden movement might make her shatter.

"FORBID IT!" Donna gritted through her teeth.

Despite the cuffs, magic built like a lightning storm, the powerful accumulation traveling along her body. Sparks in the vivid electric blue I had come to associate with Donna, flared wildly around her. Were it not for her temper I would have marvelled at its beauty.

"Come now anam cara, I only seek to protect you." Aengus pleaded, his hands held out in a defensive pose, as though he was warding off a threat.

"Hamish!" I summoned.

I knew the warrior had not moved, I could sense the presence of every wolf, it was both useful and disconcerting. I had yet to determine what to make of my new-found ability.

"Aye." He answered within my mind.

He was looking upon Donna distastefully. Searching his mind, I could see that he was offended for himself and the rest of the Varúlfur for the implication the hunter had laid at their feet, the accusation that they would desire a witch. They had said they did not like witches at the village, but I was not prepared for the hatred I witnessed within their minds, some kind of vendetta, a curse placed on all the Varúlfur, by a witch. I wanted to pry further but as the sparks of lighting Donna omitted grew longer, singing the hairs on Aengus's forearm, I let the curiosity go. The smell of burnt hair stung my nose, making me want to sneeze.

"Surround the Hunters." I replied, a silent order that to my surprise was obeyed immediately.

Quietly and deadly, the Varúlfur moved to encase the hunters. The female prisoners predicting trouble, moved stealthily to the back of the cavern, hunching down inconspicuously. I briefly wondered why none of them had attempted to leave, only to remember that they were still surrounded by hundreds of wolves, which were only recently their jailers. Unless they knew Old Norse, they wouldn't have a clue what was going on, what did they think this meant? Their deaths?

"You would move against me anam cara?" Col asked me, his eyes like the other hunters, clouding with a grey smoke that was both questioning and threatening, his body posed, ready to attack.

"You would imprison her, like Leif did these women." I countered.

"I seek only to protect her." Aengus spoke angrily at the accusation.

"You compare Leif to me?" Col asked, his eyes seething.

"Why not? Are you or are you not breaking an oath you made to her?"

Col growled long and low, the tone deadly, caused a few of the female prisoners to sob uncontrollably.

"Release her Aengus."

"What!" Aengus shouted, the giant nearly as angry as Donna.

His body rippling with power, abhorred the order.

"We are bound by oath to neither hurt them nor imprison them." Col reminded Aengus, his tone implying he was not happy with the fact.

I couldn't care less, what is it with the damn men and their belief that they owned us?

"Damn the oath! They agreed to come with us freely, Mara is queen, it's nae likely she will be leaving anytime soon, and Donna will undoubtedly want to stay with her. Mara may be your anam cara Conlaóch, but trouble follows in her wake. I will nae leave Donna here. I see their minds, the Varúlfur would kill her."

"I will not allow it. For the last time, release her." I hissed, my wolf pressing for control, rubbing herself along my skin.

Battling inwardly, I couldn't prevent my fangs from erupting, a growl escaping.

"I reject your claim Aengus, I will nae be ordered, I will nae be owned. If you cannae abide me my freedom and allow me to make my own decisions, if you cannae trust me to know my own mind, then I will never be with you. Ever." Donna said delicately, skilfully disguising the thunder contained within her eyes.

If I had been Aengus I would not have released her, that calm promised retribution for her condition, but Aengus, aghast with her omission, released the cuffs holding her power at bay. Before the cuffs had hit the ground, she released a pulse of energy that had Aengus flying across the room, smashing loudly against the far wall. With a grunt, he fell to the ground, his arm bent unnaturally.

"First you beguile me into nae noticing your intention to cuff me, prohibiting me from my only source of protection, leaving me vulnerable and weak. Then you lock me in the car like some un-trained pup who could only ever be a nuisance. Then when you can plainly see I'm no longer in danger you refuse… Refuse to release me, subjecting me to your will, imprisoning me. You arrogantly announce your desire to forbid me the use of my magic… MY MAGIC! The very essence of who I am, like I'm yours to control, and if that wasn't insult to injury, you further determine who I can befriend, and where I'm permitted to go! In front of all these people. If you can so easily disregard an oath you all up held, how am I to believe you would honour and uphold any oath you would make to me! I have never been as stressed and angry as I have been these last few days, and it was nae to do with Mara, but you!"

Screaming the latter, Donna sent wave after wave of energy flying at the ice above Aengus's head, like an avalanche the ice gave way, falling in lumps and powdered spray that landing directly onto Aengus. The younger hunters, the ones whose appearance was identical to each other's, stepped out to grab Donna. Foolish move, her fury sending them spiralling backwards into a line of waiting Lycan.

"Mara, stop this, she will listen to you." Col called from behind Donna, his face grim.

"I am of her opinion, is this not an age of equality?" I asked him, my tone more mocking than I intended.

Cursing inwardly, my heart sank when I felt a flash of disappointment through our bond. I had disappointed him somehow. A form of silent communication passed between him and the other Scottish hunter, I wished I knew what, as the Scottish hunter looked at his leader in disgust only to then stare at me, his eyes focusing on my forehead as though he attempted to penetrate my mind. My mind! No… Col would not do such a thing, he is my anam cara, doesn't that mean everything?

He wouldn't… disbelieving my own train of thought, I looked at Col, searching his smoke-filled eyes. He did! Unable to breathe, air caught in the back of my throat. He did… I saw it, saw the betrayal held within their fiery depths. He had ordered the other hunter to read my mind, because he could not. It was written on his face, radiated through the bond. I felt sick, my mind trying to understand what that meant. Every dark secret, my fears, my weakness, witnessed by another, because he, my soul mate, ordered it.

As I comprehended the merit of his betrayal, I thought I would feel anger, thought I would want vengeance, instead, I felt loss. Gasping on a sharp intake of breath, I started to hyperventilate. Images of my past came racing unwantedly to mind, my childhood, Ti's lessons that left me empty and in pain, Angelica, my only childhood friend, my punishment for hoping for salvation, and the beast… My time with the beast, and the things he subjected me to. Every tainted memory I had hoped to forget, and had been succeeding mostly in doing, came flooding back to life, contaminating my senses, and blackening what Donna called, 'my soul'.

The room and the people vanished in a blur, every suppressed feeling surfacing at once, all of them wrenching at my closed heart, threatening to destroy it completely. Images shot through me, like a blade repeatedly piercing my chest, but none as sharp or as agonisingly deep as the betrayal of Col, my light amid my darkness. The fact that I couldn't understand why it hurt so much only increased my anguish.

The wolf roared murderously as she tried to overcome me, protect me from the onslaught of emotion. I was too frail even to succumb to the beast's invitation. For the first since being a child I wanted to embrace the darkness, wanted desperately to feel nothing, instead, I was rendered useless, struggling to grasp even one cohesive thought.

Grabbing my stomach firmly, I lamely tried to hold it in, as though the pathetic gesture could stop the out pour that had firmly taken place.

"Mara! Ansgar stop!" Col commanded.

I could sense he was trying to get to me, the Varúlfur protecting their queen, denying him access. I felt like a helpless afraid child again, no longer fully aware of what was going on in the room I wanted to flee and hide as I had been trained to do, but as the pain increased with every horrific memory, I failed to find the strength to do so.

"What have you done Col?" Donna shouted, fear swimming in her eyes.

She wrapped her arms around me protectively, the action weighing me down like an anchor. It steadied me, giving me seconds of reprieve. Subconsciously, I knew that Asta and Siri were there, forming a tight circle of safety that kept me from the hunters. Where they came from I couldn't account for, I briefly recalled them not being present in the room.

"Mara, please answer me darling." Col called, his voice tormented, pleaded with me to go to him, but he was the reason for my pain, he did this.

I trusted him, stupidly believed he would never hurt me. Ti was right, no one would ever want me, not truly.

"My queen, tell me what you need." Hamish called, the chaos and noise fuelling my fears and making them more palpable.

"She needs to get out of here, I've called my brothers they have arranged for a helicopter to collect us from the nearest village, Gerd? Jerg? it will be there within the hour." Gabriella answered before lifting me from the ground. When did I fall?

"Gjerde. My queen, do you wish to leave with the vampire?" Hamish asked, deferring to my will.

"Yes" I heard myself reply quietly.

"No! Mara! Do not run from me again, let me explain." Col hissed, his voice cutting through the crowd like a beacon lighting the way in the dark.

Anger flared as I resented the power he held over me. Why would he do this?

"We cannae hold them off for an hour, ten minutes max." Hamish confessed.

I tried to push my memories back into the confines of my unconsciousness, but every time I tired, more memories surfaced.

"Ten minutes is enough for me to seal them in, they will be unable to leave until the sun rises." Donna said, her arm never leaving mine.

"That will give us four hours, do it witch." Hamish said, his voice closer than before, was urgent.

Donna relented her hold, her absence allowing the darkness more hold.

"My queen, when the witch is ready you must order the others to stand down, your men have not been ordered to inflict harm, but accidents happen, if Conlaóch is killed, so are you."

Col... the mere mention of his name wounded me further. My protectors continued talking amongst themselves, their voices fading in and out as we moved through the room seeking our exit. I heard Donna's urgent chants and Siri's quiet steps as she followed me out.

"Now!" Donna called, her footsteps quickening, rung on the floor as she caught up to us.

"Stand down, do not engage the hunters." I ordered silently, unable to locate my voice.

Col? How could he do this? I wanted to continue without looking back, some dark part of me forbade me to search for him, but I couldn't, I needed to see, needed to understand why. Turning, I found him straight away, our bond disclosing his location. Rich green eyes met mine, they were pained and filled with grief. My eyes stung as small droplets of water gathered and fell down my cheeks, the ice-cold sting they carved, crushing my foolish dream of a life filled with warmth.

"Please Mara." Col begged, blood pouring from his wounded body.

Seeing him in such a broken state only heightening my discomfort, like salt in a wound, it burned.

A Necessary Evil

Of all the horrific, and destructive things I have witnessed, nothing was as devastating and soul destroying as watching the delicate trail of water that fell from Mara's eyes. What had I done? I have seen thousands of broken men before, but Mara didn't seem to know why she was broken, it was evident in her face, and in her body. Like a child who had wondered too far in the woods, she was lost, and it was I who had led her astray.

"Please Mara." I pleaded, my chest tightening.

I should have apologised and begged for forgiveness, but how could I, I did what I had to do, what I needed to do. It is one thing to skim someone's surface thoughts but to read a mind completely is invasive and thorough. Every thought and the emotion attached to it is pulled from your mind as fresh as the day it happened, and all at once. Depending on the sort of life you had, depended on the reaction. In Mara's case, it was horrifying. But it was a necessary evil I told myself, it had to be done.

My heart beating loudly seemed to do so in disagreement, like a hammer attempting to knock some sense into me, it pounded against my chest, whispering of the wrongness of what I had done. If she was a follower of Fenrir, then why was she broken and crying? It hissed at me.

I had violated her mind and had caused her to relive every agonising moment of her short existence. The pain as her memories where ripped from her mind would haunt me forever, what kind of life could warrant that level of fear? Ansgar had stopped, but I still felt physically sick, my body trembling as I shared the pain she continued to endure. What happened to her?

"I warned you friend." Ansgar spoke sadly besides me, Mara walking away, unknowingly taking my heart with her.

"Show me what happened to her."

"You do not want to know." Ansgar answered, surprising me, if he truly believed that then it must be bad.

"You were wrong by the way, she is not loyal to Fenrir, and she has never met Sköll." He added bitterly, the fact crippling me from the inside out.

I had honestly thought I would discover some dark truth. I had hurt her for nothing, betrayed her unduly. Roaring my anguish, I was unable to process the wrongness of what I had just poured out upon her.

"What the hell happened, and where is everyone?" Aengus rumbled, a deep cut to his forehead oozed with blood, obscuring half his face.

The hunter was pissed off, scanning the vast room warily.

"That's what I want to know, you said you had claimed her, your mark is clear, why did she order the Varúlfur to attack?" Eoghuan asked, his eyes filled with concern, his stance casual.

"Col misjudged his anam cara." Ansgar answered coldly, his words like acid, scolded my veins.

I had to fix this, but how?

"What have you nae told us Conlaóch." Aengus glared, his manner accusing.

I didn't answer. My mind a turmoil of guilt and regret, fear, and agony. I could feel myself falling apart, my anam cara. For the first time since being a child I had to fight to prevent tears from forming.

Pull yourself together my mind shouted furiously, I needed to put this right, crying would not get her back. Standing eerily still, my grief threatening to unstable me, my mind hummed with activity, an attempt to overcome the torrid of emotion and create a solution. There was only one real answer, find Mara, grovel, explain, regain her trust, and love her irrevocably.

"I need to make amends Ansgar, to do that I must understand what I took from her. Show me everything." I asked, uneasy of what I would discover.

"You have already hurt her more than the monsters that plagued her dreams and haunt her every waking hour, do you really think it is wise?"

"I must fix this; do you know another way?"

Ansgar was obviously pondering the question, standing still, he stared at a dead wolf, laying a few feet away. Waiting patiently, I watched my friend as his quick intellect searched for possibilities that would not hinder her privacy further. That fact that he would protect my anam cara in such away only added to my regret, and made me realise the true extent of my error. I had sworn to protect her from harm, and yet I had effectively raped her mind, betrayed her in the most sacred of ways.

"I can think of none."

Ansgar placed his hand on my shoulder, the action forming a connection that would allow him to transfer the data that formed Mara's mind.

"Shit Conlaóch, you didn't have him read her mind?" Eoghuan hissed outraged, guessing what had transpired.

I had never heard Eoghuan angry, his brother yes, but never him.

"She is of Fenrir's blood, she didn't leave me a choice, for the sake of the world I had to be certain she was not in league with him or his sons." I answered in explanation, guilt ripping a hole through my chest.

"Reason or no, it is sacrilege, she is your anam cara, and as you have claimed her, effectively our queen."

"I know who she is Eoghuan." I snapped.

I didn't need reminding of my fuck up, I needed to make it right.

"No wonder she and Donna keep running, shit Conlaóch. Did you even ask her about Fenrir? And you…" Eoghuan pointed to Aengus "Did you bother to explain to Donna how it would be difficult to concentrate amid the threat of battle whilst she remained with you, because you know, she means everything to you. Did you ask her if she could wait for you until the coast is clear? No, you didn't. So much for all your many years of wisdom" He sighed distastefully.

"I was preoccupied with protecting her, I gave nae thought to explaining myself." Aengus grumbled defensively.

"Yes, and that's your mistake, how would you feel if she had done that to you?" Eoghuan counter remarked, his blue eyes reproachful.

"I'd bloody kill her! Shit… I' am a damn bull." Aengus confessed heavily, cursing to himself.

"Well, this is a shit day."

Finian finally joined the conversation, his legs crossed, he was laying down, his back upon the ice as though asleep. His statement about summed it up, at least the end of the day. From the happiest man to the un-happiest in less than an hour, and it was of my own making.

"You ready?" Ansgar asked me, the conversation dropped.

"Yes."

It was dark, Mara was afraid. A thin layer of ice clung to her pale skin, her hands were small, like that of an infant child, and she was shaking heavily.

"Mara, you cannot hide from me little one, I hear you trembling. Come to me child freely and your punishment will be slight."

Bravely she stood, revealing her hiding place. A man I hadn't seen before towered above her, his expression cold, stared at her with scorn.

"Come here." He ordered, in a deep, raspy voice, that made her small heart race.

"You took a bite of my bread?" He accused.

"I hungry." Mara answered, her speech immature.

"I am hungry."

The man she called Ti corrected impatiently.

"I am hungry." She repeated.

"You should not take that which is not yours. Come closer Mara."

Fear coursed through her body, afraid of what he would do. Obeying, she did what he asked, slowly moving closer to her guardian, her tiny footprints echoing forebodingly in her ears. Standing before the tall warrior she waited quietly, her quaint body frozen.

"Sit." He instructed sternly.

Sitting as told, Mara waited uncertain of her fate.

Ti returned with a large box, dropping it on the table. It banged as it hit the hard wood, Mara jumping in her seat. Taking out several loaves of bread, he placed them in a line before her.

"Greed is the first step to gluttony, gluttony paves the way to covertness. Covertness Mara, is why men have on many occasions gone to war, whether it is covertness for land, gold, or power, it all starts with greed. You have eaten, and yet you wanted more, wanted what was another's. You will sit here and eat every bit of this bread, so as to learn that no good came come from over indulgence, do you understand?"

"Yes." She whispered.

A sudden gush of snow tainted wind, flung wildly into the cabin, painfully winding itself around her and making her shiver. Catching her breath on a small gulp she stared at the bread, a small trail of water dropping on her cheek and falling quickly to the ground.

"Then begin." Ti ordered, taking the seat across from her, his powerful body unaffected by the cold.

Picking up the first loaf, she began to eat, terrified of the consequences should she refuse. Her fear for her *guardian was soul deep, his power over her, absolute. As she neared the end of the first loaf, her stomach began to hurt, her mouth was dry. Looking at her guardian she contemplated asking him if she could finish. Swallowing the mouthful of bread that had clogged her mouth, she stared at the remaining four loaves that awaited her.*

"I am full." She dared to say.

"Your mouth is dry and your stomach pains you?" He asked her, his gaze knowing.

"Yes."

"It is unfortunate then that you have not yet finished, we do not waste food Mara. Eat it all." He instructed smoothly, his expression holding no emotion.

Picking up the bread once again, she did as he asked and ate every mouthful, the bread becoming harder to chew, her small stomach full to bursting. Half way through the second loaf, her stomach revolted. Saliva filled her mouth, her body seeking relief. Heaving painfully, she emptied the contents of her stomach, the relief momentary. Without mercy, Ti placed the bread she had dropped back into her hand.

"Continue." He said coldly.

Shaking with nausea, she placed another bit of bread in her mouth, the smell and taste instantly making her want to throw up again.

"No good can come from greed, do you agree?" He asked, unmoved by her state of discomfort.

"yes." She answered, hopeful that he would release her from her punishment.

"Good, you are beginning to understand, when you have finished it all, you will never forget. Eat."

Mara was sick a further nine times before she finished the last morsel of bread, her body quivering wanted nothing more than to lie down and seek sleep.

"You did well Mara. Now to address the issue of stealing." He said, shattering any hope she had of reprieve.

"No." I hissed, allowing the memory to drop.

"And that is only her earliest memory, they are consistent in their theme, his lessons growing more profound as she grows." Ansgar explained disgusted, his eyes ablaze.

Children were sacred to the Keltoi and loved fiercely, her punishment was cruel.

"Until recently?" I asked.

"She last saw him three weeks ago."

"He treated her like that even then?"

"Yes, the other half of her nature displeases him, at least this is what Mara believes. I do nae doubt that his administrations are merely an attempt to rid her of it, and bind her to the darkness, as he appears to belong."

"Mara knows this?"

"No, but since meeting Donna, you, and the women who shared her cell, she has begun to question Ti's teachings and methods. He kept her isolated from the world deliberately, she knows only what he taught and what little she picked up when traveling."

No wonder she is so cold and un-feeling, he had been conditioning her for years, slowly extinguishing what little light she harboured within. She had learned everything from a highly methodical sadist, making Mara dangerous, but also incredibly vulnerable.

"There's something else Conlóach." Ansgar said out of nowhere, his eyes pained.

"What?" I asked, trepidation causing the hairs on my neck to stand on end, how much worse could my day get?

"She is hunted by Sköll."

"I thought you said she had never met Sköll."

"She hasn't. Mara and her guardian have been running for as long as she can recall. Assassins of every breed have searched and attacked them in an attempt to kill her, always in the shadows she feels someone is watching, but doesn't know who or what it is. But we know, his stench and foulness we have followed the world over. It is him."

"But you have not seen him attack directly?"

"No, but he has been present at every fight, observing from afar."

"Gauging the strengths and weaknesses of an enemy is common practise." Aengus added, his temper somewhat defused.

"You believe he is preparing for a final strike?" I asked, knowing it would make sense, it is why armies have scouts and send in raiding parties before battle, gauging the enemy's weaknesses and strengths before committing their soldiers, that and Sköll was nothing but meticulous.

"She felt someone watching her at the club the first night we met her." Ansgar added, a low growl of annoyance following.

Then it was him I detected, not Mara. Anger sored, my tongue hitting the roof of my mouth. I had been so concerned with Mara's distant behaviour I had missed the truth of the situation.

"If you had not been there Conlaóch there is a good chance Mara would be dead. Without the protection of her guardian, and her not yet immortal, she wouldn't have stood a chance should he have attacked." Eoghuan said, his mood the normal calm I generally associated with the young hunter.

"Aye, Eoghuan is right, Ti never returned when he said he would, I bet everything I own it's because he has been killed or captured, separating him from Mara. With five hunters who hunt him, he would nae dare make a move and reveal himself that night." Ansgar concluded.

Aengus hissed at the news, raising his hand above his head before testing the movement in his healing arm.

"Donna was there, I dread to think how close he came to her. Where did Mara go? Sköll will be searching for Mara will he no. Donna is mortal."

"Aye, and nae one to underestimate, or have you forgotten her prowess." Ansgar added, in what I assumed was a ploy to console our friend.

I understood Aengus's pain, it was my fault, my error that placed his anam cara in Sköll's path, as well as my own. Had I listened to the council of my friend and trusted Mara as she deserved, they would both be here safe.

"Aye, she is a feisty wee thing, isn't she nae?" Aengus smiled with pride.

"I will fix this Aengus, I swear it. Mara is with the vampire Gabriella, she hails from the Tepes coven, we will leave as soon as the ward drops." I promised.

"I saw the vampire and her friends stealing a mobile from an unconscious wolf, I thought nothing of it, had I have known she was securing a means to take Donna or Mara I would have stopped her." Aengus said annoyed with the fact. "I should have checked her mind, but she was a captured woman, I dinnae think it would be right given what she may have endured." Aengus confessed, his shoulders tense made me believe he felt responsible somehow.

"This is my doing and mine alone, Donna would not have left with the vampire had I not forced Mara's departure."

Aengus didn't respond but instead formed some form of resolve in his eyes. He would do whatever it took to protect them, so would the rest of my team.

"Who was the Vanir that left with Mara?" Eoghuan asked, changing the subject, and garnering all of our attention

"I do not know, Mara did not have time to speak of her." I said, curious as to why he would bring the quiet women up.

"Her name is Asta." Ansgar revealed, a small smirk surfacing briefly.

"Why?" Finian asked, sitting up to glare at his brother.

"No reason."

Eoghuan turned to inspect the icy walls.

"Like hell there isn't, why?" Finian prodded.

Turning to face us again, Eoghuan looked uncomfortable.

"It is probably nothing."

"Or it is everything." Ansgar added casually.

Clenching his jaw, Eoghuan mentally debated with the idea of sharing his thoughts.

"I did not see her face so there is no way of knowing for sure, but at some point during the fight with the Varúlfur, I felt her enter, I was consumed with the idea that I must protect her, above all else."

Confused, he waited for us to determine the reason. Without looking into her eyes, the gate way to everyone's soul, nobody could say for sure, but it would normally indicate the presence of ones anam cara.

"She is Vanir, she may have felt threatened and called for assistance, it is not unheard of." Finian answered first.

"No, it is nae possible. She is only seventeen and has nae gained access to her abilities." Ansgar added, a small smile on his face.

Walking over to the young hunter he patted him firmly on the back.

"I sincerely hope you have learned over these last few days, how nae to treat your anam cara."

"I'll try nae to be insulted by that comment friend." Aengus grunted, a mocking gleam in his eyes.

"Then you believe she is my anam cara?" Eoghuan asked suddenly fearful.

Did he not welcome the idea?

"You do not look happy brother, you do not want one?" Finian grinned.

"I do, it's just… never mind."

"We are brothers we have always shared everything."

"If this week has taught me anything it's that one's anam cara comes with a whole heap of trouble, if Conlaóch and Aengus who have lived for thousands of years can so royally screw it up, what hope do I have. No offense." He said, both Ansgar and Finian grinning widely at the innuendo aimed at myself and Aengus.

"Take nae notice of us boy, we have developed a thousand years of bad habits and bias toward the fairer sex. After all it has been less than a hundred years since this equality stuff and a millennia prior of women that deferred to the men folk, wanting our protection and aid. It was expected of men, and the women dinnae object to it.

Unfortunately for Conlaóch and I, it is a somewhat ingrained practice" Aengus explained, his mouth, stern, refuted further explanation, or further indirect insults.

"Aye, that and the fact they are nae used to people nae following their orders or questioning them." Ansgar added nonplus.

"Neither are you." Aengus said to Ansgar moodily.

"That is true, but I grew up in a household that consisted of my mother and seven sisters, as the youngest child I had little choice but to do what I was told."

"Pretty sisters too." Finian grinned, warranting a murderous glance from Ansgar.

"Huh… I've meet his sisters, they would sooner skin you then kiss you. But you are right, they are exceptionally blessed when it comes to their beauty, a complete contradiction to their less than average brother." Aengus laughed raucously, overly impressed with his comment, his mood, volatile as always, shifting full circle.

"Funny because I vividly recall your sister was rather fond of my looks, especially my mouth, she would always insist I place it between her…" Ansgar winked, the sentence left open.

Aengus's laughter died, his merriment replaced with a swift and violent rage.

"You have… My baby sister!" Aengus hissed, his eyes wild.

"Baby? She is at least four hundred years old, is she nae?" Ansgar grinned.

So easily was Aengus wound up, Ansgar has never met his sister. Normally I would appreciate the humour but how could I at a time like this?

"Idiot, he had never met your sister." I said, ruining what was destined to develop into a full-blown fight before Aengus himself would have come to remember the fact.

"Aye… I knew that." Aengus answered, his anger fading as quickly as it formed.

Of course he did.

"We have four bloody hours to wait, and you just ruined what would have been our only source of entertainment." Finian sighed unhappily, his expression disbelieving.

He looked like a child who had just had his sweets taken off him.

"Wait. Why cannae we leave now?" Aengus frowned, garnering a heated glare from us all.

"Your wee witch locked us in." Ansgar answered, before stretching out on the floor.

"Oh, crafty wee thing."

"You may as well get what sleep you can, we're nae going anywhere until the ward drops." Ansgar yawned.

"I'm nae opposed to the idea, I guess I've slept in worse places." Aengus sniffed, his eyes scanning the now empty cavern.

I guess the ward only applied to the Keltoi. On a positive note, we being the only one's present meant the alpha didn't acquire one of our women for his harem. With nothing but time to burn we made ourselves as comfortable as one could be on a bed of ice, and sought what sleep we could.

New York

"Fathers going to kill you, what are you thinking, queen of the Lycans and three Lycan generals, are you insane?" A deep male voice complained, the noise waking me from a sleep I didn't care to wake from.

"Like I said, her name is Mara and she saved my life, if it wasn't for her I would undoubtedly be dead, or worse, Leif's plaything. Besides, now she is in charge and the wolves who were loyal to Fenrir are all dead." Gabriella hissed quietly, as though despite being annoyed with the male she was desperately trying not to wake me.

"Dead? She killed them all?" Another male asked, his voice deadly, was full of authority.

"Yes, she had them rip their own hearts out. It was glorious and slightly disturbing." Gabriella added quietly.

"I would have given anything to have witnessed that." The first male speaker said.

"What is she? She is not Lycan, but not far off either." The second male asked.

I could feel his gaze studying me. Odd that they didn't have the same accent as Gabriella, especially since she had said her brothers were coming. I briefly recalled the trip to the village and the helicopter arriving, my mind stepping in and out of various memories confusing my thoughts. I gave up trying to remember the trip, but I was certain these men weren't on the helicopter.

"Were nae on the helicopter anymore Mara. We are on a plane heading for New York. These men, Gabriella's brothers, met us at an airport in Holland." Donna said happily, her hand patting me lightly on my arm.

"You have learned to read minds then?" I answered quietly, my mouth dry.

When I opened my eyes, they stung, there was absolutely no valid reason why they should, but they did anyway.

"Aye, apparently meeting your anam cara makes you more powerful." Donna said with displeasure, a small grimace flickering over her face.

As much as I liked the witch, I really didn't like that she could read my mind, especially given what Col had just done. Col... I would give anything to have never met him.

"I still cannae believe he did that to you. But do nae worry about me prying. I can only see recent thoughts and even if I could go back further I would never do that to you... never." Donna said, the truth of her words filling me with both reassurance and warmth.

At least I could trust Donna, if not my soul mate.

"I know" I said, sitting up and pulling Donna into a much-needed hug, surprising both me and her.

"I love you too." Donna said squeezing me tightly.

Love?

"I love you?" I asked confused.

"Everyone loves me" She smiled, her eyes twinkling with laughter.

"Of course they do, who could not?" I grinned, realising at last when she was messing with me.

"I know, it's a lot to deal with, I mean all those admirers, it takes a lot of humility to be as awesome as me." She said with a huge smile, fanning herself as though she was too hot.

I couldn't help but smile at my friend, her humour making me feel honoured to have her as such.

"Aww Mara, do nae do that, now I'm going to cry and ruin my makeup, and in front of all these strangers." Donna sniffed, her eyes filling with tears, her mouth doing its best not to lose its smile.

Hugging me tightly, I welcomed the embrace. Since when have I ever needed a hug? Ti would punish me for weeks if he knew I was hugging, let alone caring for someone other than myself.

'Your needs, your life should always come before another's Mara, do you understand me? There is no one person's life more important than yours, we have not come this far and fought this hard just to hand your enemies their victory". He would say, pretty much on a daily basis.

For so long I had lived by his principle, trusted in it, but now… I'm not sure I could. I would gladly die to protect Donna.

"And I you, bestie." Donna grinned, hitching her shoulders comically, her eyes filling with water again.

Wiping at her eyes, she took a deep breath and shook herself.

"When we get to New York we're going on a massive shopping spree. On me!" She said delighted with the idea.

Me not so much, I knew full well I would get no say in what items were purchased, still no blow torch for Mara.

"No, you will nae, but only because I care about you too much to have you trapesing around like a badly dressed serial killer. Have you ever heard of the phrase beautiful but deadly? Well, you have the deadly part in the bag, but the beauty part needs a bit of refining, at least when it comes to your choice of attire. A mani and pedi, some Dolci and Gabbana, and no one would ever know you were, well, whatever it is you call yourself." Donna smiled happily.

"A queen." Hamish spat venomously, irritating Donna.

"Aye and as your queen she should have the best of everything, would you nae agree?" Donna added smugly, her eye brows raised in a 'you know I'm right' arch that had a defiant flare about it.

"Aye, she should have whatever she wishes. Should she choose to wear leathers it is her right, men will still find her stunningly beautiful, nothing she wears could ever disguise her beauty." Hamish declared boldly, the other Varúlfur and Gabriella's brothers nodding in silent agreement, their eyes studying.

I didn't care for the attention, the one occasion I had designed to entertain a man only led to disappointment… and pain.

"Aye, but if you had a choice of Mara wearing leathers or Mara in a short strapless chiffon dress and French silk lingerie, which would you choose?" Donna grinned, a look of self-satisfaction gleaming brightly in her eyes when Hamish hissed, his mind betraying to us both just what version he would prefer.

"Hamish!" I called out aghast, when the mental picture he had formed quickly transformed from me being dressed in the said garment, to me removing it slowly while I beckoned him to me.

Donna obviously feeling smug, burst out laughing.

"See." Donna winked at me.

"Could I come?" Siri asked quietly, her voice hitching slightly when everyone turned to look at her.

"Come shopping?" I smiled, genuinely happy to have the little Valkyrie with me.

Ti always said they were a formidable breed, he was not wrong, I'm not even sure I could bring myself to do what she had so soon after Leif.

"Yes." She said, her voice braver than before was louder and more controlled.

I couldn't help but admire her courage.

"Of course!" Donna said, before I could open my mouth to reply. "I was hoping all the girls could go."

"A girl's day out, I'm definitely in. Asta?" Gabriella smiled, even more excited with the idea than Donna.

Her brothers frowning looked like the idea was issued from hell, the Varúlfur looking much the same.

"Shopping in New York, of course. When my parents arrive, I doubt I will ever be permitted to leave their sight again. Might as well make the most of it. Can we go clubbing too?" Asta asked, her eyes wide.

"Siri is too young, we cannot leave her on her own." Gabriella said.

"Of course, sorry Siri, I wasn't thinking, we could go cinema or theatre instead." Asta said, wrapping her arms around the girl and pulling her into a tight embrace.

"But couldn't the witch, I mean Donna, magic me in?" Siri asked, her voice muffled slightly by Asta's proximity.

"You wish to go? The clubs are very crowded, dark, and noisy. Would it not be too much?" Gabriella asked gently.

"You mean, am I afraid?" Siri said annoyed, her eye brows drawn together tightly.

"I did not mean to imply that."

"I'm a Valkyrie, we do not fear anything or anyone." She hissed, her shoulders held high.

"If she wishes to go, then you should allow her." Hamish declared, his look one of boredom.

Why should he care? Searching his mind, I was greeted with nothing but blankness. He shut me out! A quick glance at Donna showed me that he had shut her out too. Is he supposed to be able to do that? I'm his queen.

"Stop staring at me witch! The Valkyrie may be young, but she is in no way a child." He said bluntly, as though that explained everything.

However abrupt his words were, I was inclined to agree with him, to view her as a child only belittled her courage and everything she had gone through. Whether by choice or forced she would never be or think like a child again, not after Leif.

"I agree with Hamish, although drugs are still a definite no." I grinned, gaining a warm smile from Siri.

"Probably best nae to mention our night out to your folks though, the last thing I want is an angry Valkyrie parent chasing me down. Parents never believe their children are grown, trust me. My mum still rings to make sure I had breakfast." Donna smiled.

"It is only me and my brother, but it is probably best he doesn't know either." Siri grinned, her eyes filling with gleeful anticipation.

It was a relieved to see that Leif's hold, if any, was quickly diminishing.

"Girls night, yay!" Gabriella squealed loudly, her smile contagious.

"I know, right!" Donna said delighted.

Judging by the wide smiles on my friend's faces I must have been the only one who wasn't really feeling like shopping or clubbing, especially clubbing, it would only remind me of Col. All I really wanted to do was hide in a big comfortable bed, the bed Donna got for me would be perfect. I wondered if I could convince them to return to Glasgow, that way they could go out while I slept for the next decade.

"Mara!" Donna called, dissolving the very real image of the bed I had managed to form to a tee.

"What?" I said silently, the eyes of the others watching questionably.

"Hiding in a bed will nae make you forget about him. Nothing can or ever will, so putting your life on hold will accomplish nothing." She said, so only I could hear, her scorn scolding, even without the vocals.

"I did not believe that it would make me forget, only that I wish if only for a while not to do anything." I sighed, irritated with the whole situation.

"He hurt you Mara, in a way that no other has or has ever been able to. You have never known anyone capable of holding that much power over you, he holds that power because of who he is to you, and because whether you realise it or not, admit it or not, you are in love with him."

"You are mistaken; I do not know how to love, I am not even sure if I understand it."

And beside I've only known him a week how could loving him even be possible? To fall in love that quickly is nothing shy of weakness, and is stupidly reckless.

"You understand and know more than you realise. Answer me this. If Col were here right now, his life in danger, would you die if it meant he would live?" Donna asked seriously, her mouth pursed.

"If he were standing here right now, I would slit his throat for lying to me." I hissed, the thought profoundly appealing.

Huffing, her nose twitching, Donna glared at me. After staring at me as though she was waiting for me to realise something, she rolled her eyes and tutted when I said nothing further.

"No, you would nae. I do nae disagree that what he did was under handed and wrong, but he did what he thought was the right thing at the time." She said, her eyes saddening, and building with tears again.

Why would that make her cry?

The sight so vulnerable, had my eyes watering in response, I'm turning into some kind of emotional wreck, it was so much easier caring for no one. Did Col hurt her too?

"No Mara, Conlaóch dinnae hurt me, neither did he want to hurt you."

"Then why do you cry?" I asked her confused.

"Because I now know what you are and why Col did what he did. And I do nae know how to tell you without hurting you further." She said on a desperate sob, the others looking at us with confusion, Hamish frowning with concern, his golden eyes penetrating.

Hurt me? That's funny.

"Nothing could possible hurt more than what has already transpired." I said, suddenly fearful as to whether that was true.

I hoped that is was true. The pain I felt, still feel, whenever I think about what happened, was eating away at me. I never knew you could hurt someone like that, not without a physical influence, and certainly not without a lot of imagination. I doubt I would ever forget the betrayal in his eyes, I literally felt my heart crumble and fall apart, like ash scattered in the wind it was as though my heart no longer held form, piece by piece it vanished into nothingness, along with the warmth he promised me.

'Shadows and ice Mara, it is the nature of what you are, who you are. Embrace it, and you will never need fear, nothing will ever hurt you.' Ti's voice whispered in my mind, taunting me, and reminding me that I had failed his most important lesson.

I sought the warmth, and found it, and like everything that holds heat, eventually it burns, Col burnt me, and I shall never forget the agony of it. Ti was right, the shadow might be cold, dark, and empty, but at least the burn of ice preserves you.

"You are wrong Mara, Ti is wrong. It might preserve you but not without killing you first."

"Urm sorry to interrupt, but I just realised we can only stay in New York for tonight, Max. I told Conlaóch what coven I was in." Gabriella winced.

Her brothers glared angrily.

"Well that was stupid!" One of them said, pulling his mobile phone from his suit pocket.

"He is Mara's anam cara, I was being polite, how was I supposed to know he would actually turn out to be a bit of a jerk?"

"He's a hunter, you block your thoughts, say nothing and leave." The other brother said scornfully.

"You're not going to tell father, are you?" Gabriella asked hopeful,

Her eyes focused entirely on me, were wary and apologetic.

"Father."

Gabriella winced, her eyes burning, found, and remained solely on her brother.

"Seth." A sinister and alluring voice answered, a shiver of excitement, like an electric currant, spiralling through me and waking me up.

Great my beast had decided to make an unwelcome return. Like I didn't have enough to deal with. I growled, seduction and sex suddenly the most important topic.

"Gabriella told Conlaóch she is a Tepes." Seth said, staring at his sister murderously, a wicked and reprimanding gleam in his eyes.

A growl of disapproval sounded loudly through the phone receiver, making a usually loud Gabriella sit back shyly, and pull in her bottom lip.

"She owes the Lycan queen a life debt, until it is repaid she must remain with her. If Mara does not wish to be found then I will deal with the hunters, you and Lucian will stay with your sister until whatever this is, is dealt with, and get her as far away as possible. Do not tell me or anyone where you are, and get rid of your phones. Locker forty-eight b. You will find sufficient funds to go anywhere in the world, use cash only, and leave no electronic trail for them to follow."

Gabriella's father's orders were laced with anger and begged for anyone to question them.

"But father, it could be years, centuries before Gabriella pays of her debt, and …"

"You will do as I say, I will not have my only daughter in the company of Lycans, alone and un-escorted. Queen or not, the woman is hunted, her pet dogs may protect her, but they will not protect Gabriella. You will stay, understood."

"Yes father." Seth answered unhappily.

"Lucian, you understand what is expected of you?"

"Yes father. But what of the Vanir and the Valkyrie? Their relatives are coming to collect them. If they are not delivered to the coven will they not hold us responsible?" Lucian asked casually, like it wasn't really that important, but it is a courtesy that deserved some form of address.

"The hunters will not abandon a search for their women, they are probably on your heels already. There is no time to bring the them here, get rid of all their phones, collect the money, and go. I will explain the situation when they arrive. They will understand."

He said the latter with such arrogance I half guessed he would force them to if they didn't. Asta must have gotten the same impression as her face suddenly paled, alarm reflecting in her hazel eyes.

"You cannot send someone to collect them daddy?" Gabriella whispered sweetly.

"By the time you land it will be close to mid-morning, the sun up. The airport has not been built to accommodate our kind Gabriella. You and your brother may have protection from the sun but most of my men don't. We were not planning to collect you until later. The hunters will find your friends still within the airport and will search their minds regardless of whether you told them where you are going or not. They will stop at nothing to discover the truth. Is that what you want?"

"No. I would not wish it on anyone. Your advice is sound, I hope that on another occasion you will allow me to repay you for all you have done for me and my friends." I cut in surprising Gabriella… and me.

"I will assume that this is Mara. From what I understand you saved my daughter from a fate that is even now unconceivable to me. It is I who thanks you. I will delay Conlaóch if that is still what you wish?"

"There can be no forgiveness for his betrayal. I deny him his claim and want no part of him." I snarled, the beast approving of my statement. "But if you would be so kind as to refrain from killing him, I would be most grateful. I have no wish to die."

"Die? Then you have fully accepted the bond, taken the vowel? You must be a powerful woman indeed if you can deny yourself your soul mate."

"Huh." Donna tutted, her eye brows raised comically. "Power has nothing to do with it, she is just outright stubborn."

"Says the woman who has left her elska in much the same way." Hamish scowled.

"I'm teaching Aengus a lesson, no more. I have never really intended to deny his claim, only make him more receptive to my personality and needs." Donna pouted defensively.

Annoyed that they would intercede on my conversation, I mentally shouted at them to shut up. Donna jumped in her seat and Hamish winced. Serves them right.

"Apologies, they forget themselves." I said to Gabriella's father.

"No need to apologise, I understand that training dogs is harder than it at first appears, I don't envy the task laid out before you. I do however hope that in the future we can form an alliance that will benefit both my kind and yours." He stated, coaxing an undignified grunt from Hamish and the other three Varúlfur.

"I am open to reform and look forward to meeting you. Until then." I said, my eyes daring Hamish to disagree.

A fight might make me feel a bit better, help me vent. Annoyingly he just grinned, his eyes announcing loudly the fact he knew what I was hoping for, and that he wasn't going to fall bait. Irritated with the damn lord for being so arrogant I nearly forgot myself and growled. Trying to catch the error before it could reach the vampires hearing, I hastily covered my mouth, the action amusing Hamish, and the other generals.

"I'm going to slap you hard." I promised silently, the threat only making their amusement greater.

"Until then. Gabriella, Lucian, Seth."

"Goodbye father." They said in unison, just before Seth hung up.

Standing up from my seat I went and did just as I promised, slapping Hamish hard across the face. He didn't even try and stop me. Growling low, his eyes filled with heat, his scent suddenly overpowering, tantalising.

"Mara! Really? You should have realised by now that such would only turn a wolf on. The Varúlfur are messed up!" Donna scowled, pulling her long brunette hair up into a pony tail, her eyes serious.

"There is nothing wrong with liking a bit of rough witch, they say it heightens the pleasure." Seth announced, a suggestive wink aimed in her direction.

"Ugh that's disgusting." Donna said, her mouth upturned distastefully.

"Don't dismiss it until you've tried it." Seth smiled.

"Shut up idiot, she has a sufletul pereche." Gabriella clucked, mock whacking her brother over the head.

Dodging out of the way easily, her brother grinned, his attention turning to Asta.

"She has not been claimed, none the less, there are other available women."

He winked this time at Asta.

"Yeah but none that care to be used and abused, so give it a rest." Gabriella sighed, her other brother Lucian watching the display stoically, his expression reminding me of the other Scottish hunter, Ansgar I think his name was.

The amber eyed warrior who sees everything and who read my mind. I wonder how much he had told Col by now, he probably knew everything, my nightmares, my fears, Col must think me a coward.

"So, we won't be going shopping and having a night out then?" Siri asked un-expectantly.

"Not in New York, no. But as much as I dislike crowds I promise we will have our girl's night out." I said, not really believing my own words.

Did I just agree to a girl's night out? I really am damaged, but at least I'm not in any more pain, physical pain that is. Apparently now that I had let the beast out of its cage, my body changed to accommodate immortality, I got a reprieve from the bone breaking and internal gnawing. Now I just get my heart broken and my mind screwed with, and I didn't think I was in heat anymore either, win, win.

"Urm, yeah, I think you have just got used to your own scent, you are definitely still in heat." Donna broadcast loudly, oblivious to any need of privacy I wished to keep concerning the matter.

"Oh, sorry, dinnae mean to share. I get confused between what's in the head and what's nae." Donna explained, her face scrunched up in what I assumed was an apology.

But I'm not bleeding, and Hamish and the other generals aren't showing the same signs as before, wouldn't it have been the same as when I was in the village and the ice caves? Maybe they have just got used to me, and maybe vampires aren't affected by it at all? Only one way to really know.

"Hamish." I called, the warrior looking my way immediately.

"Am I still in heat or has the effects lessened." Shock flashed in his eyes, only to return to rigidly controlled, just as fast. He wasn't expecting the question or the bluntness, as such it took him a second before he answered, his eyes growing heavy with desire the longer he considered the question.

"It will last another week, at least." He finally said, his voice stiff.

"But I feel different, more in control."

"Aye, because you gave your body what it desired, which abated your urges. It will nae last long." He said, a small half smile forming on the edge of his mouth.

Is he implying what I think he is?

"It will happen again, I will lose control?"

"Aye, the longer you withstand the more urgent your need will become. You will slowly lose control as the wolf's needs grow. If you do nae satisfy the urges, she will eventually take matters into her own hands." He explained, his eyes suggesting he would be more than happy to help.

"But I'm bonded to the hunter, doesn't that mean I will not allow others to touch me?" I asked irritated by the prospect, not that he wasn't attractive, but because I didn't like the idea of disappearing again, becoming something that had no bearing on my current mind, wants.

"Conlaóch's hold on you pertains to your soul, pertains to Mara. The beast is you but not you at the same time, the wolf does nae honour oaths. In essence my queen, another lives within you, and she will bind herself to no one." He said in a manner that implied I understood everything he had just said.

Confused I didn't know what to say.

"So, I am two different people?" I asked frustrated.

"No. You are one person, but like everyone you have a duel nature. A good and a bad, light, and dark. Normally there is a grey area in between the two allowing for better control and scope to balance emotion. But because your good side is Vanir and your bad side is Warg, there is no grey area. The Vanir cannae comprehend the dark, neither do they understand it, and the Warg cannae comprehend the light, nor do they understand it. You cannae negotiate an alliance between the two as they can neither see each other or hear each other." He explained, his gaze studying.

"I have heard the wolf." I said, remembering its desires, its wants.

"Aye but you don nae understand the darkness that leads it's thinking, just as she does nae understand your reasons for what you think and want. You don nae understand each other, nor will you ever. Where others balance on what I could only describe as a sea saw swinging from one frame of mind to the other, you stand on a ledge. As you are now you hover with one foot above the dark, and one foot above the light, the smallest breeze of emotion could tip you either way. It is why you are volatile and somewhat unpredictable."

"Then the wolf does not want Col?"

"I imagine her interest in him would be only for his power and all that it would entail. She cannae feel, care or love. Should he ever displease her she would kill him without fluttering an eyelid and never think of it again. His death would only kill the light side of your nature, your soul. Unfortunately, a Warg requires no soul to exist, such is the nature of Wargs."

"Are you saying that if he died I would become purely wolf, like Leif?"

"Nae like Leif, worse, like Fenrir."

"But I don't feel like two entities." I sighed heavily.

"You are nae. You are you, but when you allow yourself to enter that dark part of yourself you become wholly dark, unable to distinguish right and wrong. For example, if you became the beast now and fully succumbed to its true nature, you would probably kill us all, at least those of us who would not serve any purpose. Myself, Kieran, Sven, and Kai, as your loyal servants, will be spared, as too would Seth and Lucian, at least until you are no longer in heat, then you would have no further use for them."

What? That's sick, there's a spider with such qualities, a black widow I believe it's called. I'm a spider.

"How often do you give in to the dark side" Seth asked, a glint of excitement dancing in his eyes.

Donna looked on the verge of laughing.

"What is wrong with you? Seriously, I know Mara is omitting some serious mojo but honestly, did you miss the part where she would kill you afterward." Gabriella shook her head, annoyed with her brother, the other brother Lucian looking as controlled and unreadable as ever.

"Seriously Mara, a black widow!" Donna giggled.

So that's what she thought was funny.

"Will you stop reading my thoughts?" I hissed.

"I really cannae help it, I don nae know how to turn it off now it's on, Sorry." She pouted, her apology unconvincing, noisily she continued to laugh.

"What's a Warg?" Siri asked.

Warg? Hamish said I was a Warg. What is a Warg? And who the hell is Fenrir?

"What is a Warg?" I asked.

"You do nae know. Col dinnae tell you?" Hamish hissed angrily.

Col! That's right, he knew? why wouldn't he tell me?

"He dinnae find out until after Hamish kidnapped you, and when he did see you again he was busy dealing with other matters." Donna smiled and winked.

Col's naked and highly addictive body was the last thing I wanted to think about right now. How am I supposed to be pissed at him remembering just how good he felt on me, inside me? Shaking myself from the memory I begrudgingly focused on the matter at hand. Donna knew that I was half Warg, but she did not wish to tell me either. She believed the knowledge would hurt me.

"Aye, I still do nae know how to tell you." Donna said sadly, her smile fading.

Astonishingly she looked to Hamish to offer explanation.

"As my queen, it is your right to know now should you wish it. But as a friend, I would advise speaking of it in private, away from the confines of a plane cabin." Hamish said calmly, his eyes portraying his belief that ultimately the decision was mine and he would oblige willingly either way.

"When we are settled then." I winced, ending the topic.

Losing my calm in the small cabin was a genuine possibility, depending on how well I processed the news. It's becoming obvious that me angry could ultimately result in the violent death of someone I had come to care for. Better safe than sorry.

"Which brings us to the subject of where we intend to go." Lucian said, his face still expertly guarded.

It must require a lot of effort to maintain his level of emotionless, unless of course he was actually emotionless, which by this point was beginning to seem like a plausible actuality. Not even Ansgar managed to remain completely stoic.

"We cannae go back to my village, it will be one of the first places they will look." Hamish announced, his generals nodding and grunting in agreement.

"Aye, they will no doubt look for us at mine and my family's home too." Donna added, leaning back in her chair.

"Bar Gabriella's brothers, they know who we all are. With their resources, it won't take much effort to learn where we live." Asta said thoughtfully.

I know, and thanks to Col even my home is jeopardised. Where should we go? Where wouldn't they think to look for us?

"Neither of you need to come. It is I who wishes to evade the hunters and the others who seek me. I am used to moving alone. It will be easier, that way none of you will be placed in a position that may prove fatal. My enemies whomever they are, do not need to be yours." I said, meaning it.

Even beyond the risk of me turning to into the wolf. I have always been hunted, will probably always be hunted. What kind of friend or even queen would I be if I were to drag innocents into it?

"No! You need me, where you go, I go. Final" Donna said angrily, her face reproachful.

"I have survived lesser odds Donna. You are a powerful witch and an irreplaceable friend I do not deny, but because you are such I will not put you in unnecessary danger."

"You would take away my choice, like Aengus did, Like Col did?" Donna asked, a sly smile edging her mouth.

"No never." I grinned, crafty witch, no wonder I had grown to like her so much.

I could hardly deny her that which she knows I hate.

"Then there is nothing else to be said, I'm staying with you." She grinned.

"Me too." Gabriella said loudly, her mouth set stubbornly.

"I know you believe you owe me a life debt, but I release you of it. As I told you before, you owe me nothing."

"I owe you everything but that is not why I choose to stay. You are my friend, I will not abandon you, you didn't abandon me." She said.

"If we do not go with Gabriella our father will brick us up into a wall, drained of all our blood, for hundreds, if not thousands of years. His temper is legendary, I cannot speak for my younger brother but I for one will not risk his wrath." Lucian said, his eyes shut as though in sleep.

"Nor I." Seth grimaced, a glimmer of fear sapping all traces of humour from his face.

"You need me too. I mean, I won't be very helpful when a fight breaks out but at least I could teach you how to channel the elements correctly." Asta smiled warmly.

True. I had forgotten about my near burn out. This wasn't going as I expected. Hamish hadn't said anything, but I knew full well he wasn't going anywhere. That left Siri. Looking at the young warrior I waited for her decision. I should force them to go home but to do that would make me a hypocrite, and no different to the hunters. They were capable of making their own choices, even if I didn't like them, I had to respect them, even young Siri.

"Oh, you're waiting for me." Siri smiled shyly.

"I am a Valkyrie, I was born for battle, there is no possibility of me returning home." She announced, truly joyful about the prospect of fight.

Shit, this wasn't what I was expecting. I must have cursed through the link that joined me to the wolves, as Hamish, his eyes filled with smugness, smiled.

Arrogant git.

"I will hurt you Hamish." I promised, a wave of annoyance tingling over my skin, stabbing at my chest.

"I look forward to it, my queen." He growled heatedly.

"Honestly Mara, you're going to have to think of a better way to punish him, his mind is warped." Donna frowned, her green eyes staring daggers at the Lycan lord.

My wolf purred, pleased with Hamish's response. Irritated with my reaction, I realised she was probably right. Unable to tear my eyes away from him, heat built, sweeping through me before filling my chest, and pooling in my belly. It was like being back at the village all over again. I hissed, desire shooting through me. The unwanted sensation was making me feel uncomfortable. I shut my eyes and attempted to ignore the fact I was surrounded by men who were annoyingly eager to fulfil my needs. I hated being a woman, such things did not happen to men, they seemed to have the best of everything. A week, a whole week, and it would only get worse. I could order them not to encourage me, but would that really stop me when things got bad. From what I've seen of Hamish, he would find a way around the command.

"Donna, can you do something to prevent the wolf from taking hold? Block out my desires?" I asked hopeful, the thought seemingly coming from nowhere.

"Nothing comes to mind, but I will think on it." She said concerned, an angry glare aimed at Hamish.

"You may wish to bear in mind Lycan, Mara has been claimed, to touch ones anam cara means your death." Donna warned.

"Aye, but should she force herself on us, no council in the world will hold us accountable, after all, we cannae disobey our queen, and the whole world knows it." Hamish said confidently, a small smirk flashing at the corners of his mouth.

"They may not hold you accountable, but they will hold me accountable." I growled.

My body tense, desperately wanted the release that Col had so expertly brought me. My wolf pushing, encouraging me to do bad things. Thinking of Col, no matter how fleeting, was a mistake, images of his ripped, perfectly formed body, lodging themselves in the innermost confines of my mind. The plane and its occupants forgotten, he was suddenly all I could see. Shivers erupted all over me, his scent as fresh as the moment I was last with him, infusing my senses. Like a gust of wind hitting dying ambers, fire flickered to life, my body engulfed in flames. Shit! Growling, needy, I stretched in my chair, the soft fabric stroking and increasing my sensitivity. The beast to my dismay happily purred encouragement, baited me to search for more, to use the men that are readily available. Damn it.

My eyes fastened shut did nothing to help, instead only make the images clearer. Hissing with frustration, my anger flared, I growled again, this time the sound was menacing.

The Varúlfur, and even the vampires growled in response. The pressure in the cabin, stifling, was becoming unbearable, I needed to get out, but where do you go when you're stuck miles above the ground.

"My queen?" Hamish hissed, his scent stronger than before, tantalising even.

He was powerful, dangerous, but more importantly he could satisfy my needs. So was the vampire, the one called Lucian, either would be my first choice, if not them, the others would do.

"Mara!" Donna called appalled.

I didn't open my eyes, but I was without out a doubt that should I open them her face would be full of reproach.

"Idea's anyone? Now's the time to share." Donna said loudly.

"Give her what she wants?" Hamish announced, his voice highly suggestive, his aura, the power that he imbued, stroking against mine.

"Shut up! I don't mean you or any of your lap dogs, she will nae be joining the mile-high club today, got it?" Donna scolded.

"She could pleasure herself." Seth added un-helpfully.

"What no! That's not an option idiot, she is in heat, she wants to mate, her hand can't do that, can it?" Gabriella hissed, annoyance lacing her words.

Donna fell unnaturally quiet.

"You could knock her out?" Siri added.

"That could work." Gabriella said.

"And if you fail you will awaken her beast and likely kill us all." Asta said quietly, her statement however heard by everyone.

"There is another option if you are sure sex is out of the question." Lucian said calmly, his masculine voice layering my skin in a warm balm that only increased the fire.

This was useless, I was going to lose this battle, I could feel my control slipping, feel the beast rising to take what she wanted. I would betray Col as he had me, and the thought stung.

"Before any of you attempt to stop me, I give you my word I will not seduce her. I move her only to offer her privacy." Lucian explained, his voice closer than before.

"Open your eyes Mara, look at me. I will make it go away." Lucian promised, his silver blues eyes soothing me, soothing the wolf within.

Placing my arms around his neck, he lifted me effortlessly, my body drawn to rest against his.

"Sit down Hamish. He will nae hurt her, I can see his thoughts. Let him past." Donna shouted.

Unable to resist Lucian's closeness I placed a kiss against his neck. Guilt hit me hard, but it didn't lessen my desire for the vampire. Hissing in response, his fangs protruded wickedly. With a speed only afforded a vampire I found myself still nestled within his arms, but at the back of the plane, our presence obscured from the others. Lowering me down, my feet touching the floor, he turned my head to face him.

His eyes so vividly bright, gazed into mine, they were studying, primal, exciting. Placing my arms around his neck I pulled him towards me, my need frighteningly urgent. Not resisting, he allowed my advance, his full mouth joining mine in a kiss that although lacking the warmth of Col's was still delicious. I moaned delighted, his sharp fangs nipping my lip. Lucian took a step forward, backing me up against the wall, his powerful body barricading me in and covering all means of escape. A strong hand travelled temptingly up my leg, the sensation truly stunning, made me remember that I only wore Col's shirt.

Col… This was wrong, only Col's hands should ever touch me. My inner voice screamed for me to pay attention, to fight and find the resolve to push him away. My body, the betrayer, didn't respond. Instead of moving away, I languidly caressed his chest, his body begging to be tasted. Growling low, his hand moved to find my waist, his body pressed tightly to mine.

Ending the kiss Lucian moved his mouth to rest at the pulse point at the base of my neck. Running his tongue slowly over the delicate area of flesh, his passionate exploration made my body to tremble, my heart beat increase. I eagerly awaited what I hoped was a bite, he didn't disappoint. Gasping with pleasure, his fangs entered my flesh.

The tension that had been building so rapidly, the urgent, painful need that gnawed, started to ebb. Hungrily, Lucian drank from me, the sensation one of pure bliss. The part of me that knew this was all wrong, recognised the danger his thirst presented, and yet I couldn't stop the hunger, the desire, that had overcome me. With every stroke of his hand and every pull of my blood, he fed my desire but extinguished my strength. The more blood he drew, the weaker I became, but still, my body craved his, needed his. I felt ashamed when Col's exquisite green eyes flashed brightly in my mind, a horrid reminder of my promise to him and my failure to keep it.

Every moment Col and I spent together etched its way in, the memory of his touch, of our time to together. His scent filled my mind with longing and begged me to be stronger, to take back control. Hissing with pleasure, my focus grew sluggish, my sight dangerously compromised. The image I held of Col wavered in and out, like a camera lens that failed to find its target. My body was heavy, exhausted.

Held tightly within Lucian's tight embrace, I didn't initially notice as my body weak from blood loss began to wane, my energy finally depleted. It had to have been Lucian's plan all along, and despite my vulnerability, I was truly grateful. As my eyes lids began to flicker, Lucian withdrew from my neck, his powerful hand supporting my head. Remnants off desire swam within his silver eyes, his expression full of conviction. I wanted to understand the reasons for his conviction but for the first time in my life, I was really tired. Cradling my head gently against his chest I felt him kiss the top of my head.

"You must learn to control your needs dragă. I have tasted your blood and like an addict I will never forget the ecstasy of it. Nor would I choose again to deny myself the pleasure you would provide. I will savour you, all of you, and will regret it not." He whispered low, his voice stiff swayed in its control, vibrated gently against my ear.

Lifting me with ease, his manner gentle, he returned me to my seat.

"You drank from her!" Hamish roared angrily, rising from his seat ready to engage Lucian.

"She is immortal. She will recover, and in the mean time she is too weak to be of any danger." Lucian said, returning to his usual emotionless self.

Unmoved by Hamish's display, he sat back down, his expression bored.

"Thank you." I said to Lucian.

Gracefully turning his head so I could see him, Lucian smiled. It was a slow smile that he wore on one corner of his mouth, it was beautiful, but like a shooting star, it was there and gone so fast, I briefly wondered whether I had seen it at all.

"Ireland." I said suddenly, an idea forming.

"Of course." Hamish smiled.

"What? What about Ireland?" Donna asked loudly, her eyes studying me questionably.

She had questions about what had happened between me and Lucian, it was written all over her face. Too tired to think coherently she would garner nothing from my thoughts. Smiling teasingly, I closed my eyes. Donna huffed.

"It is Conlaóch's homeland and remains home to most of the Keltoi. It will be the last place they will look for us." Hamish said, his anger completely dissipated.

"So basically, were going to camp in Col's back garden?" Gabriella grinned mischievously.

"Yes." I yawned.

"Your anam cara will be pissed when he finds out." Siri grinned.

"Yes, I sincerely hope so."

Nosferatu

I hate New York, as magnificent as the city was visually, the smell was abhorrent. The fact that we were submersed under a heavy down pour of rain only made it worse. Dry refuge was definitely better than wet. We were close to the Tepes coven and thus closer to Mara, but even armed with four hunters, to walk into the house of Vladimir Tepes uninvited was not to be done lightly. A vampire's ability to move beyond what even our eyes can follow, made them lethal, not to mention their strength. But to do so in their coven, in their own seat of power, made them highly dangerous. It is foolish to under estimate them. Because of the danger, we had been waiting for reinforcements to arrive, from both the Keltoi who lived nearby in Buffalo and the American faction of the Vanir.

"Why when Romania is such a beautiful country would they uproot and move here?" Eoghuan asked, his piercing blue eyes scanning the area, his nose upturned in disgust.

"It is one of the biggest cities in the world, full of humans who enjoy a vibrant night life. It is the perfect hunting ground for a vampire and unlike other cities, the tall buildings can provide enough shade for them to travel during the day." Ansgar answered.

"And the subways and tunnels." Aengus rumbled.

"I've heard there are alligators in the sewers and tunnels." Finian added, staring at a manhole cover a few feet away.

"I would nae take notice of everything you hear boy. But you could always butcher a look." Aengus grinned, shoving Finian towards the said manhole cover.

Regaining his balance quickly, he turned and threw his middle finger up at Aengus. He chuckled loudly, the rain stemming any echo the noise would have created. So, it begins between them already?

Clucking in annoyance, I started to pace. I had to reach Mara, what was taking them so long? It's been over two hours since our plane landed.

As if on cue, my thoughts read, the wind picked up, winding itself chaotically around the alley. Bits of debris flew in mini torrents that sped violently around us, signalling the approach of the Vanir. As always, their entrance was dramatic but at least someone had finally arrived. From the mouth of the alley four black cloaked figures emerged from the busy street, their large hoods obscuring their faces. Walking as though they hovered above the ground, they moved gracefully. The rain didn't seem to touch them, rolling off to the side and falling to the floor unperturbed. I envied the skill.

"Well met." I called out to our unknown allies.

"Greetings Conlaóch Ó Ceallacháin, Tiarna of the Keltoi." A hooded male replied, his voice deep and raspy.

Making themselves visible, the four Vanir lowered their hoods, revealing three males and one female. They looked to be in their late twenties, but as immortals it was practically impossible to determine their actual age.

"I am Havardr, my companions Frode, Asmund, and Runa." The large blond-haired male spoke, introducing the others, and revealing his status amongst them.

"My team Aengus, Ansgar, Eoghuan and Finian." I replied, the hunters each acknowledging their names as the Vanir did theirs.

"Your reputation proceeds you hunters." Runa, the dark-haired women said, her smile warm.

"We are grateful for your aid. You have been filled in I presume." I asked, not in the mood to repeat our plan.

"We have. I believe you have met my niece?" The one named Frode asked.

"Aye, Asta." Ansgar smiled.

"As you can imagine we have been worried. Do you know if she was harmed, is she well?" He asked, his forehead creasing with worry.

"She was safe and unharmed last we saw her." Ansgar continued.

"I'm pleased to hear it, as will my sister be." Frode smiled, his eyes lighting up with genuine affection and relief.

But then what did I expect, anger? The Vanir love their families and since conception is so rare amongst their kind, every child born is important, all of them needed to play vital roles within their communities.

The children are especially guarded, because like the humans, they are incredibly vulnerable up until the day of their immortality. It is common consensus that all mortal Vanir are never to leave family estates without accompaniment. Asta's kidnapping must have rattled them greatly. With their own towns and villages deliberately separated from the rest of the world, the only way her captors could have reached her was is if they infiltrated their town.

Known by many names the Vanir, elf or fey, depending on where you come from, are renowned the world over for their ability to manipulate the elements, water, wind, fire, and earth. They only need to imagine a wall and the next thing you know the ground is rising from beneath your feet, forming one as solid and as strong as a mountains face. Getting to the young Vanir would not have been an easy feat. In fact, I can't even fathom how they did it. The Varúlfur would not have been able to pass the wards, none can without invitation. If the elves magical barriers didn't propel the unwanted trespassers away then the animals that live within the trees or even the trees themselves would have whispered of the invaders approach, miles before they arrived at the Vanir's invisible walls. Like a security system, every living entity would have sounded the alarm, the fey whose talents lay within the bounds of earth magic would have heard the calls, and would have warned the others. Which begs the question, just who was helping Leif? And why?

"Frode was it? I am Eoghuan, it is a pleasure to meet you." Eoghuan said, grasping the elves hand, and shaking it firmly.

Surprised Frode took a moment to react.

"As it is you Eoghuan." Frode replied with a confused smile.

No doubt he was wondering why he was singled out. Satisfied he had done what he had set out to do Eoghuan walked back to stand by Finian, who was grinning widely.

"Way to make it with the in-law's brother." Finian teased, earning him a friendly shove from Eoghuan.

"Your just jealous brother." Eoghuan smiled.

"Yes I am, no worries though, she might have a sister." Finian winked.

"She does not. So Eoghuan, you believe my niece to be your anam cara do you?" Frode interceded, his face stern.

"You heard?" Finian asked surprised.

"Yes, young hunter. It is a common misconception that our talents lay only in magic. I can assure you our hearing is nearly as good as yours, and as my strengths lay within water manipulation and it just happens to be raining, your conversation was clearly relayed."

"Oh Shit, sorry brother." Finian said, shrugging his shoulders, and patting his brother on the back in apology.

Not sure what to say, Eoghuan just stood looking uncomfortable, that he would rather be anywhere else but here was clearly evident. I kindly redirected the conversation.

"Have you discovered how she was taken?" I asked.

"No, it still remains a mystery, she was well within the borders of our largest town." Havardr confessed, his eyes betraying the alarm all the Vanir must share concerning Asta's abduction.

"Your seers could not offer an explanation?" Ansgar asked.

"When they have attempted to search, they are greeted with shadows. They saw the culprits enter the town, but they held no form and travelled along a different plain. They appeared to have no definition. All they could determine was that the kidnappers belonged to the shadow, their intentions malicious." Havardr revealed.

"If creatures from the other realm are aiding Fenrir's disciple's, it does not bode well." I said, wondering what to make of the news.

There is a reason why we all fear Fenrir's release, aid from the other side only suggests he is close to broaching his escape.

"Aye, such is mentioned in the prophecy." Aengus grumbled angrily.

Mention of the first Warg always did anger him, I didn't blame him, it was Fenrir's slaves after all that viciously murdered his parents, and the reason why he became a hunter in the first place.

"Has any one spoken to Ragnar? The king refuses to bow to anyone, including Fenrir. If his people are following the dark lord, then surely, he would want to know and fine those responsible? Even acknowledging Fenrir as a power would be considered treason in his court." Ansgar scowled.

"Of course we have. Ragnar was more than displeased to discover his demons were in league with the dark lord. I thought he was going to kill everyone in his court when our seers showed him what they had seen. He was literally dragging everyone in his realm in for questioning, even the younglings. He has promised that when he discovers those responsible he will allow us to question them, so long as we give them back for him to decide their punishment and fate, which if his reputation is to be believed, won't be merciful or short lived." Runa shared, her face almost concerned for those the demon king would discover.

I did not share the same concern, but then I am not Vanir, there is a reason why they are nicknamed hippies. Personally, I would have Fenrir's servants burned a thousand times over and not share even a moments worth of regret for making the decision.

"In relation to the prophecy has it yet been discovered who or what the sun and moon is, and why the destruction of such will free Fenrir from his prison?" Finian asked, surprising me.

He actually bothered to read the prophecy, I had only asked him several hundred times. Knowing the hunter, he had probably read it the first time, his whole denial some form of self-humour. His grin aimed directly at me annoyingly declared it was the case. Abating the urge to thump him, I scowled murderously instead, his brother wincing at the gesture.

"I told you he wouldn't find it funny." Eoghuan said to his brother.

"No, but I do." Finian replied, his grin widening.

"Urm not to interrupt, but yes we believe we know who the sun and moon is and why their destruction will release Fenrir. We have notified all the species to find the young person whose name we believe translates to mean the moon. We now know that Aelius, the last of Jörg's bloodline, a Vanir who sat upon our highest council, was the 'sun', her name translated to mean just that. With her death, one of the seals to his prison was destroyed, we have reason to believe that Hati was the one responsible for her death.

The child, whoever they may be, is the last blood descendant of one of the other eight species who aided our cause, with their death the last seal will be broken, and he will be freed. We do not know from where he or she hails but we have been searching since the very hour of its birth. So far, we have remained one step behind it. We noticed that others besides us are searching for it also, and as such it has not remained static, and is always on the move. It is only by the fates that it is still alive." Havardr said, his face unreadable.

"A name that translates to mean the moon isn't much to go by." Finian grunted sarcastically.

"You are right young one, but it is all we have to go on, that and the child is different, in the sense that it belongs to no one species." Runa added.

"Wouldn't that make it easier to locate as its signature would be unique." Aengus asked perplexed, his mood foul.

Even with Donna AWOL and the presence of the Vanir irritating him, Aengus didn't care much for the rain and it was raining heavily, ironic really since he comes from Scotland, where it is always raining. I on the other hand have always loved the rain and the scent that accompanies it. It is no wonder then that my anam cara would carry the same scent, woodland under the cover of fresh rain. The thought unconsciously brought up her image and subsequently a horrid pain formed in my chest, the guilt of my betrayal re-surfacing.

"You would think so, but no, it is like finding a needle in a hay stack, and the world is the haystack. With transport so readily available, the child can be on either side of the world in less than a day. Also, we cannot see it properly, it's life force hidden behind a veil similar to what the demons have been using." Runa continued, her eyes betraying her frustration.

It was vital that this child be found. The prophecy was clear and as a Vanirian prophecy had never been wrong, it was to be believed and feared. The words of which have been ingrained within my mind since a child, as it is the case for all the Keltoi.

And the sons of Fenrir will rise in power, each raising an army that stems from the very pits of darkness from whence they were born.

Both will seek the sun and the moon, each with their own purpose. Should the sun and moon die by their hands, Fenrir will be released from his prison and the stars will disappear from the sky, for no light can withstand the darkness he will bring in his wake. The earth will shake violently, trees will be uprooted and mountains will fall, causing all bonds to break. Fenrir will go forth with his mouth opened wide, his upper jaw touching the sky, his lower jaw the earth and flames will burn from his eyes and nostrils, destroying the earth with his wrath. Later he will arrive with his armies where the final battle will take place. The blood moon will wane, and all will be enslaved to the mighty wolf, no man, no longer, can call himself free.

It was a prophecy that all immortals knew and one that begrudgingly we banded together to prevent from ever being fulfilled, the Vanir acting as our mediator, a common ground so to speak. The only thing we all agreed on besides the importance of one's soul mate and the importance of remaining separate from humans.

"How close have you come? Can you even describe it?" Finian asked.

"No, every time we have come close enough to see, another immortal has interceded, obscuring our view." Frode answered, his studying gaze fixed on Eoghuan the entire time.

Did he disapprove of the hunter for his niece? Or was he merely trying to gauge his manner?

"Another? A protector?" Eoghuan asked, no longer seeming uncomfortable but instead resigned.

"We believe so." Runa said, while searching the alley, her eyes resting on a crow that was perched on the top tier of a fire escape.

"The others have arrived." She smiled, the crow flying off with a croak.

"About bloody time!" Aengus moaned, his face set in a disapproving scowl.

Scanning the opening of the alley, four Keltoi silently emerged, their eyes, alert and mistrusting, were hidden beneath the clouded hue of our kind.

"Michael" I called in greeting, my voice commanding.

"My lord." He replied, drawing closer.

The hue within his eyes dissipating, revealing iris that were only a few shades lighter than the grey cloud that had moments ago hidden them. The new hunters bowed low, as was the proper greeting when standing before their king. Sticking to etiquette and remembering why I disliked the formalities of being the Keltoi's overseer, I returned their gesture with a slight nod of the head.

"What took so long? Look as me, I'm sodding soaked through and it smells rank here." Aengus grumbled, his broad accent making the statement almost undecipherable.

"Buffalo may be considered New York, but we had to get a plane to get here, we did not detour if that is what you imply Aengus McCormac." Michael smiled, his shoulders relaxing.

Moving to take Aengus's hand, they shook and embraced.

"It is good to see you old friend." Aengus said warmly, his mood greatly improved.

"As it is you. It has been too long."

"You will have plenty of time to get reacquainted after I have my anam cara back." I scowled impatiently, I had already wasted enough time, if we were spotted they may already be expecting us.

"Of course my lord, apologises." Michael dipped his head, his manner diplomatic.

"Everyone ready?" I asked without waiting for them to follow.

"Always." Finian announced loudly, the undertone venomous.

The house or rather sky scraper that housed Vladimir Tepes and his coven was constructed from head to toe black glass. The highly reflective surface mirroring the moon, when it briefly reappeared from behind huge storms clouds that had dominated New York's city's sky line. A human would no doubt believe the buildings dark finish was merely an architectural design, but really it was how they filtered the sun's rays, making the building a safe haven for them to live and convene. Knowing the vampires as cunning and resourceful they probably had underground safe houses and access to the tunnels that run beneath the city's streets.

"There are cameras everywhere, they know we are here." Ansgar said, his eyes scanning the area.

"Is everyone in their place, the building surrounded?" I asked, not responding to his statement.

I was aware of the fact already.

"Aye, but you know as well as I, they have secret means of escape." Ansgar replied, his tone cool.

"I will allow them five minutes to come out, if they do not, then we will go to them." I hissed angrily.

Vladimir must've known that Mara was my anam cara, the girl Gabriella would have informed him, she would have too. Mara is a queen not only to the Varúlfur but to the Keltoi. Keeping her from me would leave me no choice but to incite war against the Nosferatu. It was the last thing either side should want, especially when Fenrir's breath lingers on our necks. The large electric doors started to open, pulling me from my thoughts.

"My lord. Greetings. Lord Tepes welcomes you and invites you and your men to join him." A blond-haired woman announced from the door way, her slender frame protected from the rain beneath a large abstract awning.

"Ansgar, Havardr, you will come with me. The rest of you will remain here." I instructed, allowing my bloodline, my title, and my power to blaze around me angrily. It was a show of power, usually I abhorred the practice, but this was political and as such a necessary display of strength was required. It was expected, and Vladimir would do the same. My mother used to call it peacocking, I guess it was similar, after all, I did aim to win the girl. I smiled inwardly at the prospect of seeing Mara, even though she was livid with me. The idea of seeing her made me feel elated, I missed her, and wanted to look upon her desperately.

Entering the tall building, the furnishings were as I expected them to be, lavishly expensive. Art that stemmed from the regency period dominated the modern finish, and created the scene. The grand hallway doubled as a security check point, which with the exception of two guards standing behind a desk was entirely empty.

"This way please." The woman said, her attire similar to that of a secretary, but with a more carnal resemblance.

Following, our footsteps echoed loudly on the highly glossed marble floor, our wet state leaving a trail of water in our stead. Stopping in front of the elevators the women used a key and opened the doors.

"After you my lord." She spoke softly, her use of the English language crisp, her pronunciation suggesting she had lived in London for some length of time before her move here.

As the lift started it was just as I expected, the lift went down. Unlike normal high-rise buildings, the pent house in this instance would be found deep underground, the lesser vampires living on the top floors closest to the sun, and the possibility of exposure should the worst befall the building. As the doors opened, the woman glided out, her footsteps increasing in speed as the need to mimic human behaviour was no longer required. Able to follow step easily we past room after room until we eventually arrived at what was the modern-day equivalent of a throne room.

"Welcome Conlaóch Tiarna of the Keltoi. It is a pleasure to have you in my house." Vladimir announced, his voice still retaining the lint afforded those born in Romania despite his centuries long absent from his homeland.

"Vladimir." I answered, minus his title.

He was shielding his thoughts and it was annoying me. Smiling in response to my slight, he sat quietly, his blues eyes calculating. He was nowhere near as old as I, but his cunning and ruthlessness ensured his rise to power was swift and permanent, none of his kind would dare move against him but not for the same reason my people wouldn't move against me. The vampire's wrath was legendary, they feared him more than they respected him. Clean shaved and immaculately dressed he didn't look like the picture one would paint of him, but if you looked closely enough you could detect the danger he concealed so effortlessly. I saw it, and those who didn't would quickly be considered prey.

"Since you have misplaced your wife I will forgive you your rudeness hunter, but only because I happen to like her and despite her insistence she wants nothing to do with you, I doubt she could fight the bond forever. When reconciliation takes place, I do not wish to be on her bad side." He said arrogantly, a smirk evident in his eyes as opposed to his mouth.

As a hunter, I wanted nothing more than to run my sword through his smug face, but as a ruler, I could not. I knew he was playing games, the question was what kind of game was he playing? Frustrated and annoyed, I said nothing, my expression unreadable.

"Where is she?" I asked, attempting again to break through to his mind.

Given my age and his lack of, he couldn't keep me out forever. It was a matter of time and he knew it. Why was he stalling?

"With my daughter, Gabriella."

Daughter? She must have gained her mother's looks, I failed to see the resemblance. A truthfully answer but one that didn't disclose much.

"And where is your daughter?" I asked, unable to keep the irritation from my voice.

"At present, I do not know. I could send someone to look for her, but it could take a while." He said studiedly.

Again, the truth but the feeling he was hiding something was growing steadily.

"Tell me what colour hair would you say my wife has? I have yet to decide on the exact shade of it." I asked him, a creeping suspicion racing along my skin, my instinct once again aiding me as it has my entire life.

"I do not notice such things." He lied, the stench of it humming unpleasantly around me.

"Your first lie prince Drăculea." I accused, a flash of his true nature gleaming warningly in his eyes.

Recovering quickly, his face betraying nothing, he smiled wickedly.

"I have not yet been fortunate enough to have looked upon her, it is true. But you have already surmised as much."

"Who can tell me where she is?" I asked annoyed.

"I honestly could not say. Wherever they are, or wherever they're going, they did not share it with me."

"I find it hard to believe that your daughter would keep such information from you, and yet I know you speak the truth. It begs to question however, why she didn't tell you?"

"All women have secrets." He responded, angering me more.

"You are stalling, why?"

"Because a queen in whom I intend to grow better acquainted, asked it of me." He said, in a manner that was designed to provoke a reaction.

It worked, my temper stepping up a notch, a growl hovering in my throat.

"Your ability to keep me from your mind this long is impressive but we both know it is only a matter of time. Better you share now then have me helping myself to your thoughts" I practically snarled.

That Mara asked him was irrelevant, she had no idea the kind off danger she was in. She might be powerful but so was Sköll, and he had fought and won more battles then Mara has lived in minutes. I understood her anger towards me, understood the need to flee as she had always done, but whether she wanted me or not she would need my help, and like it or not I would stand beside her. Mara had risen quickly and was young, she had at her call an army of Keltoi and Varúlfur. It was no wonder the prince looked to gain her favour. If I were he, so would I, however his alliance would mean nothing if she's dead.

"I do not appreciate threats Conlaóch, as you may have heard. King or no, if you attempt it again in my house and in front of my people I will not let it go un-challenged!" He hissed, his upper lip curling upwards to form a smirk, his elongated fangs protruding wickedly.

"Mara is hunted by Sköll, she is not aware of this and as such has no idea of the danger she and her companions are in, as you can appreciate, the need to reach her is paramount. You may wish to consider whether you want your daughter so close to his prey." I said annoyed.

A glimmer of fear passed over the prince's face, his serene expression suddenly becoming enraged.

"And you didn't think to mention this immediately." He snapped, all pretence of etiquette forgotten.

His anger seethed, filling the room with a dark aura that made everyone suddenly uncomfortable. It was like a thousand spiders were running the length of your body, theirs legs scraping along your flesh, invading every conceivable orifice. Ansgar and I were unaffected by the illusion, but I could see from the corner of my eye that Havardr had been, his body shivering visibly as Vladimir projected his rage.

"I had hoped to find you forth coming." I replied dryly.

Instead of answering straight away Vladimir snarled, his eyes flooding with blood. The sight eerily chilling was one of pure and unadulterated wrath, the other vampires in the room, taking a few steps back.

"I told them not to tell anyone where they were going, including me… My sons are with them!" He hissed, rising from his seat.

"She is not in the city?"

"No, I am aware of every immortal in this city. I doubt they are even in this country." He said pacing, his fangs were growing increasingly longer, the prince failing to master his temper.

Not in the fucking country! Growling and restless, my mind raced. Where would she go? They would be stupid to return to Norway and Scotland, it's the first place I intended to send men, so where? Pacing just like the prince was, I tried to guess her movements. The Vanir would not harbour her, so Asta's family I could rule out. Siri was too young to have connections, and her brother so I heard was fuming to discover his sisters fate, he would kill the Lycans who accompanied Mara, maybe even attempt to harm her, although I doubt it since it was she who ensured his sisters freedom, but still, it was unlikely he would aid them.

As their queen, any of the Varúlfur throughout the world would harbour her, but again it was too obvious, both Mara and Hamish would have ruled it out as an option.

"Ansgar, are there places in Mara's memory that she would go, a place of safety?" I asked the hunter, who I could tell was also trying to determine their location.

"She is too intelligent to risk returning to any of them. Wherever she goes it won't be a place she has already visited." He said agitated with the fact.

"She could be anywhere in the world, I would have suggested a witch's aid in locating her but as she travels with one she is probably hidden behind a cloaking spell." Havardr offered unhelpfully.

Of course Mara is cloaked, the pain in the arse so called Donna is with her. If she wasn't Aengus's anam cara I would have her shovelling sand from one end of the beach to the other end for an eternity. Sighing distastefully, I studied the room trying to determine Mara's mind.

Watching Vladimir pacing the room was becoming increasingly annoying, as was the predicament we were in.

"From what I could garner through my brief conversation with Mara, she was exceptionally angry with you, some incident of betrayal that has hurt her greatly. This being said, and given her current vexation towards you, I have to believe she would go to the one place in the world in which she knows would aggravate you further. Hell has no fury like that of a woman scorned, so to speak." Vladimir said, turning to face us, his voice although underlined with venom was once again posed and calm.

He thinks Mara is being vengeful. It could be true given her current temper, but what kind of revenge could she hope to achieve in occupying a location? Unless… She wouldn't dare! I whipped my head around to face Ansgar's. The look in his eyes, mirroring my own, confirmed he had reached the same conclusion.

"She wouldn't?" I asked Ansgar, knowing the warrior had seen her thoughts.

"I warned you friend." Ansgar answered, attempting to maintain a straight face, his hazel eyes twinkling in delight at the slight Mara had predisposed upon me.

Snarling, I cursed loudly, the deadly sound filling the room. The word bitch hovered dangerously on my tongue, anger getting the better of me. Was she trying to bait me or was she just being clever?

Either way she needed to be taught a lesson, she had no idea the implications her actions could bring. The Keltoi had remained strong and feared because we stand and fight together. Every influential family, council member, hunter, and domestic, strive tirelessly for peace and unity. It was one thing for her to be angry with me and run, she was young and feared that which she doesn't understand. You could expect a bride so young, a queen so young to attempt to hide from her duties and the intensity of ones anam cara. But to deliberately usurp me in what should be our family home was a slight that could be damaging to the Keltoi. Men do not war with kingdoms they know are stable, but with kingdoms where there is unrest, like a kingdom in which their queen dislikes and outwardly defies the king, is a kingdom worth considering.

"Despite the implications of her actions, you have to admit it's brilliant, she will make a fine queen. That is, as soon as you have her under control." Ansgar said calmly, his face lined with humour.

"And if I fail to get her under control, she will become a fine enemy." I replied dryly.

Of all the men in the world, why me?

"There is that." Ansgar answered, his mouth twitching, a small grin surfacing and then disappearing just as fast.

Glad he finds it funny.

"Are you going to tell me where my daughter is?" Vladimir asked, his eyes gleaming menacingly, studied us in astonishment.

"Ireland." Both Ansgar and I answered in unison, before turning coldly and heading for the door.

"That's it? Ireland might not be a big country but it's big enough. Could you not be more specific?" He asked, his voice the calm it had been when first we entered, polite if not slightly arrogant.

"You have wasted enough of our time, I'm sure a man of your ambition and resources will figure it out." I sneered, not caring.

Ignoring a hiss of annoyance from the prince, we left the chamber, Havardr in tow when he finally registered us leaving. Looks like another long flight but at least this time, for the first time in over twenty years, I would get to see the home I love.

Warg

"What do you want Mara?" Gabriella asked, leaning out of the window to speak into a large metal box.

"The boneless bucket with the corn and coleslaw… and the green bottle." I replied, staring at the large board that doubled as an oversized menu.

"Who you sharing that with? Everyone else has ordered a chicken burger box meal?" She asked, her eye brows raised in a questionable arch.

Donna burst out giggling, the sound as always making me grin.

"Sharing? You're kidding right."

"It's just for you?" Gabriella smiled.

"I'm hungry." I said, stretching back in my chair, nonplussed.

"Ok." Gabriella giggled, ordering my food.

We had just left Dublin and were heading to county Mayo, which according to Hamish Col owned half of, along with substantial acreage across the rest of the country, including Northern Ireland.

So far, the scenery had been stunning, everything was so green and vibrant, despite being in the throes of autumn, and the ground flat one minute was disrupted by vast hills and magical forests the next. It was beautiful! It was also heart breaking, as it reminded me of Col.

After landing at Dublin and waiting for Lucian to return with the cars he brought. Donna decided to tell me why Col had done what he had and read my mind. Warg's as I now know are nothing short of evil, which explained a lot given my dark tendencies. But worse than that, I was the granddaughter of Fenrir, who is literally the big bad wolf that every immortal fear's. He was the first Warg and the creator of the Varúlfur, a demi God who favoured anything dark, twisted, and destructive on a, 'apocalyptic' level. I always knew I was tainted, that I was cursed, but now I understood the full extent of my heritage, it is a legacy of blood, of death. My grandfather is the son of Loki, the Norse god of mischief, a troublesome and untrustworthy God who enjoys nothing more than creating chaos. Probably why Fenrir is what he is, Loki's design and goal, offspring that would piss off the other Gods, disrupt the order. Fenrir is destined to enslave the world, and is the epitome of all that is evil, dark, corrupted, the first wolf, the wolf that every living being should fear. Which means my father, who wants me dead, is one of Fenrir son's, Hati or Sköll, both of whom are just as twisted as their father but not yet as strong. Instead of the knowledge giving me much needed closure, it only presented more questions.

How does a Warg and a Vanir have a child when neither can understand nor comprehend the other? The only possibility I had reached so far is that my mother was raped and being so kind hearted decided to keep me. I asked Hamish what he thought but he didn't believe the brothers raped, apparently, they preferred mass murder to carnal interludes. He also said that to the best of his knowledge I was the only offspring he had ever heard of, and a child of that linage would generally not go unnoticed. He decided that I was probably a mistake that somehow managed to get away. I doubted he was far off. From the look of pity I received from the others when Hamish told me, I assumed that such news was supposed to make you sad, injure me somehow, but in the manner one would suppose of my kind, Warg, I felt nothing. I had learned long ago I wasn't wanted, knew that my birth was tragic and unnatural.

"Mara! Stop it or I will hex you, now that's tragic, a furry bum for the rest of life, nae pretty!" She winked.

Was she serious?

"Absolutely! Now, I really think it's a good idea to stop off in Galway for a shopping trip. It will nae do turning up at Conlaóch's castle dressed like that. He may nae call himself a king, but he is, and to have his queen dressed in jeans and an Irish rugby shirt you purchased at the airport gift store is nae going to cut it. And besides, we did promise Siri a night out! We both know that Col will nae be letting you leave his sight while you're in heat." She beamed "Or his bed!" She smiled suggestively.

Bed? Not likely. I might not want to kill him anymore understanding the reasons for his betrayal, but I was still angry with him. He could have just asked me about Fenrir, he didn't have to invade my mind. He didn't trust me, and more importantly, he broke his oath less than an hour after making it.

"Aye true, but men are a simple people, we cannae be too harsh on them. Just milk it for all its worth, I would. I reckon you could get a years' worth of favours for that infraction. Breakfast in bed, massages, unlimited credit card allowance. If you play it right and bring it up at the right moment you might even get two years, at least." She smiled mischievously, her mind racing.

"Me too! 'I can't believe you did that Col, you really hurt me. I trusted you. Classic, two years at least." Gabriella added, her younger brother Seth grunting in response.

"If you want nice things all women have to do is put out, if you know what I mean." He winked, earning a disgusted look from both Donna and Gabriella.

"And you wonder why you can't keep a girlfriend. Honestly, I worry about you. Treat a woman good and she will do just about anything for you." Gabriella declared, her eyes reproachful.

"I heard that if you treat them mean you keep them keen." He interjected, his face serious.

"Aye, and how's that working for you?" Donna grinned.

Mumbling something under his breath, he didn't answer, choosing instead to focus on the road ahead.

Lucian had purchased two brand new 4x4's claiming they were untraceable, unlike a rental, and necessary for the roads we were going to be traveling on. Since we couldn't all fit in, and deciding it was better that I didn't travel with Hamish, we split up, Donna and I traveling with Gabriella and her brothers, and Hamish and his generals escorting Siri and Asta.

"So, Galway, yes or No?" Donna asked again, her eyes widening as she waited for my decision.

I did promise Siri I thought with a sigh.

"You're the best! You will love it!" She squealed delighted, Gabriella joining her in her rapture when she realised why Donna was so ecstatic.

Wincing at the sudden rise in pitch, I cursed.

"Oh sorry." Donna whispered, her excitement skilfully diverted to her face and the huge smile that adorned it.

What was she going to dress me up in this time? Tutting, I knew I was being reckless, I should be staying away from crowds. I was in heat, and who knew when I might flip out and get needy again, I already felt twitchy and irritable, which I was beginning to associate with an impending episode of 'I need sex or I will kill you'.

"Nae worry, it will all work out." Donna said innately happy.

I hoped so, because I really didn't like how it felt betraying Col. Well, physically I loved it but mentally it was a different matter. At least I wouldn't morph into a wolf, I guessed that at least I had gained better control over.

"You might want to tell Hamish our new plans. Better it comes from you, that way he will nae argue." Donna grinned.

She was likely right, which reminded me I really needed to look into the reason why the Varúlfur hate witches so much.

"Hamish." I called mentally, confident that I could reach his mind, despite the fact he travelled behind us.

"My queen?" He replied, his words clearly formed.

"We are spending the rest of the day and night in Galway before continuing on to Ashford castle." I announced in a manner that broached no argument.

"As you say my queen. May I ask why?"

"I promised them a day out, it may be the only opportunity I have to grant them their request for a while." I explained, resigned to the idea.

"Very well, I will book a hotel." He replied dryly.

He was still annoyed with my decision to go to Col's instead of hiding nearby. It was his opinion that despite Col's reasons for reading my mind, it was still an infringement of the worse kind. But then Hamish had no reason to fear my nature as the Keltoi did, or the world for that matter. I was his queen and exactly what the wolves had hoped for, powerful. The trouble was, I never intended to be queen, and I didn't have a clue how to be one. As to whether I'd be what they needed was highly debatable, if I lost myself to the temptation of darkness, I would make Leif appear no more than a child attempting to play grown up games. I sighed, exasperated with everything. How do you go from alone and un-friended to a queen of two completely different species in less than a week?

"Fate." Donna scowled. "And she is nae done with you either." She whispered, her eyes glazing over with that same white film that indicated her use of magic, of a vision.

"What did you see?" I asked, a sudden chill racing along my skin warningly.

"I need to think on it, I do nae wish to be wrong again." She said thoughtfully, a small glimmer of fear laying within the depths of her eyes.

Did she fear being wrong or did she fear what she saw? Trying to study her face she suddenly changed her whole demure and smiled widely, her fear replaced with joy. She didn't want me to garner her thoughts, annoyed, I stared as her murderously.

"This time I think we should go for the whole ensemble. Short navy dress with lace detail, stockings, suspenders, the lot." She exploded, the sentence pulling a groan of protest from my lips.

Really? Stockings, why? She's so good at averting my thoughts. How does she do it?

"Takes longer to undress you." She said mischievously.

"Well that's a stupid reason, all you have to do is hike up her dress and pull her underwear to the side, then…" Seth Interrupted, gaining a hard slap around the back of his head courtesy of Gabriella.

"Will you shut up? Animal!" Gabriella hissed loudly, her face aghast.

"You have much to learn little brother. Undressing them only ever increases the pleasure." Lucian said, his only sentence throughout the entire journey.

"How does undressing them increase pleasure, other than the fact their naked giving you better access?" Seth asked curiously, his expression doubtful.

"Anticipation, suspense, and seduction, if done properly only fuel the climax. Take your time and be attentive and you will discover that they will do almost anything you want, no matter how taboo." Lucian said thoughtfully, his attention never leaving the road.

"Anything?" Seth spoke to himself, his face speculative.

"Please don't talk about seduction." I growled, my mind only too eager to dive into the gutter, my body more so.

"Apologises." Lucian offered repentant, his eyes lingering on me through the rear-view mirror.

He was concerned.

"I'm ok." I said for his benefit, and maybe for my own.

"She will be fine." Donna said hugging me, her presence reassuring.

My life's a mess!

"Your nae the only one to think so. Make what you can of it while you can and hope that tomorrows a better day." Donna said seriously.

Make the most of it? How do you do that?

"By nae dwelling on it longer than needed. And occupying yourself with the things you enjoy." She continued, helping herself to my thoughts.

Grunting, I pondered her words. Doing the things I enjoy. What did I enjoy? Fighting, knives, welding, reading, swords, explosives, Col undressed, Col's Kiss, Col's touch, Col's tongue, Col's…

"Aye, well it might nae be best to think about him at present. It's getting a bit hot in the back here." Donna giggled.

Growling in irritation I opened the window, allowing the cool autumn air to infuse the car.

"How much longer?" I asked, unable to keep the frustration from my voice.

"About forty-five minutes." Seth said loudly.

That long? Damn it, and what the hell happened to my chicken bucket?

"You ate it already."

Ate it? When? Donna snorted, pulling unnatural faces in an attempt not to laugh.

"I don't remember Gabriella even giving it to me." I said annoyed.

Was she winding me up?

"You talking about your lunch? I gave it to you." Gabriella said, pointing to an empty discarded bucket on the floor by my feet.

How do I not remember eating a whole bucket of chicken and the sides? Fuck sake! Donna wasn't helpful, her laughter never ceasing to end.

"You still have your lemonade." Gabriella grinned, quickly picking up on Donna's amusement, the sound contagious.

Glaring at Donna un-impressed, I took the green bottle from Gabriella and opened it to drink. I guess it would do until we stopped again. Taking a large swig, I wasn't expecting the explosion of gas that burst in my mouth. Catching in the back of my throat, and with nowhere for it to go, it gushed forcefully from my mouth and nose, stinging my nose as it exited. Choking on an invisible obstruction, I coughed loudly, 'choked' would be a better description. Gabriella, Donna, and Seth burst out laughing, it was so loud it startled me. What the hell!

"What kind of drink is that?" I asked un-amused, my words leaving my mouth on embarrassing gasps.

"It's carbonated, fizzy, pop." Gabriella chuckled, her eyes twinkling gleefully.

"What?" I asked, not understanding anything she had just said.

"It's a type of drink. Try sipping instead of gulping." She added as encouragement.

Staring at the green bottle I almost considered it.

"I'll pass. They have tequila in Ireland I assume." I asked hopefully.

Who invented a drink that explodes? Stupid humans.

"Aye, when it comes to alcoholic beverages you can bet they stock it." Donna promised, her voice strained from laughter was lightening my mood.

Twitching my nose as I attempted to rid the lemonade from it, I stared out of the window and decided I had had enough conversation for today. Donna must have yet again read my thoughts as she turned and started talking excitedly with Gabriella about shoes, and the promise of a manicure. What the hell was a manicure?

"Don't answer, I don't really want to know." I said mentally, focusing instead on the lush countryside and the odd sporadic house we passed. It was similar to Scotland in its un-spoilt beauty and as such had firmly ferreted its way into my heart. I could live here, the realisation making my heart flutter. I could live here with Col, when and if I forgave him… If I survive.

The high street was busy, large crowds of people moving from one shop to the other. The old cobbled streets were crammed almost to capacity, despite the fact evenings were dark by four 'o clock. We had been shopping for nearly two hours and I had hoped that they would have been bored by now, my hope was in vain. Surely the shops would be closing soon.

"Mara, come on, the only thing we need now is jewellery and the shops close in fifteen minutes." Asta claimed excitedly before walking into a wooden fronted shop that had rings of all descriptions shimmering in the window.

Fifteen minutes, result! Walking slightly more invigorated with the idea of shopping soon completed, I entered the store, pausing abruptly when a flash of green caught the corner of my eye. Turning to get a better looked, I studied the ring that had captured my attention. A green emerald sat in the centre of a golden heart, the heart beautifully encased within white gold hands. A crown filled with tiny diamonds sat on top of the heart, and shone brilliantly, the diamonds capturing every available beam of light. It was stunning, and skilfully designed.

"It's called a Claddagh ring, it's supposed to represent love, loyalty and friendship. The heart representing love, the hands friendship, and the crown loyalty." Lucian explained from behind me.

"Then it is something you would be given? As a gift?" I asked, my eyes fixated on the ring.

It was beautiful.

"Yes, from a lover, boyfriend or husband. That doesn't mean to say you can't defy convention and buy one for yourself, if you like it." He said, his head now in line with mine as he peered through the glass.

Not intending to I drew in a deep breath, his scent traveling enticingly along my scent receptors. I hissed, heat pooling. He smelt really good. Damn it. I stepped away and walked into the shop making sure to close the door, and him, out. I hoped the men weren't thinking of coming out tonight, their presence didn't ring well for the evening.

"Mara come and look at the necklace Gabriella just got for me, it's stunning." Siri exclaimed, her face full of excitement.

Grinning, I walked over to her and studied the item that was at present being placed into a green leather box with a silk ivory inlay. The necklace was yellow gold, reminding me of Siri's hair, and a large white diamond in the shape of a tear gleamed at the chains centre.

"You compliment it well." I said, touching the object gently.

"You mean it compliments me well" Siri chuckled.

"No, I mean what I said."

"Thank you." She smiled brightly, her hazel eyes warmly reflecting her happiness.

"Ok, I think we have everything, let's go and get ready for our big night out." Donna announced loudly, her expression one of enthusiasm.

Mentally grunting I walked back out, the girls in tow, their manner overly excited. To all the gods, please give me strength!

"Do nae be so dramatic Mara, for goodness sake, I promise you will love it, twenty odd tequilas or so and you'll be humming with bliss and dancing to your hearts content." She winked, a huge grin letting on more than it should.

Something was up. What you doing witch?

"It's nae good being so suspicious Mara, honestly." She smiled, walking right pass me.

Yeah, something was definitely going on.

The walk back to the hotel, so called the 'G' hotel, was surprisingly uneventful. Given Donna's questionable behaviour I half suspected things to jump out at me at any moment, the fact that nothing did was slightly disappointing. I really needed to get rid of some of my pent-up aggression. I'd never gone two days without a fight before, what was I supposed to do to vent?

"If you can wait in the foyer, I will go and get the keys and check in." Hamish grunted, his manner bored.

He didn't much care for shopping then either. Hope he likes girl's nights out I thought dryly.

"Ok, but try to be quick, we want to shower first." Gabriella ordered, whilst maintaining a second conversation with Asta.

Scowling murderously, Hamish moved off to the front desk and checked everyone in. This was by far the nicest hotel I had ever been in. Everything was modern, clean, and expensive. Trust Hamish to book us in here, he knew full well that Lucian would be forking the bill.

"As well he should. Nae only are you a guest but we would nae be here if it was nae for the princess's error." Hamish spoke privately.

I must have spoken my thoughts aloud. How many times had I done that?

"A few." He responded, his voice containing a hint of humour, his face at the desk revealing nothing.

"I would have ended up here at some point anyway."

"Because it's Col's home?"

"Yes."

"He does nae deserve you or your loyalty."

"And you do?" I asked amused.

He kidnapped me in the first place, knowing full well Col was coming for me, and for no other reason than to produce offspring for him and his pack.

"Everything I have done, I have done for the love and betterment of my people. I may nae deserve you Mara, but I would be loyal."

"Because I'm your queen?"

"No, because I know your worth, and because I understand your nature, your wolf. I accept it, admire it even. Unlike Conlaóch who will seek to prevent her rising, I will welcome and honour it."

"Hamish, I cannot remember everything, but from what I can recall, when I killed Leif, I enjoyed it. I toyed with him, revelled in his misery. You cannot honestly welcome that. The beast that resides within me is no different than Lief's."

"Perhaps, but you overcame it, you came back."

"No, I didn't Hamish, Col brought me back." I sighed, exhausted with everything.

"And this is what Col told you?" He hissed annoyed, the sound reverberating around my head.

"No, Donna told me."

"I do nae understand why you trust the witch so." He spat venomously.

"She is my friend and has done nothing to warrant my mistrust." I fumed, irritated with his tone.

"She is a witch, if nae for them the Varúlfur would be free. They serve only their own interests." He said reproachfully, his eyes pained.

"What do you mean?"

"We were never blindly subjected to an alpha's will until a coven of witches cursed us to be so. Cursed us to have no choice but to follow our rex, Fenrir, Leif, you, or anyone else who proves to be stronger than ourselves." he said annoyed.

No wonder they hated witches, they had made them slaves. Not sure what to say in response, I took a moment to process.

"I'm sure it can be fixed. I will speak to Donna, she may know of a way to reverse it." I said finally.

If they could use magic to enslave they must be able to use it to free.

"You think we ourselves have not already tried to do so, we have been searching for thousands of years. The spell was cast so as never to be broken." He replied

"Everything can be broken Hamish, and it just so happens I'm good at breaking things." I smiled, garnering me a smile in return.

"You are nae concerned that in freeing us the Varúlfur may nae follow you?" Hamish asked, his gaze studying.

"No… My wish was to kill Leif, securing my own freedom and the freedom of the others. Being queen is not what I wanted, I will find a way too free you, then the wolves can govern themselves" I said truthfully.

Hamish smiled. Raising his hand, he pushed back a fallen strand of my hair, the gesture gentle. Lingering, he stroked the edge of my cheek, his golden eyes piercing.

"It is noble gesture to give power back to the Varúlfur, but a misguided one. Even if you found a way to free us, as the one who orchestrated our freedom you would secure their loyalty forever, they would nae wish for you to abdicate the throne." He said with absolute surety.

"How can you be sure? I am not a Lycan after all, not to mention, I'm a blood descendant of Fenrir." I cursed, slightly frustrated.

I really don't want to be a queen.

"Because I would wish for you to remain queen." He replied

"What you wish and what others wish will not be the same Hamish." I grinned.

"Aye, but they need only spend a moment in your company to realise what you are, what you can bring for the betterment of our people. You were born a queen Mara and have shown repeatedly that you will nae bow to anyone, nae even to your soul mate. You do nae have any weakness, you're strong. You are already a great queen."

"Everyone has a weakness Hamish, but thank you. It is nice to know you have confidence in me, perhaps I will make you the leader in my millennial long vacation."

It was a good idea if his prediction turned out to be right. A queen who appeared once every thousand years, that could work.

"I have nae wish to be rex, it was only ever an option because I could nae allow my brother to remain in power." He said seriously.

Taking the card keys from the receptionist, he handed one to me.

"What is it the Varúlfur want?" I asked, Hamish turning to look at me.

"You really want to know?"

"I would not have asked if I didn't."

"Very well. We do nae want to be known as the brutal savages of the immortal races. We do nae want to be portrayed as mindless beings who have only one mind, the mind of our leader. We want to be free, to make our own choices, to be seen for who we really are." He said passionately, his chest filling with pride.

"And who are you Hamish?" I asked, no longer aware of my surroundings, my focus solely on his impending response.

"I am a man Mara, who is capable of more than just brutality. I love my kin, and my kind. I value our traditions, value loyalty and friendship. I want to be defined as more than just the stigma that has been placed upon us, upon me."

Not sure what to say, I stood staring, my gaze not leaving his. What response was I supposed to give to such a statement? Still unsure what to say, I said nothing, choosing instead to place the palm of my hand over his heart. I could feel his heart beating beneath, just like mine was, just like all that lived and breathed. I knew what it was like to be slave, to be subjected to another's will. It is a life of fear, of shame and humiliation. How old was Hamish? How long had he, had all of them been enslaved? And as their queen was I enslaving them? By becoming their queen had I become like the beast? The notion didn't sit well, and left a sick feeling in my throat. Thoughts chaotic in nature filled my mind, my body frozen. I felt Hamish's heart still beating steadily beneath my palm, is it right to own it, to own his life? Do they fear me as I did the beast?

Could I change it, if I commanded it? They have to do what I say, what if I commanded them to be free? I guess there is only one way to know.

"Hamish, it is my wish for you that you will no longer be subject to my will or the will of any who come after me, that you will be free to choose for yourself, to make your own decisions and answer to your own conscience. I forbid that you will ever be bound by another again un-willing." I commanded, the words spoken with all the authority of his queen, a low hum of magic sizzling around my head.

"Mara, the bond to the alpha was forged from magic, it can only be undone by magic." He explained, raising his hand to rest upon the hand I held over his chest.

His expression was kind.

"But the fact that you would free me only reiterates what I already suspected about you." He whispered softly, leaning in, and kissing me gently on the forehead.

The gesture was unexpected, it was a side to Hamish I had not seen. It was chaste and gentle and so unlike his appearance and prior communications. It made me feel safe and I wanted nothing more than to remain as we were in that minute, hidden from the darkness I knew was coming for me.

"You are lost in thought my queen, what can I do to help you?" Hamish said gently, pulling me from my thoughts.

"Hit me, hard." I ordered, surprising myself, where was I going with this?

"What?" He frowned, equally as shocked.

"Hit me, repeatedly, until I black out." I insisted, an idea forming.

"I will nae hit you my queen." He said outraged.

Beating a woman was obviously not seen in the same light as rough sex I mused.

"I command you to Hamish, as your queen, as your alpha."

"No!" Hamish spat angrily "I will nae, nae ever."

"Are you disobeying me Hamish?" I asked, a small smile forming on the edge of my mouth.

"Aye, you damn right I'm disobeying you!" He hissed, not registering the importance of his statement.

Smiling broadly and overly proud of myself I walked off leaving him to figure it out, and to get ready for the evening. Just as I reached the elevator Hamish called.

"Mara."

"Hamish" I smiled, turning to face him.

He looked surprised and something else, an emotion I didn't recognise but truly wished I did. It made me feel elated, like a weight had been lifted, one that I didn't know I bore.

"I am free." He said cautiously, almost as though he couldn't quite believe it was the case.

"You are free." I replied happily, before walking into the waiting elevator.

Maybe tonight won't be so bad after all, one wolf down only several more thousand to go. More importantly it made me realise I could be whoever I wanted to be, I can choose who I am. I didn't have to be defined by the Warg and Vanir blood running in my veins. I am not Warg, nor am I Vanir, not really anyway. I would never belong to either race. I was a new kind of immortal, might as well embrace it I decided as the lift doors closed.

The Keltoi

After the events of the past week it was good to return to something that offered routine and a measure of control. The grounds as always were well keep, ancient trees in autumn colours dominating the private road. Driving up to my ancestral home brought a sense of peace, my home for over eight hundred years, I was glad to be back.

"You think Donna will be there waiting for us?" Aengus asked, a note of hope in his voice.

"I doubt it, but they will be close. Did you notify the guard to start looking for them locally?" I asked, glancing briefly towards Eoghuan.

"Yes, they have all received descriptions and are searching the surrounding areas." Eoghuan answered, somewhat distracted.

Nodding in acknowledgment I studied the huge castle as it finally came into view. It was just as I remembered it twenty years ago. The only difference was the cars that were parked out front. They were much better designed than the box shaped cars of the nineties.

"You happy to be home boss?" Finian asked, checking out a female we had just passed on the road, probably a tourist.

Now and again we open the gardens for the general population so as not to draw too much attention to the fact that cars are always coming and going. Ashford castle has stood for hundreds of years, since 1228AD to be precise, and as such generates a lot of interest from tourists, locals, and historians. Better to sate curiosity on our terms, then on theirs. It would be the last of the tourists in a few days. Then the gates would be closed for the winter, not to open again until the end of spring, and even then, only on select weekends.

"Yes Finian, it has been too long." I answered, just as we pulled up to the entrance.

No doubt I had a lot of work waiting for me. When we got out of the car two men came to greet us.

"Tiarna" they said, almost in unison, bowing their heads in greeting.

"My rooms are ready?" I asked the pair as I walked up the steps into the castle foyer.

"Yes Tiarna, everything has been arranged, including rooms for your guests."

"Good, thank you."

Bowing again they moved off to retrieve the rest of the baggage from the car.

"Welcome home Conlaóch" A deep voice called.

"Kyle, how are you old friend?"

"I am good, and soon to be a father." He replied, his happiness reflecting brightly in his eyes.

"Congratulations, Marie is well I hope." I smiled, taking his arm in a firm grip.

"Yes, she is well. I hear you have found your anam cara, that we finally have a queen." He grinned, peering outside towards the car.

"Indeed, I along with Aengus and possibly Eoghuan have been fortunate to find our anam cara." I admitted, not too eager to explain why they were not here.

Sighing inwardly, I waited for the question I knew was coming.

"They do not travel with you?" He asked surprised, his brow drawn together in a tight frown.

He was concerned.

"We lost them again." Finian said sarcastically, gaining him a hard push courtesy of Aengus.

"You lost your anam cara? Again?" Kyle asked confused.

How to explain the last week… Grunting in annoyance, I proceeded towards my study, making sure to glare murderously at Finian in the process.

"Finian" I called, knowing the warrior followed.

"Boss"

"Go muck out the stables, all of them, and groom the horses" I ordered.

He should know better than to open his mouth about such things, now everyone is going to want an explanation as to where my queen was and what had happened. What happens on a hunt, remains on the hunt, unless I say otherwise.

"What" Finian asked shocked, Aengus chuckling nosily.

"You really need me to repeat myself Finian?" I hissed.

Growling displeased, but wisely not arguing, Finian walked off. He was lucky, as punishments went it was mild. Should he open his mouth again however, he won't find me so forgiving.

"Conlaóch." Kyle called.

"Mara is young and has not taken to the idea of becoming a queen very well, she will be here shortly." I answered plainly.

No need to over indulge with the details.

"I see, and the other anam cara?" He asked, following me down the hall, his broad frame at ease in the large open spaces of the hallways.

"They travel together. Do not worry, they are with those who will protect them." I said, not wanting to discuss it further and not pleased with the knowledge that their protection consisted of four Varúlfur generals and two of Vladimir's sons.

Kyle must have picked up on my mood, as he didn't ask any more questions on the subject.

"Very well, I will leave you to settle in, do you need anything?" Kyle asked, pausing at the study door.

"Send Connor, tell him to bring his intelligence officer and tech team." I replied, sitting down behind the desk.

Just as I thought loads of work to sort through. Mentally sighing I leaned back in my chair, I hate paper work. Mostly it would be signatures as anything important was dealt with over the phone, but still, it was tedious. Nodding, Kyle left, Aengus, Eoghuan, and Ansgar sitting on various chairs within the room.

When the door shut behind Kyle, all eyes were on me.

"So… What's the plan?" Ansgar asked, pulling a book from the case behind him.

Good question I thought dryly.

"I'm open to suggestions" I said simply, signing the first of many documents.

"I think we should just wait here." Eoghuan said, redirecting his gaze from the window to meet mine.

"You think they will come here?" I asked sceptical.

Mara was pissed, I doubt it.

"Yes, Mara's in heat. It has been nearly forty-eight hours since… well you know." He grinned

"We all know what happens when one of her type goes without, I'm betting her companions will contact you to deal with it." He finished.

"Aye, is nae a bad shot." Ansgar added

"Your forgetting she travels with wolves." Aengus said, his response leading.

"Aye, if she travelled with just them I would be worried, but the women will nae allow for such to happen." Ansgar yawned.

The thought nearly made me snarl. If any of them laid a hand on her they would pay with their lives. What if they already had? The idea made me furious, would they dare? Hamish would.

"I agree with Ansgar. I do not believe they would allow it." Eoghuan said thoughtfully.

"I hope your right." I hissed, images of Mara and Hamish having sex hovering un-welcomed.

Shaking my head slightly, I tried to rid myself of the thought. Mara wouldn't do that, regardless of what I had done to her. She was my anam cara, I would not make the same mistake again, I would trust her. I did trust her.

"Aye, upon reflection, I reckon Donna would hurt anyone who dared make themselves available." Aengus said with a chuckle, his eyes proud.

Chuckling alongside Aengus, both Eoghuan and Ansgar nodded in agreement. I grinned, woe to anyone who pissed off the little witch. If this week taught me anything, it is not wise to anger Donna. I would wait for Mara.

"Very well, we will wait, however, I think it best the guard were still actively searching for them, just in case Sköll decides to turn up." I said, committed to the plan.

"Aye agreed." Aengus added, Eoghuan nodding in agreement.

"Aye, well, if we are all in agreement, I'm going to take a shower." Ansgar said, getting up to leave.

Not long after Ansgar left, so did Aengus and Eoghuan. After nearly two hours of signing my name, the pile of papers finally dissolved. Standing to leave, a knock sounded at the door.

"Come in"

Sitting back down in my chair, Connor and several other people entered the room, the intel and tech guys I assumed.

"You took your time."

Two hours to immobilise, I wasn't impressed.

"Apologies, we were waiting for Kieran to arrive, he does not reside on the estate." Connor explained, waiting for permission to sit.

He looked slightly alarmed but was trying to hide it, no doubt he could see I was displeased.

"You may sit."

"Thank you, my lord." He said, taking his seat, the rest of the men standing behind.

Eager to get out of this study and freshen up I didn't waste any time getting to the point.

"There is a high possibility of an attack." I said, catching their attention, all eyes on me.

"Here my lord?" Connor asked surprised, and a little doubtful, no one has attacked this castles in over five hundred years, the prospect obviously didn't sit well.

"Yes, my anam cara will be here shortly." I claimed confidently, hoping it was true. "She is being hunted by Sköll. As bold of a move it is, I have to believe he will attempt to take her from here." I finished, my fingers tapping furiously on the desk, my mood dangerously calm.

I couldn't wait to drive my sword through his foul retched heart. The thought almost pulled a wicked grin from me. It didn't, but it was close.

"I will double the guard immediately and with your permission close the gardens to the public." Connor said, his Irish accent nearly as broad as mine.

"You have it." I said, looking out of the window. "Also, I want the tech to constantly check flights to and from Ireland, ferry passage, hotels etc. You know what to look for, any unusual police reports, deaths, I want to know about it, and I want it checked out."

They would be looking for things the normal police wouldn't bother with, passengers that for no reason at all start behaving erratically or confused, maybe even having to be detained only to be released a few hours later without charge, their initial symptoms gone. Any of these things would indicate Sköll had travelled on that plane or other means of transport. It would give us a lead, and at the very least would allow us to anticipate his movements. There were only three known Wargs in existence, Fenrir, Sköll and Hati, and of course Mara is half Warg, but so far, she hadn't shown that her presence caused such symptoms to manifest in others. A Warg not unlike a powerful vampire projected their darkness, contaminating those around them. The stronger the mind the more you could withstand it, but for mortals it often caused erratic and sometimes violent episodes, temporary madness would be a better way to sum it up. However, unlike a vampire, a Warg cannot turn it off. It is common misconception that vampires belong to the dark. In fact, they lay somewhere in between, they are the shadow. A Warg is true darkness, so vile and malevolent is seeps from them like smoke from a fiery pit, tainting all that surrounds them.

"Of course, my lord, we will begin immediately." Connor said, his face fixed in determination.

"Good, that will be all."

When Connor and his team had left, I got up, walking out of the room. I was glad to see the back of the study, I was ready for a reprieve. I made it half way down the corridor when Finian came walking towards me, his face unreadable, and a little grubby.

"Boss" He called, meeting me at the bottom of the main stair case.

"Finian." I replied, my nose twitching.

The stench of horse manure was overwhelming, Finian's clothes covered in filth. Unconsciously, I lifted my hand to my nose.

"Is all done my lord." He said tiredly.

I have at least a hundred horses, he must have worked all out. Impressive.

"You know why it was asked of you?" I asked the young warrior, gauging his reaction.

"For complaining and for speaking out of turn." He answered passively.

"Good, now go and wash, you bloody reek."

I was satisfied he had taken his punishment seriously even though he was now wearing a cocky grin. Proceeding past him, Finian started walking beside me, his closeness, deliberately swamping me with his stench.

"Not by me" I ordered, trying to put some distance between myself and the young warrior.

Chuckling to himself he held his hands up in surrender, stopping, he signalled for me to go ahead of him.

"Sure thing boss."

Little shit, grinning, sure that he couldn't see the gesture, I went to freshen up.

A Night on the Town

Donna had turned our hotel suite into some kind of pre-party club, music blaring from something she called a docking station. The music was upbeat and contained no lyrics, bar the occasional one or two words that seem to be stuck on repeat. Frowning, I sat and finished off the left over Chinese food they had failed to eat. Donna, Asta, Siri, and Gabriella, dancing around the room in a half state of undress. Giggling nosily when Donna saw what I was doing she waltzed over and sat on my lap, nearly causing me to drop my chow mein. Clucking in annoyance, I glared menacingly towards her.

"Oh Mara" She chuckled softly in my ear, her demure somewhat unusual.

What's wrong with her? Her legs didn't seem to be performing as they should, she seemed unstable.

"Are you injured." I asked, visually checking her for any sign of damage, she didn't look injured, at least not outwardly.

"No, I'm nae injured, just a wee bit tipsy." She winked, signalling to Asta for another glass of wine. Tipsy? What did that mean?

"Tipsy?"

"Aye, well. Wine, spirits, beer, alcohol, it has an effect on the body." She smiled, one eye brow raised slightly as thought the action might help her focus.

"What kind of effect?" I asked, eying the two empty wine bottles I had just finished suspiciously.

"Nae anything bad, just makes you feel happy." She grinned.

She stood, retrieving a newly filled wine glass from Asta, almost immediately she started dancing again. Grinning at her behaviour I wondered why it didn't seem to be having the same effect on me. I could do with feeling happy. Forcefully being sat down and groomed, was a painless, but somewhat soul destroying means of torture, the only real benefit was having everyone here safe, and the food.

"You nae drank enough Mara, you're immortal, you need a substantial amount more than me to feel its effects." Donna called from the middle of the room.

Ah, I see. Standing leisurely, I went to stand by the bar which Seth had taken the liberty of filling, apparently the child bottles that came with the room were not adequate. Picking up a large bottle of tequila I began pouring it into a large glass that was sat on top of small the bar.

"Mara, that's a pint glass." Asta giggled.

"What? You were using it?" I asked her, unsure why she would need to mention it.

I know my education had gaps, but I knew what a glass was.

"Never mind." She added, a wide smile on her face.

Smiling back, my eyes brows raised questionably, I deduced that she must be tipsy too. Glass in hand, I started my own search for this so-called happiness.

Several large bottles later I was dancing with the rest of them, the music without words suddenly more appealing. The dancing as before was calming, I felt like nothing in the world should bother me... everything was blissfully perfect, well would be if I was naked and Col was doing that tongue thing, followed by the sex thing. I wondered what he would taste like in my mouth?

"The door, someone get the door." Gabriella shouted.

She was in the process of fastening on a ridiculously high pair of heels. Must be time to go I thought excitedly and dropping all thoughts of Col.

"I'll get it." I announced, walking bravely to the door, not a care in the world.

"Hamish, Sven." I grinned, pulling them into the room and giving them a hug before swiftly closing the door behind them.

"You're drunk." Hamish said, not able to stop a small smile from forming on his lush, very inviting mouth… Huh, his mouth… why was I still staring at his mouth?

Ignoring his comment and now a little heated, I went to go find the heels I was supposed to be wearing. I could feel Hamish and Sven eyes following my every movement. I wondered if wolves danced, jiggling around, swirling like the others were, the thought made me giggle, the sound making me pause. I just giggled, like a girl, like a girl who wears dresses and has different coloured nails. Does that mean I'm good, boring, normal?

"The cars are waiting." Hamish announced loudly, turning off the docking thing.

He smiled in my direction. I could sense his mood. He was amused, so was Sven. Must be a private joke, I wasn't getting it. All of us ready and eager to start our night, we headed for the door.

"Wait." Gabriella said loudly.

"I need to do a make-up inspection." She said, her face becoming serious before she focused in on all our faces.

"Ok, we're all good." She beamed, picking up her bag and ushering us out of the door.

Sven was the last to exit the room, making sure it was secured behind us. The journey down to the foyer was claustrophobic. The various perfumes all bunched up within the small lift made my eyes want to water. When the doors finally opened, I took a long deep breath. Walking out hastily, I was glad to be free of the thing. Asta linked arms with me as we made our way through the lobby towards the hotel's entrance. Seth, his brother, and the other werewolves were waiting by the cars, opening the doors as we approached. Slowly and lacking organisation we got into the back, the conversation easily flowing. It was nice. I was talking but without getting frustrated, and without getting a headache. I smiled as I took my seat and fastened the seat belt.

"To all the Gods, who would have thought getting into the car would be so damn difficult." Seth said on an exaggerated sigh before jumping into the front passenger seat.

"Oh, stop your whining." Gabriella laughed.

"They're in, be content with that." Lucian said, the smallest hint of humour lacing his voice.

"You decided where we're going yet?" Lucian asked Donna, his eyes finding hers in the mirror, all humour gone.

"Aye, Abbeygate street." She announced loudly, right by my ear.

Damn it!

"Oops, sorry Mara."

She giggled in apology and patted my leg.

Nodding, he started the car, Hamish and the others following in the car behind us. It felt strange this alcohol happiness, I knew I had stuff to worry about, but it just seemed somehow unimportant. All I wanted to do was dance and laugh despite the fact the smiling was beginning to hurt my mouth. Probably because my mouth had never used the muscles for prolonged periods of times, they just needed conditioning I thought with another quick giggle.

"You giggled Mara!" Donna squealed delighted, her face a picture of wonderment.

"Goal for the night, get Mara to laugh." Gabriella said, a gleeful determination twinkling in her eyes.

"Aye, I'm with you." Donna said loudly, leaning in with Gabriella to take a photo of us together on her phone.

"Hashtag, Mara giggled." Gabriella laughed.

"What?" I asked confused

"Hashtag." Gabriella looked at me. "You know, hashtag." She prodded.

Confused, I just pouted awkwardly.

"Never mind." She laughed again. "I will explain when I'm not under the influence."

Influence of what? Confused, my head fuzzy, I bit my lip and opened the window. It was late but much like Glasgow the air hummed with life, I could almost see the weaves of air around me like tiny threads that swam through the sky. Tonight was going to be good, I felt it. Instinct. My cheeks ached but I couldn't get the smile to leave. This happy drink really works. Content, I watched cars pass and listened to the distance and various tunes that flowed into the streets. I don't think I've ever felt this relaxed. Ever.

"STOP! Lucian stop." Donna shouted, making everyone but her grunt in response.

Rubbing my forehead, I turned to glare in her direction.

"I think you burst my ear drum." Gabriella said, twisting her neck, and rubbing at the ear closest to Donna.

Instead of apologising, Donna leaned forward in her seat, pointing out of the passenger side window.

"Here, Lucian." She said in deep concentration.

Satisfied they had stopped where she directed, she sat back, a huge smile on her face. Lucian and Seth got out and opened the doors, the other car doing the same.

Convening on the edge of the pavement, we greeted each other as though we hadn't seen each other in an age. It was weird, but I participated in it anyway.

"Right, ground rules, no cheating, no stealing and… that's all I've got." Donna broke off, walking gracefully, if not a little unbalanced, into the small court yard that hid the clubs entrance.

Siri, Gabriella and Asta shrugged their shoulders, smiles and grins covering their faces. After a few seconds, we were following Donna into the club, Seth, and Lucian up front and Hamish and the others encasing us from behind.

My heart racing, I entered the club, Hamish on my tail. The lighting and music drew me in. It was a different type of music then the music playing back in the hotel and in the club in Glasgow. It had a fast beat but also had a slow back ground beat, so dancing slowly or fast didn't seem out of odds with the song. It was good, really good, and it had lyrics you could sing to if you wanted.

"What kind of music is this? I asked, to whoever happened to be listening.

"A mixture, dancehall, pop, reggae, I guess." Gabriella smiled.

Instantly everyone started dancing, our bodies taking on a mind of their own. My eyes soaked up the atmosphere, the energy from the patrons infectious, beguiling.

Definitely a good night I mused. Walking past my friends to stand in the middle of the dance floor, the enthralling and varied beat made me feel… beautiful maybe, I don't know, aware of my body, whatever that is.

Ignoring the humans, I allowed the melody to move my body for me. My hips were loving this style of music, my mind more so. It was making me think of Col's deliciously ripped body and the feel of his mouth upon my flesh. I hummed with pleasure and wished him here, despite knowing I no longer liked him, or did I? Was I still mad? I couldn't remember, was I?

Closing my eyes, and licking my lips, I lost my train of thought, remembering instead the way he tasted, the memory making my stomach fill with heat. Little flutters of suspense ferreted their way across my frame as though something soft was being teasingly brushed against me.

A large hand found my waist. It held me tightly as though at any minute I might disappear. Opening my eyes Hamish stood before me. I smiled at him as I continued to dance care free, pulling him closer to me in the process.

Broad shoulders and golden eyes didn't object to my closeness. Moving closer, my hands rested upon his chest, my body turning slowly, my hips swaying. He hissed low, the sound sending shivers, that glided along my flesh and embedded themselves deep into my muscles. It felt so good, my body relaxing, my mind trapped in the moment. No other thought existed but the sense of touch, my body was on fire.

Col felt so good, his touch perfect. Another hand slowly made its way up the length of my arm, stopping at my neck. Gently he moved my hair, my neck fully exposed. A soft mouth hovered temptingly against it, a delightful breath making my heart pound chaotically within my chest. Heedfully, automatically, I pushed my hips further back, my back curving against him. I purred when Col's mouth finally landed on my neck, the gentle and suggestive stroke of his tongue pulling a heated moan from my lips. His kisses ceased, frustration weaving its way around my limbs, they felt heavy, cheated.

"Col" I whispered mournfully.

The hands that held me suddenly let go, the firm body departing. Irritated, I wanted to know why. I turned to find Hamish looking at me, his eyes pained.

"What's wrong?" I asked, trying to determine what had just happened.

I scanned the room for friends I knew were nearby, what had happened?

"You said Col." He replied, his jaw clenched.

Why was that an issue? Dizzily, my body aching, I realised something was off. A small breeze ran its way along my skin, I shuddered at a complete loss, where did Col go?

"Where did he go?" I asked Hamish, my question angering him.

Moving forward, he pulled my face towards his, his hands locking my head in place.

"It was nae his touch that fuelled your desire, it was mine… You must have known it was me." He breathed softly, his eyes pinning mine, searching for something hidden within their depths.

The closeness felt familiar. Confused, I stepped back.

"He was not here?" I puzzled.

I looked at Hamish for explanation, my mind spiralling, unable to hold form.

All emotion left Hamish's face. After staring at me for what seemed like a minute, he turned and walked away, leaving me standing alone in the middle of the busy night club. What just happened?

A new song sounded, and the thought was gone. Allowing the music to capture me, I started dancing again.

"Mara, I got your drink." A friendly voice called.

Slow is Good

The pressure from the shower felt good, hot water scorched my back, pushing the tension from my shoulders. Groaning pleasantly, I turned into the spray, my eyes shut, and allowed the hot jets of water to run over my face. Placing one hand on the steamed glass I was failing to rid the image I had of Mara from my thoughts. Her naked wet body was glistening as though we had just stepped out of the pool all over again. Without realising what I was doing I ran my hand along the length of my erection. Moaning with pleasure, my strokes firm, Mara's hot mouth came into view, her unknowing but curious eyes looking up at me. Perfect breasts swelled with need as she lay beneath me breathless, a drop of water traveling temptingly down her flat stomach, catching in the tight curls of her…

KNOCK KNOCK KNOCK…

"WHAT." I growled frustrated.

"Boss."

Damn it! Turning the water off, I opened the shower door and got out.

"What do you want Eoghuan." I almost shouted, grabbing a towel and exiting the bathroom.

"Hamish is on the phone." He called from behind the door.

Hamish. What does he want? Wrapping the towel around me, I opened the door. Eoghuan was standing there red faced. He must have run with the phone. Shit, Mara. Is she ok? What happened?

I grabbed the phone from him before he could pass it.

"Hamish" I snapped.

If anything has happened to her, I swear…

"Conlaóch."

Hamish said my name like it was toxic.

"Mara has need of you."

"She's in trouble?" I asked, pulling on some trousers, Eoghuan still hovering in the door way listening in on the call.

"She is safe, but in need of you."

"Be more specific." I snarled, reaching for a clean shirt. Bloody werewolf.

"Apparently, your treatment of her was nae enough to put her off you, nor is the fact that she is drunk. She wants only you, thinks of only you." He said, his tone suddenly becoming flat and unreadable.

Wait, she's drunk? Need… Growling low I understood the need. Images of her naked body came spiralling into focus. Instantly hard, I attempted to fasten my trousers. It was difficult.

"Where are you?" I grunted, the tension returning to my shoulders.

"Halo, Abbeysgate, Galway." He answered before hanging up.

"I'll get the car." Eoghuan said, grabbing his phone from my hands.

Not responding, I followed, my thoughts one minded. The possibilities of her need were endless, so many things could be done. Focus. I needed to get to her first. She was in heat, what bright eyed genius thought plying her with alcohol was a good idea. What if I wasn't in the country. My lust was now riding alongside fury. 'Nor is the fact that she is drunk'. Hamish's sentence came back to me. Was he hoping to make her more palpable by lowering her inhibitions. Growling dangerously, I knew the shadow had entered my eyes. Hamish was going to pay dearly, well as soon as my anam cara was placated that was, her needs first. With that thought, my mind quickly turned back to the gutter. Grinning wickedly, I was only too happy to fill that void.

After seeing me exit the castle with Eoghuan, car keys in hand, the rest of the team followed, piling into the back of the car, no questions asked. The hour it took to get to Galway was torturous. All I could think about was possessing her, so much so that when anyone attempted to ask something I couldn't bring myself to hear. I briefly recalled Eoghuan asking his brother whether he should talk to Asta at the club or wait in case she had been drinking also. Had Mara still been untouched I would have worried about that too, but she had been claimed, is my wife, is mine. She needed me, if I didn't fulfil her needs she would go elsewhere, the Warg that resided within her would make sure of it.

"This it is." Eoghuan announced, turning off the sat nav and peering out of the window.

I felt like I was on the hunt again, the true hunter coming forward, the emotions, mistakes made, love, need, all of it giving me direction. I needed her, not just physically, I needed her full stop. Getting out of the car I walked up to the club geared for war, I would win this battle, she would leave with me, she will not fight, and she would let me sate her desire, let me possess her mind, body, and soul.

Growling, aware of everything around me, I entered the club, the others at my heels. Donna's loud laughter caught my attention, where Donna was, Mara was. I turned in that direction, Aengus pushing in front of me, no doubt because he had heard her to. She was there in private booth, three vampires and a Valkyrie beside her, but no Mara. A small glimmer of fear caused me to scan the bar and back booths in case the need had become too much for her, and she had, as I feared, found solace in another. When I didn't see her, I let out a soft sigh of relief and continued towards Donna.

She was staring at Aengus, her face trying it's best not to reveal how happy she was at seeing him.

Donna stood up unsure, the vampires with her perceiving danger suddenly switched to high alert, their eyes filling with blood, their bodies poised for a fight. As much as I would love to see how that fight played out, I wasn't interested in them, I was here for Mara.

"Where is she?" I asked the witch, my voice deadly calm, was barely human.

"How did you know we were here?" She asked.

Hissing, my hunter despairing, volatile, I stared at her. Afraid, she shuddered and pointed towards the dance floor.

"She has been dancing since she got here, she's in the middle somewhere." She said, glancing back towards Aengus, her surprise in seeing us not yet leaving her face.

Walking into the large crowd of dancing bodies I felt for the bond and let it guide me towards her. After pushing through a multitude of people, I saw her.

She was beautiful, breath taking. Loose golden curls cascaded over a short navy dress that moulded to her curves and ended temptingly at the higher end of her thighs. She was dancing, her eyes closed, her body moving enticingly to the thrum of the music, swerving, and curling in a manner that had me moving towards her like iron to a magnet. Uncomfortably hard I couldn't see anything else, no one else existed. As though she knew I came for her she opened her eyes. Ethereal blue eyes meet mine as though there was nowhere else for them to look upon. Her mouth turned up into a smile that set my body alight, and like a predator, I bridged the gap between us, one hand claiming her waist the other gliding over her cheek to rest behind her neck. Her eyes were hungry, her mouth inviting, without a word being said, I lowered my mouth to hers, and kissed her.

Like heroin in a vein the kiss was ecstasy. Inflamed, I hissed, pulling her closer, until I was convinced no gap existed between us. The mould of her body fit mine perfectly, the heat between us unfathomable. I had held back before, conscious of her innocence, but tonight the hunter was relentless. Growling suggestively, I left the warmth of her mouth, my eyes blazing into hers. My hunter was challenging her to run, offering her the promise of bliss never ending should she heed, stay with us. My predatory intent coaxed her movement backwards. Slowly, my eyes not leaving hers, my hand gently guiding, we left the crowded floor and exited the club through the fire exit. Once outside, sure that none could witness, I claimed her mouth again, the action almost desperate.

She moaned against me, the sound tripling my pleasure and making me tremble with anticipation. Backed towards the hood of a car she halted her retreat, her hands exploring my chest and back hungrily, her breathless gasps enticing me to commit sin.

Lifting her with ease I sat her upon the cars bonnet, running my hands up her thighs. They were like soft silk, warm and inviting, and yet it wasn't enough just to hold her. Reluctantly, I broke away from her lips and the sweet taste of her mouth and arched her backwards, pulling her hips to rest upon mine. There are times when slow is good, but this wasn't one of those times. I wanted her badly, and I wasn't in the mood for gentle cooperation.

As though her thoughts mirrored my own she leaned forward with a seductive curl and sank her fangs into my shoulder, her fingers urgently pulling at the zipper of my trousers. I hissed tormented, the pressure from her bite sending my head reeling. Damn she was hot! I wanted to rip her clothing off and expose her perfect form, but the thought of anyone else looking upon her prevented me from doing so. Growling with annoyance, I wished we were away from the possibility of prying eyes. There was no way in hell I would be able to postpone the urgency in time to get her anywhere. I would have to take her here, then spend the rest of the evening… week, making sure I had tasted, seen, every inch of her flesh. The idea allowed my imagination to run wild. Would tying her up be considered imprisonment? I would make sure she enjoyed it. It would be torture for her, but of the pleasurable variety. Grinning at the notion, I lifted her from the bonnet so that she sat within my palms. Holding her tightly to me I hissed when her hands gripped me tightly, slowly moving up and down my erection. Every stroke pulled a groan from my mouth, leaning in, I claimed her tongue again.

Guiding her back against the bonnet I took her hands and forced them above her head. With one hand, I held her wrists in place, my other hand scooping beneath her to lift her up and down against me. I needed to be inside her, needed our bodies to be joined together. Damn it! This wasn't going to work, I was too tall, and the damn European car was too low down. Cursing, frustrated, I pulled her up to lean against me. Moving past the car, Mara held tightly against me, I couldn't help but breath her in. She grinned, a seductive curl to her mouth when I lent her against the brick wall, running opposite to the club. Lowering her legs almost reverently, I knelt before her, my eyes hungrily holding hers. Lifting her dress slowly I kissed my way up the tops of her thighs, taking more time when I reached the soft spot between her hip and groin. Fuck she smelled good, her heat and scent making me almost feral. Desperate to be inside her, my fangs erupted, the force of their arrival almost savage. Hooking my fingers through the edges of her silk lingerie I pulled them partially down, sinking my fangs into the soft curve of her groin. She screamed, pleasure escaping from every pore on her body, the sound and scent, feeding my hunger. I wanted to explore her more vehemently, place her legs over my shoulders so I could feast on her desire, but her need, my need, was far too great for pleasantries, foreplay was a no go.

Standing, I kissed her passionately, lifting her legs and wrapping them around my waist once more. Pulling the thin strip of silk aside I entered her body with deliberate force. The cry she emitted was heaven to my ears, her hiss of pleasure a balm of delectable heat that drove me wild. She's mine.

Entrapment

"Don't be gentle." I commanded throatily, and unnecessarily, he hadn't been thus far.

But still the need to say it was paramount. Growling low against my ear, the vibrations from the soft rumble, teasing, he whispered in an un-recognisable voice.

"I wouldn't dream of it."

With that he thrust once again, the wave of ecstasy that followed staggering. It was painful, but damn fucking good. Hissing my approval, I pulled his mouth back to mine, desperate to taste him. I moaned loudly as he continued to send me into wave after wave of unbearable and unrelenting pleasure, the likes of which coursing feverishly throughout me. Gasping for breath as the pressure built, I felt as though I balanced on the edge. I was so close to release, so close to earth shattering bliss, that my mind was on the verge of shutting down, my thoughts sluggish. I briefly recalled that this may not be the best thing to be doing, for a reason that was important, or still is important.

"With me Mara!" Col ordered, his voice dominate but thrilling, snapped me from the thought.

Meeting his eyes, I locked onto the green/grey depths that demanded my acquiescence. They brimmed with power and authority, the whole idea of surrendering my control to him, pushing me closer to the edge. No longer able to contain it, the fire blazed uncontrollably, my body painfully trembling when release finally rocketed throughout me.

With no breath in my lungs I couldn't scream like my throat seemed to think it should, instead, breathlessly, I dropped my head onto Col's shoulder, while he continued his torture, his closeness and ferocious energy claiming my entire being. Ownership permeated through the bond, and despite disputing it, my mind, my body, craved it with such clarity and acceptance I found myself dazed. What the fuck.

"Look at me darling." Col hissed, the fierceness of his tone both compelling and revealing.

He was close.

Raising my eyes in a dream like state, I met his gaze, his urgency evident as well as something else. A dark desperation, a need that was great and all consuming. I wanted to determine the need, wanted to understand what I was seeing, but like before it remained a secret, a forbidden piece of knowledge, I wasn't supposed to have. But I wanted it, wanted it like I needed air to breathe. It was so important I understood, so important that I have it, a tear fell from my eye in silent desperation. I felt it fall as Col finally found release, his body coiling tightly only to relax again, his roar of ecstasy echoing around me.

Time stood still, at least it felt as though time stood still, I can't remember how long we stayed connected, un moving, but it felt safe, felt right. Even as my thoughts seemed to refocus and absorb the situation, I didn't want to move. I had sex with Col, again. But I didn't regret it, even if I was still mad at him. I should be mad, at least that's what I thought, but some annoying buzz of happiness keep whizzing through my thoughts rendering anything too complex to diminish and loose form.

After holding me to him a minute longer Col reluctantly pulled away, lowering my feet back to the ground. Gently and in silence he straightened out my clothing. I almost wanted to smile at the way he was doing it, it was as if any sudden movement might ignite trouble.

"What you are doing?" I asked, amusement lacing my words.

"Rearranging your clothing." He said, his intellect studying me, his eyes on edge. "Were you crying?" He asked alarmed.

"What? No." I said, quickly wiping at my face to see if I had been. Was I? Maybe… Change of conversation was required.

"I want to put your cock in my mouth." I said with all seriousness.

Well that worked well, I grinned as Col's entire expression shifted, the look of his face a treasure.

"What…Mara." He hissed, the shadowed hue returning to his eyes.

"Damn it, don't change the subject." He said, trying to regain his composure.

"But I want to know what you taste like." I baited further.

Growling low, he swept me up in to an embrace that instantly cloaked me in warmth. I shivered when his mouth found mine again, the gentle stroke of his tongue driving me crazy. I could no longer claim I didn't like it, nor could I complain about others enjoyment of it. It was amazing, even minus the warmth that comes with Col's kiss I thought, remembering the kiss I had shared with Lucian. The kiss with Lucian! Shit! I cheated on Col. My guilt must have filtered through the bond as he suddenly stopped to stare at me.

"What is it anam cara?" He asked, those damn knowing eyes reading me.

I was tempted to not say anything, but I knew he witnessed the guilt I felt, and guilt could only mean one thing, I did something I wasn't supposed to. Damn it!

"Don't be angry." I said lamely, chewing on my bottom lip whilst trying to look as innocent as possible.

"Mara."

"Well you know I'm in heat and that the Warg in me makes me slightly aggressive and unpredictable."

"Yes." He growled deeply, dangerously.

"Well... It was a long flight to New York and my wolf started to get demanding and to stop me changing fully and risking the lives of everyone on the flight, including mine, because any damage to the cabin would have potentially caused the plane to crash... Urm."

"WHO! Who touched you." He hissed, his hands clenching into tight fists as power I had never seen him emit before came pouring off him dark and deadly.

"It was just a kiss...! There may have been stroking... but I tried not to, my mind was not connected with my body. It wouldn't listen to me." I said panicked, shit he was going to kill him.

"It was Hamish, wasn't it?!" He said far too calmly, his shadowed eyes blazing murderously.

Fuck, fuck, fuck.

"No, it wasn't Hamish" I replied, maybe too fast, as he quickly turned and stormed into the club, leaving me behind. Oh no!

"Donna." I screamed mentally, running into the club after him.

I should have made something else up, I should not have told him the truth. The power he radiated reminded me of my guardian Ti, how is it possible to masked that much power?

"Mara."

Donna answered just as I made my way towards the booth I had left her in, Col nowhere in sight.

"Col is going to kill Hamish, he thinks he kissed me. He didn't let me get as far as stating it was Lucian."

"You kissed Lucian! I knew something happened." Was her reply.

"Really Donna! That's what's important right now!" I said astonished, my eyes scanning the club for Col.

"Ok, I'm on it." She said, the connection somewhat weak.

I swear I heard her giggling just as the link ended.

I had just pushed my way through the crowd to reach the booth, when a large body came flying through the air, knocking two bystanders aside with it. Oh shit! I was about to make my way over to see who it was when Col came stalking up, his sword held high. His features were set in ice cold determination, the sight sent a slither of fear coursing through me. So naturally, I jumped in front of him, blocking his advance. Since when did I start doing such stupid things? Idiot! Stopping abruptly, I thought he was about to attack me, and I'm sure he would have, if not for the recognition of who I was reflecting in in his eyes.

"Get out the way Mara." He said smoothly

"I swear Hamish did not kiss me, I would not lie about it." I said desperately, stubbornly standing my ground.

He stared at me, his eyes wild, before finally lowering his sword and leaning in so close his controlled breath shimmered softly against my lips.

"But someone did, tell me who Mara, before I decide to kill all the men who travelled with you, just to be sure I got the right one." He whispered menacingly, truthfully.

He really would, he would kill them all. Because someone touched me. I wanted to smile but something inside warned that he wouldn't read it the same way I did.

"I will tell you, but I have terms." I said recklessly, moving if possible even closer to him, our mouths separated by a margin so small it was almost non-existent.

And just to ensure it didn't go horrible wrong I slowly and suggestively licked my lips. He hissed when he caught the gesture.

"Their death is non-negotiable." He snarled, but at least the ice cold of his eyes was abated a little, a flicker of fire dancing within the iris.

I have his attention, now what would I have to trade for Lucian's life?

"I think you will find I can be quite persuasive." I said, bartering for the time I needed to think of a deal.

"Mara." He warned, the fire in his eyes dissipating.

I needed to say something now, what? What do I say?

"I will leave with you now, no objections, no fight, no argument." I said, taking hold of the front of his shirt and arching my body against his.

"You are leaving with me regardless." He smirked.

"I promise not to leave your room or your bed until I am no longer in heat." I added quickly.

He growled heatedly. Is it working?

"I can restrain you, just in case?" He asked, his free hand falling to rest on my lower back.

"you mean tie me up?" I asked breathlessly.

"Yes, and even after you are not in heat you will sleep where I sleep every night."

"So long as you give me your word you will not harm any of my companions."

"I haven't finished with my terms, you will also promise that should any sexual need arise you will come and find me immediately, you will also come to me if you feel the wolf rising, and you will never run from me again." He finished, his voice hinting that no further negotiation would be made regarding the matter.

Was it a good deal? I couldn't think straight this close to him, all I could conjure up was images of me tied to his bed, Damn being in heat!

"Do we have a deal?" He whispered arrogantly against my mouth.

"Deal" I agreed, hoping it wasn't a huge mistake.

Bloody hell, I felt like I'd made a deal with the devil. What had I done? My mind wasn't its usual quick and methodical norm. Was it being in heat that was making me dim?

"It's the alcohol" Donna giggled from beside me.

Whipping my head around, I locked eyes with her, was she there the whole time? Shit they were all there, watching, all eyes on our exchange. Even Hamish was there, his face, unreadable, was swollen and covered in blood.

"I'm sorry Hamish, he jumped to conclusions." I whispered mentally, not sure if freeing him from my compulsion also freed him from the link we shared.

"It is of no bother my queen, I had shown him as much myself, he hit me because of a different matter." He replied, the link still present.

What! He knew!

"Did you show him everything?" I asked, turning away from Col agitated.

If he knew! If he bloody knew…

"If you mean does he know about Lucian, then yes. He has witnessed my memory of the event, He has already dealt with Lucian but nae before he viewed Lucian's memories, more specifically, one of us dancing together." He continued through the pack link, a small hinge of amusement lacing his voice.

The bastard! Obviously after seeing the event he knew it was unavoidable and had decided already he wasn't going to kill them. He tricked me! Turning around as realisation struck, I slapped Col around the face.

"You bastard! You had already decided there was no need to kill them and you let me make a deal anyway."

"I did what I had to do to ensure nothing of the sort would happen again, so technically, you have saved lives." He said smugly.

Oh, I'd never wanted to beat someone so much, how could he do it? One minute he has me soring with pleasure the next I'm considering murder. He is making me insane!

"A deal is a deal, we're leaving." He said with a cocky half smile. "After you darling." He added, pointing with his arm towards the entrance.

I wanted to break it, how did this happen… fucking hell. Scanning the small circle of friends, I tried to relay a message of help. They all averted their gaze, Really! Donna was checking her nails whilst trying to hide a massive smile. My shopping trip and her weird behaviour suddenly made sense.

"You knew this was going to happen, didn't you?" I accused, making sure to shout her name mentally at the same time I spoke, 'It's unlikely you will leave his bed' she had said earlier.

"It was a possibility." She admitted with another giggle. "See you in a week." She laughed.

I'm going to kill her!

"Mara." Col called, holding his hand out for me courteously.

"I believe your exact words were 'I will leave with you now, no objections, no fight, no argument.' He grinned wickedly.

Damn it! I'm never drinking again. Refusing to put my hand in his, I walked, shoulders held high, towards the entrance.

Family Ties

It had taken a lot of restraint not to kill Lucian and Hamish, regardless of the fact Mara was in heat, they both knew the punishment for touching another's anam cara. Legally it was my right to kill them, and initially I had wanted too, still wanted to. That I didn't, was merely for Mara's sake, not because I thought it justifiable. Hamish was no longer under the alpha's compulsion that would have compelled him to do as his queen commanded, and Lucian knew better. He could have drunk from her minus the kiss and eager exploration of her body. The vision still vividly clear made me growl viciously, they may not die for what they had done but their punishment was far from over, I wasn't done yet. Besides, the deal was her idea, why dismiss what will give me the time I needed to repair our relationship, I grinned as I followed Mara from the club. I'd make sure she enjoyed her incarceration.

Mara was waiting by the road, her body rigid, her temper flaring wickedly about her. Arms folded across her chest, her mouth fused in a defiant pout, she looked psychotic. People passing unconsciously granted her a wide berth. Probably for the best I mused, whilst going to stand beside her.

"Mara." I called, making sure not to get too close.

If I'd learned anything at all these last couple of days, it was to respect her space when she's pissed. I grinned mentally whilst unconsciously rubbing my jaw. She ignored me.

"Mara, I apologise for misleading you. When the opportunity presented itself, and given all we had gone through, I thought it would allow me the time I needed to speak with you. About who you are, and those who hunt you. I will not expect anything other than your ear whilst you remain by my side" I said gently.

Turning, her mood still foul, she glared at me murderously.

"I was coming to you tomorrow anyway." She hissed She was.

"I did not know that, again I apologise." I sighed.

Why are women so difficult to read?

"I was, as you may recall, more hunter than man, it is as you know my legal right to have them killed, I wanted to, as I'm sure you know. I didn't, because I do not wish to ever hurt you again." I added truthfully.

I doubted I would ever forgive myself for the wrong I had poured upon her. If it cost me their deaths, then so be it. Obviously, my words were sinking in, as her shoulders relaxed, the fire in her eyes lessening. Finally, I was getting something right. Exhaling a small breath of relief, I cautiously moved closer to her. I wanted to wrap her in my arms, but instinct told me it would be pushing it.

"Then you will free me of the deal?" She asked

"Once I have told you all I know about you and Sköll, yes."

I didn't really want too, but again, if that is what it took to regain her trust, then it was a price worth paying. Ansgar was right, I had been impatient. I had known her less than a week. I had to trust that she would share with me when she is ready, anam cara or not I had expected too much from her.

"What has Sköll got to do with anything?" She asked me, her anger fully diminished.

"It is he that hunts you."

"Why?" She asked, coming to stand in front of me.

I had thought about this a lot since Ansgar revealed the knowledge. The only possibilities I could determine was that either she was his unwanted daughter and he wanted to erase the mistake, or worse, and what I feared the most, is that she was the one we have all be searching for, the child of prophecy, the one whose name translates to 'moon'. I had meant to look it up this evening but then Hamish called.

"I will explain everything, but I would rather we did so where we can be free of prying eyes." I said, unconsciously searching the streets for danger.

"Ok" she said, surprising me.

This had to be the first time she had ever agreed to anything I had asked of her. She must have registered the shock on my face as she smiled broadly, the sight stealing my breath away. So beautiful.

"Ok" I said, a low hum of joy lacing the word.

Gently wrapping a stray lock of hair around her ear, I smiled.

"Let's go home anam cara."

"Is this really necessary?" Mara asked, while I finished tying her to the large antic bed frame.

Not really, no, but I hadn't been able to shed the thought since the first time I had her restrained. I grinned, sure she couldn't see the gesture.

"You said it yourself Mara, you have a habit of running, it is important we discuss everything, not just for your own benefit but for all your friends. They have refused to leave you, so they too are now in danger to." I explained, trying to disguise the heat in my voice.

Maybe restraining her was a bad idea, conversation was no longer the most important issue at hand. Focus. Her hands and ankle secured I went to sit in a chair by the wall, not that it really helped with the desire to ravish her, but it had to be better than sitting next to her.

"Ok, so where would you like to start." I asked her, my voice husky, dripped with lust.

Damn it! Someone is trying to kill her, think! She obviously noticed my desire for her, her eyes growing heated before slowly drawing in her lower lip. Held between her teeth, she released it on a soft hiss, desire licking my insides.

Coughing gently, Mara cleared her throat.

"Start with Sköll, I already know I'm part Warg and part Vanir, I don't really know what a Warg is still, but I know enough that it can wait." She said.

She's half Vanir. How is that even possible?

"You know this how?" I asked her, my mind still trying to figure out how a Warg didn't immediately kill her mother. Warg's cannot stand the light, external or internal, its excruciating for them.

"Asta recognised it, she taught me how to manipulate water. Apparently, I have a knack for it." She smiled proudly.

"What else can you do magically?" I asked, somewhat stunned.

A Warg that can control the elements, no wonder he wants her dead, she threatens his very existence. If anything, the fact that she exists proves that darkness is not an absolute, but rather a choice. It would have to be a choice, because if the son of Fenrir, he who was born in the pits of darkness, he who cannot abide the light for he is darkness himself, if he can father Mara, then he chose it, embraced the light, literally embraced it when he slept with Aelius.

This changes everything. The very basics of our belief systems, our understanding of good and evil, well regarding Warg's at least.

Wait. But it was not Sköll who took Aelius. 'We believe Hati is the one who took Aelius' the Vanir had said. That means that Hati is her father and not Sköll. Hati.

"Mara what was the name of your guardian again."

Is it possible?

"Ti" She whispered, almost as though she never wished to utter the name again.

Ti, could he have shortened his name? But why? In case her thoughts were read? No hunter alive had ever seen his face, they would not automatically link Ti as being Hati. I tried to recall the memory Ansgar had shared with me from Mara's childhood, so I could view her guardian. He was tall, the same height as Aengus, and like him was powerfully built. His hair was a lighter shade then Mara's, almost silver, and his eyes… Were in every way, shade, and shape, the same as Mara's.

"I don't think he was merely a guardian Mara." I grimaced, irritated for not connecting the dots sooner.

I had met Aelius, her eyes were blue too, but more like a navy blue then the ethereal ice blue that Ti and Mara shared. But her features were similar, why didn't I notice that before? Their hair colour was the same too.

"What do you mean?" She asked me, her puzzled expression studying.

"Have you ever noticed both you and he have the exact same eyes?"

Her eyes were unique, in all my years I had never seen any like them.

"I have never really thought about it, why?"

"The colour of your hair, the colour of your eyes, your features and build, they are genetic markers, traits that are passed down to your children." I explained.

"Children." She whispered carefully.

A wave of pain passed through the bond, her tongue hitting the inside of her mouth. The sudden arching of her brows clearly relayed her anger. I understood the pain, it's one thing to have a guardian treating you that way, but a father…

"Yes, you said his name was Ti, Ti could be short for Hati. I spoke to the Vanir a few days ago, they said that Hati had abducted one of their own, a woman named Aelius. The two have never been seen again. You look like her, her hair colour, her features, they are the same as yours."

I wanted to continue, but the look on her face as she processed the news made me pause.

"Mara."

Raising her head, Mara looked at me, her eyes covered in a wet sheen that made me think she was about to cry. I wanted to go to her, to shelter her from the news, but I hesitated. Would she want that?

"Are you saying that Ti is my Father?" She whispered

"Yes, and if I'm right, you are the last blood descendant of Jörg, your life the last obstacle to Fenrir's escape."

"Fenrir…Wait Jörg, as in mother earth?" She said quietly, her eyes shocked, seemed to be finding it difficult to determine what that meant.

"Jörg, wife of Odin, mother earth, it was she who created the Vanir. They serve her, serve the earth. It is why they have access to the earth's magic. Your mother was her great, great, great granddaughter I believe."

"Ti said my family wanted me dead, he meant Sköll didn't he?" She asked, her eyes turning cold.

"It is likely, the Vanir have been trying to find you so they could protect you, they would not have harmed you. If you die Mara the last seal that holds his prison together will be broken. He will be free." I said, realisation setting in.

Shit, Mara was the key to everything, if she died, we all died. I needed to inform everyone, she cannot be taken.

"You need to summon your army Mara, I have sufficient land to house the majority…"

"Wait!" Mara interrupted, her brow creased in worry.

"You don't know for sure if I am, you're just guessing."

True, but it made sense, everything was connected. Sighing, I realised she was right, we needed to know beyond a doubt. I need to contact the Vanir, have them come see her. If anyone can confirm it, they could. Standing, I went to retrieve the phone from the bedroom dresser.

"What are you doing?" Mara asked suspiciously.

"Making sure I'm right." I replied, dialling Herlta's numbers, the queen of the Vanir.

Damn it, I hope I'm not right!

Memories from the past

I had no idea what language Col was speaking in while he continued to pace restlessly across the room, in deep and hurried conversation with whoever was on the other end of the phone. Sighing, annoyed I could not eavesdrop on the conversation, I tried to reposition myself on the bed. So far being tied up wasn't as enjoyable as I had hoped it would be. I sighed again, unable to keep the feeling of disappointment from the small sound.

Col must have noticed, as he stopped to look at me, his gaze steady, was overly assessing. What did he see? Pouting, too tired to determine his mind, and no longer caring what I thought he might be seeing, I stared bored at the ceiling. It was bland, the whole thing a solid mass of white, a complete contradiction to the lavishly furnished room. But at least the bed was comfortable, really comfortable. Yawning deeply, I closed my eyes. I could feel Cols eyes on me, I should probably stay awake to get more information, I doubt he was done talking, but if I really was this seal child…thing, then sleep was important, right? And besides, it's not like I could go anywhere tied up. Resigned, and with Col once again pacing, I waited for sleep to find me.

"Get up Mara!"
"I can't" I answered weakly, pain radiating furiously from the large wound marring the inside of my leg.

It was bleeding heavily, the blood, so potent in its quantity, was dominating my sense of smell. I tried to keep the wound shut, cold blood pumping through my fingers and pooling beneath my fallen body.

"Get up Mara!" Ti repeated, his voice as always, commanding.

He would not move to help me, but for a moment I thought I saw a flash of worry flicker in his eyes. No, the blood loss was making me see things, Ti doesn't care enough to worry, especially about me. I tried again to stand, but again I couldn't. Why wasn't the wound healing like the others were, why this one?

"It's not healing, I think the femoral artery has been severed." I said, my thoughts growing sluggish.

I'm so tired. Ti growled in displeasure before finally coming to look at me. Kneeling on one knee, his claret stained sword still held in his hand, he quickly scanned the area before pulling my hands away, revealing the wound. The pressure that was stemming the blood flow was lost, the artery instantly spitting out more jets of blood.

"The blade of Hodr." Ti muttered to himself quietly.

"You must get up Mara, I cannot do what needs to be done here, we are exposed, there may be others." He added louder

I knew he was right, but I couldn't stand, I was so tired.

"I'm tired." I manged to whisper, my eyes, heavy, beginning to close.

"If you sleep, you will not wake." He hissed in my ear, violently shaking me with his free arm.

I will die. Maybe that wasn't such a bad thing, I was tired of fighting, tired of Ti's relentless training, tired of the pain that came with it all.

"I'm ready." I breathed, no longer bothering to try and stop the bleeding.

I'm not afraid to embrace death.

"Damn it Mara! Get up, get up now!" Ti spat, pulling me up harshly, the pain excruciating.

My damaged leg refused to bear any weight. Dangling pathetically from Ti's grip, my breathing was shallow, the cold wind doing nothing to clear my mind.

"He cannot have you Mara! My father can never be free." He snarled, dragging me hurriedly towards the water's edge.

"You are ready Mara, you are strong, stronger than you know, do not give up now, fight! Get up and fight!"

His words left me confused, not the words themselves, but the voice of his command. It was a tone I had never heard him use before, but a tone I had heard others use. The voice of a parent who just witnessed their child ride their bike without help for the first time. He was proud of me. It was probably just imagined, a silent fantasy of mine that I had been secretly carrying, but still, made-up, or not, it made me want to fight, if not for any other reason than he would never think that the pride was misplaced, that I would remain worthy of anything other than his normal contempt.

Ignoring the pain, and the increasing call to sleep, I forced my legs to hold the weight. Dizziness swept over me, the pain increasing to unbearable levels. Somehow, maybe by the grace of fate herself, I managed to stand.

"Good Mara." Ti spoke encouragingly.

Every step was agony, my mind relentlessly tempting me to succumb to its desire to sleep. Only for a minute it seemed to scream, Only I knew that the 'one minute', would be eternal.

"We're nearly there." Ti said, approaching a small boat that was moored to a flimsy wooden dock.

When we finally reached the boat Ti lifted me on board, releasing the rope that anchored us to the shore. Almost instantly the rivers current had us propelling forward. Laying me on the deck, he left me to enter the cabin, returning seconds later with a decorative wooden box. Inside was a small green bottle with a cork stopper. Removing the stopper, he lifted it gently to my lips.

"You must drink it all." He instructed.

The liquid had a strong taste, not unlike aniseed, it made me heave.

"What was it?" I asked, finishing the last of it, my head falling back towards the floor, my eyes drooping.

"A gift from the sun." He answered, a flicker of pain dancing in his eyes, his voice almost reverent.

"You will live Mara, sleep now." He added, his expression quickly returning to its normal stoic self.

Sleep was no longer a choice I thought as I…

"Wake up Mara!" Col called from somewhere close, maybe to the left of me, I wasn't sure.

"No" I half growled, half moaned, not a chance.

I'm still tired, just because he happened to finish his phone call, doesn't mean I should be awake. The dream of Hati and my near death bothered me. I went to sleep so I didn't have to think about him, so of course my dream would have to include him, wouldn't it! No escape from reality for Mara. But then I guess it's not really a dream if it actually happened. Do people dream of memories? Maybe I wasn't even asleep. Confused, and a little bit freaked out, I opened my eyes on a loud sigh.

Col was standing above me, a glass of water in hand.

"You're lucky." He grinned, before placing the water on the night stand.

He wouldn't have!

"You would have regretted it." I hissed, before fixing him with a defiant, I dare you to disrupt my comfort stare.

"Oh really." He grinned, a low hum of a growl following.

Slowly and deliberate he sat on the bed beside me. Pausing for a brief moment, he then proceeded to lean over me, his mouth at my ear.

"I'm going to count to ten Mara, if you're not out of that bed by then, you will learn the true meaning of the word 'regret'." He promised, a soft breath grazing my ear, sparks of excitement skimming down my neck.

Ppfft… the true meaning, please. Unaffected by his warning, I didn't move. I was comfortable, nothing or no one was making me get up, and if his punishment is sex, it's not really much of a punishment, is it? Plus, I wouldn't be required to leave the bed either, so…bring it.

"One." He counted, a playful glint in his eyes.

"Two."

"Three." I counted for him.

"Four." He added, just as I was about to open my mouth and announce the same.

"Five." He whispered against my mouth, his hands slowly finding and holding my wrists.

He must have un-tied me at some point, because I was no longer restrained. Why didn't I notice that?

"Six." He continued.

"Seven."

"Eight."

Col growled, the low vibrations making me purr. I'm not moving! I'm not!

"Nine, last chance Mara."

"Ten." I hissed, before giving him my most wicked smile.

I don't think he appreciated the smile. Lifting me up off the bed as though I weighed nothing, he flung me over his shoulder, my hands grasping at the back of his shirt in an attempt to balance myself. What the hell is he doing?

"Put me down!"

I tried wriggling free, but I was so far over his shoulder, I was literally hanging by my legs. He had one hand pressing down on the lower of my back so that I could make myself upright and the other hand, or rather arm, pinning my legs to his chest. I couldn't even kick in this position. Annoyed, I summoned my fangs, I can't move, but I can bite. The idea made me smile.

My fangs puncture the thin layer of his shirt like it was made of sugar paper, the pressure from the bite and the taste of his blood instantly making me think of sex, or more precisely, sex with Col.

From the hiss he emitted when the bite hit home, I was sure that his thinking matched mine. So why was I still on his blasted shoulder?

The flooring, which from this position was clearly visible, changed from carpet to tile. Is this the bathroom? Why the bloody bathroom? Not that I minded sex in the bathroom, I honestly think I would be happy having it anywhere, but we were on a huge bed, why deviate from that?

A few steps in he stopped, leaning forward slightly. A heavy spray of water followed, it sounded a lot like a shower, why...? Bastard!

"Don't you dare Col! Don't, do not do it!" I hissed alarmed.

He didn't listen.

Dragging me off his shoulder, he placed me directly under the shower. The water, ice cold, seeped into my body, my mind if not before, was instantly alert. Sucking in a deep breath, the cold causing temporary shock to the system, rows of goose bumps erupted all over me. Shaking, I looked up at Col. He was stood safely out of the waters reach, a look of self-satisfaction covering his face, his eyes smugly declaring a victory. So, he thinks he bloody won, does he?

"You look cold, would you like me to warm you up darling?" He grinned, his eyes brimming with laughter were highly suggestive.

My mind wanted to say no, not after that, but my body was saying yes please, please be thorough, I'm chilly everywhere. I hated my body, it was treacherous... But he didn't need to know that.

"That's very thoughtful, but I'm sure I can sort myself out." I said confidently, slowly removing my dress.

My eyes were locked onto his, a cool grin at the edge of my mouth.

"Is that right?" He muttered slowly, the laughter in his eyes dying.

"Yep."

Turning, I adjusted the thermostat to warm, not that I felt the difference, but it didn't cause me to shiver.

The dress off, my back to Col, who I could tell was still watching, I undid my bra. Holding it out to the side I let it fall to my feet. Then remembering that slow was sexy I hooked my thumbs either side of my knickers, slowly pulling them down, making sure to keep my legs together. As I reached the knees I was required to bend forward, this pleased Col, who hissed loudly behind me, his pleasure as always, increasing my own.

"You sure you don't need a hand." He growled low, the bond betraying just how eager he was to help.

Naked, I turned to face him, the water caressing my body.

"No, my hand will do." I replied almost as a whisper.

I was winging it, I wasn't sure if what I was about to do was sexually enticing but I wanted to do it anyway, I enjoyed him watching, it was nerving, but thrilling at the same time.

A smoky cloud filled his eyes at my comment, his gaze quickly darting to my hand before returning to find my eyes. He was eager before, now he was practically on the verge of leaping for me, I could feel the tension in the bond, the raw primal need that echoed between us.

"Mara."

He merely uttered my name but the way he did it made my stomach flutter, my breathing hitch.

Feeling bold, I gently ran my fingers across my lips, slowly altering their course, they made their way down to my chin, neck, the length of my chest, stomach, until finally, I reached my destination. The suspense had my heart racing, Cols eyes hungrily watching.

Intense heat was my reward when unabashed I caressed and manipulated my own pleasure. A breathless gasp of desire escaped my lips, my eyes closing. Why have I never considered this before?

Col growled, the low vibrations telling me he was near, closer than before. I opened my eyes. Col had removed his clothes and was kneeling before me, his wicked mouth hovering millimetres above my hand. Reverently he slid his hands around my thighs, gripping my bottom and guiding me closer to him. At this proximity, I could feel his warm breath, the delectable sensation had me unconsciously licking my lips. His touch was gentle, and yet the tension I felt through the bond was turbulent, almost as though he fought an internal battle. I was about to ask why, or maybe complain at his lack of attention, when he grabbed one of my legs and sat it over his shoulder.

Moving my hand out of the way, he teasingly kissed me, his warm mouth replacing my hand, fingers. It was torture, granted it was of the good variety, but still, what's he thinking? He was touching me, but barely, like a gentle caress that whispered against me only to leave before my mind could fully comprehend its presence. Frustrating didn't quite cover it, I wanted him on me, in me, his tongue hungrily exploring.

Annoyed with his teasing I tried to pull his head towards me, forcing him to taste me fully. He didn't move but I was sure I caught the faint impression of humour pass between us.

Before I could protest, he lifted my other leg, placing it over his other shoulder. The action lifted me higher, catching me off balance. Not thinking, I placed my hands out to the side to steady myself, my hands slipping slightly on the steamed glass. How was I supposed to force his cooperation now? Frustrated, I hissed, my body trembling with need.

"Damn it Col."

I attempted to roll my hips, hoping it would draw his mouth fully against me. It didn't work, my hips caught in a vice. Another flash of amusement passed through the bond, a gentle laugh vibrating against my core.

"So impatient." He breathed with another languid stroke of his tongue.

The sensual swipe of his moist tongue pulled a delightful moan from my lips. Standing up abruptly, my pleasure halted, he placed my feet back on the floor. Whipping me around before I had time to react, Col pinned my hands against the tiled wall. Holding them in place with one hand, his other hand pushed against my lower back, forcing it to arch towards him.

"Keep your backed arched, don't move." He ordered.

Slowly he ran his free hand up the arc of my back, when he reached my neck, he gently moved my hair out of the way, lowering his mouth to the base of my neck. I felt his fangs grazing, his low stubble leaving trails of blissful heat. Every inch of my neck, shoulders, back was tasted, explored, before he finally moved in, his hard body encasing me. My body rippled furiously, not sure how much more I could take. I needed more, desperately needed more.

"Please" I pleaded, almost as a whimper, my teeth clamping down hard on my lip.

"You need me?" Col asked, his voice although heated, seemed to contain a smile.

"Yes"

"Then say it Mara, tell me you need me" He whispered against my ear, his tongue softly pulling on my ear lobe.

I had no idea that such a small gesture could evoke so much pleasure, the ear! I nearly whimpered again, my body, turning to mush, was finding it difficult to stand on legs that were gently shaking.

"I need you anam cara."

Broken

Watching Mara pleasure herself had nearly been my undoing, never in my life had I seen anything so damn sexy. She was stunning, her desire clouding and illuminating her eyes. It was mesmerizing, her failure to include me though, needed addressing. I had planned to tease her for hours to teach her a lesson, but apparently, I could only manage minutes. Watching the water roll down her arched back, hearing her soft moans was too much, and when she called me her 'anam cara', the hunter no longer cared for her education. Possessiveness and need exploded within, the hunters need to sate her, to claim her, all consuming. Just the idea of being inside her had my body coiling tightly, my fangs extending. She was mine the hunter declared, the savage need to please her, the dominant thought.

Using my foot, I widened her stance. Held in a vice, her hands remained pinned to the wall. With my free hand, I pulled her hips back, forcing her to bend further, her perfectly sculpted arse encasing my erection. Eager, I entered her roughly, the less than smooth action making her gasp, her head falling back to rest on my shoulder.

Fuck she felt good, her entire being capturing mine. I could never tire of her, never be without her. With that in mind, my pleasure spun wildly, my head swimming. In an act of pure dominance, I grabbed her hair, pulling her neck to my mouth. My fangs pounding, were desperate to penetrate her flesh and join her to me in. Without thinking, my release in sight, I sank my fangs in deep, a blinding rush of ecstasy following. My soul was inflamed, Mara's soul bending to accommodate mine. I felt the closeness of her essence, pushing, fighting to reach my inner light. Our energy blended together, before blazing erotically and infinitely about us.

My whole sense of self was overcome with feelings of love, need, euphoria. It was wholeness in its purest form, oneness. It was everything, meant everything. With this clarity of mind, I could no longer postpone the fury and inevitability of our union. With a final heart rendering thrust Mara screamed out, her climax racketing through her body and taking me with her.

Breathless I couldn't move, my body like hers, trembling. Aftershocks of desire was passed chaotically between us, happiness in every form, filling my chest. For the first time in an age I felt weak, tired, and yet all I could think about was taking her again.

"I love you Mara."

Mara tensed, her body soft and pliable one minute, rigid and stressed the next. Her energy, essence, unfolded and separated from mine. The quickness of its departure, wrenched at my heart, causing me to tremble, not from loss of desire, but from the icy chill that has somehow managed to fill the room. Shit. We were there, together, whole, but just like that Mara had switched it off, locked it away.

"Mara, I don't expect you to say it back." I whispered against her ear.

Please don't walk away. Turning her to face me, I turned off the water and held her against me. She said nothing but didn't push me away or attempt to leave. Progress.

"I'm broken." She said unexpectedly, a frown that was mixture of desperation and confusion painting her face, her eyes covered in a wet sheen that broke my heart.

"You're not broken Mara, where is this coming from?"

"I see it, when we are together, your light encasing me. It fills me, seeps into my soul, pushes the darkness back.

Love hovers in the centre, or at least I think it is love. I don't know, but whatever it is, it sits there ready to be taken. Instinct tells me that it's mine, that all I have to do is reach out and take it. But when I do… my hand passes through it, like an illusion, it holds no true form. The more I try to grab it, the more it fades away… I don't think it can abide me, the light? Love…it fades because it rejects me, shies from my touch, my taint. If I cannot reach it, then theoretically, I cannot Love."

"I don't believe that Mara, you're my soul mate. If I could not be all that you needed, and if you could not be all that I needed, our bond, union, could never exist, and yet it does."

"How can you be sure that it does? I mean… you just said you loved me, I'm guessing your admission isn't based on want or ideology, but on something more concrete, a feeling based on your prior knowledge of love, your understanding of it. I don't know…" She sighed, her brow creasing. "I like you, a lot, care for you even, and when you touch me I'm flooded with warmth that otherwise I am unable to feel. You are the only one who has ever made me feel anything but the cold. But if you die, I have a suspicion that it would do no more than piss me off, a loss of something that I greatly enjoyed. It wouldn't destroy me. Isn't that what love is? The idea that if that person was to cease being, you would be devastated, crippled. That you would no longer wish to live because a life without that person no longer holds any appeal?"

Damn, that was cold! She basically just said she was ok with me dying. Lifting my shoulders high, I tried to hide the pain her statement had caused. If she were any other woman, she would be callous. The only reason I didn't get angry was the look on her face. Her eyes were the eyes of someone who had been wondering for days, lost and without direction. Her statement, although wounding, contained no malice. She did not intend to hurt me, probably didn't even know that such words could or would.

"You have spent a life time in the shadows Mara, forced and conditioned to feel nothing, to ignore emotions. You are learning all over again, of course you will struggle to feel anything. In time, you will. Take Donna for example, if she were to die, it would hurt you, would it not?"

"Yes, but I don't know why, it doesn't make sense. I feel the need to protect her, to trust her, even against my own thinking. It is an instinctual trait; my mind pushes me to do what she asks even if I don't fully comprehend why. My attachment to her, wasn't a conscious choice." she frowned again, the expression one of pure frustration. "I do not choose Col. I react. There is no conscious thought when I flip from one frame of mind to another. Whether it is to inflict harm or to protect, it just is, a decision made that I had no part in. The Warg, Vanir, I'm ruled by my nature, not by my will." She sighed sadly, a small droplet of water running down her cheek.

"You chose to become the wolf, to protect you friends and defeat Leif."

"Yeah, I guess..." She sighed "Maybe I am over thinking it."

"You said that I am the only one who has ever made you feel warm, do you mean literally? Or figuratively?"

To all the gods I hope she means figuratively.

"Literally."

I mentally sighed, what did that mean?

"I have never felt warmth, heat of any description, until you touched me, when physical contact ends, I feel nothing again." She explained, walking out of the shower.

Wrapping a towel around her I guided her back into the bedroom, my mind racing. Her father's conditioning is complete, to not feel anything…it must be. Perhaps that's why he left her, not because he was taken or killed but because he had finished, succeeded in breaking her.

I need to speak to the Vanir, they will know what, if anything can be done about it, what it means.

Mara had slept for over twelve hours last night, the queen of the Vanir arriving a couple of hours ago. Not surprisingly she was eager to meet my hybrid wife.

"Get dressed Mara, there is someone I would like you to meet."

Kings and Queens

The start to my morning with Col had been perfect, right up until the point he said, 'I love you'. Honestly, I feel bad about it. I know that love is supposed to be a predisposition of finding one's soul mate, but I don't love him, although I think I want to. Instinct tells me he is mine, that we should be together, are meant to be together. Also, I think about sex a lot when I see him, but that's most likely due to the fact I'm in heat. I don't gush at the sight of him like Donna does with Aengus, and I don't worry about him getting hurt, in fact, I have already hurt him myself and didn't feel even a little bit guilty about it. That's not love, is it? I didn't lie though, when I said I saw the light within him, I did. Its calls to me, begs me to partake. It was there the very first time we were together, the pull of its allure growing with every union. I wanted to take it, I tried to, but like my experience with all things that holds warmth, I couldn't. Perhaps that's the keys to loving him, to understanding love, I must be able to take it, but how can I when it's not letting me? Frustrated I followed Col down the ridiculously grand stair case, my eyes fused to his rather tempting backside.

"Stop checking me out Mara, we're about to meet Herlta. She is the queen of the Vanir, our meeting is important, as are political niceties, I need to think of matters that aren't warped with sex." Col growled.

"I'm not checking you out"

I so was. He looked good, and felt even better, it's hardly my fault, and then there's the way he tastes, smells, talks…

"Mara!" Col stopped, turning to face me.

His eyes were clouded with that grey smoky mist that told me he was either turned on, or about to kill someone, either way, both did it for me.

"What?" I asked innocently.

"You are thinking of sex, your want of it is passing through our bond and enraging my hunter. I cannot do politics when all I can think about is sating your desire." He explained, his eyes moving up and down my body leisurely.

"Politics is boring anyway, there are so many things we could be doing, for example, I still haven't gotten to taste your…"

"Don't say it, don't think it!" Col interrupted with a heated hiss, a passing staff member grinning widely.

"Fine."

Sighing, or maybe sulking, I made the last few steps down to Col, doing my best not to think of anything remotely linked to sex. Damn it, if you really think about it, most things are. I decided that inspecting furniture was the best option.

The castle was as one would expect, massive, and richly furnished. It had all the ancient features that makes you wonder about its history, but with all the modern perks, it was beautiful, if not extravagant. I like it, not so much the space as it could perceptively hide endless dangers, but it was ok. I missed the bedroom Donna had created for me though, that room really was perfect. Maybe Col would move in with me and Donna, Aengus too I suppose. Grandeur wasn't really my thing, this castle, glorious as it is, didn't feel like a home. It was more like a retreat you would treat yourself to, stay for a few weeks and enjoy something new. Ireland was beautiful, nearly as beautiful as Scotland, but theirs the operative word, 'nearly'. It doesn't matter how beautiful it is, it's not home. A sudden sadness filled me.

"Col, can we live in Scotland?"

I would live here if I must, but sometimes places attach themselves to you, the highlands of Scotland claimed me long before Col did.

"You don't like it here?" He asked, his green eyes studying.

"It's big, and there are a lot of people here, I miss Scotland… will always miss it."

"You are hunted Mara, more people, means less attempts on your life."

I guess…

"More people is tactically beneficial; however, they literally live in the castle, with us, all the time. Multi-living and my wolf won't work in the long run. You must see that as a permanent solution you would be putting your people and their families at risk. You can't be with me every minute of the day just to ensure nothing happens, and when I said I missed Scotland, it wasn't a momentarily longing, it is a longing that is pulling at my very being."

Standing outside large double doors Col seemed to be pondering my statement. His eyes briefly met mine before he opened the huge doors.

"I will see what can be done." He answered, with a small smile that made me feel like the most important person in the world.

"Thank you." I smiled.

Taking my hand in his, the power that he so effortlessly hides suddenly blared around us. The sight and magnitude of his true power sent an eerie chill racing along my spine. The shadowed hue was not in his eyes, but you could tell he meant business. I thought the Keltoi were friends with the Vanir, what's going on?

Entering the room, I quickly understood, I was meeting the queen, but not only the queen. Seven people were in attendance, each of them with their own veil of power. They were all dangerous in their own way, but two of them, both men, were cloaked in a darkness that was completely enthralling. As always, the pull of the darkness was greater than the pull of the light, I had the sudden urge to go and run my finger through the dark aura they emanated, wrap it slowly around my fingers, and then draw it in for a kiss. What is wrong with me? It wasn't the men I wanted, it was the power they held. Shaking myself internally I reluctantly diverted my gaze and focused on the room.

It hummed with magic and loosely controlled tension. Just what kind of meeting was this? Hamish was here, he was the only Lycan, and was obviously bored. He was sat on one of the nine chairs that was placed around a large circular table. He got up when he saw me enter behind Col.

"My queen." Hamish said simply, before rising and pulling out one of the chairs, motioning for me to sit.

Leaving Col, I went and took the seat offered. As soon as I sat, the rest of the guests followed suit. Col sat on the other side of me, the others choosing a chair closest to them. When everyone was comfortably seated, the doors closed, a lash of fiery magic that flickered across the ceiling, walls, and floor, sealing the room. I raised my eyebrows, the thought of being locked in here with strangers putting me on edge. My fists clenched tightly, a low growl hovering in my throat. This isn't good, I could sense my wolf rising, it didn't help that the stranger's gazes were fixed on me. Col must have sensed the danger and uncertainty of my thinking as I felt his hand rest upon my leg, his warmth and light instantly reassuring.

"Thank you all for coming on such short notice, I understand that we are pressed for time, so I will get right to it." Col said to the room, his voice clearly saying, 'pay attention'.

"May I introduce my queen, and queen of the Varúlfur, Mara, and her general, Hamish."

The strangers in the room gently inclined their head, first to me and then to Hamish, but not a word was uttered.

"Mara, may I introduce you to the leaders of earth's races." Col pointed to the closest stranger with a slight nod of his head. "Valac, high druid, and representative of the human race. He is as you may have deduced human, and yet immortal. The world of man no longer believes in magic, nor are they aware of the existence of other races living amongst them. The Druids of Cernunnos are to the humans, non-existent. Only humans that are born to, or are found to possess the gifts that were once common place amongst their kind can become, or will ever know of their existence. We do not speak of them to anyone. It is imperative for the succession of mankind that they are left unheard of. The closed mindedness of man and their quick use of destructive technology when exposed with the threat of the unknown cannot be tested." He explained.

Good job he did, not because I would have blabbed, but because I've never heard of them. Questions flew through my mind, I know so little. Biting my lip, I didn't say anything, I got the impression that this wasn't the time for a chit chat.

The High Druid seemed ok, he was the shortest immortal I have ever met but he was still close to six feet. He had grey, silver hair that hung loose about his shoulders, and a young almost cherub like face. His appearance didn't quit fit the strength and sternness that radiated from him.

"Next, we have Nefta, Mother of the Valkyrie"

The woman looked fierce and like Hamish somewhat bored. She had long black, blue hair that was held up by some form of half jewellery, half battle helm concoction. She was stunning, in an observe from afar kind of way.

"Vladimir Tepes, Prince Drăculea, lord of the Nosferatu, I believe you have spoken before." Col said, a flash of annoyance skimming across our bond.

I grinned and inclined my head to the prince. He was one of the two men with that darkly tempting aura. He looked like Lucian but with a more evil twist about him. He grinned back, before meeting Cols eyes, his grin turning sinister. Not a fan of my husband then. A good wife would have been affronted for him, such a small gesture from the prince but one that held a lot of meaning. I should have been, but instead I found it amusing. That alliance he wanted now seemed like a spectacular idea. How many times could

I get the prince and Col in a room together? And what would happen? Who would survive?

Col placed his hand on my shoulder, his warmth infiltrating my mind, the idea good before, suddenly felt cold. Did I really just think that? I looked up at Col, an apology in my eyes. Col eyes were controlled, emotionless, and yet I could sense he wasn't angry, concerned, but not angry, good.

"Herlta, Queen of the Vanir, Guardian of the light."

She was even more pixie looking than Asta was, a fragile, dainty being, and yet I suspected that to treat her as such would be a mistake, a painful mistake. Like with Col she harboured a light, so bright, I felt as though I was looking directly at the sun. It burned, but on second glance, I couldn't see anything, just the small elf, her peculiar glance making me feel…odd, dirty even. I didn't like it, so I looked away, somewhat confused as to why I was still calm, and not pissed with her, 'I'm judging you' eyes, masterfully disguised by a, 'I'm far too sweet to be judging' smile.

If she thought I didn't notice, she was wrong, bloody woman.

"Fumi Achike, High warlock, Voice of the Hexan."

Damn he was tall, he made Hamish look short. He reminded me of one of the Zulu warriors I had seen pictures of. Powerfully built, his dark brown, almost black eyes were empty. A lick of fire filled them briefly before vanishing, bad thought? Posturing? Warg in heat?

"Ragnar Draconis, Lord of realms, King of demons."

The king winked, the gesture immediately followed with a wicked grin. Col growled, his grip on my shoulder tightening ever so slightly. This was the other temptingly dark aura man. Not able to help myself, I licked my lips, the action not missed…by anyone.

Col wasn't pleased. Hamish chuckled through the pack link, his first shared thought since this stupid meeting started.

"As you have all been informed I have reason to believe that Mara is the daughter of Aelius, who we now have reason to believe was the last surviving blood descendant of Gaia, the final key, who's demise will ultimately free Fenrir. I also believe that Mara's father is the son of Fenrir, Hati, and that he has for whatever reason guarded Mara, keeping her alive, a complete contradiction to what we know of Warg's, their nature, and prophetic legacy. Of course, none of what I believe has yet been confirmed, which is why you are all here. We must be certain, but more importantly, and as I'm sure you all agree, Fenrir cannot ever be released. Every precaution should be taken, every suspicion investigated."

"Agreed" Fumi mumbled, his voice as I imagined it would be, deep and raspy.

The others declined to speak but nodded in agreement.

"I suspect your belief that Mara is Aelius's daughter is correct, and with your permission Mara, I would like to be certain." Herlta smiled at me, her judging vibe no longer noticeable.

"And how would you be certain?" I asked suspiciously.

If it has anything to do with mind reading she can piss off, been there, done that. The queens smile grew wider, a slight hint of humour flickering in her eyes.

"Do not fear little one, there will be no infringements on your mind, I need only sense your fey magic. Like a DNA test, a person's magic is unique to its heritage. Aelius was my greatest friend, if you are her daughter and not just one who is similar in appearance, I will know instantly."

"I've only learned water manipulation, I have not attempted any other elements yet." I said to the room, my suspicion abated.

"The grandchild of Fenrir, capable of wielding the earths magic…dangerous for all." Valac mused aloud, with a not too friendly tone attached.

He did it in such a manner you would half believe he didn't mean to speak aloud, but I know a threat when I hear it, no matter how well disguised. I couldn't help but growl, probably not the best reaction as I probably just proved a point. I hate politics… Col's grip on me tightened again. If he dug any deeper he was going to break the skin, and the pain, regardless of how insubstantial, was bating my wolf. Unconsciously, I rolled my head, absorbing the scents in the room, an unwilling act that spoke much of my wolf's intention. My fingertips were freezing, a quick glance showed that they had started to turn blue, a thin layer of ice sprinkling my nails and slowly climbing to my knuckles.

"Must you forever be a fool Valac, one does not threaten a Warg and then expect them to ignore it. Young the queen may be, but in no way stupid, she understood your meaning well. If I were you, I would guard my tongue, lest we leave in less numbers than we arrived." Ragnar said, his words crisp, dripped with contempt.

Safe to assume they don't get on well, I can see the dislike. Druid or not, his blood if I wish it, will fill my belly, and quell my thirst.

"It was not a threat, merely a fact. It is the earth magic, that, combined with the strength of the other races, imprisoned Fenrir. If his half breed granddaughter has access to that magic, there may come a day when she is more powerful than he. The darkness has a greater hold on her than her fey counterpart. I would even dare to say that she inherited more of her father's traits than her mothers, the Warg's strength and power magnifying her fey magic, but whilst retaining overall control. Her Warg blood is corrupting the great mothers pure magic."

"The mothers magic cannot be tainted, it is light in its purest from, no darkness can withstand it." Herlta interceded, a look of annoyance aimed in Valac's direction.

"How can you be sure? After all a 'Warg' did mate with a 'Fey', that in its self should have been impossible. Her Warg father further going against his nature by ensuring she survives. What reason would a Warg have to preserve another life, unless that life had benefits linking and aiding their evil plans?" Valac continued, his voice grating on my every damn nerve.

"If Aelius was his life mate than perhaps their bond neutralized or at least illuminated his predisposed nature, the darkness if you like lessening to a degree that enabled him to understand, however small, a measure of regard or even love. If this was accomplished then he may have protected his daughter because she was just that, 'his daughter'." Fumi grumbled, his deep tone speculative.

"Indeed. There are only four Wargs in existence, if you include Mara. We have presumed that based on Fenrir and the actions of his sons, like that of their father… they are soulless, as we know Fenrir to be. But did he begin life soulless? He has lived since the beginning of earth's history, that knowledge long lost to us. It is possible, and as I have often believed… that life begins pure. But is at some point during an individual's life, corrupted." Herlta frowned, her tone like Fumi's thoughtful.

"This is not a philosophical debate, such can be discussed at another time, we have more pressing issues, like the fact that Mara has captured the undivided attention of Sköll and that my daughter refuses to leave her side." Vladimir sneered, his eyes vexed, filling with blood.

I was following their conversation but with great difficulty, not that I didn't understand what was being said, but because of the closed space, the dark alluring aura from Ragnar and Vladimir tempting me to do bad things, and the damn presumptuous comment made by Valac taking full hold of my mind. While they sat debating 'what if's' I was fighting the urge to spill the druid's guts on the table and hang his entrails round my neck like a necklace. I even visualised my self-standing naked in front of a mirror, his intestines framing my face, his blood painting delicate patterns against my creamy skin. As far as attire went it looked good, licking my lips, I knew it would taste even better. My hands were now completely frozen, my fangs hidden behind my closed mouth, cutting at my lips. Pressure was building up inside me, the wolf refusing to let go of the slight.

"Mara?" Col's voice drew my gaze, my eyes meeting his the minute he uttered my name. "Fuck" was his response, his eyes instantly filling with smoke.

Hamish's head whipped round to look at me, his eyes briefly relaying worry before regaining control.

"My queen, If I may, I recommend we leave now." Hamish's words swam through my mind, but did little to diminish my vision, or desire.

"You idiot" Ragnar spat at Valac, "what have you done? Release the wards warlock, it is time to re-schedule this meeting."

"Mara, look at me." Col called, my eyes like before finding his immediately.

I could sense he was trying to reach me on some kind of personal, love induced level, but his light, however bright, wasn't getting through. The darkness within wrapped its self around my heart, the tendrils my imagination created, carrying a rotten black tar into all that held life. I saw Col, but I didn't see him, like a picture he became nothing more than an object that bore resemblance. Slowly I stood from the table, the air around me turning into clouds of mist that floated eerily in the room, its movement, if any, defying nature.

The mist grew darker as the air grew colder. Like the coldest winter, on the highest peak, the frozen air burnt my skin, my breathing growing shallow, my heart beat falling quiet. The beat was so hard to define it was as though all life was seeping from me, an un-living image of me remaining in my stead. The words and mutterings of the others in the room no longer held meaning, intangible nonsense, nothing mattered but the threat that had been made against me. That thing of a man, that heart that was beating loudly not six feet in front of me, that was my true purpose. Bursts of magic fired against me, the pressure from the blasts letting me know that I was being attacked, but the effect of their idiotic attempts not debilitating me in anyway. The warlock would have to wait his turn.

With little effort or recollection, I now stood behind the druid, his white hair the perfect back drop for the soon claret staining. Yes…red on white, the livid contrast, a perfect canvas. Fear from the druid drifted to the forefront of my mind, the delight it gave me made my mouth water, my hunger intensify. Running my hand through his hair, the gentle movement, almost a soothing gesture, made the druid shiver. I felt a small smile form on the edge of my lips, an internal sigh of contentment that gave a sense of profound peace, freedom. A hunter came and stood beside me, his warm hand falling to rest on top of mine, he was powerful, appealing, but he wouldn't understand this longing, wouldn't allow me to be free. No… He will send me back to my cage.

"Attempt to stop me hunter and you will die with him."

Pain that wasn't mine, ferreted through my body, the hunter cursed and fell to the ground. The annoyance this caused me was illogical, bordering on maddening. Who dare harm what is mine. Mine…the hunter belongs to me somehow, if that is so, then they are harming me. Furious, the druid was no longer the priority, the warlock however, was.

"What the fuck are you doing Fumi?" A vampire hissed.

"They are bonded, if I cannot hurt her directly then I will do so by any means, all be it an ally."

Sparks of orange lightening forked through the air, its target the hunter, and secondary me. No longer caring for the slow provocative kill of the druid, my wolf ripped through my skin, my fur a sense of true self, a favourite dress that bestowed power.

Like a shield I was impenetrable, indestructible, but the hunter's skin held no such protection. Why wasn't he fighting? He is strong, exceptionally so, he could prevent this. Pausing, something didn't feel right, instinct warning me that a trap lay waiting. The orange lightning struck the hunter in his chest, the acrid smell of burnt skin and clothing dominating my senses, before the pain from the hit could relay within me. A scorching sensation of blue flame encased my chest, the pain not having the desired effect, pleased me. The fact that he hurt the hunter though, did not. Sure that there was a trap I endured another three indirect hits before the hunter growing weak became a problem I couldn't ignore. Undiagnosable thinking had me believing that I couldn't survive his death, the foreign thought not carrying alarm but certainty. The death of the hunter, a tactical misfortune that I might never recover from, even though he was nothing less than a pawn, a servant at best.

The Lycan jumped in front of the hunter a second before I had made the decision to do so myself. The pain ended, the hunter safe. I turned my focus on the tall warlock who had flames in his eyes, and dancing within his palms. In less than a second I was stood in front of him, the fog spiralling through the air, an extension of my body and will. The grey tinted mist rolled out, winding its way up his legs, his torso, and then his neck. His rich ebony skin paled as the fingers of fog locked him in place, just as they had the druid. Unable to move, the flames in his palm grew larger, his eyes ablaze. Heat peeled from his body, the heat hissing briefly before being completely consumed by the icy clouds that had locked onto his soul.

A quick kill no longer necessary, my fur became skin once more. Slowly, I stood naked before him, the frozen air refreshing. The flames the warlock controlled continued to grow, steam filling the room as he battled my cold embrace. A flicker of annoyance edged its way into my thoughts, the steam was ruining my view, obscuring my vision for what I had imagined, an artistic kill. A small trail of blood ran down my chin, my fangs so far extended having punctured my bottom lip. The taste of blood, even my own was sensational, the blood of an enemy, would be divine. Lifting my hand in an almost reverent manner, I ran my frozen finger tips across the warlock's mouth, his breath, silent, fettered against my finger tips and carried within, subtle notes of fear. Delighted, razor sharp claws pierced my frozen nails, so black they seemed to absorb what little light remained in the room. With one finger, I punctured the warlock throat, just above his Adams apple, like a scalpel, I sliced my way down, a straight red line that ended at his pelvis, his clothing a flimsy barrier that did nothing to lessen the cut.

"Mara stop!" The hunter pleaded, his voice, gravelly, said much of his current strength.

"He attempted to kill me, and you, least you have forgotten, an incitement of war, if ever there was one."

"You attempted to kill me, is that then an incitement of war?" The druid hissed.

"You what me dead druid, suggested it, within my hearing and within the hearing of kings and queens, I consider that a premeditated attack, war… is indeed imminent human. But let's be clear who initiated it. It was not I… but I will finish it."

Calmly, I slid my hand into the warlock's gut, blood coating my arms nearly to the elbow. I took a minute to gaze into the warlock's eyes, the flames now nothing but faint sparks, his pain not heard, but visible in every pore of his body.

"Damn it Mara, stop! Herlta please, bring her back before it's too late." The hunter demanded, a desperate edge to his voice.

"To get involved is to declare a side, we must remain neutral, regardless of the outcome." The small woman replied.

"Fuck neutral! No matter how bad you think Mara is right now, she still has a soul, is still capable of overcoming the darkness. Fenrir does not, Mara may have killed a few hundred men, but he has annihilated entire civilizations for no other reason other than he enjoyed it. Her life is all that keeps him from the world, if she is lost, then we may as well surrender now."

"Conlaóch has a valid point, Mara is better than Fenrir, and if she is the last descendant then we have no choice but to ensure she isn't corrupted." The Valkyrie announced.

Their conversation drew another smile from my lips, it was amusing to think they could alter the outcome, to believe they can place me back into that cage. I am who I am, and require no permission to be so. With that thought, I pulled the intestine free from his body, the iron rich scent, the perfect perfume to match my outfit. Draping the large organ around my neck several times, I ripped the excess off. It seemed a waste, but too much would ruin the look. As my imagination promised, the blood created stunning streaks that coated my flesh. No longer alive, I let the dead warlock drop to the ground, the magic that locked us in, ending with him.

"Where might I find a mirror?" I asked the room, whilst casually inspecting my new look.

Fire

Stunned, and in incredible pain, I couldn't find the words to even attempt to answer Mara's question… a fucking mirror, so she can admire her work, this can't be happening, it isn't real. A pinching pressure on my forearm pulled my gaze. It was Herlta, a look of regret in her eyes. It is happening, it did happen…Mara, what have you done? Unashamed, and without the slightest bit of fear she stood in the room wearing Fumi as an adornment, a fine piece of jewellery she wanted the world to see and admire her in. The druid lost the contents of his stomach, the acid stench infusing the small space, and making the heavy scent of death even more putrid. I didn't understand… why couldn't I reach her? I dropped the thought when the doors to the room burst open. Donna was standing in the entrance, her hands on her hips, a stern pout on her mouth.

"I leave her with you for less than a day and this is what happens." She frowned at me, her eye brows arching in disbelief.

Anger pulled me from my stunned silence, is she blaming me for this?

"I did not cause this."

"You put her in a closed room with seven powerful and thus dangerous strangers, two of whom are so dark in character they border on evil, and then expect her not to find the enthralling catnip like aura not the least bit compelling, corrupting." She huffed.

"You cannot be effected by the energy source of another." I said annoyed.

Mara was staring at Donna, a faint gleam of recognition registering in her stormy eyes. This pissed me off further, she can remember the witch but not me, I'm her damn soul mate.

"It may not affect you, but it effects a Warg, in the same manner a Warg affects others who are close by. They absorb the essences of another, as well as project. The darker the aura, the more appealing, and subsequently, the more they take into themselves. She literally drew it in with every breath she took."

I was unaware it worked both ways, nor did she send anyone else mad like her Warg relatives. Sighing, I sat down on the closest chair, my gaze on Mara. She was now slowly rotating in front of a large polished brass shield, her reflection allowing her to see what she obviously thinks is a master piece. Hamish was sat leaning against the wall, his features set in a stern scowl as he kept watch on his queen. I couldn't begin to imagine what everyone was thinking, Mara…saviour of the world, but in her spare time likes to wear your organs for clothing, oh, and be very, very careful about what you say, do, or imply, lest she decide to turn your head into a hat.

How was I supposed to repair this damage? It was witnessed by the most important people on earth, the witches will see it as an act of war, the only saving grace, he attacked first.

"Why are we still sealed in, the room should have opened when Fumi died, not that I'm complaining, the view is somewhat spectacular after all." Ragnar asked, a slight twitch of his jaw the only indication he meant what he said, that and his far too studying eyes.

"I would appreciate it if you didn't observe my wife which such keen interest."

Of course a demon would think a 'blood and entrails' covered woman 'spectacular', not even Hamish was his normal eye wondering self, apparently, he had limits even with Mara.

"It is a small room, and a naked woman is hard to pass up, especially when she has such an eye for detail."

"You're insane." Donna nearly choked.

"I do not deny it." Was Ragnar's response.

Donna's eyes went wide, her eyes glued to his forehead. She looked at me, a nervous shake of her head before shuddering. I knew she could read thoughts, another thing I would need to address, what she saw I could only guess, the mind of a demon king… probably made Mara look like a girl scout.

"So why are we locked in?" Vladimir hissed impatiently.

Glancing briefly at me, he altered his gaze to land on Donna. "You locked us in" He demised, a slight hint of vexation evident in the barely audible click of his teeth.

Being that she was the only one who could, it made sense, a fact I would have gotten to sooner if not for Mara's 'complete loss of words' actions. But worse, and more disturbing, her naked, all be it blood stain body, still turned me on.

"I didn't lock you in, I locked Mara out. There are families in this castle with young children. The warlock's screams were so loud I could hear him from the stables, it doesn't take a genius to guess something went wrong, which generally means, Mara's gone bad." She sighed dramatically, her mouth fused into a' I knew it' pout.

Annoyingly she did the right thing. Mara in this state, free to roam… Scotland is no longer a 'I will see what I can do' option. The Keltoi have strong Irish and Scottish links, even some Welsh. I have just as much land across the three countries. The Isle of Skye would be the perfect home for Mara, remote, surrounded by stormy seas, separated from the main land, and with an extremely sparse population. I also have a currently unused castle there, yes, Isle of Skye it is.

"So, little fact I have learned about Mara, when she uses her fey abilities all her darkness is pushed back, so people, how do we trick her into using her fey magic?" Donna asked within my mind, the fact that she used the word 'people' prompting me to assume she had communicated to the room.

Since everyone but Hamish turned to look at her, my suspicions were confirmed. The pack link probably the reason she failed to include him, that or she doesn't care much for his opinion, either way, it was a good call.

"Interesting piece of knowledge, she mentioned she had only attempted water manipulation. Perhaps given that she showed a like for Fumi's fire I can ask if she would like to learn how to create it." Herlta spoke.

"I would be cautious with any invitation, she is suspicious by nature, your over share with thoughts earlier is bound to have compromised her trust capabilities." Nefta warned.

Indeed, who in the room would she trust? It certainly wasn't me, she was more than happy to sit back while I literally burned. I had hoped she would have come to my aid, the bond pulling her to me, so I could make physical contact, allowing every damn bit of light I possessed, to attach, and pull her back through the darkness.

"Do nae beat yourself up, she wanted to go to you, but she knew it was a trap, one that she believed would put her back in, 'the cage'." Donna smiled.

She did? Things aren't as bad as they appear then. 'Cage' interesting description, she is aware there are two parts to her.

"Aye, and in answer to your first question, the only person she will trust right now is Hamish, he is her loyal servant. The problem though is that if he does nae keep a tight grip on his thoughts, Mara will learn of our intentions, and there is no guarantee he will help." Donna frowned, before perching on a small side table and staring at Mara.

"I'm bored, un-lock the room witch." Mara demanded with a half snarl.

"Hamish said he will help." Donna shared with me and the others. "I placed a timer on my spell, it will not unravel for another ten minutes." She spoke aloud, in answer to Mara's request.

The storm in Mara's eyes flared once again, the grey swirly mass picking up speed. Her head tipped slightly to the side before those empty eyes raked up and down Donna's. A slight hiss escaped her lips, a small trail of blood escaping her mouth and running down her chin.

"Tread carefully Donna." I warned, her telepathic abilities proving useful, despite how uncomfortable it made me knowing she could read my thoughts.

"My queen, since we have time to burn, perhaps we could make them productive." Hamish said, standing from the floor, his face a mask of boredom.

Mara turned to face him, her manner questioning. A quick inspection of Hamish's physique pulled a hint of a grin from her blood-stained mouth. I knew exactly where her mind had drifted. Unable to hold back my thoughts on the matter, I growled low, capturing Mara's attention and gaze. She smiled, the gesture cold.

"No need for jealousy hunter, you are all welcome to participate."

She licked her lips before turning to look at Ragnar and Vladimir, her eyes lingering on Ragnar more than I liked.

Not fucking happening!

"If any of you touch her I will kill you."

"Don't be a prude Conlaóch. You will be surprised how many men can find pleasure with just one woman to play with, four women, if the others are game." Ragnar grinned.

Donna did choke this time, her face scrunched up in a look of complete disgust.

"Urrgh, nae thank you." She managed to get out.

Nefta and Herlta declined to answer at all, Nefta looking as though she found this whole situation suddenly amusing. Valac refused to look anywhere but his hands, the druid not saying a word, even telepathic. I suspect after throwing up so much he wasn't feeling great. I imagine he didn't want to draw Mara's attention.

"It's not going to happen Ragnar." I said in a manner that would end this conversation all together.

Ragnar grinned before sighing. He looked at Mara with a moments worth of longing before resignation crossed his face.

"My queen, as you are aware, I will always do as you ask, your desires, my desires, your goals, my goals. If pleasure is what you seek, so be it. However, it was not my original thought. War has been declared by both the witches and the druids, as powerful as you are, you have more power available, power that currently you are unable to access. As Herlta is fey, and our ally, I thought that given we are all in one room, you could request she teach you how to access the other three elements, thus giving you greater strength for the coming conflict." Hamish said calmly, his body language indicating that ultimately, her will, will decide.

The man was more intelligent than I gave him credit for, highly skilled in slight of word. The whole dynamic of his sentence and tone of voice negated any threat, or self-suggestion. It was simply put, but Mara would find nothing about his statement or idea un-trustworthy.

"Pleasure can be provided anytime, knowledge of this importance is harder to obtain." Mara said in response, her voice half animal, was thoughtful.

"Indeed, my queen, and to learn from one of the most powerful fey magic users, it is an opportunity that will not present its self, perhaps in many a lifetime." Hamish offered.

"You will share your knowledge?" She asked Herlta.

"Do nae offer your aid too freely, she will nae believe it." Donna warned.

The witch was smarter than I gave her credit for too. She obviously understood Mara better than I do, the fact was slightly infuriating. Pride aside, if it works, then I have no choice but to admit I need Donna around, even though the bloody woman is a pain in my arse.

"I am willing to share my knowledge, but I would ask for an alliance between the fey and the Varúlfur, and between you and me. Since there is no guarantee that once you have learned all there is to learn you will not then break that alliance, I would ask that it be forged in blood and by our inherent magic. If you break the alliance, your fey magic will be severed, forever out of your reach, and vice versa. If I were to break the alliance I would lose my magic, in the same manner. This would ensure that neither one can gain from the alliance failing."

Mara seemed to be processing the pros and cons before turning to face Hamish.

"What are your thoughts on this?" She asked him.

"It would be prudent to mention, that a fey with no magic, would become mortal, bar the exception of heightened senses, the queen would practically become human. If you were to lose your magic, you would remain as you are now, but without the ability to access the elements, since you have only basic knowledge of water manipulation at present, you risk little. By entering into this agreement, the queen is bargaining her life, the gesture says much of her commitment to the alliance, if it fails, it will be she who is set to lose the most." He answered.

"It almost seems too good to be true." Mara mused, her tone suspicious.

"Someone has to be the first to make assurances, and I had hoped to gain a preconditioned favour by being the first." Herlta explained, standing, and making her way over to where Mara stood.

"There is a catch." Mara grinned, her prior suspicion absent.

"If life has taught me anything, there is always a catch" Herlta smiled, her gesture warm. "I want your full cooperation and support in bringing me those responsible for the abduction of my people, by Rex Leif, the Varúlfur involved, and those who aided, regardless of species."

"A hunt…" Mara grinned again, the small action, pure evil. "We have a deal."

I shuddered, the hair on my neck raising, there was something in the way she uttered the word 'deal' that was foreboding. The others must have had the same feeling. a despairing silence hanging in the air. Donna visibly paled, her eyes a white coat of mesh that shielded her true eyes, a vision, what did she see?

"We have five minutes, why not get started now, what element appeals to you." Herlta asked, her warmth infused voice, restoring the hope Mara had just stolen.

Mara lifted her hand, the fresh blood painting her nails. Placing her finger in her mouth, she sucked on blood soaked tip, a low hum of happiness following.

"Fire." She grinned.

"Very well, I will show you how to create a flame as a token of intent, and because we have a few minutes, beyond that, I must insist on the oath."

"Noted."

Herlta gestured for Mara to sit, which to my surprise she did. Hamish took one of the seats beside her, Herlta taking the other. Still in pain I remained where I was, on the opposite side of the table. Silently, I prayed to the mother Gaia, hoping that she would pave a way for Mara to return. Nauseated, I watched Herlta open her hand so that her palm was facing upwards, with a light nod of her head she indicated to Mara that she should do the same.

"Have you ever been burned, by a flame?" Herlta asked Mara

"Yes."

"Remember the sensation, the pain, hold onto it with your mind, envision your hand amongst the flames. Try to recall every detail, the colour of the flames, the smell and movement. See it flicker through your fingers, lisps of smoke, escaping on the air.

"Am I supposed to feel pain?"

"No, but remembering the pain helps you to better understand the essence of fire."

"I see."

"Some find it easier to close their eyes, one's imagination, creating a clearer image."

Mara closed her eyes, concentration marring her brow. A minute passed in silence.

"Can you hear it Mara, the flames song? it speaks to you, the particles for its creation are being drawn in from the air, you are drawing them in." Herlta leaned forward slightly, a glimmer of surprise in her eyes.

I made a quick glance around the room, everyone was watching, even Valac was paying attention, everyone waiting to see if she could do it, if it Gaia's magic, so pure, could bring her back.

"I can hear it." Mara whispered.

I wasn't sure if I imagined it but their seemed to be a softer edge to her voice.

"Good, let its voice carry you, guide you, keep the image of fire in your mind, see it rise from your hand."

Like the rest of the room, my eyes were drawn to her palm, I didn't know who was concentrating more, me or Mara.

"Look." Donna squealed excitedly, and from within my head.

"I was already watching, I would appreciate it if you could refrain from mental screeching."

Irritated, I flung Donna a heated glare, a strong smell of smoke redirecting my gaze. From within Mara's palm, a small column of white smoke was rising in the air, its origin an inch above the centre of her hand. Growing thicker, small sparks of orange gave the impression of glitter floating within the smoke, before a single orange flame took form, its varying and colourful tones, dancing, the small breezes in the room, carrying it back and forth.

"That's it Mara, now allow the fire's voice to take control of the flame, once you have given over control you will have the power to command it. A king does not wield the sword in battle, he commands his men to wield it for him. His strength not derived from one, but from the absolute power of the many. Surrender yourself to the flame, and the flame will surrender itself to you."

Mara's eyes remained closed, her forehead creased in deep lines, I tried to determine her train of thought through the bond, but I could sense nothing.

"Her aura is changing." Donna whispered, her voice subtle carried hopeful anticipation.

I couldn't see aura's, but I trusted Donna's ability to do so. Leaning forward on my chair as I eagerly watched on, I almost forgot to breathe, please Gaia. The flame in Mara's hand grew, the orange flames mingling with blue. Another foot higher, but still the flame was restricted to the narrow column she had begun with.

"You must surrender Mara, elemental magic cannot be controlled, it must be led, it is a partnership, not a dictatorship." Herlta instructed softly.

A low growl escaped Mara's lips, the tone not aggressive but determined, more importantly it suggested emotion. I couldn't help it, hope flared. I tried to rein it in, lest Mara noticed and grew suspicious. Hamish eyed me in annoyance, Donna swinging her gaze to mine.

"Hamish said if you fuck this up he will beat you." Donna frowned, a quick grin hitting the edges of her mouth.

Instead of replying with a sarcastic comment that would only rile both Hamish and I up, I flipped him the finger instead. Damn wolf.

My leg started tapping lightly beneath the table, this is taking too long. Slowly my hunter was becoming on edge, I could practically envision my 'hunter self' pacing back and forth in my mind, his eyes wild. Worse, the small room allowed Mara's 'I need sex' scent to invade the air, coating every part of my body. It was making me hungry, and not in a three-course meal kind of way. My mouth closed, I ran my tongue over my top teeth, my fangs hadn't appeared but the hard lumps of gum above my canines told me they would soon if I didn't get out of here. Once their out, there's no getting them back in, not until the hunters appeased anyway.

Not that Mara would mind but I wasn't really feeling an audience, especially after Ragnar's earlier comment.

Mara's eyes flung open "grow" she whispered, her features calm, her voice more so.

The moment she gave the command, the fire erupted, it was like someone had just turned on a gas valve, the flames, wild, rocketed towards the ceiling, the heat and fury making everyone pull their faces back, some even pushing their seats further from the table. Surprise had me standing up, the pain in my chest intensifying. I growled painfully before falling back to my chair with a grunt. Worry permeated through the bond…Mara. The flame died instantly, the heat with it. I found Mara's eyes, the ice blue iris filled with concern.

Donna jumped up from the side table overly excited, water in her eyes.

"It worked!" She squealed, before running and pulling Mara into a huge side embrace. She let go quickly, stepping back with a horrified expression on her face. Slightly heaving, Donna leaned against the table.

"You should shower Mara, warlock is nae a good look… or fragrance for you," Donna managed to spit out, her heaving growing worse when she noticed she was now wearing warlock too.

Donna's face paled further, I couldn't help the small grin that surfaced, Hamish's sudden laughter almost turning it into a smile.

"The barriers down… I hate you… Hamish." Donna said, running out of the room, both hands covering her mouth.

"Please tell me I didn't eat him." Mara said, unwrapping Fumi's intestine from her neck.

She looked straight at me, her thoughts on what she had done concealed from everyone's inspection, however, there was a glimmer of shame that passed between us. Her shame.

"You didn't eat him." Hamish said, pulling his shirt off. He offered it to Mara.

"Thank you." She said as I growled.

No, not happening. Fucking men and my wife! That was it, the final damn straw, my hunter was enraged. Ignoring the pain, I shot up from the table and stalked towards Mara. Pulling the shirt Hamish had given her from her hands I threw it at him before shoving him against the wall. Turning, I grabbed Mara, throwing her over my shoulder.

"Col, what the hell." Mara hissed.

Too many male scents on her flesh, none of them mine.

"I swear to all the gods if another man makes himself even the slightest bit available to you, even hints at being interested, I will destroy them." I fumed, walking out of the door.

Legacy

To my surprise, the meeting went well. Granted Donna held my hand the whole time, but still, I didn't turn, and nobody died. It was a good day and after the last seventy-two hours of Col's eye-opening imprisonment, I actually felt… happy. Turns out being tied up can be fun, who knew.

"Mara please…I mean honestly hen, seventy-two hours of just you and Col and your mind is still drifting to sex." Donna sighed, the gesture false.

I smiled, Col replicating the gesture. He seemed more at ease, as though finally I wasn't stressing him out. Clutching my thigh beneath the table lightly he stood, putting his chair away. This time around our meeting took place in the middle of a meadow, a patrol of guards circling from a distance.

It was Donna's idea, and a good one. Herlta the fey queen had appointed me a fey teacher. Upon everyone's insistence I was to channel at least four hours a day, thus ensuring my wolf stayed calm. I didn't mind, after what I had done to Fumi it was a good thing. I felt bad, not so bad that I felt the need to apologise, but bad about the way I killed him. He was the one that started it… so technically, it was his own fault.

"Are you ready Mara?" Herlta asked.

Col held his hand out for me to take. Standing up from the table, I did my best to look like a queen. The idea of embarrassing Col didn't sit right, especially after the last few days we have spent together. It was important to him, so, still not quit understanding why, it was important to me.

"I'm ready."

Stepping away from the table I went and stood in front of Herlta, five fey chancellors moving in and encasing us in the centre. We were about to enter in to a blood oath, an alliance. I do not really recall much of the wolves' dealings when last we met, but Donna filled me in on most, Col and Hamish on other things. It was a unanimous vote from all the leaders that the agreement be entered into immediately. During a private conversation with Hamish, we also decided that for the safety of our people, I should be a queen who cannot rule by absolute control, and that I should release them all from blind obedience, making sure that if I ever became lost to the dark irrevocably, I couldn't use them for my evil inklings. I still wasn't sure how that was going to be implemented but I knew that it should. I would remain their queen as an undefeated alpha, the strongest, and would still remain mentally linked to every wolf, but without the power to overt my will. Of course, if they defied me in my presence I could still make them submit, but in a worst-case scenario, 'Warg gone rouge' they can never be an army for dark forces, not unless they chose it.

"Please except these blades." An unknown fey said, holding two identical blades towards us.

I took the blade from his hand, the texture and design highly crafted. The almost Celtic looking design reminded me of Donna's money clip. It seemed like so long ago when we gate crashed the wedding. Donna started giggling.

"Good times." She whispered into my thoughts.

I grinned. From the corner of my eye I saw Col gently shove Donna. I couldn't see but I was betting Col had a threatening gleam in his eye, all serious and snarky.

"Aye, someone needs to pull the stick from his arse." She half snorted before catching herself.

"You are about to enter an agreement that will bind you, Mara Ó Ceallacháin, Queen of the Varúlfur and queen of the Keltoi, and you Herlta, queen of the Fey, Guardian of the light, that will bind your magic. So long as the alliance stands, you will both retain Gaia's gifts. If the pact of peace is broken, your gifts will be lost, never to be possessed again. Do you both understand?" The fey who handed us the knife asked.

"I understand." We both said.

"Make your cuts, and join your hands." He instructed.

Taking the blade, I ran it across my palm. Normally such a slight cut wouldn't garner a response, but like heated metal, the blade burned, my hand inflamed. I growled low, my teeth elongating. My wolf snarled in the back of my mind. It cannot rise now. Using some of the breathing tactics my fey teacher, 'Ether' taught me, I drew Gaia's pure air into my lungs, envisioning the threads of magic the air contained, knotting together, a barrier of light that would keep my wolf at bay. Tense, I failed to offer my hand, Herlta taking hold of it for me. Our hands joined, an extra measure of calm swam up my arm and chest, the sensation, like that of Col's warmth, further pushing the Warg back. Feeling in control once more I lifted my eyes to Herlta. She smiled, reassurance covering her face.

"Repeat the oath."

Col had woken me up this morning, the oath written on a small piece of paper. He was also naked and delicious, Damn it! I silently cursed. Focus.

"Allies we stand, united we are, in cause and in deed. May the goddess witness our pledge, her divine eye guide. Our blood we join, our magic the price. Peace be ensured, the fey, the Varúlfur, the Keltoi as one. Bless us with the light, the strength to withstand. Let that which is forged never be undone. The light of creation, a beacon in the night, the darkness not withstand. Our alliance, is our bond, our alliance, is our legacy."

A bright light engulfed our hands, the burning sensation from the cut evaporating. Herlta smiled and let go of my hand. Lifting it up I noticed the cut had healed but like the scar on my thigh it hadn't disappeared. I wasn't quite sure what I expected but I was a little disappointed the earth didn't quake.

"It is a constant reminder of the pledge you have made, much like the oath and mark we share." Col whispered in my ear, his arms circling my waist.

I leaned against him, his closeness pulling a small smile from my lips. Licking them, I turned and faced him. His forest green eyes relayed happiness, his gaze as always, seemingly gazing into my soul.

"What are you thinking?"

"That I'm happy." I said, meaning it.

Granted, I was still hunted, twisted and unpredictable, and not to mention the granddaughter of Fenrir, who is still emotionally inept, but right now, in this very minute, I couldn't make those things matter. I was learning, the more time I spent with Col, Donna, and my friends, I was beginning to understand normal, and I liked it. Love hovered on the tip of my tongue, but like before it didn't come, but for the first time in my life I believed that it could, that it will.

"Then your day is about to get better." He half grinned.

"How so?"

"Mara!" Gabriella called.

"I decided, based on merits of good behaviour over these last few days, that it's probably safe for you to see your friends."

I snorted, Good behaviour, I was tied to a bed while he did magical things to me, pretty difficult to get into trouble.

"You don't agree." He said with a look that said he could always change his mind.

"I'm not going to argue with you anam cara." I smiled.

Before he could speak again I placed my mouth over his, warmth and electricity, infusing my senses.

"Urrgh, get a room, minors are present… Ppfft." Gabriella teased.

A low rumbling growl, vibrated against my chest, Col wasn't happy with the interruption. Moving away from Col, I grinned. He took a step with me as though he intended to follow. Stopping, I swept him a sideways glance.

"I'm sure you have lots of king things to be doing, I will see you later."

"I said you could see them, I didn't say alone."

"I'm not alone, there's five of us, six if you include that hunter… who won't let go of Asta." I frowned.

He is one of Col's team, a twin, why the hell is he drooping all over Asta? She didn't seem to mind, but still, Asta's fragile, pure. I didn't like his roaming hands. I was obviously glaring with daggers in my eyes, as the hunter shot me his most intimidating glare. At least I thought it was, it wasn't overly impressive. What the hell happened? It's only been three days since I last saw them, I was angry, a sudden need to protect her ripping a snarl from my mouth.

"See, you shouldn't be alone." Col said, garnering another snarl.

"Who's he, and why is he touching her? Better yet, why are you letting him?" I hissed.

Col tried to grab my arm when I stalked towards Asta, and the far too big and dangerous for her man. Asta jumped when she saw me coming, the hunter stepping in front of her, shielding her from my view. His eyes clouded with grey smoke, his fangs protruding from his mouth. So, it's like that is it. Furious, my temper soared, my breath hitting the air with an icy chill. I growled, gaining the attention of a group of nearby guards.

"Damn it Mara, what are you doing? They are anam cara!" Col hissed behind me, successfully grabbing me from behind.

His arms laced their way around my chest, pulling me tightly against him.

"You lie." I hissed.

"It's true." Gabriella jumped in front of me. "His name is Eoghuan, he is Asta's anam cara." She said softly, her eye brow raised in a verifying arch.

I froze, my eyes studying hers for the truth before finding Eoghuan's. I sized him up, scanning his body. Asta was small, dainty, Eoghuan was not. The fact that he could very easily hurt her was wearing with the notion she was his soul mate; my logic didn't like the dynamics.

"Is it true Asta?" I asked softly, not wanting to frighten her.

Asta stepped out from behind Eoghuan, the hunter didn't like this, his arm moving protectively in front of her. She stopped, looked at him, and then at me. She smiled her shy smile, her cheeks reddening.

"This is Eoghuan, Mara, my anam cara."

It's true.

"You are bonded?" I asked her, my temper was fading but I still wasn't happy.

Her face went bright red, her mouth opening and closing slightly, I guessed because she didn't know what to say.

"They are. Asta is his wife." Col answered for her.

"Did he hurt you?"

He didn't like the question, he growled, Asta placing her hand on his chest.

"She's is protecting me, she means nothing by it." She said to him.

He looked at her, his smoky eyes slowly vanishing, bright blue eyes taking their place. He gazed at her, like Col did me, that un-graspable emotion that reminded me I'm tainted. I sighed. Eoghuan pulled her against him tenderly, before returning his attention to me.

"I would never hurt her, that my queen would seek to protect her, honours me." He said, in that same hypnotic Irish lilt that Col had.

Col grunted behind me. I got the sudden feeling that the hunter's words were the product of his glare as opposed to Asta's revelation.

"You are happy?" I asked her.

Her face lit up, her smile radiant. Happiness was pouring from every part of her, it was like the first time I met Herlta, but this time when I looked again that light was still there.

"Yes, very happy."

Eoghuan smiled with her acknowledgment, a glimmer of pride dancing in his eyes.

I sighed, and then grunted resigned.

"Fine… But Eoghuan, I swear to all the gods, if I so much as see her frown you will pay greatly for it."

Asta's face paled, but perhaps out of fear for her anam cara she kept a semblance of a smile on her face. Eoghuan looked pissed by my comment, but after another grunt from Col, said nothing. I elbowed him in the ribs, he winced.

"I'm warning you woman, I have a dungeon." He grumbled in my ear, before sucking on my ear lobe, I melted against him with a soft hiss, my irritation forgotten.

"Ok, so… urm." Gabriella started.

"Boss." One of Col's guards called, his breathing laboured.

I turned as Col did, both of us picking up on the seriousness of his tone. He looked worried, about what he had to say or about what Col's response would be? Either way, it didn't look like good news.

"What is it?"

The guards jaw twitched.

"He is here." He said.

Who is here? Damn stupid man, could he be any vaguer? Col obviously understood as he tensed before snarling.

"Everyone in the castle now!" He shouted, far too close to my ear.

Wincing, I hissed. Eoghuan didn't need be told twice, lifting Asta into his arms, Asta looking embarrassed, he started running towards the castle. Begrudgingly, I had to admit he obviously felt as protective over her as I did. The rest of the guard began ushering everyone in the same direction. Shouts and orders started, they seemed to come from every direction. Hamish, who I don't remember being around, came running towards me, Sven in tow.

A loud bang had my head wiping towards the sky, a flash of electric blue light exploding. The neon edge of the circle grew in diameter, lightening filling its centre. What the fuck. Col grabbed my arm, the action catching me my surprise. Instinctively I went to hit him, before realising he was only trying to help me.

"What's happening?" I asked, letting him drag me along.

Hamish and Sven were now behind me, their eyes on our surroundings, I could tell through our link it was serious, Hamish and Sven calling all wolves to arms.

"There is a Warg close by." Hamish answered.

"Herlta and her chancellors have confirmed you are a blood descendant of Jörg, the child of prophecy. Ragnar has summoned his demons to aid us, the fey have erected a shield wall." He continued.

Shield wall? The bang, I looked at the sky, the blue mass now fully covering the estate.

"Yes, my queen."

Col was shouting orders in Gaelic, his men, hundreds of them surrounding us, their ancient weapons gleaming under the high suns glare. They literally came pouring from every conceivable direction, where the hell did all these men come from? I've seen men around the castle, but this many.

"We are talking about one Warg right?" I asked.

You would think they were preparing for dooms day, shit… excessive much. Hamish grunted in annoyance, grabbing my arm, and spinning me around. Col spun around with me, his clouded eyes wild.

Hamish stepped closer, grabbing my shoulders. His eyes were furious, his aura no longer hidden, darkened the air around us, the un-natural bend of the air trapping the sun's rays.

"Look at me and listen closely. Do not underestimate the danger you are in, one Warg is as destructive as a league of demons, more so. You are powerful my queen, but you are young, he is not. You are the fate of the world, your death is the enslavement of everyone you care about, who they care about, families, children. You will do what your king says, you will not take risks, you will let men die if it means you will live, am I clear!" He hissed.

Taken a back I didn't say anything, my heart thumping loudly. Col had stilled too, his expression caught between surprise and concern,

"Promise me my queen, promise me you will listen." Hamish pleaded, his eyes softening.

An overwhelming emotion passed through the pack link, Hamish's memories and feelings flooding my mind. I saw myself the first time we had met, and every encounter since. So many emotions mingled with images, some hard to decipher, but one above all, the feeling of absolute despair, the thought of me being harmed, the thought of losing me ripping a whole in my chest. I couldn't inhale, my breath caught in an uncomfortable lump that wouldn't give way. A streak of wet ran down my cheek, my chest feeling as though it was catching on fire. What is this? It was like Col's betrayal, but so much worse. The world grew out of focus, nothing held any meaning, nothing could ever matter without her.

"This is what it feels like, when the idea of someone you love may be taken from you." He whispered in my mind.

"Promise me." He asked me again aloud, his eyes pained.

Another tear rolled down my cheek, my mind trying its best to understand what this meant. *"You love me?"*

"Yes, my queen."

"I promise."

A Call to Arms

The sounds of men running from room to room seeped through the bottom of study door, the castle humming with activity. Herlta, Ragnar, Vladimir and his sons sat, opposite me, Hamish, and Mara to my side. Aengus burst into the room, the rest of my team following behind.

"They are both here, my lord." Aengus rumbled, his face set in a deep scowl.

Hati and Sköll. I growled along with most of the room.

"You are certain?" I asked, not really needing to, they wouldn't give me false information.

"Aye my lord." Ansgar answered.

Fuck, I glanced at Mara quickly. Ever since her exchange with Hamish, she had been unusually quiet. Expecting her to argue about the sanctions I had placed upon her, I didn't know what to think of her sudden cooperation. Something happened between them, a private conversation that I wasn't privy too. I tried to ask her about it, but she said nothing, her eyes drifting to closed thoughts. When I attempted to learn from Hamish I got the same solid wall he used to guard his mind. I could press, could force my way through, but it required attention I couldn't currently give.

Wargs stalked the grounds, ready to take Mara from me. With most of earth leaders here, why stop at just her, they would take as many as they could, making the coming of their father even less of a challenge. I shouldn't have waited, I should have called everyone to arms sooner, now we were at a disadvantage. With the exception of Ragnar's demons and Herlta's fey warriors nothing could get through the barrier her men erected for her protection. As its stood, we were under prepared, the fact playing havoc on my temper. With just one Warg our odds were balanced, two was pushing it. There is a reason we hunt them away from our homeland, the elite are battle tested, my team could take Sköll, but not without civilian casualties, a lot of civilian casualties. Humans losing their lives is one thing, losing my people is a different matter entirely. There are young children here, young minds cannot fight a Warg's madness, cannot block their darkness from corrupting their thoughts. We need to go out and destroy them, sooner rather than later, lest our children and young ones start killing each other.

"Are they together?" Ragnar asked.

"Nae, we do nae believe so." Ansgar said somewhat distracted.

"Are all the younglings secured?" Herlta looked at me, worry etched into her face.

"Yes, anything that could be used as a weapon has been removed from their vicinity."

"Aye, we even took their shoe laces." Aengus cut in.

Ansgar's distracted face kept pulling my attention, he was in deep thought, his jaw constantly rolling. He was obviously processing something of importance.

"What is it Ansgar?"

His golden eyes locked onto mine, deep lines creasing his forehead. He grunted before quickly glancing at Mara, who was still staring out of the window in a dream like state.

"I have a theory, but if I'm wrong it could prove fatal. Either it's the truth or a trap that's been years in the making." He said finally.

"Speak." I frowned, not happy with the look he gave Mara, that his theory involved her was clearly evident.

"No one has ever seen Hati's face, we do not know what he looks like. There are two Wargs prowling the estate, their movements almost suggesting that one is pursuing the other. You had a theory that Mara's guardian Ti, was Hati, I have seen Ti's face, as have you. If we can match it to the second Warg then we can be certain her guardian was indeed Hati, but more than that, if he is, he may be here nae to aid his brother but to protect Mara as he has before."

"Mara's guardian was her father?" Seth asked, a look of disbelief hovering in his eyes.

Ansgar revelation drew everyone's gaze, including Mara's. Vladimir sat further back in his chair, his expression thoughtful.

"Why would a Warg protect his daughter? Her very existence is all that stands between them and their victory." Ragnar spoke up, his eyes finding and remaining on Mara.

"That's the question, you have heard my theory, perhaps if I could meet him, I could determine whether it is correct." Herlta said.

"The problem with your theory is that Aelius is dead. If they were bonded, her death would have turned him into a soulless creature just like his father." Vladimir added.

He made a good point.

"Unless she's not dead." Lucian spoke up.

Everyone's gaze fell on him. It would make sense, the missing piece of the puzzle. It would explain why he had never harmed her, why against his very nature he raised her. She's alive.

"A gift from the sun." Mara whispered from under a bowed head.

"A gift from Aelius." Ansgar said to Mara.

She looked up at him, her eyes pained.

"Why would she leave me with him, why have I never seen her?" She said, her sadness slamming into my chest, the emotion quickly turning to anger.

Hamish moved closer to her, pulling a stray lock of hair from her face.

"It was the greatest act of love my queen." He said gently, lovingly.

I fought to keep in a growl, he was her general, her adviser, she needed him, but always he pushed against the line, one small gesture too far. He looked at me, his face stoic before taking a step back. He hid it well, but I could tell that step was painful for him. Is that it, is that what his outburst was about earlier? Is he in love with her? Damn the pack link! The promise, what else was promised, what didn't I hear?

"He is right little one, so long as you were the only key, your life was assured. A child, even with the smallest amount of Warg blood, is a child that would have been deemed too dangerous to live. Aelius knew this, Hati knew this, if you were to have any chance at life, at reaching your immortality, earth's races needed to believe you were the last blood descendant. Now we know you are not." Ragnar said, the undercurrent dangerous.

Hamish growled, moving to stand before Mara, myself included. My team's hands hovering over their weapons, everyone in the room growing tense.

"There is no proof Aelius is alive, and even if there was, what condition is she in? Two keys are better than one." Herlta spoke up in Mara's defence.

"That Hati is here to protect her is proof, what if there are other children like her out there? Siblings. We have all witnessed Mara's strength and her inability to control the Warg within her. She has an army of Lycans at her disposal, Lycans that will do whatever she says regardless of the consequences. As Valac pointed out, she has all the ingredients to becoming Fenrir and more, all that is needed now is the correct settings." Ragnar hissed.

"He is right." Mara said, her gaze heavy, landing on Ragnar. "I cannot control it, but as for my army, I have found a way to free them from my compulsion, and as for my magic, if ever I become what you all fear, I am certain the fey queen will volunteer her death, so I cannot wield earth's magic. It is why she suggested the alliance in the first place, is it not? My Warg would never understand a powerful queen that would sacrifice herself, her power, for the benefit of others, she would never have suspected your true intention." Mara said to Herlta.

Herlta smiled, a warm glow filling the room.

"Your intelligence far surpasses your years. It was indeed our true intention, but I knew you would not only except, but understand."

Mara didn't say anything but nodded in agreement. She turned to face me, a sad smile on her face. I wanted to wrap her in my arms. Hugging isn't really my thing, but her distress no matter how well she concealed it, set off my protective instincts. Right now she needed me, needed comforting. Doing the second-best thing, I placed my arm around her back, drawing her body into mine, to the room it would seems as though I was shielding her, nothing more. With the things Ragnar has said no one would suspect any emotional reasoning behind it.

"The wolves have tried and failed to remove the curse for millennia, if you could prove this claim, and with the shared alliance between you and Herlta, I will concede that the risk of you living is acceptable."

"I do not require your permission to live demon king, if you want me dead feel free to challenge me. As for your proof, Hamish is my proof." Mara hissed, her fangs cutting her lower lip.

Hamish stepped forward, a low growl rumbling from his chest.

"Hamish, as your queen, I command you to attack Ragnar."

An evil grinned passed over Hamish's face, his face contorting into a half man, half wolf configuration. His muscles flexed as he adjusted to the larger form such a change required. He snarled, his slightly elongated jaw gleaming with razor sharp teeth. Ragnar sat back in his chair before regaining his composure, a mask of indifference lowering over him. Instead of attacking, Hamish remained where he stood, his lethal gaze focused solely on the demon king. Mara let go of me, moving to stand by Hamish. Pushing up onto the balls of her feet, she lifted her mouth to his ear. With all the voice and authority of an alpha, she hissed.

"Kill him Hamish. Do it now…I insist upon it."

Mara had never mentioned freeing Hamish, a fact I only learned from reading his thoughts, she never said anything about her pack. I could hear quick breaths being drawn, none of them yet to be exhaled. My eyes kept drifting between Hamish and Ragnar, could she really have found a way to free them all? And if so, why wouldn't she mention this to me? Hamish growled, the ferocity of it putting everyone on high alert. Then just like that, it was over, Hamish's face returning to normal. He smirked at Ragnar before turning to face Mara.

"No, my queen." He grinned, his eyes sending her a message that was meant just for her.

"Well that puts a whole new spin on things." Vladimir piped up, a sadistic edge to what I assumed was a smile.

"Indeed." Lucian added.

"Of course, the fact that you are what you are, and no longer able to manipulate the Varúlfur, you may discover you are a queen of few." Vladimir speculated.

"She remains alpha of all alpha's, the undefeated. Our people will follow her, recognise her as their leader, their queen. That she would free them of the curse will only secure their loyalty. So long as she remains an enemy of Fenrir, we will stand by her." Hamish defended with an irritated hiss.

"If I lose myself to the darkness Hamish will become king, everything is in place." Mara said, before moving to look out of the window again, her expression sombre.

"You have made him your beta." Ansgar asked her.

"Yes. If you will excuse us, I must meet with Donna and discuss my plans regarding this matter. Hamish." Mara called, before heading out of the room without saying goodbye, Hamish as always, practically on her heels.

As a king, I knew why she didn't discuss her plans concerning her people, but as her husband. it pissed me off, I had kept nothing from her. Sighing, I knew I was overreacting, my hunters restless state getting the better of me. It's not like we have had much time to talk, nor had I asked her. Mara's days are spent with Hamish, her nights with me, no matter how I looked at it, it was a problem. The more I thought about it, the more I'm convinced he loves her, maybe even as much as me. Unlike me however, he says the right things. Frustrated, I sat back down at my desk, everyone staring at me. The dilemma would have to join the queue, first problem, Sköll.

"Do you think you can find him without confronting Sköll?" I asked Ansgar.

"Hati? Aye, it shouldn't be an issue."

"Take the team. If you can, speak with him through the wall. If his reasons for being here are as you suspect then he will want to see Mara, he should agree to let you read his mind, make it clear he will not have access to her otherwise, and bring him to me first, you know where to take him."

"Aye my Lord."

Ansgar left, Eoghuan, Finian and Aengus exiting first.

"Are you sure that's wise?" Ragnar asked.

"You have a better suggestion, other than killing my wife?" I hissed, my temper flaring.

"I have no wish to kill your wife, after all, she is exactly my kind of woman, beautiful but deadly." He grinned. "I merely wanted to stir the hornets' nest, so to speak, Mara riled up, is truly stunning. Wouldn't you agree Lucian?"

Ragnar's laughter was deep and throaty, how he learned of Mara and Lucian was something I planned to find out. That Vladimir's eyes filled with blood made me lean towards him. Keeping my face as impassive as I could, given my current state of vexation, I focused on Vladimir.

"About that, I have been meaning to bring it up. As you're well aware I could have your son killed, instead, and because I have no wish to displease my wife, I will settle for a life debt. He will remain here under my command for the period of five hundred years. If he fails to live by my rules, he will spend those years in my dungeon, starving."

Lucian didn't say anything, but I caught a shot of blood fork into his eyes. He was not happy with his fate, this pleased me, it was exactly my intention. Vladimir didn't manage to conceal his displeasure. Furious, layers of menace peeled from his body, the air stifling. It was an impressive display of malice, but not enough to change my mind.

"What he did was done in good will, she would never have lived with herself, had she killed everyone on the plane." He hissed.

"Draining her blood was an act of good will. Kissing her, enjoying her body, was an act of self-gain. He enjoyed it, so much so, he made it clear he would do it again, regardless of the fact she is mine." I growled, my hunter failing to calm.

You do not fondle another man's wife as an act of good fucking will.

"She is in heat, what man wouldn't kiss her back?" Vladimir spat.

"You forget I have read his mind. He does not regret what happened, he would even now, with his fate laid before him, do it again."

Vladimir turned to face his son, his face marred in unrelenting anger.

"Is this true?" He snarled.

Lucian's jaw twitched before he turned his head to meet his father. Keeping his gaze, Lucian didn't so much as flinch.

"Yes."

Vladimir struck him hard across the face, the impact sickening. Lucian didn't make a sound, taking the punishment in his stride. Lucian was Vladimir's heir, his confession and lack of will would be seen as a weakness, a weakness in an heir, is a weakness in the father, and in the Tepes coven. Lucian rolled his jaw calmly before looking at me, his silver/blue eyes, piercing.

"You have read my mind, you know what could have happened. I could have pressed for more, I didn't. None the less, I accept that I over stepped. I will serve my time." He said smoothly, the Romanian tang, although subtle, still lingering in his accent.

"Good. CONNOR."

The door opened, Connor entering the room.

"Tiarna."

"This is Lucian, he will be joining Cael, make sure he's where he's meant to be."

Connor frowned.

"You are placing him onto an elite squad?" He dared to ask me.

"You have a problem with that?" I snarled, the hunter's hue entering my eyes.

"No, my lord." He answered quickly, his head slightly bowing.

"You may not be Keltoi, but you will fight with them as though they were your blood brothers. If you fail to pull your weight, if you place any of them in danger, there will be no further mercy. You will serve the rest of your time beneath my castle. Understood?"

"Understood." Lucian said, standing casually from the table. "Take care little brother."

Inclining his head to Seth, he ignored his father, turning, and leaving the room with Connor. Still seething, Vladimir sat back down in his chair. Ragnar finding the whole situation highly amusing. If the demon king was resorting to creating chaos then he must be bored, the sooner he leaves, the better for everyone.

"I have had assurances from Nefta, and Valac, they will offer their full cooperation in the continuing battle against Fenrir's forces. I have yet to hear from the Hexan, but given the circumstance I expect it may take a while to replace Fumi. That leaves you three. So, what will it be? Will you call your forces to arms? Or will you allow Fenrir to reign?"

"Your cause is my cause; the Vanir stand with you." Herlta smiled.

Leaning forward she extended her arm, gripping my wrist, likewise I gripped hers. A small volt of electricity flew between us, a pledge acknowledged by the Gods, the seal that would mark our pact has been made. Withdrawing my hand, Herlta's royal crest rested on my wrist, just as mine was upon hers. I lifted my eyes to Ragnar, waiting for his decision. His steel coloured eyes held my gaze, his demeanour giving nothing away.

"I will stand with you hunter because the darkness has over played its hand, and because the balance is off set, but understand, if you fall in battle, I will see to it your queen dies with you." He warned, not as threat but as a promise.

I grunted in irritation, before mentally sighing. I will protect Mara with my life, but even I must admit that without her soul she cannot live.

"A promise I sincerely hope you keep."

Just as I did with Herlta, a pact was made, the demons coat of arms less than a centimetre above the Vanir's. My eyes turned to Vladimir. He sneered, but held out his hand, just as the others did.

"I do this for the love of my people. When Fenrir's forces rise, I will stand with you, but in all else, do not expect my aid."

Not saying anything I placed my grip into his, another crest to add to my collection. Vladimir stood, his temper still far from being contained.

"If we are done, I must return to New York." He hissed, his son Seth, standing with him.

Vladimir turned to face him, a lethal snarl escaping his fanged mouth.

"You will remain to protect Gabriella." He spat before stalking out of the room.

Seth didn't move, his mouth half open as though he was about to disagree, wisely he didn't. Looking awkward, he just hovered unmoving in the centre of the room.

"You can remain in the rooms already provided you, do not get in my way, and stay away from our women." I ordered with a threatening scowl.

Waving him out of the door, he left looking somewhat perplexed. Making a slow spin in the hallway he tried to determine what direction to go off in, finally deciding on left. It was the wrong way. Snarling, I picked up the phone. How many foreigners am I going to have to babysit?

"There is a young vampire named Seth, he just left my study. Make sure he gets where he's supposed to." I grumbled.

Three hours had passed, and I still hadn't heard back from Ansgar and my team, nor had I seen Mara. When I found Asta in the Hallway and asked if she had seen her, she gave me a shy smile before making an illogical excuse and leaving.

Against my suggestion and blatant hint, Ragnar declined to leave, more demons arriving by the minute. I didn't mind the strength and skill they brought with them, especially given the circumstances, but where there are demons, there is chaos. It was only a matter of time before something happened, the magnitude of which, yet to be determined. With so much to do I had no choice but to trust that Ragnar would control them, which only made my unyielding temper fouler. To say I was in a bad mood was putting it lightly, I was a storm in a tea cup, the slightest provocation and it would be hell to pay. My people must have picked up on this, as every time anyone passed me they immediately lowered their heads, moving when possible, further from me.

Grunting, I rolled my neck and shoulders and entered the common room. As always, the large hall was full of my people, a gathering area they would convene, enjoying the company of family and friends, knowing that within this castle they were safe. A slight pang of nervousness hit me, for the first time in years I questioned just how safe they were. A question I started to ponder, before my gaze fell on Aengus. He was sat on one of the large side benches, Donna perched in his lap, her arms draped around his neck. I'd been waiting, worried for three fucking hours, and he along with Eoghuan and Finian were sat in here, all casual like, damn smiles plastered on their faces. It was more than enough to break the damn tea cup. Furious, I let out all the days frustration, my pent-up anger, in one single growl that had everyone freezing on the spot. Eoghuan and Aengus lowered their women to the bench. My men, including Finian and every other solider in the room, standing to attention. Even the horde of demons that were sat on the other side of the room stood, however they did so with weapons in their hands, a look of 'Am I going to attack' gleaming wickedly in their eyes.

Donna stared at me before a look of 'oh shit' crossed her face. She swung her head up to face Aengus.

"Ansgar didn't report to Conlaóch." She said, her face etched in worry.

Aengus's eyes suddenly filled with concern, Eoghuan and Finian looking at each other, a panicked expression passing between them. Aengus growled, his face reddening as his temper soared.

"Boss, he was on his way to report to you an hour ago." Aengus confessed stalking towards me.

I was furious, but with the confession, alarm was quickly taking over.

"You did not question that he had not returned." I rebuked. "What happened?"

Realising that my anger was aimed at my men, everyone else in the room started to take their seats again, however in the nature of people they remained hushed, curious to learn the reason for my outburst. This wasn't the place to be speaking of such.

"Nae worry, they cannae hear anything now." Donna perked up, a dramatic wave of her hand, the air around us flexing with various hues of blue before resettling to its normal clear visage.

"You know how I feel about you reading my thoughts Donna." I hissed.

"Aye, you and the rest of them, but now is nae the time to be so bent about it." She moaned, her tone a reprimanding one.

Given the circumstances I was willing to let her tone slide, however her belief that being Mara's friend somehow gives her permission to question me would not stand much longer. She looked at me, the defiant purse of her mouth telling me what she thought on the matter.

"I mean it Donna, I am a king, you may be good for Mara, but you will respect my title, what patience I have is growing thin." I snarled, just for her hearing.

I must have put more threat behind the comment than I thought, she took a step back, instinctively seeking safety by edging closer to Aengus.

Little did she know Aengus could not save her from my displeasure.

"We made contact with Hati, you were right, he is Mara's guardian. He said that he was here to protect Mara. Of course, we were nae prepared to take his word. He was nae happy about it, but he finally agreed to let Ansgar read his mind. We took him to the fort, he is locked in the white room. Ansgar dismissed us. He said he was going to report back to you, that we would be called when we were needed. That was, as I've said, an hour ago." Aengus rumbled.

"In what direction did he go? At what point did you all split from each other?"

"He took the east path, we separated close to the armoury." Finian explained with a sigh, concern and annoyance flaring in his eyes, he was pissed with himself, worried for Ansgar.

"You and Eoghuan will go search for him, Aengus sound the alarm, everyone is to assume the worse has happened, find my wife, take your witch with you! Down the privacy spell Donna, I need to warn everyone."

Finian and Eoghuan nodded, Eoghuan spinning around to pull Asta into a tight embrace.

"I love you." He whispered against her ear. "Do not leave this hall anam cara, promise me you will remain in here." He told her, before gently cupping her face with his palm.

Nervously she smiled at him, her expression a mixture of love and fear.

"I promise." She said finally.

Leaning forward she kissed him goodbye.

As soon as Eoghuan withdrew Donna pounced on Asta, hugging her tightly. Softly, Aengus pulled her away.

"We have nae time Donna, we leave now."

Nodding, Donna followed, a sorry look aimed at Asta. As Donna left the hall, her eyes cloaking in a white mesh, briefly locked onto mine.

"Find her hunter. It is time, he has come for her." She said in a ghostly voice, before disappearing down the hall.

The despairing growl that built in my chest pulled the attention of the room, fear and anger feeding the deadly baritone. He dares try and take her from me, the dark vile bastard will get his due. Enraged, I felt the grey smoking abyss enter my eyes, my strength flaring and sparking around me. This time everyone stood, man, woman and child, uncertainty reflecting in their eyes.

The demons hissed and growled, my energy and lethal intentions riling them up for carnage, for blood. Every eye was on me, every civilian eye afraid. My men pulled their weapons, their grey violent hue, swimming, waiting for the command they knew was coming. Mara's face hovered upon the surface of my war enthralled vision. Like a hologram she held form in every thought, every sound, every intention. The thought of losing her, of her death, filling me with a dread that only made my hunter more fearless, more focused on the kill. Sköll stood in the way of all that could be, stood like a double-edged knife, ready to rip her away from me. Under the mantle of a king, my hunter was in full control, a guardian of the light, ready to destroy the encroaching darkness. With a deafening roar, all my passion, all my intent radiating within, Sköll's fate was sealed.

"We stand as one, brothers in blood and in cause. We are the swords that steal the taint of darkness, who quell the might of evil. Guardians of the light, of life and of hope. We will this day honour our calling and purge the darkness from our lands. To arms! For now, we hunt." I called to the room, the command greeted and acknowledged with the thunderous beat of weapons being beaten against the hard-wooden tables.

The sound resonated throughout the large hall. Quickly, responding thumps joined in the blades song. Coming from every direction, every room, every station across the estate. The slow chilling thrum was a declaration of our coming. It says 'we know you're here'. Some march to war by the sound of drums, the call of the horn, but for us, it is the sound of our metal, and the promise… you will die by it.

Turning my back on my men, I strode from the hall determined, Mara will not die this day. We will be victorious, I have to be.

Into the Woods

I left the study glad to be out of the damn room. My wolf was tetchy, and I still couldn't fathom how to begin dealing with Hamish's declaration of love. Despite his early impressions and abduction, I realised I was fond of him, and not because he smelled divine, looked divine, but because he was more than anyone gave him credit for. He let me into his head, shared every private memory and thought, his entire life laid bared before me. Every weakness, every shame, love, desire, pain, all of it. The length of his life, his knowledge, experience, now belonged to me, and he asked nothing in return, not verbally, and not in thought. He had literally given me everything, the scope and measure of his gift leaving me trapped in a half-dazed stupor, my young mind trying to catch up, comprehend and respond.

I thought my life was tragic, convinced myself that no one could ever understand the darkness, the pain...I had been so naive.

"My queen, your friends have arrived." Hamish whispered from beside me, his cold breath sending a delightful chill racing down my spine.

Sighing softly, I forced myself to focus on the present. Whilst stuck in the day dream I somehow managed to walk to one of Col's many gardens, the how and why lost on me for a moment.

"You arranged to meet with them all in private earlier, before the ceremony." Hamish clarified for me, my head whipping around to frown at him.

I did? yes, I did. Damn it.

"You gave me a gift Hamish, one that I am honoured to possess, but your timing was…"

"Inconvenient." He finished for me, a slow smile crossing his mouth.

"Yes."

"I dinnae want to risk never having the opportunity."

Because my stupid uncle and father had shown up, I thought to myself on an internal snarl.

"Aye, that and your reckless, unpredictable and stubborn." He grinned.

I grinned back, the conversation helping me to stay in the here.

"Mara! Ppfft, off all the tailored, fancy gardens, why did you insist on this unruly one?" Gabriella complained noisily.

"It's secluded, walled, and the furthest away from the castle, but still well within the shield wall." Siri perked up, with what looked a lot like an eye roll.

I smiled at the sight of my friends, their light infused energy lifting my spirits and dimming the gloom. Hamish chuckled.

"Clever deduction little Valkyrie." He smiled.

Siri blushed before delivering him a shy grin.

"You know, Siri will be a stunning woman when she has finished growing, not to mention smart and lethal. Right up your street." I nudged Hamish in the side.

Hamish grunted.

"She is a child, unlike women who can imagine anyone into adulthood, I see her only as that, all be it, intelligent, and less annoying."

"Mara, honestly, really…him." Donna huffed.

"Any woman would be fortunate to have Hamish. If not for the fact I am bonded to another I would be the first in line." I scolded silently.

Donna didn't answer but pursed her lips in disagreement. I felt Hamish's eyes on me, the gaze penetrating. Did he hear that? I really needed to learn what to share with the pack and what not to share. How many heard that? Have heard most of my private musings?

"Only those within a certain range will hear, I have given you the knowledge of how to be more guarded. And aye, I did hear." He said, his voice even from within my head holding great affection.

"Not to complain, but could you not speak in the head, it's weird, and you all make ridiculous faces, I feel like I'm watching a foreign film that has no sound." Asta giggled.

Gabriella snorted, and Siri grinned.

"I was just thinking the same thing." Gabriella laughed.

Not able to help it, and not really wanting to, I smiled, my chest filling with joy.

Donna's eyes started watering, her hand moving to cover her mouth. She gasped a little as though she was trying to keep something in. I felt my brow creasing as I tried to figure out what she was doing.

"You realise… what just happened?" Donna half sobbed, half gasped for air.

You lost your mind? Was my first thought, followed by, you're choking? Hamish started laughing, the low vibrations casting his humorous vibes our way. Everyone's faces broke out into wide smiles, even Donna's, although hers looked trapped between two 'not quite right' angles.

"Ppfft no… You felt joy Mara, like actually felt it and understood that you were feeling it. It made sense to you." She smiled, a small tear falling down her cheek.

I felt joy…and understood it. Somehow the revelation made my joy even greater, the feeling encompassing my entire body, my skin tingling. It felt like the air was cleaner, the concept and my perception of feeling, healing, freeing. Am I fixed? Does this mean that I can love?

Donna got all excited, her stance stuck somewhere between getting ready to jump and remaining rigidly still. Flutters of electricity erupted all over me, my mind humming with an overload of emotion, positive emotion. All of the feelings were familiar but instead of being confusing and alien they now felt… undeniable, natural, instinctively belonging. I don't know, something…something.

"Right." Hamish grinned.

Yes right. Having always been. My cheeks were hurting but it didn't diminish my happiness.

"You fixed me Hamish." I said, before throwing my arms around his neck, pushing myself up onto my toes and hugging him.

"Not fixed my queen, educated. You were denied such emotion, grew up unaware, unknowing. I have given you my knowing, my awareness." He explained, returning the hug.

"Group hug!" Donna squealed before wrapping her arms around me.

I grunted with a smile, her hug knocking some of the air out of me. Another pair of arms encircled me, Gabriella's, and then quickly following Asta's.

"Urm, I'm happy for you, honest, I'm just not feeling 'group hug'." Siri said, her voice sounding like the biggest smile.

Donna let go, forcing Gabriella and Asta to do the same.

"Not feeling it?" Donna grinned wickedly.

Siri stiffened, her eyes growing slightly wider.

"No" She said, holding out her hand in a sign that said 'stop'.

Gabriella, Donna and Asta looked at each other, a silent message passed between them. Turning their eyes on Siri, they smiled mischievously.

"Group hug." They called in unison before running towards her and sweeping her up into a tight embrace.

Listening to them laughing, I remained were I was, Hamish's arms still holding me tightly against him.

"As much as I would like to remain like this, time is running out, we must get down to business." Hamish said before lowering a small kiss onto my head and releasing me from his hold.

Sighing, I knew he was right, now wasn't the time for emotional celebrations, I'd got plans to make, and actions to take, so to speak.

"Where's Sven?" I asked Hamish.

He was supposed to be here already.

"I'm coming my queen, two minutes out." Sven replied.

Despite being glad he was on his way, I couldn't stop the small snarl I emitted. I really had to do something about my constant over share. Damn it, since Hamish and Sven called all local wolves to the castle, I now had at least twenty newcomers here and another thirty-odd answering the call, and who were currently en-route. Hamish had also contacted his pack, all of them flying in from Scotland on private jets.

"About that, they have landed at Knock. They should be here in just over an hour." Hamish said, a slight hinge of humour lacing his voice.

I hissed, obviously he thought my over shares were amusing, which it wasn't. What about when I'm with Col? It's bad enough knowing Donna, Hamish and Sven can pry, now hundreds are coming, all of which can potentially, if not physically, join in on my, 'not to be shared in public' time. Donna snorted before giggling.

"It is a bit of dilemma, isn't it?" She said, eyes twinkling.

I growled low, my happy buzz fading. Why couldn't I have learned the useful stuff first, instead, I'm landed with emotional 'not useful in a bloody fight' baggage. Hamish gave me the knowledge, so why the hell was it taking so long to get through? Damn stupid brain. Irritated, I started prowling, the occasional mumbling of curses leaving my mouth. My never too far away anger started to grate on me, my Warg self-growing impatient and hungry. For blood? Death…No.

"Sex." Hamish leaned down and growled in my ear, the delectable vibrations hitting all the right spots.

I stopped, my body tensing before little bursts of desire licked at my insides. Warmth filled my belly, my tongue sensually gliding over my lips…yes, sex. Donna grabbed my arm and shook me hard.

"Nae now Mara, we're here for a meeting remember." She arched her brows at me, her features reprimanding.

I hissed annoyed with her interruption, a dangerous snarl following. My head felt sluggish again, fleeting, the good work my friends had made in abating my darkness, quickly diminishing. Hamish pulled my head around, his golden eyes locking onto mine.

"My queen, your enemy stands before you and behind you. Let us prepare for their demise before perusing one's desires." He said, his gaze commanding.

A faint, barely audible giggle pulled my attention. My eyes landing on Siri, she was looking at the floor, a small grin plastered to her face.

"What's so funny?" Gabriella asked, giving Siri a slight nudge to the ribs.

Siri's head shot up, a flash of surprise in her eyes.

"What."

"You were giggling." Asta smiled.

Siri's face looked appalled.

"Aloud?" She asked uncomfortably.

"Yes aloud."

A pink tinge started to colour her cheeks, her eyes shooting to Hamish before returning to the ground. My original train of thought forgotten, I found myself overly curious. She's embarrassed. Donna smiled.

"It was funny." She said awkwardly "It rhymed."

Donna started snickering, Asta and Gabriella looking slightly confused. I wasn't sure if I looked confused, but the odds were good.

"What rhymed?" Gabriella asked.

"Let us prepare for their demise before perusing one's desires." She grumbled, in what I thought was meant to be an imitation of Hamish's deep and heavy Scottish accent, that she attempted it in her very feminine voice made the whole jibe comical.

Hamish grunted beside me, his response only adding to the growing blast of glee that swept over me. I couldn't help it, it just came from where ever such an episode is created, bursting out before I even registered what had happened. Everyone was quiet, just looking at me, a look of complete shock radiating on every external visage.

Slowly they started to smile.

"Did I imagine that?" Donna asked.

"No. That was definitely a laugh." Gabriella grinned.

I smiled, overly pleased with myself. Not that I did anything or planned to, but still, I found myself feeling rather proud.

"I feel like I just witnessed my child taking their first steps." Donna let out on a long happy gasp.

Ppfft, that was taking it too far. Scowling at her I went and plonked myself on a half-overgrown bench. Where the hell is Sven?

"Here." He shouted before jogging through the garden gate.

He took a breath before regaining his composure, another twenty or so wolves entering the small garden behind him. All of a sudden, the small wilderness felt crowded. Why are all immortals so big? Ignoring the question, I ran my gaze over the newcomers, they didn't know it yet, but they would be the first. Not wasting anytime, I stood motioning for Donna to come stand by me. I only got a few minutes to speak with her before I was dragged into another one of Col's diplomatic meetings, but Donna was confident she could make the process of freeing my people from the alpha's compulsion, faster, amplifying my reach. Of course, as with most things magical, and un-tested, it was better to make sure first, just in case something went horribly wrong, like accidentally messing with their heads etc. With that thought all eyes locked onto me, a brief flash of 'shit' registering in some of their eyes. Donna laughed.

"Nae worry boys, I'm awesome." She winked.

They didn't look convinced. I couldn't remember the exact words I used with Hamish, but I was pretty certain that what I was going to say was close enough. They would naturally still defer to a stronger pack member as is the nature of wolves in general, but they couldn't be forced. If they really didn't like what was being asked, they could walk away, have a choice.

"Just in case there are any doubts let me make this clear. I am Mara, Alpha of all Alpha's, Queen of the Varúlfur. I am the granddaughter of Fenrir, daughter of Hati, half Warg, half Vanir… I linger between darkness and light, between good and evil… I will not lie and tell you that I can control into what void I drift. I cannot… but it is my hope that someday, I can. There is uncertainty whenever my name is uttered, I do not blame you if you hold such sentiment. I have done, and am doing all that I can to ensure that no matter what future lays ahead of me, the Varúlfur will not, and cannot ever be used as pawn's again. My fey magic is linked to Herlta, the fey queen, she has promised that if ever I lose my battle with the residing darkness she will break our alliance denying me the ability to channel. Furthermore, it is my intention to free all Varúlfur from the alpha's compulsion, something I have had success in. Once free, there is no obligation to acknowledge me as your queen, you are all, if you wish it, free men, your fate, yours to decide. You will not be pursued; no attempt will be made to sway your mind. I know what it is to be kept against your will, to be subjected to another's will. I do not know what kind of queen I will be, but I know I will not be that queen." I paused.

Hamish would not like what comes next, the thought only just coming to me. But it had to be done, the risk was to great.

"Hamish Halvorsen is my beta, if I fail, he will succeed. Before this day is done, he will pledge to me his oath, he will promise that if I fail, he will oversee my death. I ask that even if you choose not to follow me, in this, you will follow him." I finished to the sound of Hamish's long and deadly hiss.

Licking my lips, I ignored his reaction, my mind made up. I understand now what it is to rule, it's all so clear. To rule is to love your people before your own interests, to place them above all, to protect, and ensure the continuation of the race.

"You cannae ask this of me Mara." Hamish's voiced filled my mind, his anger and grief flooding in with it.

"If I were you, and you were I, can you honestly tell me you wouldn't do the same, that it wasn't what's best for our people."

Hamish growled, the thunderous pitch deafening, he swore before storming off, his departure breaking my heart, a slow chill piercing my chest. Donna started to sob, I looked at her taken aback. Her tears seemed to be contagious, my eyes watering in response. Sadness overwhelmed me, my lungs struggling for breath. Keeping it at bay, I forced myself to get on with what I had come here to do.

"Are you ready Donna." I asked, my voice no matter how well I tried to hide it, quaking.

"Aye." She whispered, another tear staining her cheek.

Walking closer to my men, I motioned for Sven to step forward, he would be the anchor.

"Donna is going to project my command, to make sure that it works I will afterward command you to complete a task, this will allow me to determine whether it was successful. Once freed you can choose to stay and potentially die, or leave to live another day. The choice is yours alone, no one will stop you." I explained.

Turning slightly, I nodded to Donna I was ready.

Sparks of electric blue shimmered and blazed across her hands, lifting them into the air she uttered a melodic chain of commands. Weaves of neon blue spread from her finger tips, wrapping, and forming links that joined my men together, a string of soldiers, held by her magical cord.

"Now." She whispered, her presiding sadness lingering in my mind.

"From this day forth you will do only as your conscious permits, you will choose what path you wish to tread as free men capable of making your own choices. You will be bound to no man, woman, or child unless you wish it to be so. Never again will any one person have absolute power over you, not me, and not any that come after me." I commanded with all my conviction, my strength, and my title.

Donna's magic unravelled, the lashes of blue recoiling and returning to her body. My men looked at each other briefly before looking at me.

"Hop on one leg." I ordered, with the same amount of power and authority I exercised just moments ago.

No one moved, one by one they started to catch up, understand what that meant. Just for dramatics and feeling as elated as I did when I freed Hamish, I decided to throw everything into another pointless command.

"Twirl like a ballerina."

Donna laughed. Sven grinned.

"No, my queen." He chuckled, the rich sound making me smile.

"Very well. Silently, I'm glad, it's not a vision I think I would have ever forgotten. Congratulations, you are the first of a new dawn of Lycan. Free."

Satisfied it worked, I sat back down on the rickety bench, soon the next lot would arrive, my plans thus far going as planned. Sven came to kneel in front of me.

"My queen, I offer you my allegiance, as my queen, my ruler, and my alpha. If you ask it of me I will pledge in blood and enter freely into the bond."

I didn't know what to say, like an idiot I just stared, my stupor growing worse when the rest of the men adopted the same position, their words echoing Sven's. Donna elbowed me in the arm.

My mind was racing, I just freed them of a bond why would they choose to be tied into another one?

"Mara, you should probably say something." Donna smiled.

Yeah, but what.

"I am honoured and accept your allegiance; however, I require no blood bond. Not because I do not value what you offer or because I do not believe you worthy, but because it is not safe to offer me such. I trust that you of all people understand why." I said, my attention swinging to Sven.

"I understand my queen, a precaution I hope will remain unjustified." He smiled before standing.

"So now we know that was a success, what now?" Asta glowed.

"I need to find Hamish, but you are all free to do as you please. Thank you… for everything."

"Where are you Hamish?"

Stalking in the direction he left in, I waved good bye to my friends, the action hurt, the sudden feeling I may never see them again, causing an icy, and terrifying chill, to wind its way up my spin. I wanted to turn back, but how could I? Stick to the plan Mara! You must, or everyone you love will die. Painfully, my steps forced, I left the garden and them behind, a sinking feeling in my chest.

I'd been walking around the estate for over an hour and I still hadn't found Hamish. On top of that he was ignoring me, knowing full well I was aware he could hear me. I was furious, my skin itchy. My wolf wanted out and if he didn't bloody answer me soon I might be tempted to let it. Sighing, I narrowly avoided a patrol of armed men who came pouring out of a side door. The giant store house had a familiar lingering scent. A bolt of aggression fuelled adrenalin, rolled its way around my head, Hati was in there. I growled, eager to confront him. Not now Mara… soon I would deal with him. The guards eyed me suspiciously before it suddenly dawned on them who I was.

"My queen, forgive me, but Tiarna Conlaóch told us you were not permitted outside the castle at this time, I would be honoured to escort you back." One of them said, his words followed by a subtle bow.

Permit me! Scratch furious, I was raging. What does he think I am, a damn lap dog? I was seriously tempted to thump the guard, kick him a few times in the head. Instead, rather oddly, I came to the conclusion, it wasn't his fault. Well that's new, another gift from Hamish's many years of wisdom? He was lucky, yesterday's Mara and he would have been bleeding out already. Raising my eye brows slightly, I tried my best to keep my face passive.

"That won't be necessary, but thank you. My husband, however good his intentions, forgets I'm a big girl, and a Warg at that. I'm young but even my under developed intelligence understands that remaining within the wall is a wise decision, and since the Warg's can't pass, I should be fine. If you happen to see him, please relay that message in full." I smiled sweetly.

The guard paled.

"All of it?" He asked, a glimmer of panic entering his eyes.

"Would it be easier if I wrote it down for you, that way you can pretend you didn't know what it contained." I grinned.

The guard seemed to be pondering it when Ansgar came bowling around the corner. His golden eyes locked onto mine, a scolding frown following. Damn stupid men.

"What's the problem here?" Ansgar asked, striding towards us.

Mentally cursing my luck, I knew that Ansgar wouldn't settle for a note, the man is far to bloody smart.

"No problem." I smiled, quickly turning to walk back the way I came.

"Mara." He called.

Urrgh… Stopping, I turned back around.

"Ansgar."

"You should nae be here Mara." He said, waving the guards away.

"So I've been told, I'm looking for Hamish, have you seen him?"

"Aye, I passed him a few minutes ago, he said his men had arrived. They have been allocated rooms at the hunting lodges."

"And where will I find the hunting lodges?" I smiled.

"You hear that Hamish, I know where you are."

Ansgar frowned again, his jaw straining.

"I cannae let you go there Mara. It's on the other side of the estate and too close to the shield wall. Conlaóch will have my head if I let you wonder off alone."

"If you wish to escort me, then do so, but we both know you can't stop me. Point me in the right direction lest I beat the information from whoever I run into next." I hissed.

"Fuck woman, why cannae you just do what your told?" He growled.

"Because this is important."

"I will take you, but we will return as soon as you have spoken to him, that's the conditions. I must speak with Conlaóch, contrary to belief, that too is important." He rebuked.

"I accept your conditions."

Ansgar grunted before turning back down the path he came from.

"Keep up." He said before breaking into a run.

By the time we reached the lodges my lungs were on fire, my legs reduced to jelly. How bloody big is this estate? Pulling in a long breath I tried to calm my breathing.

"Hurry up, I'll wait here." Ansgar instructed with a sharp intake of air.

I shot him a, 'I will take as bloody long as I want' stare, before jogging towards the nearest cabin.

"Hamish, will you please just come and talk to me?"

I walked into the closest cabin, ten pairs of golden eyes swinging my way. Yet again, still no response from Hamish. Fuming, I growled low, my fangs cutting my bottom lip. Those golden eyes suddenly became hungry eyes, slowly they undressed my body. Low hisses and growls filled the lounge, my heart beat picking up speed. My wolf liked the attention, a lick of a grin edging my mouth. Teasingly, I ran my tongue over my lips, the slow, deliberate movement, capturing their full attention. Pulling my bottom lip in, I bit down hard, my fang piercing the sensitive flesh. A small drop of blood escaped my mouth. Catching the droplet with my finger, I slowly licked the blood from its tip, a suggestive purr sent their way.

"Hello boys" I smiled. "Tell me where I can find Hamish and I promise to play nice."

One of them stood, a cocky smile etched into his masterfully crafted face. Delicious.

"Our lord is currently unavailable my queen, perhaps there is something we can help you with." He winked suggestively.

Unavailable, is he? We shall see.

"Now that you mention it, there is."

Unzipping my jumper, I pulled the garment off, dropping it to the floor. My eyes on the wolf that had stood, I walked towards him, slowly pulling my t-shirt off in the process. In just my bra and jeans I leaned up and kissed him on his chin, my tongue slowly darting out to taste his bottom lip. The un-named wolf growled, his hand falling to rest on my lower back. A couple more wolves stood from where they were sat, their eyes burning red hot trails along my body. My wolf howled within my mind, overloads of sensation making me hum with pleasure. Another hand glided across my stomach, a flutter of excitement creeping through my chest. Hamish came bursting through the door.

"You've made your damn point, enough!" He growled. "Get your fucking hands off her."

Snarling, he shoved the closest wolf out of the way before grabbing my arm. Spinning me around, he started dragging me from the cabin.

"Another time boys." I smiled, before disappearing through the doorway.

Not saying anything Hamish led me into a smaller cabin that bordered the woods. Entering, he released my arm, sitting down in a large arm chair.

"Talk." He said simply, refusing to look at me.

"I'm sorry."

His jaw twitched before his eyes fell on me, the rich golden gleam, softening.

"As you should be, you have nae right asking me to do that, I would nae do it, I cannae." He confessed, his manner weary.

"No Hamish, I'm sorry that I upset you, I'm not sorry for asking. It has to be done, you know that. For the sake of everyone's future, you must swear it." I sighed, a small dash of anger altering my mood. I hate me.

The anger returned to his eyes, a low menacing chill filling the room.

"No." He seethed.

Hissing, I sent him a scathing look.

"You can't let emotion cloud your judgment, it's a failsafe Hamish. It may never happen, but in case it does, you're the only one I trust to do it."

The look Hamish gave me after I made my comment made me take a step back, a sliver of danger bolting up my neck. He stood up slowly, his eyes wild. Stalking towards me, I refused to sacrifice more ground, standing still, I held my head high, a defiant flare about me.

"Do nae let emotion get in the way?" He hissed, the under tone deadly. "I love you Mara. If you understood what that meant, if you had the faintest idea, you would nae ask me to kill you."

"Somethings are more important than love." I spat back.

"It's easy for you to say, who do you love? Who have you ever loved?"

I paused, trying to think of a response. Who do I love?

"I love Donna, but if a had to kill her, I would." I smirked.

"That's nae even close, the love between friends in no way compares. I do nae love you as a friend Mara, I love you in the same way Conlaóch loves you. You exist in every fibre of my being, you are the air that fills my lungs, the blood that feeds my heart. What you ask is impossible, I will nae be blood bound into being your murderer."

"Fine, maybe I don't get it, but you can still choose to act above emotion, attachment. Yes, it may hurt, yes, it is morally wrong, but it remains the right thing to do, for everyone." I implored.

I was so angry, so pent up, why is he being so damn blind? I started to pace, every step thumping my anger up a notch, my fangs refusing to recede. My skin started growing itchy again, the irritating condition creating an emotional whiplash that coursed tiredly about me, pissed off, understanding, turned on, sad, confused, insatiable, calm. I cursed, frustration, the overall winner.

"Really, you really think it's that simple?" Hamish hissed.

"Yes."

"Then prove it Mara, prove that emotion, morals, hold no such limits, that it's all so... easy. Sleep with me."

I froze, I didn't really know what I was expecting him to say, but it definitely wasn't that.

"I don't understand, what would sleeping with you prove?"

"Your married Mara, belong to another man. Conlaóch loves you, say what you want but I know you love him too. That love will prevent you from sleeping with me. You cannae do it, because you cannae bear the thought of hurting him, betraying him. Knowing that, knowing what it would do to him, will always far exceed everything else, will prevent you from doing what you deem 'the right thing'. Do you nae see Mara, just as you cannae hurt him, I cannae ever hurt you." He explained, his voice softening.

"You're wrong, this is more important than me, him...you. This is beyond love, loyalty, this is the fate of the world were talking about Hamish. You know what I will become, just like Fenrir, maybe even worse."

Hamish swore in frustration, even going as far as to physically shake me.

"I will nae do what you cannae do Mara, do nae be a hypocrite."

"And if I can, and would, if I prove I would do whatever was necessary, will you enter into the oath?" I asked him, my mind determined.

Hamish frowned, an expression of absolute disbelief reflecting in his eyes. He snarled before running his hand over his face, the gesture laced in weariness.

"Aye." He said quietly "But Mara, even if you could, you would nae be able to live with yourself afterward. I'm trying to make you understand…"

I cut him off, reaching up, I pulled his mouth down to mine, and kissed him. Col will hate me but not as much I hate me. Fate was cruel to make me his anam cara, a sad joke that he didn't deserve. I've always know I was a lost cause, the only difference now is that I have people who mean everything to me.

I'm cursed, a taint on everyone's lives. A darkness, like a sand storm, that chokes the life out of everything it passes. The promise of my death, a promise that cannot been broken, is the only surety any of them have, the only hope of surviving me. I trust Hamish, my Warg trusts Hamish, he is the only one she will let get close, the only one who can destroy her. Everything in me wanted to pull away and run to Col, to feel safe and cherished within his arms, but I had been a hindrance for too long. Now with my enemy knocking at the door it brought everything into perspective. There was a reason I always felt like an outsider, because I am one. There is no place for me in this world, I am the darkness, the knife in everyone's chest. Tears streamed down my face, my heart crippling, numbness separated my mind from my body, my soul weeping in despair. The Warg was in her element, but ultimately, her pleasure, was my demise. I love you Col.

So it Begins

No longer in my casual attire, I was geared for a fight, my hunter restless. Walking through the castle I had an entourage of men at my heel. So far, Sköll had manage to remain un-detected, not attempting to cross the heavily armed perimeter my men had formed. I had a sick feeling in my stomach, my thoughts repeatedly returning to Mara. I had everyone looking for her, but still nothing. Neither had Finian and Eoghuan returned, all my men missing. That I was alive was the only indication that Mara was alive. Not long after leaving the common hall I had an overwhelming feeling of despair, grief hitting me like a hammer, it was so powerful, so saddening, I felt my eyes water. I was afraid, something had happened, she may not be in physical pain, but she was still in agony.

"My lord." Connor called.

He was escorting a young guard with him. There were so many new faces since I returned, the young guard, just another one to add to the list. He paled when he saw me, but kept his nerve.

"Connor."

"This is Patrick, tell lord Conlaóch what you just told me." He ordered with a stern arch of his brow.

The guard clicked his jaw before he spoke.

"I have seen the queen my lord, she was with Ansgar three hours ago." He explained.

Relief swept over me, if she was with Ansgar, she was safe.

"Where were they going? Were they injured?" I asked.

The guard looked slightly confused by my question.

"They were not harmed my lord, Ansgar sent our patrol away, but as I left I heard the queen mention she was looking for someone named Hamish."

Of course she bloody was, I couldn't help it, I snarled, the guard taking a step back.

"Did you see where they went?"

"No, but they were at the armoury when I saw them."

"My lord, the queen's men were allocated accommodation at the hunting lodges, if she was looking for Hamish it is the mostly likely place he would be." Connor added.

"That will be all Patrick, dismissed."

The guard leaving, I turned to Connor.

"When did Mara's men arrive?" I asked

"About three hours ago, the time line fits."

Indeed, and if Ansgar escorted her it would explain why he never reported in. My tongue hit the inside of my cheek, my mind racing. It didn't explain why he still hadn't reported in though.

Even if he did take her there why hadn't they come back? Calculating, I tried to determine at what time the sudden bout of grief hit me. Just over two hours ago, maybe a little longer.

I had sent them there deliberately, knowing that they were far from the castle and far from me. I hissed, pissed that what was meant to be a positive had been spun into a negative. They remained on the estate essentially, but it was a good thirty-minute run, an hour if you followed the road round. A loud commotion dragged me from my thoughts, my head swinging in the direction of the disturbance.

Gabriella and Seth came speeding around the corner, stopping abruptly not two feet in front of me.

"Finian and Eoghuan found Ansgar, he is in a bad condition. He said Mara is being attacked and something about Connaught woods." She spoke quickly, her face etched in worry.

Connaught woods was the name of the woods the lodges were situated in. Growling, fear for Mara gnawed at my insides, my chest tightening.

"Connor, you will stay and protect the castle, expect an attack, Sköll would not have come here alone. He will try and distract our forces, keep us from the real fight."

"Yes, my lord." He said, running off in a hurry.

Finian and Eoghuan came trudging around the corner covered in blood, Ansgar hanging limply between them.

"What the fuck is he doing here?" I called, hurried steps leading me in their direction.

"He insisted on seeing you, wouldn't take no for an answer." Finian hissed, his manner telling me he strongly objected.

Lowering him to the floor, I knelt down to speak with my friend. He was cut up badly, his wounds angry. Long slashes obscured half his face, blood freely running from his wounds. That he would insist on finding me in this condition spoke volumes. Whatever he had to say, it was important. Opening his eyes, Ansgar's pain filled expression made my temper sore. Grunting, he tried to speak, blood escaping his mouth.

"We have under estimated Fenrir's reach." He hissed painfully "stronger than… we thought. He has found a way to enslave morning stars, Sköll leads them against us." He choked, his eyes struggling to remain open.

Shocked, my heart fell into my stomach. How? … Ansgar grabbed my arm.

"Mara plans too…" His eyes closed again.

"To what?" I shook him gently. "What does Mara plan?"

"Unburden…us. She is planning to…" He passed out before finishing, my mind spinning. Ansgar didn't look good, his injuries upon closer inspection, life threatening.

"Get me Herlta, Ragnar, now! Find Donna."

She's going to leave me, leave all of us. Furious, I stood, my power peeling and radiating about me.

"Pull in every man that isn't needed for the castle defences, contact our allies, I want as many people fighting with us as possible. Cael! You and your team leave for Connaught woods, now, I will follow behind. Mara is the priority. Do not engage the morning stars."

"Yes, my lord." Cael called, nodding his head, Lucian and the rest of Cael's team following.

"You two. Take Ansgar, see that he gets help, stay with him, do not leave his side. Finian, Eoghuan, with me."

Ragnar manifested in front of me, his face grim.

"You have been looking for me."

"Sköll is attacking to the east, Mara is there. Your demons can get there quicker than we can."

"Say no more." He said, preparing to transport himself.

"Wait. Fenrir has enslaved morning stars, they fight for him, Sköll leads them." I said, the extent of that knowledge filling me with dread.

Morning star is the name given to a soul that departs from its body, 'morning' meaning new dawn, a new beginning, and star because as its leaves and rises the bright light resembles a star. It is a journey, a passage of one life lived, another to begin. I had witnessed the leaving of one's soul, to capture and then enslave them…how was it possible? All those people denied the right to move on, forced to serve Fenrir. Ragnar's eyes blazed murderously, the cool tinge to his face a cold hard visage that promised death to all those involved. Humans portray demons as the servants of evil, the scourge of hell, but in reality, they have no allegiance. They are chaos, destruction, saviours, and condemners. They belong to no one place and travel between worlds, worlds that number in the millions. Their task not to serve good or evil but to ensure that every soul remains where they are meant to be, that no one interferes with the basic universal laws of life and death. Only in death are we permitted to travel to different times, places and lives, fate deciding your course. The balance of nature in every world perfectly formed to sustain life, darkness, light, all of it a delicate line that holds the universe together. Demons are not born, but chosen, pulled from different worlds for their skills as warriors, sentenced to live as eternal soldiers, war mongers, assassins. when a demon dies, they die forever.

That Ragnar was pissed was understandable, Fenrir had infiltrated his domain, messed with the order and stolen knowledge that changed the dynamics. Basically, in the grand scheme of life eternal, the game of gods, the rules have been broken, Fenrir is cheating. Demons exist for the sole purpose of ensuring this very thing never happens, that the playing field remains level, as Ragnar is their king, in the eyes of the gods, known or unknown, it was his fault.

"You have seen this." He asked, his voice not human but a deep gravely imitation of a beast.

The sound horrifying made even the most battled tested soldiers shudder, myself included.

"My most trusted man refused critical medical care to make sure I learned of this." I answered dryly.

"We must reclaim the souls, see that your men do not engage them." He hissed before disappearing, a cold gust of wind filling the void he just created.

Like I needed to be told, I'd already told my men as much. Snarling, my hunter was pacing, I should be running to my anam cara, not stalling to instruct my forces.

"I want Herlta here now!" I shouted, frustration and anger lacing every god damn syllable.

Stalking down the halls I went in search of the fey queen. She would know how to defend against the morning stars without the need to fight them, but more importantly, she could save Ansgar. If needed our weapons can be used against them, defeat them, but to kill a morning star, is to wipe them out of existence. To kill an enemy is one thing, but they were pawns, slaves. We did not kill innocents.

Every step taken, increased my hunters rage, I had never felt so much desperation. Slowly my inner self was becoming wholly dominant, a wild yearning, wailing in my head. The smoky hue that had not left my eyes since the common hall, swirled, the embers within growing hotter by the minute. It was not a good sign, but no matter what attempts I made at calming myself I couldn't. Every thought was coated in a snarl, like a hound the continuous bark demanded I attack, that I seek what is mine, and kill all whoever stood in my way. This feeling was new to me, but from our history I knew what it meant, I was in danger of becoming what the humans called a 'hell hound.'

Humans, witches, fey, every living being has something within that forces you to choose who you are. For humans it is the easiest, good person or bad person, either way, for mankind, it is never too late to turn back, to make amends and choose a new path. But for immortals, each with a power unique to their race, the choice when made is nearly always permanent. The Keltoi are powerful, guardians of the light, keepers of balance, but in the way of nature, for every good there is always a path to the wicked. Taking the form of a 'mac tire cú', wolf hound, was forbidden, a law that had not be broken for thousands of years, and for a good reason, for us, it was the path to a soulless existence.

Fionnghall the king that reigned before my father Conall was the last. The power the form gives you, a hundred times worse than the addiction of heroin. Every turn blackened your soul further, weakened your resolve. The kings craving for the power was insatiable, after the seventh transformation he was unable to turn back, an evil twisted beast all that remained. The fey were forced to summon their most elite, the tuatha dè danann 'tribe of the gods', their finest warriors, altered my magic. Led by the then fey queen Danu, and together with the Keltoi, the wild hunt oversaw their destruction.

"Conlaóch." Herlta called urgently, her light infused voice helping me to push through the hunter's thrall.

I was stood outside, the sun nearing the horizon, soon it would set, darkness descending.

"I have heard." She said sadly. "We can hold the morning stars, but I cannot free them, such work can only be accomplished by Ragnar." She paused, her sadness spreading, a single glistening tear rolling down her face. "The balance has shifted, Fenrir should not have been able to do this, all those souls… If there are deaths, I fear he will claim our people too."

My thoughts immediately went to Ansgar, my friend for so many a century, I would not let Fenrir take him, I cannot.

"How do you catch the morning stars? Is it possible to wear the trap?"

Her brow creased in thought, her gaze slowly meeting mine.

"It may be possible, the magic in your blades…in theory they could hold a soul. If we can imbue them in the event of death, the soul would not rise but be drawn in. I have never done this before, I will have to consult, but in principle, it could work."

"Make it work, the more people we lose the more he will gain, we cannot afford to strengthen his armies."

Nor can I bear the thought of my people being forced to fight for Fenrir, forced to kill their loved ones. It would taint them, make them as twisted as their master, condemn their souls to eternal darkness. Herlta nodded before hurriedly moving off.

A split-second decision had me running towards the armoury, Fenrir had fucked with the odds, changed the game to roll in his favour. Our only chance of winning now was to do the same, break the rules. Sometimes to fight a cheat you must become one, do what they least expect. I had a key advantage, someone who knows how to play his game, an ace in my sleeve, Hati.

Hati's ice blue gaze pierced through the one-way mirror, he could see me, us. I held his gaze, my eyes every bit as calculating and empty as his.

"I don't think this is a good idea." Finian said from beside me.

I don't doubt he's right, some way or another it is sure to back fire, but right now, I didn't have many choices. He would protect Mara, would die for her. If I could read his thoughts, I would learn, understand the true thinking of a Warg, knowledge that would ultimately aid me in the ongoing fight. Against Finian's warning I unlocked the door. Hati watched me closely as I entered, his stance, cautious and un-trusting. He didn't say anything, the tall warrior not in the least bit afraid. He drew in a long slow breath, a glimmer of anger creasing his mouth.

"You wear my daughter like a musk hunter, her scent lingers on every part off you." He sneered, the statement almost sounding like an accusation.

"Mara is my wife, my anam cara." I said simply.

A low snarl flew from his mouth, icy clouds carrying the sound. The floor glazed over, a frozen vein cracking noisily along the floor. My eyes followed the forked shard, the jagged points stopping millimetres from my feet. A warning. He smirked, the gesture as cold as the ice he controlled.

"Sköll has breached the wall, Mara is being attacked."

His smirk vanished, his eyes no longer blue became a thunderous grey, flecks of silver bursting within.

"He cannot have her, she is the last blood descendant or Jörg." He hissed

"Aelius is not alive?" Finian interceded from behind me.

Hati's eyes swung to his, a look that said, 'of course not' edging his mouth.

"She is dead. Her morning star was stolen, my brother has her hung around his neck, another trophy for his collection."

"She has not left this world, this why you have retained your soul." I mused aloud.

"Yes. It is a fate Mara will share if you do not let me out." He growled. "Mara is the key, but she is also strong, once he has broken the seal, they will use her as a weapon."

The room was magically sealed, a prison that would hold almost anyone. A hundred years' worth of layers coating the small room. Eventually he would peel them back, but at the very least it would give me decades to find alternatives means of imprisonment.

"The man who read your mind is gravely injured. I will need to read you again."

"You will let me go to her?" He asked with a half snarl, half command.

"Yes."

Finian grunted behind me.

"I want your word." Hati demanded, a dark mass swirling around him, jet black claws exploding from his fingers, the ridged tips, catching the light.

"I give you my word, but we will fight for her together." I insisted, the hue in my eyes turning slowly to flame.

"Deal."

We left, ready to head towards Connaught woods, just as we were entering the vast woodland a group of demons flashed next to us.

"Which of you is Conlaóch." A large horned demon asked, blue flames dancing in his eyes.

"I am Conlaóch."

Waving his arm, two demons moved forward, my hand instinctively reaching for my weapon. The large demon grinned.

"Ragnar wanted us to give you these, they are from the fey queen. She has instructed us that they are to be worn around your neck. Also, Ragnar has a gift for you, he said it will redistribute the balance. However, once we have resolved the issue, he wants it returned." He explained, placing heavy emphasis on the word 'returned'.

My brow creased, my eyes darting to the objects in their hands. What could he possibly give me that would even the odds?

Catching my confused look, the massive demon chuckled. Stepping forward, he motioned to speak with me in private. Moving slightly to the side he leaned down to my ear.

"Ragnar wished me to tell you this. What he gives, he wants back, if you do not he will take it by whatever means necessary."

"What is it?"

"It is an amulet, I cannot say much more, but he said it will allow you to become and return safely."

What the fuck was that supposed to mean, scowling, I pinned the demon with a scathing look.

"That's it?"

He laughed again.

"Our king gets bored easily, he like to mess with people's head, it entertains him. It is all he said, but knowing him, it will make sense when it needs too."

Grunting, I didn't say anything further, what would be the damn point! Fucking demons. Taking the amulet, I placed the tooth like object around my neck. Walking back to my men Eoghuan passed me another long chain. Herlta's crest was carved into the centre of what looked like an over-sized rain drop. Lifting both chains, I placed them inside my shirt, my men doing the same. We had left before she could enchant our weapons, these must be the alternatives. Not wanting to waste any more time, I entered the woods. Hati paced impatient to be gone, a dense mist unravelling from his body. He growled when he saw me.

"The scent of blood carries on the wind." He hissed.

I pulled in a long breath, the wind and all its contents licking at my senses. The air was fresh, but it was there, sitting in the background, blood. For it to have reached this far, there must be a lot. Snarling, my anger destructive, I broke into a run, Eoghuan, Finian, and Hati, racing with me. The tree's passed in a blur, my hunter regaining control of my body. The smoke in my eyes was growing hotter with every intake of air, the oxygen stoking the embers within. A wild desperate keening filled my head, my entire body inflamed. Mara's face hovered in front of me, her soul beckoning. A snarl, more beast than man, erupted from my chest, the lethal edge meant for my enemies, for those who would dare hurt her, steal her from me. I'm coming Mara.

"Fuck Conlaóch, you're on fire." Finian cursed.

Darkness descends

Heat licked its way across my body, delectable shivers of pleasure racing along my skin. The wolf was lean, powerful, his strong arms pinning me to the wall. I hissed, the impact forcing the small sound to escape my lips. My most trusted servant growled, his sharp fangs nipping and pulling on my lip. He pulled the buttons on my jeans before pulling them down over my hips. I grinned, his eagerness to please me and his haste in doing so, would be rewarded. Hamish paused, his hands still clinging to my thighs, his mouth lifting slowly away from my throat. Irritation flared.

"Continue." I ordered.

I did not hide my vexation, it was clear in every possible way, and yet still, he did not move. A low snarl was my response. The wolf's golden eyes shut down, the heat and desire they had held fading. He took a painful step back, I took a deadly step forward.

"My queen." He bowed, his gaze, not being able to withstand, gliding over my body.

"I have a need soldier, fulfil it."

A growl that didn't make it past his lips rumbled deep in his chest. The man was beautifully designed, his pained expression only adding to his appeal. His giant frame was built for games of domination. I licked my lips, the thought intriguing. Tipping my head to the side, I tried to determine the best way to use him, he is my trusted aid after all, I could allow him to chain me, cut me.

"I cannae my queen, if you had really wanted me to touch you, you would nae have your wolf in your eyes." He said, a brief look of regret flashing over him. "Forgive me Mara, it was wrong to push you. I should nae have allowed it to come to this." He scowled, a sad impression marring his face.

His words might as well have been foreign, not one word of it made any sense. Is he rejecting me? Furious, I took another step forward, my fangs slicing my lip.

"Are you, or are you not, my servant?" I hissed, a dark mist forming, the dense fog rolling around my feet before twirling sinisterly into the air.

"I am."

"Then continue."

He hissed again, forcing himself to move further away. His departure a clear 'no'. The small wisps of fog started for him, their erratic and jumpy movements, reaching, seeking.

"Then I no longer have use for you." I said, my claws ripping free from my flesh.

What a disappointment, I had such great hopes for this one.

"Your servant was acting in your best interests, he knew that he alone could not fulfil your needs, so he summoned me. Forgive my lateness." A gravelly, seductive voice, spoke from behind me.

Turning quickly, I studied the newcomer, the door had not opened, how did he get in here?

"Have we met before?" I asked him, my eyes darting between him and Hamish.

The tall demon looked familiar, his dark and chaotic aura pleasantly enthralling. Hamish hissed in the demon's direction… what am I missing?

"Yes." He grinned, his eyes lingering on my chest. "My name is Ragnar, you invited me to pleasure you, do you not recall?" He asked.

I glanced at Hamish before returning to the demon, why do I not recall this? He was not lying, and I could tell that Hamish knew him. Something about this was not right, my instinct rubbing me in all the wrong ways. Tingling at the base of my neck confirmed foul play. Hissing, my body shuddered, my skin burning. Within my flesh I felt the movement of my bones snapping, realigning, growing. Ragnar removed his shirt before un-hooking his trousers. He grinned as he slowly walked towards me.

"Do not touch her." Hamish snarled, his face contorting, the soldier's wolf, forcing its way to the surface, the bones in his face reshaping, lengthening.

The demon did not stop, reaching me, he grabbed my hair, pulling my head towards his. My mouth was practically against his, the pain sending little flutters of danger spiralling about me. My anger diminished, curiosity standing in its stead. Steel coloured eyes held me to him, my body humming with excitement. Hamish flung himself at Ragnar, but he didn't make contact, the demon sending a fiery wave that had Hamish flying into the wall. The impact was loud, the warrior hitting at an awkward angle, he groaned but got up, a murderous look in his eyes.

"An invite, is an invite, once given, it cannot be revoked." Ragnar laughed, the dark tinge making my mouth salivate.

"The invite stands." I purred, my tongue caressing his bottom lip.

"You're fucking insane." Hamish spat at Ragnar.

Pushing off from the wall, he went for him again.

"No young wolf, I am chaos."

Hamish didn't reach Ragnar. He lost his footing, the room violently shaking. Fire and smoke filled and clogged the room, the ceiling caving and falling in huge lumps around us. I could no longer see Hamish, but I could scent his blood.

"Both fate and I have plans for you." He murmured seductively against my ear.

Hot fumes crept up my neck, his hands, like bellows of smoke, wrapping around me. Every nerve was on fire, my body, a furnace, that grew hotter by the second. A low hum of ecstasy teased against my lips. What was left of my clothing turning to ashes, gently flaking to the ground. Ragnar growled, one large hand going around my throat. Squeezing, he placed his mouth on mine, a clawed hand scrapping up my thigh. The burn from the cut sent shivers of pleasure soaring through me. Opening my mouth on a gasp, he skilfully placed his tongue inside, a dance, an urgent need, sent to consume, to conquer.

"Only a Warg would enjoy my torture, and enjoy it you will." He breathed against my mouth, his hard body drawing me closer.

His clothes gone, he lowered me to the ground, the room, and my surroundings, vanishing in a blur of smoke and flame. No longer in the cabin, we were somewhere else. My back connected with a hard surface, I growled not happy with the dominate stance of him towering above me. He grinned, a wicked edge to his mouth, the arrogant display of play, humouring me.

"I'm going to hurt you Mara." He promised on a pleasure driven hiss, hungry eyes, devouring my flesh. "But unlike other women, your limits are without end, my pleasure, will also be yours."

He leaned up, my legs parted for his still standing position. His clawed hands pulled me down against him, the deep bit of their sting truly sensational.

"You promised me pain, pleasure…you better deliver." I warned with a deadly flash of fangs.

Ragnar's eyes found mine, the steel iris within, turning into molten lava. A slow grin spread across his face, a wicked ripple of power warping the air.

"I will deliver."

"Wake up Mara."

I grunted, my body sore. I didn't want to get up, I felt so tired, like I have been running for days, my muscles burning.

"Wanted or not, you're getting up." Donna shook me.

I opened my eyes, the low sun stinging them. Donna's face was inches above mine, a scowl that was laced with worry, coating her face. I looked around unsure of my surroundings.

"Where am I?" I asked.

"The woods by your men…" Donna started.

"Connaught woods." Aengus rumbled, cutting in.

I was with Hamish. I kissed Hamish. Donna's scowl vanished, her eyes widening.

"You dinnae." She hissed.

She got up off the floor and stormed off, a loud slap followed. Sitting up, I glanced in the direction Donna had walked off in. Donna and Hamish stood staring at each other, obviously some form of silent argument was taking place, the sight puzzling. Asta's right, it does look weird. I was on the ground just outside of the cabin, or what was left of the cabin. What the fuck happened? Standing, I walked to the debris, trying to recall my thoughts, it was difficult, a deep thrumming pain winding around my limbs and disrupting my thought process. The last thing I remembered was arguing with Hamish, and then the kiss. How did the house fall down?

"You have no memory of what happened next?" Hamish asked me.

His words snapped me from the thought, my head turning in his direction. I had not noticed before, but he was badly injured. Guilt coursed its way through my blood stream, did I do that to him?

"Nae you my queen, Ragnar did this. He took you, beyond this world. We came across your body five minutes ago, despite previous searches in this area. You have been gone for over two hours, however time moves differently in other worlds, I fear you may have been gone a while, days, maybe even weeks." He said, my brow raising.

What? That's not possible, I would remember being gone for any length of time. Hamish's eyes filled with guilt, his jaw clenching.

"I pushed you too far Mara, you made your point, but in doing so, you became the wolf. Whatever happened..." He hissed, anger sparking all over him. "It is my fault."

"Nothing happened." I said defensively.

"Just because you cannae remember it happening, it does nae mean it dinnae." Donna pursed her mouth, her eyes scanning my body.

I looked down, following her gaze. What the fuck was I wearing? Is this silk? I ran my hand over the material, the soft, almost dress, slip, shimmering. He did take me. I didn't know what to think, my mind racing for answers as to why. What happened? Panicking, I started pacing, it was one thing ensuring I got Hamish to enter into the pledge, it was another to think I went off with some random man, let him touch me. My eyes flung to Donna's, my thighs were burning, the pain reminding me of prior blade cuts. I wanted to look, but I didn't want to look. What would it confirm? I started crying, I already hated me, what's beyond hate? Aengus looked distressed when he noticed my silent tears, Hamish having to turn away, a downpour of guilt tarnishing his entire expression.

"It's ok Mara." Donna said soothingly, her eyes watering.

No, it wasn't ok, it was never going to be ok. She walked up to me, drawing me in for a tight embrace. Gently she ran her hand back and forth against my back, her head resting against mine.

"Forgive me my queen, we are running out of time. Donna said you needed her aid before I can return her to the safety of the castle." Aengus grimaced, an apologetic gleam in his eyes.

Donna scowled at him, a stern brow raised. I wanted to be swallowed up, but he was right, more was at play here then my disappearance. My people needed me.

"Hamish, you will enter into the pledge" I asked him, my voice steady.

Wiping my face, I stood tall, my emotions pushed back to the furthest part of my mind. They would not help me, not help anyone.

"Aye."

He came and stood in front of me before falling to one knee. Offering his hand, I took it, our hands gripping on to each other's wrists.

"I, Hamish Halvorsen, swear before all here who stand witness, before the gods, that should you ever lose your soul or be lost to the darkness…I will kill you." He said gravely, his grief and pain dominating the pack link.

Donna placed her hand over ours, a hum of magic brushing over my hand, wrist, and arm. Tingling, almost burning sparks, pierced my skin, like a thousand tiny needles stabbing. The sensation lasted only seconds, when it was finished, Donna lifted her hand.

"It is done." She said.

I lifted my arm for inspection, upon the inside length of my arm, runes, Norse runes, marked my flesh. Starting from the wrist, two columns, side by side, ran nearly to the elbow joint.

"It indicates that a pledge exists between you and Hamish, nae worry, it doesn't stipulate what the oath is." Donna said.

"Could you please call all your men?" Donna asked Hamish.

He took a second, looking at me, and then Donna, before nodding his head. Turning, he left. Once Hamish had vanished around the corner Donna pulled me to the side, so our faces were not in Aengus's line of vision.

"You cannae leaves us Mara." Donna's said, her saddened voice coating my thoughts.

I sighed, I should have known she would find out.

"It would be suicide, without us, without Col, you will nae last long. The longer you remain in your Warg state, the harder it will be to return." She warned.

"My mother is alive Donna, I am not the last key, my death is the only guarantee that the people I love do not get hurt, killed."

"Your forgetting that your death will also be Conlaóch's...I have seen a future where you are happy Mara, this vision is based on you staying, when you decided to leave, it disappeared, now all I see is death, darkness...I do nae see anyone's future." She frowned, her face etched with fear.

I took a step back, my eyes studying every inch of her face. She was telling the truth. Donna pursed her mouth, a little angry grunt sounding from her throat.

"I would nae ever lie to you Mara." She rebuked.

"I know, it just alters things."

I was about to talk further when a thunderous crack sounded above us. It reminded me of glass breaking, but on a gigantic scale that burst my ear drums. Everyone's head swung to the sky. The shield was failing. Large forked rivets were spreading along its entire surface, black infused fog flooding through the small gaps. Fuck.

"We need to go." Aengus called.

Running towards Donna, he went to pull her. Donna swiped his hand away.

"He is nae in yet, I need to free the wolves." She said

"Where are you all Hamish?"

"Behind you." He said, bursting through the tree line at a sprint, an entire force of Varúlfur behind him.

Not waiting for them to stop, I motioned to Donna that I was ready. Like before, Donna's magic grew, the long threads of magic whipping through the air and attaching themselves to my people.

Unsure, some of them stopped, Hamish shouting for them to continue forward. Using the same words as I did in the garden, I uttered the words that would free them. The command given, Donna released her hold, Aengus pulling her against him.

"It is done, we must go now." Aengus insisted, his eyes constantly darting between the wood line and the sky.

"Forgive me Aengus, but I cannot leave Mara, I must be here." She said, a delicate apology held in her eyes.

Aengus growled before focusing on her, He was about to say something, but after a small pause, his eyes softened. A glimmer of fear crossed his face before he nodded.

"You stay by my side, please Donna." He pleaded.

"Aye, always." She promised with a sad smile.

"I need a weapon." I said to everyone, my eyes looking around as if I might happen to find one laying about.

"Here."

Aengus removed a set of large curved daggers from his back. He handed them to me, his face grim.

"You stay close too Mara, Conlaóch will have my head if anything happens to you, which means he will have Donna's too." He grumbled, his eyes serious.

"I will behave warrior, I promise."

He grunted before nodding his head. I don't think he believed me, but he didn't say anything further.

"Aye, your damn well better behave." Ansgar grunted, the raven-haired warrior running up beside me. He pinned me with a, 'you fucking will" glare, before looking at Hamish.

"They are pushing through the wall… they will be here in minutes. We do nae have enough time to return to the castle, we must fight and hope that aid comes." Ansgar frowned.

Hamish stalked up, standing by my other side, his eyes trained on the trees.

"We should at least try to make it to the burial ground, the ground has a natural dip and incline, it will give us an advantage we do nae have here." Aengus suggested.

"Aye, let's go."

Not delaying further, Ansgar stepped up behind me, pushing me forward. Aengus sweeping Donna up into his arms. At a run, we headed for the burial mound, the air rushing past me. A sliver of fear crept up my back, my eyes darting to Donna. Her admission had changed everything, my plan no longer an option. What do I do now?

All of us were pulling in deep breaths, our eyes focused on the low rumbling sound that came from the direction we had just vacated. The black and grey fog that seeped into the sky was clouding above the tree line, slowly moving closer towards us, the deep and deadly thrum, traveling with it. Sven came flying through the trees, another wolf with him, they were both in wolf form, but somehow, I still knew it was Sven. Just as he was about to hit our defensive line, both he and the other wolf stopped, a barrage of snarls escaping his muzzle. The odd thing was that I knew what he was saying. *"There are hundreds of them, a giant white wolf leading in their centre."*

Sköll.

"He has an army of morning stars." Sven added, another sinister snarl tumbling from his chest.

Both my eye brows shot up, what the hell are morning stars? Sven's golden eyes stared into mine.

"Souls that have not moved on to the next phase." He hissed, the sound carrying only in my head. *"He has found a way to enslave them."*

I didn't know what this meant, what the implications to this knowledge would mean for our chances. Hamish relayed the message to Aengus and Ansgar, both letting out a deafening roar. Anger was evident in their every movement, every expression. Not good news then.

"Show me." He demanded, his eyes on Sven.

Sven slowly lowered his head, in what I thought was a nod, Ansgar staring at him, his eyes glued to his forehead. His face was calm but then quick as lightening every feature morphed into a lethal scowl, large heinously sharp canines exploding from his mouth.

"Conlaóch needs to know about this, someone needs to get to him." He said, his eyes scanning the crowd.

"You, and you, with me. The quickest path through is nae far from where our enemy lays waiting, you two are the fastest, we will go together in the hope that at least one of us makes it." He instructed, two large wolves stepping forward.

They looked at me. I nodded my head when I released they were waiting for my permission. Ansgar's gaze quickly fell on mine.

"If you allow your Warg control, we will lose, everyone here will die." He said, deep worry reflecting in his eyes.

"I will not let you down." I promised.

He grunted before regally inclining his head. With a last look at Aengus, he sped off with the two wolves. Just as he vanished from sight, the first lot of soldiers strode through the tree line, a low lingering fog, swimming around their feet. My eyes struggled to focus on the men, their forms transparent, an eerie and unnatural glow shimmering around them. There were wolves, fey, Valkyrie, and many others, all of them with tortured expressions. Souls... my head swung to Hamish.

"They have no body?" I asked.

He looked back, a brief flick of worry crossing his mouth.

"Aye, they are souls, all their strength from this life but without the obvious weakness, they are already dead, so cannae physically die." He grunted.

How the hell do you defeat a force of undying powerful beings?

"You can kill them, but you would be phasing them out of existence, they will have no rebirth." Donna said, a tear rolling down her cheek.

"Aye, a soul is weak against man-made matter, you should be able to harm them, my blades would kill them, as would the daggers you hold." Aengus explained.

"Can we not free them from his hold?" I asked.

"We do nae know how he stole them, without that knowledge, we cannae know how to free them." Donna said sadly.

I glanced at the trapped souls, more, and more of them, pouring out into the open, a pang of sadness welling up and coating my heart. They didn't deserve this, I didn't even know this was possible. In all my thinking regarding the fight with Sköll, the final fight against the darkness, not once did I consider an army of bodiless souls marching towards me.

"It should nae have been possible Mara, what he has been done defies the laws of nature, of order. He has done what the gods forbid." Donna hissed.

"Then the gods will intervene?" I asked, a little bit of hope entering my voice.

She shook her head.

"Maybe, when they learn of it, by which time it will be too late." Aengus grunted.

Hamish came and stood beside me, his hand briefly running the length of my arm.

"Once they have all arrived they will attack, stay with Donna, if our forces reach the point of defeat, she will use her abilities to bridge you beneath the mound. It will give you more time, allow reinforcements to arrive." He said, his tone implying I will not argue. "I'm sorry Mara…I should nae have kissed you back, I should have just agreed, then he would never…"

I placed my hand on his arm.

"Don't, this isn't the time. What happened, what didn't happen, we can deal with later. I'm not mad at you, I don't blame you."

How could I, it was my fault, all of this was my fault. Hamish snarled for my benefit, his eyes scolding. I was pretty sure he was about to verbally scold me but then the air started buzzing, an irritating pitch that made the air grow static. I looked at Donna thinking it was her, she looked at me shrugging her shoulders. Not Donna then.

"Be ready." Aengus shouted, his smoke-filled eyes aimed at the enemy.

Everyone was tense, the electrified air only making it worse, all was quiet bar the haunting thrum that came from the trees.

It was chaos, blades, and blood, colouring the air. Just as Hamish had predicted they would, they attacked the moment they were all amassed. Sköll thus far, had not joined in, his ghostly apparitions sweeping down upon us in a tidal wave of tainted fog. I have never seen anything like it, they hit with a combined force that lifted the first two rows of Lycan into the air, their bodies flying over us before crashing into the trees behind. Donna was next to me, a blue shield coating her body, streaks of forked lightening exploded from her finger tips. The smell of burnt wood, flesh, tainted the air, but compared to the blood, it wasn't nearly as overpowering. As Aengus had promised the steel blades were keeping the souls back, but with so many of them, our men were quickly falling. Second by second they gained more ground, our clearly outnumbered army, dwindling fast. The carnage was baiting my wolf, my emotion a hurricane that was quickly leaning towards violent rage. My head felt like it was going to burst, my will, bullying it into cooperation. I wanted to fight, wanted to feel the blood cleanse my skin, but I had promised to stay close to Aengus, and out of fear of condemning an innocent soul, I refused to use my daggers, not for them. My eyes found Sköll's, they are for you, I shouted, the words silent. As though he heard my threat, his eyes found mine, a look of utter disdain crawling along his face. I kept my eyes on his, my fangs slowly edging out of my mouth.

"I will kill you." I mouthed just for him.

He smirked, a cold malicious glint in his dark eyes, lifting his hand, he beckoned me to him. I took a step forward, ready to accept his challenge, Donna's hand grabbed my arm.

"Do nae, it is what he wants." She warned.

I hissed, Sköll laughed, the dark twisted sound resonating clearly, even amongst the carnage. Hamish's anguished roar caught my immediate attention, my eyes searching for him. He was favouring his left, his arm pressed tightly against his right side. Even from here I could see the blood, the rich claret stain, soaking his clothes.

"Hamish." I called.

"Stay where you are Mara, give me your word." He said, his desperate command whispering in my mind.

I ignored him. Donna hissed as I ran towards him. I could feel Sköll's eyes on me, his sadistic gaze scorching horrific trails along my back. Just as I was about to reach him, I suddenly remembered I was half fey, I cursed to myself for not previously having the thought. I wouldn't use my blades out of fear of hurting the innocent, but I could use my magic. It would not kill them, but it would push them back, maybe even weaken them. I knelt down beside Hamish, his face was pale, a grey tinge to his skin. Not focusing on his injuries, I focused on the air. I pulled in a deep breath, the taste of the atmosphere infusing my senses. Pushing my wolf back, I allowed the information on the air to take precedence within my consciousness. Amongst the movement of power and bodies, I could see the threads that structured the air, the loose cords flowing wherever the wind carried them. They were so clearly defined, I could play them like a stringed instrument. I summoned them to me, each string, pulling taunt. I could see the pressure building, a whip ready to be lashed. The noise of the battle slowly faded, the gentle thrum of air all that I could hear. My breathing slowed, but still I bended the air further, again, again, until there was no longer space for it to condensed and fold any further. A sharp stab of pain penetrated my shoulder, the severity, nearly making me lose my grip. Hissing, I remained focus. Guiding the threads, I aimed them at the main force, the enemy that pushed tirelessly against our front line. The air cracked, the pressure creating giant torrents within the invisible cage I had created. Clouds, like those you would find in a storm, swirled together, a large swirling mass, filling with power. I grinned. It had not been my design to create such a force, but I was pleased with the outcome. Satisfied with my work, I let go.

The recoil from the pressure sent me flying back. Crashing into the side of the mound, I rolled over, ignoring the pain the impact wrought. I wanted to see what I had unleashed, wanted to witness what I hoped was mass destruction. The storm lashed out as I hoped it would, a hurricane in the form of a whip, cutting across the sky. When the tip connected with the ground, an enormous crash burst through the trees, the earth and trees that stood closest, flung into the air, catching, and flying at our attackers. It did not hit them all, but it hit enough for us to strengthen our stance. The Storm lashed a further three times before the pressure gave, the air returning to its original form.

"Hello Mara, impressive, but ultimately inadequate."

I pulled the blades from my back, the over-sized holder making the action slow and awkward. Sköll stood in front of me, his stance arrogant. He looked like my father, but unlike my father's cool blue eyes, his were grey, chaotic, and terrifying. Wary, I stood slowly. Everything in me told me to run, the thought angering me. I would not run from him. He smirked, the gesture cold.

"Do you know what this is?" He asked, lifting a small medallion from his chest.

I recognised the design, Odin's compass. It was masterfully etched into a silver metal. I didn't respond, guessing that the question was rhetorical.

"This is your mother, Aelius." He sneered.

"Is that supposed to injure me? I never knew my mother." I sneered.

He grinned, his Warg momentarily contorting his face before returning to its previous form.

"Your friends are losing Mara, but you can save them...I lead the morning stars, if I die, they will return to my father."

He couldn't have dropped a bigger hint, he wanted me to fight him, but why not just attack already if that was the case? Because he wants me to change, I thought, wants me to become my most powerful self.

"No one knows you're here Mara, your hunter is not coming for you. The wolves you sent, never made it."

The wolves I sent...but no mention of Ansgar. I kept my face impassive, my eyes guarded. If Ansgar made it, then they were coming, his assumed advantage would be lost. Circling him slowly, I didn't say anything.

"If you want to kill me so much why are you stalling, why not attack already?"

"I'm waiting."

"For what?"

"I want to see the despair on your face when those you love die, then I will kill you." He smirked, his intelligent eyes beaming.

Like a ticking clock they seemed to be counting down, a plan in motion, a goal soon to be achieved. I snarled, even with the risk of having him at my back, I turned, looking for Donna. She was still next to Aengus, her face pale. The shield she had made stood, but like a broken light bulb, it flickered, her magic fading fast. Aengus must have been aware, as he drew closer to her, his huge body acting as a second shield. Hamish was still on the ground, I couldn't tell if he was moving. I sent a command to Sven.

"Protect Donna."

The large grey wolf that was Sven, turned his head in my direction, his gaze passing me and landing on Sköll. Several wolves turned and started flying up the hill towards me. Sköll laughed.

"You're making it so easy Mara, you're bringing them right to me." He mocked.

"No! Do not come to me, to Donna." I shouted verbally and mentally.

"Donna has refused our aid, she threatened to electrocute any who came to help her, and not you." Sven replied.

Of course she did. Damn it, I can't let any more die, I can't.

"I do not need your help, hold the lines, keep everyone away from me." I warned my pack.

My men stalled just as they neared me, their expressions torn. I sent them a look that said, 'stay the fuck away." before turning to face Sköll. Rolling my head slightly, I pushed the tension from my shoulders, a low snarl erupting from my chest. Sköll grinned wickedly, the sinister lines of his face only baiting me further. A spike of anger lashed through my mind, the fiery slash cutting me from the inside out. My fangs dropped, my strength grew, but by some act of magic, I managed to remain in control. The ground beneath Sköll and I froze over, like liquid nitrogen it happened in seconds, a freezing mist rolling across the earth in chaotic and eerie spirals. The sun dropped below the horizon, darkness descending.

My inflamed skin gave way, a brilliant white coat of fur taking its place. A huge, cold infused breath, hissed from my snarling mouth, my mind and emotions calming to an instinctual driven state.

All I saw was prey, an enemy. There was no feeling, no rage, just silence. Every sound, scent was crisp, the information uploading to my mind at an incredible speed. There was no darkness, no light, but a perfect state of balance, for the first time in my life the path was clear, un-tainted, un-biased.

Flashes of light flew around me, men falling from the night sky. My wolf wanted to look, but sensed that they were no threat, the only real danger was Sköll. My eyes refused to leave him, his body contouring, ice, and mist swirling over him. Some of the men that appeared from the air, attempted to wound him, his fog, like hands, locking around their throats and flinging them to the side. I moved closer, my movements cautious but lacking fear. I was ready.

His change complete, a large white wolf stood in front of me, a mirrors image of my own. Sharp jagged teeth dripped with saliva, the air warping with every movement of his body. Muscles rippled beneath his coat, his liquid silver eyes, filled with hate. I positioned myself on a slight incline, my beast instinctively claiming higher ground. He snapped his jaw in my direction, a fake lunge towards me. Fearlessly, I didn't flinch, a low rumble building in my chest. I heard Donna scream, I knew that this was wrong, that something had happened, but my wolf refused to allow it any power over me. It was a distraction, a tactical move that would break the equilibrium. Sköll growled, the anger fuelled sound rubbing along my fur. I was not playing his game the way he wanted me to. I lowered my head, a long and deadly snarl wisping through my teeth. We had postured long enough. Pushing on the balls of my feet, I leapt towards him.

Mac tire cú

The scent of blood was getting stronger, we were close. My eyes burned, my entire body on fire. Finian had said I was on fire, he meant it literally. What Ragnar said suddenly made sense, 'you can become and return safely.' I had become the mac tire cú 'hell hound'. It must have been Ragnar's design, the amulet allowing for the change minus the dark, soul destroying taint that came with it. The use of the hound's strength and power, re-levelling the balance.

I remained in control, the same man, but with a rage enthralled edge to me. I ran alongside Hati's wolf, both of us speeding through the woods. Finian and Eoghuan were trailing, but not by much. Mara had been injured, a scolding wound to her shoulder. It was when our bond relayed her injury that the mac tire cú took hold. It was painful, my bones snapping with nauseating effects. I stumbled as the change spread throughout my body, but out of fear, desperation, I pushed myself forward. The giant black hound rippled with power, primal needs, and aggression, lacing every thought. I could understand the pull to possessing such power, it certainly changed the odds. I kept pace with the Warg easily, my body just as large as his, wider in the chest. It felt good, the lithe movement and increased sensitivity, painting the world in a whole different perspective. It was beautiful, the colours all the brighter, the smells, fresher and more informative.

The un-mistakable sound of battle reached my ears, my hunter howling as we drew nearer to our destination. Muscles burning, we picked up speed. Racing, the woods held no true shape, a mass of colours and smells that washed over us, blurred, and distorted our surroundings. Hati howled, the dark sound tearing through the air, carrying on the wind, and penetrated the flesh. It was like a deadly whisper that crept into your soul, warned that death is coming for you. Another wave of pain struck me in the back, a deadly roar soaring through the night. Mara.

Hati's head swung to the right, my head following.

Our angle of destination adjusted, we broke through the last of the trees. The sight before us was carnage, demons and Varúlfur fighting back to back while masses of souls swept around them. Enslaved fey had walls of earth jutting up from the ground, dividing and weakening what little men remained standing. My men's attention on the fey, bodiless Valkyrie flew from the sky, attacking from above. I could see Cael and his team defending Aengus, Lucian speeding between demons and men, his exceptional speed preventing the souls from breaking through their tight defensive circle. Aengus was still standing, but Donna was on the floor behind him, Sven, one of Mara's generals, at her back. Not seeing Mara amongst the main force, my eyes whipped across the scene.

Hati pushed past me, a mirage of frozen mist flying around him. I left in the same direction, trusting he would lead me to Mara. I tried to feel for her through the bond, but I couldn't detect any emotion, nothing to guide me towards her. Finian and Eoghuan didn't follow, instead they ran towards Aengus, their weapons held high, a low deadly snarl announcing their coming.

Reaching the far tip of the mound I finally saw her. I had never seen Mara's wolf form, but I knew it was her. Another giant wolf had her pinned to the ground, his large muzzled jaws clamping down on her back. Her white fur was completely matted in blood…her blood. Hati roared, the deafening pitch carrying small particles of ice, thousands of make shift razor blades speeding through the air, embedding themselves into his brothers back. Sköll's head whipped to the side, just as Hati reached him. Leaping onto his back, both Hati and Sköll rolled down the small hill. Mara got up, her legs giving way. Collapsing to the floor, she whined, the painful hiss enraging me.

My hunter went wild, an overwhelming blast of emotion coursing through my body. Panic flared in my chest, my will forcing it back down. My logic understood that she would not be safe until Sköll had fallen, ignoring the urge to go to her, I raced past, entangling myself amid Hati and Sköll. The flames that flickered across my body hit their icy visage, loud sizzling hisses tainting the air. Clouds of grey smoke swam within their frozen banks of fog, the combination of the two making the whereabouts of each other difficult to determine. Relying heavily on my senses I stalked towards Sköll. He had gone silent, but he was still here. A brief flicker of fear crept up my spine, would he try and double back to Mara? Suspecting that he would, I slowly made my way towards her, making sure not to make a sound, give myself away.

The mist was thick, but I could see her outline, she was alive, I could hear her heart beating, the erratic pulse begging me to go to her. It took every ounce of strength to remain where I was. Hunkering down in a natural ditch I laid close to the ground, my eyes on the mist encircling Mara. I pushed the loud clatter of fighting to the back of my mind, focusing on the sounds nearest to me. My breathing slowed, my body almost in at trance like peace. The flames I wore like a cloak crawled back, instead off licking the air they danced along my fur, the small wisps somehow understanding the need to remain concealed. Ready, I watched, waiting.

I didn't wait long, the stagnant mist suddenly coiling, a small breeze pushing it around. My muscles tensed, ready to launch at a moment's notice. The outline of a large wolf's head slowly appeared, a silent snarl fixed onto its face. A low hum of a growl vibrated in my chest, my eyes burning wickedly. Anger lashed and howled, demanding I reach her now. The mac tire cú and I did not like his closeness, she was ours to protect, ours to cherish. Drawing in a hushed breath I forced myself to be patient. He was close to her now, really close. One more step…

The growl I had been holding tightly, flew from my chest, my body flying into action. At full speed, I ripped through the night, my heavily sharpened jaw tearing into his neck. The doused flames sparked to life, the fire singing his fur. Blood filled my mouth, the iron rich liquid, feeding my rage. Sköll locked his jaws onto my shoulder, his daggered canines chomping to the bone. I snarled, but did not let up. Hati must have heard the disruption, his large wolf bursting through the mist to hit Sköll on the opposite side. Unrelenting, we ripped into his body, the frozen ground, mist, clinging onto my flesh, an attempt to freeze me in place, render me useless. Forks of sharpened ice sliced through my skin but still I held on, refusing to let go, to give up.

Again, and again, we tore, bit, clawed. Tired, bleeding, my body was weakening. The pain was so great my mind refused to acknowledge its existence, a welcomed numbness dulling the pain. Sköll finally stopped fighting, a low keening pain escaping him in sporadic bursts. I fell back, Hati taking his human form. Blood covered his skin, long tares brandishing his body. Leaning down he ripped a medallion from Sköll's neck. Lifting it, he reverently brought it to his lips.

"Aelius." He murmured against it.

"We must capture his morning star." I managed to say.

What's the point in killing him if Fenrir can still use him? Hati turned to face me, a slight nod of the head in agreement. Like Hati, my body had returned to normal, and like him, I was covered in numerous wounds. With great difficulty, I took the pendant Herlta had given me from my neck, it, along with the amulet, were all that survived my transformation into a 'mac tire cú'.

Hati took the pendant from me, kneeling over Sköll, and placing an open hand above the icy ground. The ice that covered the earth started to reshape, the result, a long, heinously Sharp dagger, the highly reflective surface, catching and distorting the moon.

"My lord." Eoghuan called, Finian climbing the hill behind him.

They both looked tired, an angry slash crossing Finian's jaw. I grunted, acknowledging the fact I heard them.

"The morning stars have dispersed. The demon's caught as many as they could, but most got away." Finian's jaw clicked, a flash of anger swirling in his eyes.

"Donna and Hamish are badly injured; Aengus and Mara's men are heading back to the castle." Eoghuan added, his gaze falling on Mara. "Shit." He hissed.

Running over, he picked up her limp body, gently settling her against his chest. I tried to get up, so I could reach her, my limbs stubbornly refusing to budge.

"You." Hati called to Finian. "I need you to hold the pendant above his heart, I do not want to risk another force sweeping in to steal it before it is contained."

Finian nodding, taking the pendant from his hand. Moving to the other side of Sköll, Finian knelt, the pendant dangling centimetres above the centre of Sköll's chest. Not wasting any time, Hati plunged the dagger into his heart, blood bubbling around the hilt. He did not remove the knife but turned it three hundred and sixty degrees, the cut becoming a gaping hole. Hati's face remained impassive, his eyes watching his brothers face suspiciously. Pulling the knife from his chest he then sliced open Sköll's throat, bloodied spray coating Finian and Hati in a fine mist, Finian spat before cursing in Gaelic, an angry glare aimed at Hati.

A strangled gurgle escaped Sköll's throat, a last laboured breath hissing past his lips. I listened for a heartbeat, wanting to be sure that his life truly ended, I couldn't find one. A flash of relief coursed through me, my eyes drifting to Mara.

"Eoghuan, bring her to me."

"Not yet." Hati hissed "Get ready." He said to Finian.

At his tone, my attention returned to Sköll's lifeless body. Just like ones I had seen in the past, his morning star started to rise. It was so small, the light blinding. The greatest volume of light shone at the top, a line that still clung to the body stretching from the bottom. It was hard to imagine that something so pure, so beautiful, existed somewhere inside Sköll. Finian lowered the pendant directly onto its top, the large teardrop absorbing the light. Trapped within the prism, Sköll's soul flickered, the sight reminding me of vividly bright fire flies, swirling within a sealed bottle.

"Is it done?" Finian asked.

Hati looked at him before turning his attention to Mara, a sad gleam flashing in his eyes.

"The demons cannot be trusted with Sköll's soul, someone among them is aiding my father. Do not allow Mara to have it either, it will over time corrupt any who possess it." Hati warned, whilst gently sweeping a strand of Mara's hair from her face. "I did what I thought was best, I did not know how to raise her. I thought only of preparing her for the reality of her legacy. There are others… others who serve my father, just as powerful as you, maybe more so. Do not ever leave her alone, do not trust anyone with her."

Finian helped me to my feet. I winced, pain lacing its way up my sides.

"I will protect her with my life." I promised.

Hati grunted, his hand tightening around the silver medallion he had took from Sköll.

"It is not enough hunter; every enemy of my father needs to protect her, with their lives." He hissed.

Mara stirred on a small groan. Regaining consciousness, she opened her eyes. Fearing the wolf would be within them, I let out a long relived breath when her vivid blue eyes locked on to mine. When she realised Eoghuan was holding her, she hissed, pushing against his chest until he let her go. I grinned, that her normal defiant self was present, was a good sign.

"Damn stubborn woman." Finian grunted, a slow grin curving the edge of his mouth.

Ignoring everyone, including her father and Sköll, she got up from her knees and walked towards me, a small limp in her left leg. I could see that she was in pain, but as per usual, Mara hid it, her face set in a, 'I refuse to acknowledge I'm in pain' scowl. When she reached me, she smiled, were it not for the blood on her face, it would have been stunning. I smiled back, running my hand over her face, my other hand pulling her waist to mine.

"I learned something today, something really important. I have also learned that time is a precious commodity that can leave you without warning, So…" She leaned against me, her legs standing on tip toes, her mouth hovering over mine. "I love you, Conlaóch Ó Ceallacháin." She whispered against my mouth.

I hissed, my whole-body energizing and filling with pride. The wash of emotion was overwhelming, my hunter's possessive urgings forcing me to draw her ever closer. Mara winced but didn't complain, a little grin annihilating all self-control. Not caring who was watching, I kissed her, the passion filled exploration hinging on desperate.

"You realise you're both naked, right? Not to mention joined together and with an audience." Finian chuckled.

Shit, growling. I broke from the kiss. Desire swam in Mara's eyes, the sight pulling another growl from my chest.

"I don't mean to interrupt but you are all needed back at the castle, there have been many casualties. As you suspected a second force was sent against us." A silver eyed demon said, his gaze falling on Sköll.

Hati moved towards Mara, Finian and Eoghuan doing the same. The demon noticed, taking a step back, he lifted his hands in warding fashion. Mara hissed at the demon, a flash of anger passing through our bond.

"I come as a messenger of the fey queen, I mean no harm." He said, his eyes switching from one person to the next, a weary gleam twinkling within.

"Take the body back. We are on our way." I instructed.

The demon nodded his head before moving to retrieve the body.

"Make sure there are clothes waiting for us at the armoury." I added.

It took us a lot longer to get back, our bodies aching. As requested, clothes were waiting for us, along with a crying Gabriella. I put on my clothes trying to delay whatever news she was going to share. Her expression said it all. Someone who means a lot to one of us had died. My thoughts immediately went to Ansgar, a sharp stabbing pain piercing my chest. Refusing to lift her gaze, a fully dressed Mara went over to speak with her.

"Donna?" Mara guessed, her eyes filling with water.

Gabriella sobbed, a slight shake of her head. Slowly she lifted her face, her blood shot eyes falling on Eoghuan. Eoghuan froze, his head slowly shaking in a disbelieving manner. He tried to speak, but nothing came out, his face twitching with a backlash of emotion.

"No." He finally gasped.

Gabriella burst into uncontrollably sobs, Mara's pain at the news ripping at my insides. She didn't say anything, but I saw her, knew that she was dying inside, felt the tsunami of emotion wash over her, and subsequently, me.

"Eoghuan." Finian called to his brother, sadness marring every inch of his face.

"No, she is not. No. No." Eoghuan's chest fell forward, his breathing caught between a roar and a desperate sob.

Finian took a step back, realisation reflecting in his eyes, if Asta is dead, then today he loses his brother. Eoghuan will not be without her, cannot be without her. The inseparable twins will be no more. Mara flung herself into my arms, her un-expected dash catching me off guard. I took a step back before pulling her in for a tight embrace, my mind refusing to accept that my young friend may not make it to the end of the day.

Eoghuan's grief quickly turned to anger, a low snarl escaping his strained mouth. His despairing gaze flung to the castle before he ran towards it, the hunter's smoky hue claiming his eyes. Finian fell to his knees, his head falling to the ground. A loud despairing roar sounding from beneath him, birds scattering from the trees. Hati leaned towards the hunter, a dominant aura flaring about him.

"What loss you feel in no way compares to the loss he feels. Get up! Your brother needs you." He commanded with a hiss.

"I want to see her." Mara breathed against my neck. "Please, I need to see her."

Hati's words seemed to have had an effect on him, the young, black-haired warrior, rising to his knees. He looked at Hati, an anger fuelled gleam in his eyes. His wound had only just begun to knot together, the large cut along his jaw still losing blood. Standing, a look of calmness swept over his face, resolve manifesting in his stance. He inclined his head to Hati before walking towards the castle, the rest of us following close behind.

Morning Star

I don't understand, how did this happen? Asta was well within the castle, she should have been safe. Tears stung my eyes and stained my cheeks, emptiness filing my chest. Col had not let go of me, his presence, the only thing keeping me from lashing out. I wanted someone to pay, to blame. She was my friend, gentle, kind, she knew what I was but still she stood in my corner, me, who didn't deserve such friendship, didn't deserve her. Gabriella walked behind me, her hand clinging to the back of my t-shirt, her sadness pouring from her very soul. She had not stopped crying, Siri standing by her side. I wanted Hamish to be here, but his injuries were still too raw, too dangerous to chance. It was the same for Angsar, both of them still fighting for their lives. Col had not mentioned his friend, but every time the hunters name was mentioned I felt the knife in his chest.

The bodies of all the dead had been placed in the large common room, the count at well over a hundred. Families and loved ones stood around their fallen, sadness radiating for every pour. Of those, at least forty lost anam cara, their partners, whether male or female, standing over them. The Vanir had managed to trap their souls, preventing them from being taken, the only blessing to an otherwise tragic day. Resting on the chest of each dead was a morning star, some were caught within blades, others jewellery. It was because of these traps, that most did not realise the loss of a loved one until after the battle had ceased.

The demons had left before we even made it back to the castle, taking with them all the enslaved morning stars they had managed to catch. I was glad that they left, I had business with the demon king but now wasn't the time. The fey had stayed, wanting to remain, to guard and oversee the ceremony. They were going to release the morning stars, their living soul mates choosing to travel with them. Tears started to well up again, the love that swept through the room unfathomable.

Eoghuan had not left Asta's side, still within his arms he held her to him, her lifeless body draped against him.

When they fey released the souls, the anam cara who survived will take their own lives. At first, I was surprised, but then I understood, what is life without your soul mate, but a gaping hole in your chest, a half-life, an empty life. To keep them was to deny them passage to the next place, I silently hoped, a better place.

"Mara." Donna called

I turned to face my friend, her face bruised and swollen. She was on crutches, Aengus acting as a second shadow, following her every dip and step, ready to catch her at a moment's notice. She huffed when he stepped on the back of her heel.

"Sorry." He mumbled.

Despite the situation, it brought a small smile to my lips. I left Col's arms to give her a gentle embrace, her scent of cherry and vanilla pretzels making me long for a different time, a simpler time, when I couldn't feel, couldn't hurt.

"It is time." Col breathed against my ear. Both Donna and I watering up again, a grief ridden tinge to our demure.

Col walked into the centre of the room, myself on one side, and Herlta on the other. All eyes were on him, us.

"We have fought and today we have won, but as you all know our victory was achieved at a heavy price. We have all lost someone we love, the pain of that loss will never leave us, a scar we will carry for an eternity. It is with thanks to Herlta that we did not lose them to the darkness, that they will have rebirth, a new beginning, a new life. To protect the morning stars this room will be sealed, no one can leave or enter. For all those that have yet to depart, say your final goodbyes, bring your anam cara forward."

A slow mutter swept through the room, goodbyes, and tears, passing between broken hearts.

Eoghuan stood, Asta's vivid red hair cascading over his arm. Finian walked behind him, one hand on Eoghuan's shoulder, the other gripped into a tight fist. His face remained stoic, but his eyes were bursting with pain, a haunting abyss that had his iris's flickering between hunter and man. I did not know Finian well, but I could see the despair, the grief of losing his brother. That he was still alive, instead choosing to die, had to make it a hundred times worse. He was being selfless by letting him go, a quality I hoped that I could possess but doubted I did.

Eoghuan dropped to his knees, Asta cradled in his arms. Every anam cara adopted the same position, their soul mate, like Asta, held tightly against them. Behind each of them stood another single person, Finian behind Eoghuan, other loved ones behind the rest. Friends and relatives from the un-bonded morning stars brought their souls forward, laying them at the feet of Eoghuan and the others. Necklaces, brooches, and blades of every description and design, rested on the floor beside them. With the exception of the those who stood behind the line of anam cara, everyone returned to the edges of the room, their gazes turning to Col.

Col lifted his hand, summoning a group of people to step forward. A woman with long black hair, and striking blue eyes, stopped behind the line where Finian stood, a fiddle in her hand. Lifting it to her shoulder, she played a long captivating note that instantly made my heart stutter, my breathing strained. The men that followed her out started to play various instruments, the same stirring tune making the whole room fall into a compelling silence.

"May the light guide and shelter you, may your souls once again be made whole." Col said over the melody, his right hand raising like a salute, his green eyes locked onto Eoghuan's.

A single glistening tear fell from Finian's eye, his gaze fixed to Col's raised hand. A shot of sadness wound its way through my chest just before Col swept down his raised hand. It was a command, taking my eyes from his, I watched as one by one, the men that stood behind the kneeling, drove their blades through their backs and into their hearts. I gasped, a soft choke hovering in my throat, why? My mind was racing…Finian, why did he have to do it? … His brother, my heart broke for him.

"He is his only living relative." Donna cried, her sadness amplifying mine. *"They had only each other, and then Asta…"* she didn't finish the sentence.

Someone tapped on my shoulder. Turning I was shocked to see Ti, Hati. His eyes, my eyes, filled with pain. He held out a long broad sword, the blade etched in Norse drawings, the hilt a large Viking dragon with sapphire eyes. I took the blade not understanding, my mind wondering why now of all times he would single me out. He pulled a medallion from his pocket, hanging it around his neck.

"I did the best I knew how, I realise it was not good enough, that I have no right to ask." He knelt in front of me, clutching what I now remembered was my mother to his chest.

Col's hand fell to my back, his body closing in on mine from behind. I licked my lips confused, tears running down my face.

"You are my only family Mara. I understand that my words mean little, but know that I did love you, will always love you. Something that before Aelius would never have been possible. Please, I need to be with her."

A flash of anger had me biting my lip, my breathing hedged with a low snarl. He had no right…Love…Love me, I fail to see the love. I was an object, a thing that he was left with, and he made sure I knew it.

"Your mother is the only one who ever loved him, their time together short. When she died, he didn't know what to

do. Compared to his childhood, yours was normal, kind. He does love you Mara, he is telling you the truth." Donna sighed.

I wanted to hit him, the only reason I didn't was out of respect for the many in here mourning their dead. Cols arm reached around my side, his hand gripping the sword with me, his fingers sliding, and locking between mine.

"I have read his mind Mara, it does not alter anything, but it is the truth. I will help you." Col whispered over my shoulder, his warm breath gliding over my cheek.

I shook, not quite sure why, my mind a whirlwind of different emotions, none of them sticking long enough to make sense of anything. I couldn't breathe, my body failing to recognise the need to draw in air. Ti's eyes stayed on mine, an apology held within their ice cool depths. His brow creased slightly, the most, and only emotion I have ever witnessed.

"When was I born?" I asked him, my eyes studying every line and arch of his face, a sudden need to remember bursting forth through my thoughts.

"December 28th, thirty-two minutes past midnight, 1990, Loch Katrine, Scotland. It was your mother's favourite place, she said the earth was seeped in magic, majesty, that it was the heart of the Gods." He sighed "I could not speak of it Mara; the day of your birth, was the day of her death."

"Mara, if you are to do this, it must be now, it is time." Col said.

I stood a minute longer, my heart torn. It felt like mercy and I wasn't sure I wanted to give it to him.

"Forgive me Mara." Ti said.

I tried to hold it back, hold them in, but I couldn't. I never believed I would shed a tear for him, and yet hot tears fell down my face, a million butterflies fluttering around my stomach. Col's grip on my hand tightened. Guiding the sword, my body unwilling to move, Col positioned the blade over his heart, my mother's medallion still clenched tightly to his chest.

"I forgive you." I heard myself whisper, just as I plunged the sword into his heart.

I staggered back, Col preventing me from moving far. Lowering the sword, I watched my father dying, his expression peaceful, grateful.

Herlta's voice reached the room, an almost song like utterance that wound its way around your body, filing you with hope. It was light infused, the breeze swirling around the room, carrying a mirage of golden wisps that coloured the air. I knelt next to Ti, his breathing weak. His was clinging to life, but barely. I was about to touch him, some kind of last minute effort to be close to him, but I didn't, a small bright light leaving his body just as his last breath hit the air. I had never seen anything like it, my eyes unable to part with the magical glow. It rose slowly, an identical light rising from the medallion. Slowly and together they twirled, danced into the air, spinning, and winding around each other. It was beautiful, a sense of wonderment that cleansed my soul.

I glanced around the room, hundreds of the same lights dotted the air, a universe of stars swimming above me. I couldn't speak, couldn't find the words to describe what I was seeing. I felt like I was witnessing something divine, something beyond my understanding, beyond the scope of this world. I stood slowly. Turning, I tried to see all of it, every eye in the room, facing the stars.

"How will they get out?" I asked someone, anyone who would answer.

"They will find a door and pass through it." Col said, wrapping his arms around me.

A door.

"Beyond our vision?" I guessed.

"Yes."

Donna came and stood by me, the stars reflecting within the green gleam of her eyes. I linked my arm through hers and watched with her until every morning star had departed.

"What happens now?" I asked Col.

He turned me around to face him, a soft expression in his eyes.

"We rebuild, prepare." He said with a gentle sigh.

"I will always be hunted, won't I?"

He grunted, the sound unhappy. Clenching his jaw, he swept his hand over my face, cupping my head. His eyes locked onto mine, all his love shining within.

"Not you Mara, us, all of us." He rebuked with his famous half grin. "It's you and me Mara, let them come. We will be ready."

I would like to thank my test readers for all your help and support during the writing of my first novel.

Daniel Large
Lesley Kerr
Catherine Coe
Trindy Farquharson
Donna Booysen
Vicky Bogle
Jennifer Algieri
Lynsay Bogle
Jillian Campbell

Thank you to all my readers, I hope you enjoyed reading: A Legacy of Blood.
If you can spare a minute please feel free to leave a review, good or bad.
I'm always looking to improve on my work and am grateful for any advice and feedback.
Yours sincerely

Salena Lee

Look out for the next book in the: A legacy of blood, series

Book 2: Morning Star

Imagecopyright:2017SalenaLee

Salenalee.com
Follow me on Twitter or Facebook

Prologue: Morning Star

I had been two months… Those months had been torture, for me, and for all those who lost people they loved. I had hoped that with the death of Sköll things would become easier, instead, the more I learn, the more I realise easy is not a word that exists within our world.

There is a saying the humans use 'time heals all things', I had heard immortals use it too, but from what I've seen, felt, time heals nothing. All that time does, is make hiding your pain easier, more natural.

So many question kept buzzing around my head, so many answers evading me. Why? Why her…Why me? Out of respect for those grieving, I had kept them to myself, tried to push them back and ignore the annoying hum that accompanied them. But the more I refuse to acknowledge, ignore, forget, the more I give myself to the wolf.

Every day she grows more powerful, every minute acting like a push up, building her core strength. Instead of attempting to control her, I find myself wanting her company. It probably didn't help that I was cooped up, restless, bored. It was a daily battle, light verses dark… a combination, I could never truly be free of, a fight, I am sure to lose at least fifty percent of the time. Now was one of those times. I could sense the build in momentum, the graduation of the inevitable. A wave of evil, of a dark twisted void, was coiled, ready to lash and announce herself the winner.

It's far from normal, reassuring. The darkness my wolf imbues, holding me prisoner. She coats every internal and external surface with her dark sap, like skin, like blood, it is the part of me that holding me together, protecting me from the barrage of grief that threatens to overwhelm me. She calls to me, my wolf, a tempting thrum that promises me retribution, vengeance. The pain of loss, of injustice, is the catalyst pushing me closer to the brink, closer to her reasoning.

My thoughts were maddening, bordering on desperate. Pain laced its way around me, a noose that was tightening by the second. I need help, I need someone to listen… But who? … Who would understand the pain, the nature of what I am, the fear, the grief, the nauseating despair that refuses to leave me?

I am a Warg… A daughter of tainted blood, a wolf, a nightmare that poses as a dream… Weaves of light induced hope latch onto me, anchoring me from the storm that has taken hold of my heart, my emotions. I understand the importance of their presence, understand the need to have them in place. I am the key that binds the blight of true evil, and yet I am myself the seed of such an evil.

The light my love ones infuse me with, prevents the growth of violence, but it also prevents my revenge, the knowledge only increasing my anguish. A nasty taste layers my mouth, the idea of not hunting my enemies, contaminating the storm with an uncontrollable rage, rage that batters against my consciousness, like giant waves against a cliff face. I know my protectors mean well, but they do not understand the dark need that hammers within. In this one goal, I need to be free, need to exact my revenge, to make right the wrong, the injustice wrought upon me, upon those I have learned to love, cherish.

I should warn the others, should fight harder to prevent the outpour…but for the first time in a long time, I don't want to. Not because I don't care, don't love… But because revenge is the driving force, the constant nagging that wanted me to pay attention, listen and obey. There are those who would help me, loved ones that have proven that they always have my back, but when I try to open my mouth to voice my despair… Nothing comes out.

They wouldn't understand.

I snarled, the deadly sound baiting my wolf. There is only one real solution…

Morning Star
Book 2: A Legacy of Blood (Series)
Salena Lee

Printed in Great Britain
by Amazon